THE EXCEPTIONALS

CLARA HOWELL

Lulu.com
https://www.lulu.com

To my mom and dad,
for always supporting me, encouraging me,
and raising me to follow God.

1

AILA

We had always been taught to fear the Exceptionals.

We were told that they were dangerous, containing otherworldly powers that no human should ever have. We were told that they were corrupt, with abilities that were wild beyond our understanding. We were told that if we ever saw Exceptionals, we should report them to a trusted adult so they could be taken care of immediately.

There was no mistaking an Exceptional. They were clearly marked, always on their left hand, always with an X that could've been mistaken for a birthmark if it weren't for the fact that it appeared overnight. That's why no one wore gloves. No one wanted to risk being mistaken for an Exceptional.

I used to think there was only one thing worse than being an Exceptional: seeing one and not reporting him. Seeing one and knowing that if I didn't report him, anything he did would be on me.

In my sixteen years, I had only seen an Exceptional once. Even now, eight years later, I can close my eyes and recall every detail of that fateful day. The crisp air that nipped at our fingertips, the warm scent of freshly baked bread that leaked from the bakery, the laughter that carried on the wind…and the kind, hazel eyes of Chase Kader, my best friend.

Chase and I were eight, one year younger than my brother Warren. We'd been friends since birth, tied together by our mothers' friendship and the nearness of our houses. I didn't have a single happy memory without my brother and my best friend in it. As long as I had the two of them by my side, I had nothing to worry about.

The three of us walked home together every day after school, winding between the wagons, stone buildings, and gridlike streets of Bedrock. On that day, we chattered excitedly, discussing our plans for holiday break and how we would celebrate the establishment of the Nicolin dynasty on the upcoming Throne Day. The air was cold, turning our cheeks pink and our hands dry, but none of us wore gloves.

We were passing the bakery when I saw it, a mark on Chase's hand that hadn't been there a moment ago. I stopped abruptly, and so did the boys, tracking my gaze to Chase's left hand.

"Maybe it's nothing," Warren said, worry filling his voice as we stared with wide eyes. "Maybe it's just dirt."

"It can't be, and you know it," I responded. "It's the mark." My voice caught on the words as I struggled to understand. A pit of dread had formed in my stomach.

"No, it's not." Chase withdrew his hand with a jerk, hiding it behind his back. "I'm normal, like you. I'm not an Exceptional. You *know* me."

"We have to report him," I said.

"No," Chase begged. "Don't, Aila, please don't."

Chase's pleas fell on deaf ears that day. I ran straight into the bakery, blurting the news to Baker Rae before the door had a chance to swing shut behind me.

I watched through the bakery's picture window as the Exceptional Police—which we called Expos—surrounded Chase. I stood, my palms pressed against the glass as one of the Expos pulled out a swath of cloth and pressed it over Chase's nose and mouth. I only looked away when Chase collapsed into the arms of another Expo and was carried away.

Baker Rae did not let Warren and I continue our walk home until all traces of Chase and the Expos were gone. Warren started out with long strides, forcing me to jog in order to keep up. As soon as the bakery disappeared from sight, Warren turned on me, his face startlingly pale, his eyes hauntingly hollow.

"Why did you tell, Aila?" His voice trembled as he spoke. "No one had to know."

2

I shook my head. "We had to report him. We'd get in trouble if we didn't." Warren continued to stare at me in shock, so I added, "It's not like anything bad is going to happen. They're just going to make him better, and then we'll get him back."

"You don't understand," Warren said, tears welling in his eyes as he shook his head. "They lie to us, Aila. They don't make the Exceptionals better."

With that, Warren spun around and ran up the street, leaving me to finish the walk home alone.

It had taken me two years to finally accept that Chase was gone, that he was dead. Because even now, eight years later, I had not seen Chase Kader again.

I was reported as an Exceptional on my sixteenth birthday, by none other than my brother Warren.

Until that point, I had thought the only thing worse than being an Exceptional was seeing one and not reporting him. I was wrong. There was nothing worse than the betrayal I felt when someone I loved called the Expos to take me away. For the first time, I truly understood how Chase Kader must've felt when I reported him on that winter day so long ago.

But by then, it was too late.

2

STORM

It was an unusually warm day for mid-March, and the entire town had spent the week chattering about how perfect the weather was for preparing the fields and getting a head start on the planting season.

Which meant I was as far away from the fields as I could get.

The crooked streets of Ferrol were deserted at this time of day, so I didn't have to worry about anyone wondering why I was heading in the opposite direction of where I was supposed to be. The youngest kids studied in school, and the mothers and daughters busied themselves with housework. Everyone else was out on their farms, breaking their backs while trying to break the ground.

I scoffed. It was a waste of time. In the end, the only results were a few more corn kernels toward the stew, and a few more coins toward the taxes.

I took the long way around the Security Station, which had big windows that looked out onto the street and always made me feel as though I was being watched, and finally broke out onto a broad road that led away from the crowded little town. There, taking refuge from the heat in the little swath of shade cast by the nearest building, was a carthorse and his driver.

"Danin," I said to the man by way of greeting as I swung myself into the back of his wagon. It was empty for now, but would soon be filled with supplies from Carsley Market. Danin made money selling those supplies to townspeople who didn't have the time to make the trip to Carsley.

"Storm Dawson," Danin grunted. "You come to steal a free ride off me again?"

I flashed a grin. "My presence is payment enough."

"Say that one more time, and you'll walk to Carsley," Danin muttered, but we both knew the reason he had been waiting in the shade on the side of the road wasn't to give his horse a break. Danin slapped the reins against the horse's back, and the wagon jerked forward as we pulled away from the town.

In all honesty, calling Ferrol a town was generous. Everyone here was condemned to be an impoverished farmer, just like his father before him, so the "town" was really just crooked rows of tiny homes surrounded by miles of fields. Everything else—from the butcher to the blacksmith—was found in Carsley, the trading town just a few miles up the road.

Carsley Market was my refuge, and more often than not I wasted entire days wandering between the colorful stalls and aromatic booths that lined the streets at the center of Carsley. Red banners stitched with gold hung across streets, green and yellow awnings separating one booth from the next. People wearing bright cloaks bursting with color selected goods from the array of even more colorful fruits and vegetables. The market teemed with light and life until it seemed like the very streets were breathing. I much preferred it to working under the hot sun in the fields, getting yelled at because I wasn't living up to the standards of my elder brothers.

Besides my parents, there were ten of us in total, all boys. Garrick was the oldest at twenty-five, and eleven-year-old Jonan, who we called Jon, was the youngest. I was four years older than him, and yet I was the one who my family thought didn't belong, and they made sure I knew it.

It didn't help that I hardly looked like anyone else in the town. Everyone in Ferrol was fair-skinned and only tan in the summer, but my skin was perpetually bronzed. My mop of brown hair and dark blue eyes starkly contrasted everyone else's pale complexions. I had no idea why my parents decided to adopt me when I was four years old, and they made it clear that they had regretted the decision ever since.

To be fair, the fact that I often skipped work in the fields and was sometimes dragged home by the Securities after being caught stealing food didn't help my case.

The first time I stole, it was from a little family-owned vegetable stand I used to pass on the way to school. I ended up sneaking back that night to leave them a coin I'd picked off an official visiting from the Stone Cities. These days, I stole from any vendor who dared to look away, and in the packed streets of Carsley, it was too dangerous to pay them back. But I kept stealing, because I wasn't doing it for myself. Most of my spoils went to Jon late at night when everyone else was asleep. My parents didn't see what I did; Jon needed extra food, or he wouldn't survive growing up in a town like Ferrol. And because he was the one person who saw me as a true brother, not an outsider living under the same roof, it was my duty to provide for him.

Jon was smaller than other kids his age, but that hadn't been an issue until five years ago when the plague swept through the country, hitting Ferrol and other filthy, impoverished towns hardest of all. Jon's case had been the worst, and although he had miraculously survived, he had never quite recovered. My parents noticed that he struggled to keep up in the fields and let him continue his education beyond the normal age of eight, but they didn't realize how much the plague still affected him.

They didn't know how the slightest activity taxed him physically, or that he came home from school exhausted even when all he did was sit at his desk for the day. They didn't know how hard it was for him to keep up with the other boys when they were playing tackleball behind the schoolhouse. They didn't know how the hunger that was part of the daily lives of everyone in Ferrol was so much worse for him when he needed all the energy food could give.

He would whisper these things to me at night when our brothers were fast asleep, begging me to keep his secrets. He didn't want our family to see him as weak. So, three years ago, I started stealing. No matter how angry others got at me, I never told them the real reason behind my theft.

The wagon bumped over a rut in the road and rattled closer to the squat buildings of Carsley. The plague had hit Carsley, too, just like the rest of the Rosan Empire, but not all towns had been affected equally. The capital of Rosan and the surrounding Stone Cities had been hurt least of all, but hadn't bothered to lift a finger to help ease the suffering of places like Ferrol. If the plague had taught me anything, it was that the Stone Cities didn't care. If I had the chance to steal from them, I would do it so without remorse.

Danin slowed the wagon as we rolled into town. I rose to my feet and clapped him on the shoulder. "Thanks for the ride," I said, then vaulted over the edge of the wagon and onto the ground. Danin grunted in response, then nudged his horse forward. I slipped down the street between the two nearby buildings and headed toward the market.

Shouts, chatter, and laughter echoed off the buildings as I drew close, and the cobblestone walkways between the stalls quickly became suffocated by crowds and heavy heat. Thick scents of fried vegetables, freshly cooked meat, and roasted almonds hung in the air. The merchandise at each of the stands was as diverse as the people that wove between them. One stand boasted jars filled with multi-colored jams while beaded necklaces hung down from the ceiling of another, and still a third stall displayed carved figurines painted in bright colors. I felt myself slowly begin to relax as my eyes roved the stands, seeking a place where I could slip a loaf of bread away without being noticed.

I spotted a stall and started toward it, but hesitated when I saw who was attending the stand. *Omar.* Nearly every time I stole from him, he caught me before I got away. He had a sharp eye, and merchants were quick to hire him to tend their stands. I turned to keep searching when a flash of movement caught my eye. Before I could make sense of what I was seeing, a small hand darted from beneath the scarlet tablecloth and seized a piece of bread.

Omar was twice as fast. He seized the wrist in an iron grip before it could disappear. With one jerk, he pulled a small, pale boy from beneath the table. My stomach dropped. *Jon.* I immediately shoved my way through the crowd, ignoring the cries of protest as people stumbled out of the way.

7

What was he even doing here? Wasn't he supposed to be in school? Omar raised a hand, and I closed the rest of the distance with a lurch, sliding between the two of them with my arms wide.

"Stop!"

Omar's arm jerked to a halt before he could land his blow. He glared at me in recognition. "Storm Dawson," he snarled. "Stay out of this."

Jon grabbed my hand from behind. His palm was slick with sweat.

"He's just a boy. He meant no harm," I said, shoving my brother further behind me.

"He stole from my stand!"

"Did he really? As far as I saw, the bread never left the table."

"Of course it didn't," Omar said scornfully. "I catch all thieves."

I noticed that some of the shoppers had paused, casting us furtive glances and slowing the flow of traffic. As far as I knew, someone could've gone ahead and alerted the Securities. I scanned the street, the wheels in my head spinning. "He can pay."

Omar narrowed his eyes. "Don't you try to fool me, boy."

"Just give me one second."

Omar opened his mouth to protest, but I was already dragging Jon a few feet away.

"Jon—"

"I can't pay." Jon's face was flushed, his hand still clutching mine. "I'm sorry, Storm. I didn't think."

"What are you doing here?" My fear turned my words terse, and Jon flinched.

"You said you might not be able to make it out of the fields, so I thought—"

"No," I interrupted. "You must *never* steal, okay? I'll always take care of you. I promise."

Jon's eyes were brown pools of distress. "I can't pay," he repeated desperately.

Omar watched us impatiently from just a few steps away. It was only a matter of time before he interrupted. I reached for the bread that

8

was still in Jon's hand, and he passed it over willingly. "See the booth selling spices, next to the one with the red tent?"

Jon's eyes scoured the street, and he nodded slowly.

"When I say so, run between those stands and towards home without stopping. Okay?"

I didn't wait for a response. I whipped around and approached Omar, lifting my chin to meet his narrowed eyes. But I was still a few feet away when I tripped, losing my balance and careening into Omar.

"Watch it, boy!" he snarled, shoving me away from him.

I stumbled back and he brushed off his clothes, glowering. "So can he pay or not?"

I smirked. "He's from Ferrol, Omar. Of course he can't pay. But he can *run*!"

I shouted the last word as Omar's face twisted in understanding. "*Securities!*" he bellowed.

Out of the corner of my eye, I saw Jon spin around and sprint down the street. I took off in the other direction, and as I ran, I heard Omar's enraged roar behind me.

"*Dawson!*"

I grinned, running my thumb over the silver embellishments on the gold ring. It had been way too easy to slip the ring from Omar's pocket when we collided, and it ensured he would send the Securities after me, leaving Jon alone.

I pushed my way through the crowd. An angry shopper shoved me back, and I toppled into a nearby wooden table. The table tilted and fell. I crashed to the ground, painted beads raining onto the cobblestones around me. The vendor's furious shouts echoed after me as I shoved myself to my feet and sprinted for the nearest alleyway. I tore through another stall, sending colorful scarves tumbling to the ground, then veered left, breaking away from the crowd and ducking into the shadows between two buildings.

Water arced up behind me as I stumbled through a puddle that had not yet been dried by the morning sun. I barely reached the street on the other side when I heard the splashing of Securities behind me.

I gritted my teeth. They were closer than I thought.

I broke out onto the street and turned sharply left. The people in the crowd drew back, parting in confusion. The Securities darted out onto the street behind me, and I risked a glance over my shoulder. There were four of them, and one called out for the crowd to stop me as I swept into another alleyway. My eyes landed on a beam above me. It stretched between two rooftops, and I took two more running steps then jumped.

I just barely managed to wrap my arms around it. Grunting, I pulled myself up and laid on the beam, gazing down into the alleyway as the three Securities rounded the corner. Their heads whipped in every direction, their eyes scouring the narrow alley.

I tensed, waiting for them to look up, to spot me, but they didn't. One muttered something to his comrades, and they all took off at once, their boots pounding the sodden earth. I waited until they disappeared before swinging down from the beam and dropping to the ground.

I looked in the direction the Securities had gone, turning the ring in my fingers, wondering if it would bring too much suspicion if I tried to pawn it off. I let out a breath of relief, turned around...and ran straight into another Security.

Right. There had been four of them, not three. I spun around to make a break for it in the opposite direction, but somehow the other three Securities had come up from behind without me noticing. I glanced at the beam above me, but one of the Securities grabbed my shoulder and shoved me against the wall before I could jump.

"Nice try, kid," another Security sneered as he snatched the bread and the ring from my hands. The man pinning me against the wall grabbed my shoulder and angled me in the direction of the Security Station, where I'd be questioned and reprimanded. Again.

But for some reason, that didn't bother me as much as it should have. I might have been captured, but Jon had escaped. To me, that's what really mattered.

The Securities were not gentle as they all but dragged me home later that evening. I fought part of the way, but quickly gave up when one of them threw me on the ground and drove his boot into my gut. Now that the adrenaline from the chase had worn off, all I felt was exhaustion. They'd kept me in the Security Station nearly all day, yelling at me and demanding payment for what I had stolen. Eventually, they realized I had nothing except the clothes on my back, and only then did two of them decide to take me home.

My house stood in the corner of Ferrol on the outskirts of town, so there wasn't much commotion as the Securities dragging me down the street. The sun dipped toward the horizon, casting a golden glow across the fields. Normally, it would've been a pretty sight, but I was too worn out to enjoy it. My family would be angry that I skipped work in the fields, and they wouldn't be much happier when they learned what I'd been doing instead.

All except for Jon. The main reason I didn't want to return home was because I flinched at the thought of facing his guilt. I didn't even have the bread to console him.

As I predicted, the expression on my mother's face was one of pure fury when she opened the door to find me standing there, bruised and disheveled, flanked by two grim Securities.

"Storm Dawson," she snapped. "I don't even know what to say to you."

I didn't reply; I'd learned it was best to remain silent in these types of situations.

"You cause more trouble than you're worth," she muttered, shaking her head at me. Her gaze flicked to the Securities. "My sincerest apologies. This won't happen again."

She said that every time, but we all knew there was nothing she could do to stop me, besides possibly chaining me to a post. But then again, she'd need to find the money to afford the chains first.

My mother reached out to grab my arm and pull me inside, then suddenly froze, her hand quivering in midair.

I followed her gaze, and my next breath caught in my throat. Time seemed to slow as all our gazes zeroed in on my left hand, which looked different than it had five minutes ago. There, clear as day, were two brown lines that intersected to form an unmistakable X. My head began to spin. I felt disoriented, as if I was in a dream instead of reality. Somewhere, deep down, I supposed I had never thought it would happen to me.

I snapped out of my stupor and ripped my hand away from my mother.

"You're an Exceptional," she whispered.

"No, I'm...it's not..." I grabbed the hem of my shirt and began frantically scrubbing at the mark. "I'm not!"

"He's an Exceptional!" My mother's voice was clear and strident. "He has the mark!"

I heard my father's gruff voice come from somewhere in the house. "Nova, what's going on?"

"This isn't real," I said, folding my left hand protectively against my chest. I slowly backed away from my mother, who was staring at me with wide eyes, as if I was a stranger. "This can't be..."

The Securities moved in behind me, and I stumbled a few steps to the left. Should I run? If so, where to?

"Nova?" my father called again, stepping through the door. In one sweeping gaze he took in my mother's shocked face, the Securities' grim expressions, and the way I cradled my hand. My four brothers that were closest to me in age filed out behind him, then froze in the space between my parents.

For a moment, none of us spoke as the reality of the situation slowly sank in.

My father broke the silence. "What's going on?"

His words flipped a switch. Everything happened so fast I hardly had the chance to react. One of the Securities grabbed me, wrenching my left hand out in the open and revealing the wretched brown X to a chorus of gasps. He shoved me back, pinning me against the wall of the house.

"Wendell, get the Expos!" my mother shouted. My brother raced off, and I felt a jolt of panic.

"Stop!" I strained against the Security's grip. "Get off!"

Up and down the streets, doors to neighboring houses started opening. Families wielding lanterns stepped into the night, summoned by my cries. I shouted and struggled as the second Security began to push back the crowd.

"Get inside your houses! He could be dangerous."

"Boys, get inside, quickly," my father instructed, practically pushing my brothers through the door.

A few neighbors hesitantly returned to their homes, but most clustered closer, forming a ring around my family and our house. I heard shouts from beyond the crowd, and Wendell broke through, followed by three figures dressed in plain gray uniforms. My heart stuttered.

The Expos.

They wore helmets that were painted white, the visors obscuring their faces and concealing their identities. One of the Expos relieved the Security of his position and took over holding me against the wall. The other joined the Securities in trying to keep the crowd at bay.

A few feet away, I saw the third Expo extract a folded strip of cloth from a pouch at his waist. Only then did I stop struggling. There was no escape. As soon as I inhaled whatever was on that cloth, I would be dead.

"Storm!"

My head whipped around as Jon darted out of the house, his eyes wide with terror. He started toward me, but my brother Fabian grabbed him around the waist and pulled him back.

"Stop!" Jon screamed, punching Fabian's arms. "Let me go!"

I felt a sudden spark of determination and fought against the Expo with renewed vigor. "Jon!" My voice was raw. I couldn't leave Jon behind. They couldn't make me.

"What are they doing to him?" Jon cried, his voice cracking in desperation.

"He's an Exceptional!" my mother called shrilly.

"Stop!" Tears were running down his cheeks. "You're hurting him!"

He was scared, but his terror was nothing compared to mine. This was the last time I would ever see Jon, and the thought nearly paralyzed me. The Expo with the cloth hesitated, as if allowing me to say final words of goodbye.

I forced myself to stop fighting. I forced my voice to remain steady. I lifted my head, meeting Jon's gaze one last time. "It'll be okay, Jon." I blinked away the tears that had sprung into my own eyes. "It'll be okay."

I had never said anything further from the truth, and Jon knew it. He twisted around and threw himself into Fabian's arms, his sobs muffled by my brother's shirt.

The Expo with the cloth stepped up to me, obstructing the view of my family. Looking through his visor, I was surprised to see that he seemed young, almost my own age. As I peered closer, I caught a glimpse of his hazel eyes.

They begged me to trust him.

That was the last thing I noticed before the Expo flattened the cloth over my mouth and nose. I could only fight for so long before I was forced to suck in a strained breath.

Everything went black.

3

AILA

My eyes fluttered open. I was lying on my back, a stone ceiling stretched above me. It was so similar to the one in my bedroom at home that I almost rolled over and let myself fall back asleep. But then I felt the stiff bed against my back, noticed the stone walls and floor, saw the thick iron door on the opposite side of the otherwise empty room, and only then did my memory catch up with me.

I was an Exceptional. I had been reported, and the Expos had come.

And somehow, I was alive.

They'd made a mistake. That was the only explanation. Somehow, they hadn't used the right herb concoction on the cloth, and as soon as they realized it hadn't killed me, they would come in and finish the job. I swung my legs out of the bed and stood up abruptly, the cold floor stinging my feet. They had taken my shoes, but other than that I wore the same clothes I had woken up in this morning. My gaze darted around the cell, searching for a way out before the Expos discovered me.

But before I could even take a step, a loud clanging from the door made me freeze. A metal panel near the bottom slid open, and two brown eyes peered coldly through a slit, pinning me to place in the center of the room.

The eyes flicked away, and I heard a man say, "This one's awake."

Someone in the hall responded, but my mind spun too fast to make out the words. *This one's awake.* The man hadn't been surprised. He'd acted like I was supposed to be here, alive and well and standing in the middle of the room. And judging by his words, there were more Exceptionals that were alive.

The man on the other side of the door turned his attention back to me. "Brone will be with you shortly," he said, then slammed the panel closed.

I didn't know who Brone was, but I knew immediately that I didn't want to find out. I rushed to the door and planted both palms on the cool metal, searching desperately for a handle, a lever, anything. But other than the little indent for the panel, the door was smooth and solid. The rest of the walls were the same, even and windowless.

My hands shook as I stumbled back to the bed, barely reaching it before my legs gave out. I was alive, and that was something, but I had the terrible feeling that things were only going to get worse from here.

I didn't know how much time had passed when I heard movement on the other side of the door again. It had been a while, but not long enough for my shock to wear off completely.

Never in a million years had I expected Warren to report me. I could still hear the words he'd said back on that day when I turned in Chase. *Why did you tell, Aila?*

The scorn in his voice had remained in the things he said for days afterward:

If you were really his friend, you wouldn't have turned him in.

Is that how you throw away your eight years of friendship? With betrayal?

And, of course, the sentence that made me want to curl up in a ball and shut out the rest of the world forever, even now:

It's your fault Chase is dead. It's all your fault.

A few months later, Warren had stopped saying those things. He'd stopped saying anything to me unless he absolutely had to, only things like, "Can you pass the butter, Aila?" and "Mother wants us to buy groceries at the market before Father comes home from work." But he would never quite meet my gaze; his voice was glaringly empty of its old affection.

I had never imagined that he would end up doing the same thing he had shunned me for. We had drifted apart, but I hadn't realized just how far the chasm between us had grown.

But that's not what scared me the most. What scared me was if Warren had been the one to become an Exceptional, I would've done the exact same thing.

We'd all heard the stories, rumors whispered during lunch at school, the tales exchanged in hushed voices in candlelit rooms. Once, I overheard my father's friend, telling of a family who had learned their son was an Exceptional. They refused to report him, and the next day, their entire home was gone, the wooden hog's pen the only sign that anyone had ever lived in that field. Another time, when a boy in my class at school returned from a trip to the sea, he told me that there had been an Exceptional discovered in a nearby town. When his family passed through on their way home, nothing was left, not even the stone Security Station building.

If Warren had become an Exceptional, I would've reported him out of fear for the consequences, just as I had done to Chase.

Once more, Warren's biting words rang in my ears. *It's your fault Chase is dead.* But now, sitting alive on the rigid bed, I was beginning to wonder if even that was true.

Noise sounded once more on the other side of the door, muffled whispers exchanged between several people. The door swung open. A young man stepped through, dragging a chair behind him. He stepped aside to reveal the other man standing on the threshold.

Brone. I didn't need to know anything besides his name or see anything besides his eyes to know that this was the man behind the murder of Exceptionals. This was the bad guy, the evil mastermind, the man whose name sent shivers down my spine.

He was a tall man with square shoulders and graying black hair. His cold, calculating gray eyes fixed me with a piercing stare. He wore a dark uniform with black boots and gloves, and when he stepped into the room, he brought an air of authority. The other man retreated into the hall, and as soon as Brone was seated, the door to the cell swung shut, leaving the two of us alone. I tried to swallow, but my throat had gone dry.

Confidence, Aila, I told myself, but it was hard to find strength when I was facing the man who held my fate in his hands.

When he spoke, his voice was cold and collected.

"Neither of us are in the mood for a long conversation, so I'll keep it short. Do you know why you are here?"

I nodded, and when Brone didn't respond, I said, "I'm an Exceptional." My voice caught on the last word.

"And do you know who I am?"

I swallowed hard. "You're Brone."

Brone dipped his head slowly, and part of me withered. The deeply buried, barely acknowledged hope that I had somehow been rescued from the Expos was crushed, forcing me to look reality straight in the face.

Brone leaned forward. "Let me tell you about the Exceptionals." He stood up abruptly, standing before me like an intimidating tower, his expression stoic. In fact, I had not seen any flicker of emotion cross his eyes since he entered my cell. He was as dispassionate as the stone walls surrounding us.

"There is a common misconception about Exceptionals." His voice was a commanding rasp. "Many believe that anyone can become an Exceptional at any point in their lives. In truth, people only become Exceptionals the second week of each month, and newly discovered Exceptionals have only ever been between ages eight and eighteen."

I would've been surprised if I wasn't too busy remembering how to breathe. Only a man whose entire life was devoted to capturing Exceptionals would have noticed these patterns.

"Exactly twenty people become Exceptionals each month," Brone explained. "That means two hundred forty Exceptionals a year."

I sucked in a breath. *Two hundred forty.* Brone did not at all seem fazed that he was ruining the lives of that many children and families a year. But then, he did give this speech twenty times a month.

"Besides that, the manifestation of Exceptionals is completely random. It is not hereditary nor based on town or status or gender. *Anyone* between the ages of eight and eighteen can become an Exceptional." Brone fixed me with his icy stare. "And you are one of the unlucky people who did."

I flinched and looked away.

"Of course, you know why Exceptionals are dangerous."

"Their powers," I said. My voice sounded hoarse.

"Yes," Brone agreed flatly. "Their powers. Every Exceptional has one unique power, manifested before they turn nineteen. It's always there, simmering beneath the surface, but not all Exceptionals discover their powers right away."

I felt a surge of disappointment. I had been holding onto the faint hope that I would manifest super strength and be able to punch a hole in the wall and run to freedom.

"So here you are, in the place we call the Olum, a newly manifested Exceptional with a power on the way." Brone dropped back into his chair and gazed at me intently. "And now, Aila Vinn, you have a decision to make."

My gaze snapped up in surprise, and I didn't know whether to feel hope or dread. The cold glint in Brone's gaze made me think it should be the latter.

"You have two choices," he continued. "The first is death."

I felt a sudden irresistible laugh bubble in my throat. This didn't seem like it was going to be much of a decision at all.

"The second," Brone said, watching me carefully, "is to join the Exceptional Police."

The humor drained out of me immediately. Join the Expos? An image flashed through my mind of the emotionless figures, stealing life after life away from innocent children, hidden behind helmets and visors. How could I ever become one of them?

I thought of the gloves that perpetually covered their hands. How many Expos had been Exceptionals without anyone knowing? Did Earl Nicolin even know?

19

"This would mean that your time, your power, and your life would be dedicated to helping the Exceptional Police and working for their cause." Brone leaned forward. "Keep in mind that, in doing this, you will also be working for Earl Nicolin and therefore serving the entire country of Rosan."

I sucked in a trembling breath, my mind spinning and my chest tight. Was it worth working for the Earl of Rosan, our ruler, if it meant I had to be one of Brone's heartless Expos?

Brone cast me a final stare before he stood up and crossed to the iron door. He knocked on it twice, and the door swung open. The young man swept inside, grabbing the chair before retreating into the hall. Brone turned to me and grabbed the handle of the door.

"The choice is yours," he said. "You have one week to decide."

He pulled on the handle, and the cell door swung shut.

As I stared in the face of the black iron door, I realized I had been asking myself the wrong question. I should've been asking another one entirely.

Was my life worth ruining the lives of so many others?

It took me three hours to decide.

I spent every minute feeling as though I was balanced on the edge of a steep cliff, trying hard not to fall. One moment I was wracked with fear, and the next, wracked with guilt. In the end, I supposed I had known what my answer would be all along. Between joining the Expos or death, there wasn't much of a decision.

The guards checked in on me a few times every hour. They pretended as if they wanted to ask if I had made my decision yet, but I could tell from the way they lingered, surveying the room with a penetrated gaze, that they were really there to make sure I hadn't manifested my power. Clearly, Brone didn't want to risk letting anyone escape.

The next time a guard opened the slot, this time to deliver a plate of food, I hurried across the cell and dropped to a knee in front of the panel. "I've made my decision." The words left me in a rush before I could change my mind.

The brown eyes on the other side studied me carefully. "Already?"

I swallowed hard and nodded. The guard continued to stare, and it took me a moment to realize he was waiting for me to say something.

I took a deep breath. If I was going to make this decision, I couldn't do it while second-guessing and regretting. I had to make my decision and commit. Besides, this was what I wanted. I *wanted* to stay alive.

I lifted my chin, forced my voice to remain steady, and said, "Tell Brone I've agreed to join the Expos."

4

STORM

By the time the door handle turned, I was awake and ready to run.

I should've been dead. The reason I was still living and breathing and plotting escape was beyond me, but I wasn't about to waste the opportunity. I must've been awake for at least an hour. When I first woke, I laid stiffly in my bed for several minutes, trying to understand where I was, or if I was in a dream. Even now, every time I caught a glimpse of the glaring brown X on my left hand, I felt jarred all over again.

After I had gotten over the fact that, no, it hadn't been a dream, and yes, I was in fact still alive, I quickly realized three things.

First, the bed they had put me in was extremely comfortable. It was actually *soft*, unlike the hard ground I was forced to sleep on back in Ferrol. If this is what came with being an Exceptional, it wasn't all that bad.

Second, I realized there was no way to escape. I had felt along the stone walls, stood on my bed and reached for the window, and tried to break the brass doorknob off the wooden door. It was no use. I was trapped.

And finally, I realized with a wave of confusion that I was *supposed* to be alive. I hadn't accidentally woken up in a morgue with other dead bodies, or worse yet, a grave. I had woken up in a locked room on a soft bed. They'd known I would wake up. They had prepared for it. But whatever that meant, I didn't want to stick around and find out. I needed to get out of here. I needed to get back to Jon.

22

I sat on the edge of my bed, facing the door with my muscles tensed. I expected that someone would be sent to check on me sooner or later.

What I didn't expect was for that someone to be a boy who couldn't have been more than a year older than me.

I was on my feet the second the door clicked open. The boy backed into the room, laughing at whatever was going on in the hall. I scanned him quickly, my eyes catching on the gloves covering his hands before I noticed the dagger at his waist.

The boy backed a few more steps into the room before swinging around, a half smile on his face. He froze, his eyes widening.

"You're awake," he said, and I promptly lunged forward and shoved him against the wall.

Before the boy could react, I ripped the dagger from his scabbard and sprinted out into the hall. His shout of alarm echoed after me as I whipped around the corner and darted left. Then I saw it. At the end of the hall, several men and women had collected, swords strapped to their waists, blocking the way.

I slowed to a stop, hesitating. I had one dagger, and there were at least ten of them. I glanced over my shoulder, but the other end of the corridor ended in a wall. Which meant there was only one thing to do.

Without warning, I bolted toward the guards, swinging my dagger in front of me to part them. They pulled back to avoid the blade, and I charged through without resistance, feeling a thrill of triumph. But before I could take another step, one of the men stretched out his leg and tripped me. I stumbled in an attempt to regain balance, but another man slammed his shoulder into mine, sending me sprawling back onto the floor.

Immediately, the guards fanned out and surrounded me. One stepped forward and pressed his black boot onto my chest, pinning me. Another ripped the dagger from my grasp. I let my head fall back and stared up at the ceiling, but the sight made me pause. The stone walls arched up to a peak a few dozen feet above, and an intricate crystal chandelier dangled from the ceiling.

So, I was miraculously alive and had woken up in a lavish mansion. Things couldn't get much weirder.

A guard stepped over me, obstructing my view of the ceiling with a smirk. The dagger dangled from his fingers. "Next time, you might want to arm yourself a bit more before you charge ten trained guards."

"It was worth a shot," I retorted.

"No, I don't think it was," a cool, commanding female voice interrupted. The guards immediately parted to reveal a woman with brown hair cut in the straightest line I'd ever seen. Her pale green gaze was so sharp I half expected her to order my execution, but instead she just said, "That's not the way to make a first impression. I assume this is the newest recruit?" She directed her question at the guard still pinning me to the ground.

"He is, Commander White. He recovered from the valerian root sedative before we were prepared. He attacked Chase when he entered the room."

The woman's—Commander White's—eyes flicked around the group with concern, and a few of the guards quickly parted to let the boy who had entered my cell step through.

He and the commander seemed to exchange silent words with just a glance, and then Chase said, "He was awake and standing when I entered the room. Something in the sleep sedative must've been off."

The guard pressed his boot harder on my chest, and I shifted uncomfortably on the ground. Chase's gaze darted from me to the guard. "Lighten up a bit. You're hurting him."

The guard snorted and opened his mouth to respond, but was silenced by a sharp glance from Commander White. The hall fell silent as she studied me once more, her expression curious. I clenched my jaw impatiently. The ground was cold, my chest hurt from the boot of the guard—who had ignored Chase's request—and I didn't like the feeling of being a specimen under examination.

After another long second, I said, "So are you waiting for me to tell my life story or what?"

"Let him up!" Commander White barked.

The guards immediately shifted to give me space. The man standing over me removed his boot from my chest and grabbed my collar, yanking me roughly to my feet. I shoved him away just as roughly.

"What's your name?" the commander asked, drawing my attention back to her.

I met her cold green gaze head-on. "Storm."

"Last name?"

I rolled my eyes. "Dawson."

"Mr. Dawson. You are an Exceptional."

I snorted and wondered if it was stupid to try running again. "Thanks. I hadn't noticed."

She narrowed her eyes at me, then spun to face the rest of the guards. "Who prepared the sleep sedative for the cloth?"

It was the second time I'd heard it referred to as the sedative. Not the *death sedative*. They hadn't tried to kill me. They hadn't *wanted* to kill me.

Everyone turned to Chase, and with a start, I recognized his hazel eyes. He was the boy who had gazed at me reassuringly through his visor, back during my capture.

But he was also the boy who had forced me to breathe in the sedative, so I wasn't about to go around becoming friends with him.

Chase said, "I got the cloth from Emer."

"Thank you, Mr. Kader." Commander White turned to the guard who had been holding me to the floor. "Chadrick, find Emer and have her refresh on the sedative guidelines and confirm she is using the correct amount of valerian root."

The guard snapped into a salute, tossed me one last glare, then hurried down the hall. I couldn't say I was going to miss him.

"Mr. Dawson." I glanced toward Commander White. "Tell me, what did you do after you woke up?"

"I tried to escape." And I would probably try again.

"How?"

"By attacking Chase and stealing his dagger."

"And what did you do next?"

25

I was confused by this interrogation, this building, this entire situation, and I was through with it. Ignoring her question, I said flatly, "Why am I alive?"

Commander White raised her eyebrows. "Would you rather be dead?"

I opened my mouth, but she began speaking to the guards before I could say a word. "Wake up the rest of the recruits, and bring them to lunch. I will speak with them in my office afterwards."

"Wait, lunch?" I sputtered, but everyone ignored me as all but two guards and Chase peeled away, disappearing down the hall.

"Lyle, show Storm the refectory," the commander said. "Then the three of you are dismissed for the rest of the day. Good work." She turned to the guard who still held the dagger I'd stolen, and beckoned for him to return it to Chase. "This wasn't your fault," she told him in a gentler voice as he resheathed the weapon. Chase nodded once, and then her eyes landed on me again, just as scrutinizing as before.

"It's clear that you're a fighter, Mr. Dawson, and that will either be a good thing or a bad thing for us." Her piercing gaze stared straight into my soul. "Let's make it a good thing." With that, she spun on her heel and strode off down the corridor.

Without another glance in my direction, Lyle started down the hall after her. Chase and the other guard followed, and for a moment I considered making another break for it. I reluctantly decided against it, which turned out to be a good decision. The three of them led me down a labyrinth of corridors, and I was lost in about thirty seconds.

Stone walls raced up into vaulted ceilings, and high above, arched windows let light to pour in. Intricate paintings and vibrant tapestries hung on the walls, and dark oak doors dotted the halls. Some hung open, allowing me to see into classrooms, lounge areas, and even larger halls. It was a stark contrast to what I had expected the Expo base to be, although I did notice all the windows were too high to see through. I had no idea where we were in the complex. Any of the doors could lead outside or just to another room.

"If you're not going to kill me, why don't you just let me go?" I said, raising my voice to ensure the guards in front of me heard.

"Not going to happen," Lyle said without even turning around. "Just be happy you're alive."

I opened my mouth to respond, but Chase cut me a glance and shook his head sharply. I was about to snap at him to leave me alone, but I remembered that I still didn't know what these peoples' deal was, and I bit my words. The guards finally stopped before a door that hung open. The sound of chatter poured through the opening and into the hall. Lyle gestured for me to enter, but the second I stepped through the arched doorway, I drew to a halt.

The room that stretched before me was undoubtedly the eating refectory. It looked big enough to fit every building in Ferrol, and it was filled with five sets of wooden tables and benches that spread across the length of the room. Platters of food covered an entire table on the far side of the room. However, it wasn't the room that surprised me most, but the people inside. They were all ranging from about eight to eighteen and sat leisurely at the tables, jabbering and laughing as they ate.

And all of them had a brown X on their left hand, standing out like a bright flame burning in the night.

"They're all Exceptionals," I whispered. I twisted around to find Lyle and the other guard were gone. Chase was the only one left, and as I watched, he pulled off his left glove to reveal the brown X on the back of his hand.

"That's impossible." My head whipped back and forth between his hand and the roomful of very many, very alive Exceptionals.

"And yet here we are."

I gaped at him. "Am I dreaming?"

Chase laughed, a genuine laugh, the kind I hadn't heard in a while. I didn't quite know how to respond, so I was grateful when he said, "Don't worry, Commander White will explain everything to you after lunch. Grab a plate and some food from the table on the left then find a place to sit and eat. I'm sure you're hungry."

I was starving, but I was so used to constant gnawing in my stomach that I hadn't even noticed. I started toward the food table, then paused when I noticed Chase wasn't following. "You're not coming?"

Chase shook his head. "I'm out of training," he said, as if that explanation answered the question instead of raising more. "I'll see you after lunch."

As he disappeared through the doors, I made a beeline for the platters of food, piling as much meat and fruit and bread on my plate as possible before finding a seat at an empty table. Even though I was confused and worried about Jon to the point that it hurt, it wasn't hard to enjoy the meal. It was like going to Carsley Market, except all the food was free. I didn't even know what half the stuff was. I dug in, and for a moment I felt all the stress drain out of me. If only Jon had been here to enjoy it with me.

That thought killed my mood, and I was scowling at my plate when I heard footsteps approaching. I glanced up as a boy maybe a year older than me strutted between the rows of tables. Judging by his wide, darting eyes, he was another new Exceptional. He slammed his plate down on the table across from me with such force that the entire surface trembled, all while glaring at me as if it was my fault he was an Exceptional.

He was taller than I was, and well-built, dressed in richly colored clothing made of fine material. Judging by the light brown shade of his skin, his dark hair and eyes, and the fact that he was wearing a clean pair of boots, he was from a Stone City.

My suspicions were confirmed when he dropped into his seat and growled, "I'm only here because this was the only open bench. If it wasn't for that, no one from Travertine would stoop so low as to sit with a street rat."

Travertine. Because it was the closest to Rosan City, the capital, Travertine was the most prominent Stone City. At least one member of each family worked for the Earl, meaning everyone in that town had more money than they knew how to use. I felt anger burn in my stomach. There he was, dressed in his perfectly tailored clothes and practically ignoring the food on his plate, while Jon and I suffered in poverty with the rest of Ferrol.

28

Biting back my fury, I smirked across the table at the boy. "At least my father doesn't work for the same government that took you away to die."

The boy slammed his palms down on the table and shot to his feet. "You take that back!"

"Wow, you're stuck up *and* you have a temper."

"Watch your tongue, street rat!"

"You're just proving me right, rich boy."

The chatter of the Refectory died away as people began to turn and stare in our direction. The boy noticed and quickly dropped back into his seat, glaring silently at me over the platter of fruit. I just went back to eating my meal, and the noise of the room slowly returned to normal volume.

Over the next half hour, new Exceptionals trickled in, until there were five of us in total. The youngest was a girl who was probably around nine years old, and the oldest was a young man nearing eighteen. Besides the rich boy—who was still glowering at me—I could tell that the third arrival, a thirteen-year-old girl, was the only other one from a Stone City. They both looked like a fish out of water, so clearly unaccustomed to difficult situations like this one.

I finished my meal before the rest of them and suddenly had no desire to continue sitting here and pretending to be content. I stood abruptly and swung my leg over the bench.

The boy from Travertine looked up at me through narrowed eyes. "Where are you going?"

The other new Exceptionals stopped eating and glanced up to watch.

I wasn't about to give them a scene again. Ignoring the boy, I turned around and strode between the tables and out the door. I took the first right, but I made it no more than three steps when I heard the sound of rapid footsteps behind me. Someone grabbed my arm, and I whirled around furiously.

"What?" I snapped.

The Travertine boy released me and crossed his arms. "They never said we were allowed to leave the Refectory," he said.

"They never said we couldn't." I turned around and started down the hall once more, the boy matching my every step.

"You won't be able to escape," he said. "The Exceptionals are dangerous. Someone would have made sure this place has strong security."

Another corridor branched off of the main one, and I hesitated, considering my options. "Stop talking about them like that. You're an Exceptional too, rich boy. And besides," I said, continuing straight down the hall, "I've been in worse fixes."

"You're going to get in trouble," he said, trailing after me.

I reached an intersection of halls and paused to contemplate. "You are, too, if you keep following me."

"I'll turn you in."

I stopped and spun to face him, smirking. "To whom? The same people who captured you and brought you here? Are you gonna go crying to your *father*, rich kid?"

"Stop calling me that!" he snapped.

I shrugged and turned back around. For a moment, the boy was silent, and I hoped he had given up and gone back to the Refectory. But then he said, "You're lost."

I was, but there was no way I would admit that to him. I peered to the left and the right, but all the infuriating corridors looked the same.

"Face it. You're not getting out of here," the boy said.

I gritted my teeth, hating that he was right. But once more, I kept my frustration suppressed. "I'm not the only one who needs to face the truth. We both know you're only following me because if I find a way out, that means you'll be free, too."

The Travertine boy fell silent once more. I could practically feel the anger radiating off him. The hall in front of me had a broad staircase at the end. Maybe we were underground, and that would lead me to the ground level. I started towards it, and to my annoyance, the boy followed.

When he spoke, his voice trembled furiously. "I'd *never* need help from a criminal, you scrawny, worthless, lazy—"

"Woah, don't use your whole vocabulary in one sentence."

The boy's face flushed with rage.

"Storm!"

I spun around to see Chase striding down the hall in our direction, his face etched with relief. He threw a questioning glance at the Travertine boy but passed by him, drawing to a stop in front of me.

"We've been looking for you. What are you doing out here?"

The boy sneered. "I told you that you'd get in trouble."

Chase glanced at him again. "Aris, right?"

The boy jerked his head with a scowl. "Aris Castillo." He spoke the name like it was supposed to mean something, but I was tempted to keep calling him rich kid just to spite him.

"Right." Chase blinked at him. "I hate to break it to you, but you weren't in the refectory, either, which would mean you're in trouble as well."

I coughed to hide a chuckle. Aris's eyes widened in anger, and he took a threatening step toward Chase.

"Watch what you're saying," he snarled, jabbing a finger into Chase's chest. "My parents both work for the government, and I live in Travertine, which, if you didn't know, is a Stone—"

"Excellent," Chase interrupted, brushing Aris's finger off his chest as if it were a pesky fly. "I'm from Bedrock. It's nice to meet someone else from the Stone Cities."

Aris stared at Chase, and I mirrored his shock. Chase didn't fit any of my preconceptions about people from the Stone Cities, and although I insisted on hating every person who lived there, Chase seemed to contradict all of the stuck-up, insufferable stereotypes.

"Commander White is waiting to speak with you," he said, becoming serious once more. "I'll take you to her office."

Chase started off down the hall, and I quickened my pace, so we were walking in stride. Aris lagged behind, clearly angry at both Chase and me and maybe just life in general. I dropped my voice and leaned toward Chase.

"You're really from the Stone Cities?"

He blinked. "You think I'd lie?"

"We all do crazy things to get what we want."

31

Chase pursed his lips, his eyes searching my face. "Do I want to know why you weren't in the refectory?"

"I was looking for a restroom," I said, studying a passing tapestry with sudden interest.

"Storm." Chase waited until I turned back to him. "Don't try that again, okay?"

"What are you talking about?"

"I know I just met you today, but it's easy to tell from your little stunt after you woke up what type of person you are," Chase attempted to catch my gaze, but I ignored him. His voice hardened as he repeated, "Don't try to escape. Do you understand?"

"I wasn't—"

"*Storm.*"

I looked at him.

"You're safe here," Chase said, "but the second you go out there into the real world, it's anybody's game. You have to understand that."

I didn't respond. Chase didn't understand; these people may not be the Expos everyone thought they knew—or even Expos at all—but even if I was safe here, I couldn't stay. I needed to get back to Jon, and I couldn't do that while I was cooped up with the same people who had dragged me away from home in the first place.

We stopped in front of one of the many wooden doors, and I heard the commander's voice coming from the other side. Chase placed his hand on the handle, but instead of opening it, he leaned toward me and muttered, "Stay calm in there. No matter what, you *have* to stay with the Insurgence."

Giving me one final look, he pushed open the door and ushered Aris and me inside

5

STORM

I swung around just in time to see Chase close the door in my face.

The Insurgence. I didn't know what that meant, but it was clear that whoever these people were, they were not the Expos. Part of me wanted to believe that was a good thing.

But the other part of me wanted nothing more than to get back to Jon, and I was growing worried that doing so wasn't going to be easy.

"Mr. Dawson, Mr. Castilllo, nice of you to join us."

Commander White sat on the far side of the room, behind a large wooden desk that separated her from where the other new Exceptionals perched on the edge of their chairs.

"Please, have a seat," she said, beckoning to two adjacent chairs, giving Aris and me no choice but to sit beside each other. She waited until we grudgingly dropped into our seats before continuing.

"We were concerned to hear that you had left the cafeteria." Commander White stared at me with her pale green eyes, like she knew it was my fault.

"We got lost while trying to find the restrooms," I lied easily. After years of fibbing my way out of robberies, the words flowed from my mouth without hesitation, but I could tell by the way her lips pinched that she didn't believe me.

"Before we begin," she said, returning her gaze to the rest of the Exceptionals, "how many of you have parents that work for the government?"

Aris and the teenage girl I had suspected of being from the Stone Cities raised their hands.

Commander White leaned toward them. "Let me make one thing clear," she said, her voice suddenly harsh. "Your parents work for the same government that had the two of you taken away to be killed."

The girl flinched, and Aris's gaze hardened with anger. He opened his mouth to speak, but the commander cut him off.

"We aren't planning to kill you, and you'll be completely safe as long as you follow our orders," Commander White said, "but the second you decide to go running back to your parents, we'll send you straight to the Olum."

I hadn't heard of the Olum before, but it wasn't hard to guess what it was.

"So you're not the Expos, then?" The oldest boy spoke up from the other side of Aris, his voice holding a note of hope.

Commander White chuckled. "No. No, we are not the Expos. We are the Insurgence."

Our response to the declaration rippled through us like a stone dropped in water. Everyone seemed to sag simultaneously in relief, but at the same time frown in confusion.

"The belief that the Exceptionals are taken away to be killed is only a half-truth," Commander White explained. "Not all of them die. We are able to reach some of the Exceptionals before Expos do. There are many rules to Exceptionals that will be explained in due time, but the most important is this: Exceptionals only manifest during the second week of the month. We call this Mission Week, and we do our best to have as many small groups in as many towns as possible and get to the Exceptionals before the Expos do." Commander White leaned forward. "And that's why we need you."

Of course. That's why she'd called me a recruit. They didn't just rescue Exceptionals; they employed them.

"The more people we have, the faster we can respond." Commander White made eye contact with each one of us in turn, her gaze meeting mine last. "The faster we can respond, the more lives we can save."

34

I stared back at her, my mind racing. Not only did they give us food and shelter, but they gave us a purpose. As long as I could remember, my entire life had been devoted to keeping Jon and myself alive. The thought of having another goal, something greater, made my heart thud wildly in my chest.

Suddenly, becoming an Exceptional seemed like the best thing that had ever happened to me.

"Exceptionals are vital to our cause," Commander White said, "simply because the rest of us don't have powers."

I had heard that the powers were what made Exceptionals so dangerous, but clearly Commander White didn't fear them. In fact, her tone was one of respect. I frowned, wondering if I was misreading her voice.

Or maybe the government had been lying to us. Maybe its corruption went deeper than I knew.

"There are many types of powers, each one unique. Some Exceptionals have enhanced senses while others have extra speed or strength. Before you turn nineteen, you will manifest your own ability. If you agree to the conditions of working for the Insurgence, we will give you food and shelter and train you to use that ability in exchange for your service."

I studied her warily. "What are the conditions?"

"Good question," Commander White said, and I heard murmurs of interest from the other Exceptionals. "First, you'll have to train before we deem you fit to go on missions. We need each one of you to be able to follow commands, move quickly, and make logical decisions. You also need to learn about the geography of Rosan and the layouts of different towns, so you don't get lost on the missions."

I nodded, imagining the look on Aris's face when I crushed him in every type of physical competition.

"There is one more thing," Commander White added. She tossed me a warning glance, and I felt a sudden sinking feeling in my stomach. "Exceptionals are not, under any circumstances, allowed to leave the Insurgence Base unless they are on a mission."

I sucked in a breath. They wouldn't let me leave. They wouldn't let me go back to Jon. *Jon.* I thought of the last time I'd seen him. His face had been buried into Fabian's shirt, and he'd been sobbing. I'd left him. There was no one else to look after him, no one else who understood him. Suddenly, the urge to see Jon again was so strong I wanted to scream.

Instead, I dug my fingers into the wooden arms of my chair with renewed determination. I needed to get out of here. I should've known better than to believe I'd actually find a good life at the Insurgence.

"Now," Commander White continued, oblivious to my sudden change in emotion, "is there anyone who has an issue with the terms of agreement?"

A silence settled over the group as we all shifted uncomfortably. I doubted there was an Exceptional in the room who *didn't* have an issue with the conditions, but there wasn't much of an alternative.

"Very well, then," Commander White said, looking unsurprised by the lack of response. "The five of you will—"

"I have an issue," I blurted.

Commander White blinked. "Excuse me?"

I pushed my chair back and slowly rose to my feet. "I have an issue with the conditions," I told her. "Specifically the last one."

Commander White stood, too, just as slowly. "I'm afraid the conditions are nonnegotiable. In order for you to become a member of the Insurgence, you must agree to all terms."

"Well, I don't agree."

The commander looked taken aback. "Are you sure?"

"Yes, I'm sure," I snapped. "I'm not going to allow myself to be imprisoned here."

Commander White gritted her teeth. "This base is a safe haven, not a *prison*—"

"Then why can't we come and go freely?" I laughed scornfully. "I'm not agreeing to anything. *I'm not joining.* Let me go home."

Commander White straightened her spine. Her initial shock had worn off, replaced with a hard expression. "I'm afraid, Mr. Dawson, that is not an option."

It was my turn to be surprised. "What?"

"We cannot let you leave the Base without permission, and I do not give it."

"But I didn't agree to the conditions—"

"I'm afraid we cannot let you go, whether you agree or not," she said regretfully. "The survival of the Insurgence depends on secrecy."

I stared at her for a moment longer, my heart pounding in panic. Then, before anyone could react, I spun and bolted for the door.

I was surprised to find it unlocked. For all this talk of staying in the Base, they were making it painfully easy to go wherever I wanted. I burst into the hall and veered right. I had no idea where I was going, but in my short time here I had come to understand that the Insurgence Base was huge. If I could just find an unlocked door, maybe I could hide out in a room and let things die down before searching for an exit.

However, I was barely halfway down the hall when someone stepped from an alcove in the wall, blocking my path.

It was Chase, and he looked annoyed.

"Did you listen to a thing I said?"

I could've kept running, but for some reason, I stopped short. Maybe if Chase heard me out, he would give me some help. "I can't join the Insurgence. My brother is back in Ferrol. I'm not leaving him."

"You don't have a choice," Chase said.

"Actually, turns out I do, and I'm choosing to get out of here." I tried to step around Chase, but he matched my movement.

"Storm, you aren't *listening*—"

I was done listening. I sidestepped Chase and started down the hall again.

"Storm, wait!" he called after me. "Please, hear me out!"

I ignored him, and to my surprise, he let me go. I reached an intersection of hallways and slowed, trying to remember which one led back to the Refectory. Maybe it would also take me to some sort of exit.

"Storm!" I heard Chase call from behind me. "I'm sorry."

There was an unexpected note of warning in his voice that caused me to turn around, just in time to see a man step into my path. His fist collided with the side of my head, and everything went dark.

I woke up to find myself staring at a familiar ceiling. But of course, it was not the ceiling of my home, which meant I wasn't any closer to getting back to Jon. I sat up and groaned, rubbing my temple where the guard had made contact. The punch had been effective; I could feel a bruise forming. I wondered how many times the man had done that to stop an Exceptional from trying to escape.

A beam of light from the setting sun sliced through the window above my bed, casting the door in a golden glow. I felt a bolt of panic. I'd been unconscious for several hours, which meant I had already wasted too much time. I swung my legs out of bed and stood, only to stumble as a fresh wave of pain shot through my head. The room swirled around me, and I braced myself on the nearest wall, closing my eyes against the stars that sprung to my gaze.

The sound of a key turning in the lock caught my attention, and my eyes flew open. Four guards armed with swords pushed their way into the room, then cleared the way to let Chase step in behind them. I glared at him, although if I was being honest, he *had* tried to warn me.

"I'm not agreeing to anything," I spat. "Keep me locked up in here for all I care. I'm not working with the Insurgence." With that, I crossed my arms and turned my back on them, fixing my gaze resolutely on the stone wall.

The silence that followed stretched on so long, I wondered if the soldiers had left without me noticing. Then Chase said, "Let me talk to him alone."

A mumble of unease rippled through the guards. "You're unarmed—" one woman began.

"That means he can't steal a weapon from me, which I'm sure he'd do the second the door closed," Chase replied. There was a pause, then he said, "Storm won't hurt me."

It was true. Chase wasn't the one who wronged me, and I wouldn't harm an innocent person. I continued to stare at the wall as I heard the guards file out of the room, shutting the door behind them.

Then I said, "You aren't going to change my mind."

"Storm—"

"*No.*" I turned around to face Chase, my voice leaving no room for argument. "I've made my decision. I'm not joining."

Chase hesitated for a moment, then nodded his head slowly. He dropped down to sit on the floor and leaned his back against the door, turning his face up toward the window. The warm ray of light slanted across his face, making him look younger and more trustworthy than ever. I paused, then perched myself on the edge of my bed, a silence settling between us.

Finally, Chase said, "You're safe here."

"I'm a prisoner here."

"No, you're not—"

"They say I'm not allowed to leave, and the second I try, I'm knocked unconscious."

Chase paused, then said, "Okay, fine, but you're still safe here."

"Look." I waited until Chase met my gaze. "My life has never exactly been a bed of roses and riches. I don't *care* about being safe. I care about Jon."

Chase's expression softened. "Your brother?"

I nodded, my throat tightening.

Chase sighed and let his head fall back against the door. "Storm, we've all had to leave someone behind that we loved when we became Exceptionals." He looked wistful, and I immediately wanted to know more about the day when he became an Exceptional. In the short time I'd been here, Chase was the only teenager who seemed to have any sort of standing in this place. He'd told me himself that he was already out of training. I didn't know what training was, but if Chase was beyond the status of most teens his age, he must've been young when he was recruited.

I wondered who he'd left behind all those years ago, what memories plagued him at night.

I shook my head. "The difference is that I'm making an effort to get back to him."

Chase's entire demeanor changed. He straightened up, his jaw clenched, and his eyes sparked with a sudden ferocity. "Stop. *Never* say that others haven't made efforts to get back to our old lives," he said sharply. "None of us *wanted* to leave our friends and family. No, the difference is that we were smart enough to realize how dangerous it was. If we went back, we would put the whole existence of the Insurgence at risk. That's why no one can leave. What makes you think you're the exception?"

I slammed my fist down on the sheets of the bed. "I need to get back to Jon!"

"No, what you *need* is to stop being so selfish," Chase snapped, and I flinched. He shoved himself off the ground and crossed the room in my direction. "I understand that you want to see Jon again. Believe me, I know how it feels. But every time you try to get what you want, you're putting others' lives at risk. By endangering the Insurgence, you're endangering the lives of all the future Exceptionals we could possibly save. People could die, Storm, and for what? So one self-centered boy can see his brother again?"

I stared straight back at him, but felt a stab of guilt.

Chase must've, too, because suddenly his expression softened, and he took a step back. "We all had to make sacrifices, Storm," he said quietly. "I'm not saying it's easy, but it's necessary to make the world a better place."

If Chase wanted me to feel ashamed, he'd succeeded. I lowered my gaze, and he lingered a moment more before turning and starting back toward the door. He paused with his fingers resting on the handle.

"Trust me, Storm. If it were safe to go back, I would've done so ages ago," he said, then swept through the door.

6

AILA

I had known joining the Expos would be far from fun and games, but I hadn't quite realized to what extent this would be true.

First of all, I remained locked in my cell for the majority of the day. Brone said he would move me to the girl's barracks once he deemed me to be trustworthy, but until then, a guard named Jax escorted me from my cell for training and meals in the Common Area. That was it.

Second, the training was not at all what I'd anticipated. Deep down, I'd been expecting it to be something like recess at school, with sunshine and laughing children. But it quickly became clear that not only would I be prevented from going outside the Olum, I wouldn't even get the chance to *see* outside. The stone corridors were windowless, and training sessions were held in a large, cavernous room. Also, no one was laughing.

Not even remotely.

The training was tiered in three levels. Once I reached Level Three, I would be allowed to participate in Recruitment Week. Until then, I started at Level One.

"Training Level One" was really just another way of saying "spend all your time and energy trying to discover your power." On the first day, I spent two hours concentrating on my hands and trying to get water to flow out of them. I then moved to running in circles in an attempt to manifest super speed. I wrapped up the day by staring at a board across the room, trying to see if I would develop enhanced eyesight and be able to read the numbers on the board.

The first six days were so horrendous that I considered pretending to be diseased when Jax pounded on my cell door the seventh morning. I was pleasantly surprised when, instead of escorting me to my regular training room, he led me to a new one.

The new room was even larger than the one I'd been training in before. It buzzed with activity but lacked the structure of the other room. A group of teens sparred with a variety of weapons to my left while a few Exceptionals practiced shooting bows and arrows at the targets to my right. Others were racing through a series of obstacles, overseen by an instructor.

I turned excitedly to Jax as a group of trainees ran past on their jog around the room's perimeter. "Did I advance to the next training level?"

"Not yet," Jax grunted, pointing across the room. With disappointment, I recognized my fellow Level One trainees, standing at the base of a twenty foot rock wall. The large, rectangular stone pillar stood in the corner of the training room, towering above everything else.

"Every seven days, there is a competition between Level One trainees and select Level Two trainees," Jax explained. "You already know that you can move up the levels by manifesting your power, but you can also beat a Level Two in these competitions. Looks like you're scaling the rock wall today."

I rolled back my shoulders, lifting my chin as I approached the group. As long as I could remember, I had spent hours struggling to scale the nine foot walls that divided properties in Bedrock, fighting to keep up with Chase and Warren. I'd never quite succeeded. Once, I had even fallen, twisting my ankle so bad that I was on bed rest for the next two weeks. But the second I was cleared to stand, I was back at it again, chasing after the boys.

This rock wall was just like those stone walls at home. All I had to do was find the cracks, use the ledges, and I'd be well on my way to Level Two.

I joined my training group as a cluster of Level Twos gathered next to us. The instructors, clad in dark uniforms and incapable of smiling, called one member of each group forward to compete. Very few from my group made it to the top ahead of a Level Two, but those who did clambered down to rejoin us with grins of triumph.

Only four Level One trainees remained when I heard my name called.

"Aila Vinn, competing against June Palmer."

I sucked in a breath, my heart racing in my chest. As I stepped forward, a girl from the Level Two group joined me at the base of the climbing wall. She had dark brown hair that fell in curls across her shoulders and bright hazel eyes. My heart clenched. Her eyes reminded me of Chase.

Focus, I told myself sharply. If I performed well today, Brone might finally move me out of the cell. He might finally trust me. I couldn't mess up.

"You ready?" the girl asked, offering me a friendly smile as we craned our necks to study the wall.

"I haven't tried it before."

She shrugged. "I'm sure you'll do great."

"Contestants ready," one of the instructors droned.

June stepped away, positioning herself on the side of the wall that was around the corner. I eyed the path ahead of me one last time.

"Three...two...one...*go!*"

I launched myself at the wall the moment the last word left the instructor's mouth, already reaching for the next handhold. My fingers curled around the tiny ledge as I hoisted myself up a few feet, following the path I had just mapped out in my head. I heard June's breathing as she scrambled up the wall, but the edge of the wall hid her progress.

I continued to climb, but my foot slid against a tiny ledge halfway up. I gritted my teeth, straining to keep my grasp on the thin handholds. The Expos had provided me with basic uniforms consisting of pants, shirts, and boots, and I wished I had thought to take off my boots before we started. They weren't exactly ideal for climbing a stone wall.

The handholds became smaller and further apart the higher I climbed, slowing my progress. I could hear June pulling ahead and forced myself to move faster. I was only a few yards from the top when one of my feet slipped. I let out a shout as I lost my footing completely, which left me hanging fifteen feet in the air, clinging to the wall with just my hands. My boots scrabbled against the wall in search of another foothold.

"Are you okay?" I heard June's voice from around the corner. She had heard me and stopped advancing up the other side of the wall.

I gritted my teeth, unable to respond from the effort it took to keep from losing my grip. My hands were beginning to ache, my knuckles turning white with strain.

I heard movement on the other side of the wall, and a moment later, June's head poked around the corner. Her eyes widened when she saw my situation.

"There's a foothold right beneath you—no, to the left a little bit—no, back to the right, down a little more, and—" June made a frustrated sound. "Oh, I'm just coming over."

With difficulty, she started to climb down to my level and around the corner. I waited until she was a few feet below me, ready to direct my feet to the ledges, before I acted. I kicked against the wall and started surged forward, scrambling upward with renewed vigor, ignoring my aching hands. Finally, I threw an arm over the top of the wall and pulled myself onto the flat top, gasping for breath as I collapsed onto the platform.

Moments later, June clambered over the edge, panting. She fell down next to me, and two of us lay there, drawing in rapid breaths.

"I win," I said at last, pushing myself into a sitting position.

"You cheated," she accused.

I shook my head in denial.

"You knew what you were doing the whole time."

I paused, then relented with a nod. I had planned my entire route beforehand, deciding where I would "slip" before I even got on the wall. "But that wasn't cheating," I added quickly. "They never specified the rules. I just decided to bank on you being a nice person."

June narrowed her eyes. "That's low."

"You're just jealous you didn't think of it first."

June laughed. I leaned over the edge to where the two instructors stood, mumbling amongst themselves. The Level Two instructor, a thin man with dark eyes, was nodding grimly as my instructor, a tall woman with a pointed nose, made sharp, aggravated gestures. The Level Two instructor caught me looking and narrowed his eyes.

"We should probably head down," I said, pulling back from the ledge.

June nodded, and we made our way to the staircase next to the rock wall, which led back down to the floor. She stopped me before I started down.

"You should eat dinner with us tonight," she said. "I noticed you've been sitting alone."

I blinked in surprise. That wasn't exactly unusual for me. After Chase became an Exceptional and Warren started to ignore me, I had grown used to spending my lunch hour at school eating in solitude.

But June had noticed me. She'd noticed me and was offering me a place at her table.

"Will you?" June pressed. "I know our table may seem boisterous at times, but we'd love to have you."

It'd been a long time since someone had gone out of their way to talk to me, so long that I almost didn't know what to say. "Sure," I said at last, and we started down the stairs to the main level.

The instructors met us at the bottom, their faces twisted into disapproving scowls. My Level One instructor spoke first.

"Aila Vinn. After some discussion, we have agreed that, although you did win, you will not be advancing onto Level Two."

I felt my heart drop.

"Why not?" June said immediately. "She beat me, so she gets to advance."

My instructor stared down her nose at June. "She beat you, but not fairly. She did not follow the rules."

"What rules do you have against someone using their brain?"

"*June.*" The Level Two instructor glared at her with his beady eyes until she fell silent.

"Our decision is final," my instructor said sharply. "You can try again next week, but you will not be moving on to Level Two today."

"Actually, I think she will."

All four of us started, and I twisted around to see Brone striding past the crowd of Level One trainees. His gray eyes met mine for a bare second before darting back to the instructors.

"Brone," my instructor said, lowering her head and stepping back, but not before I saw her eyes flash with fear. "By all means, enlighten us with your opinion."

"What Miss Palmer said was correct. Never in your instructions did you specify how the trainees were to get to the top of the wall, just that they should. Miss Vinn used her head and was able to beat her opponent. I think that type of cunning is worthy of praise, not punishment. Wouldn't you agree?"

"Of course." The words couldn't seem to stutter out of my instructor's mouth fast enough. "Of course, sir."

The Level Two instructor nodded so aggressively I knew he'd have neck pain tomorrow.

"Well, I am glad we are in agreement." Brone offered them a tight smile, then turned his attention to me. "Well done, Miss Vinn. I hope to see you continue to perform so admirably in Level Two."

With that, he spun and disappeared through the doors, as if he'd never even been there.

The instructors muttered to each other and shuffled off, calling out the names of the next two trainees and leaving June and me alone. She beamed at me, her eyes bright.

"Great job, Aila! Come on, I'll introduce you to some of the people in Level Two."

"June, wait." I grabbed her arm, stopping her before she could walk off. "I just want to say...thank you. For defending me."

June just smiled. "I was only pointing out the work you'd done already."

She turned back around, and I followed after her, realizing I had just made a friend in one of the most unlikely places.

46

The Common Area was as vast as the training rooms, but filled with tables instead of equipment. Instead of heading to one of the round tables in the corner, where I usually enjoyed my meals in silence, I quickly pinpointed June at a long rectangular table and started in her direction. She waved when she saw me and scooted over to make room at the end of the bench.

I sat down with my plate of food as June returned her attention to a boy with rugged features and startlingly pale hair. I had often seen him during training, attempting to be an overachiever in just about everything, always the center of attention. Now, he was on his feet, acting out a tale with exuberant gestures.

"—I was running like mad, and the guy was chasing me," the boy said, blue eyes glowing with the heat of the story. "The sky was clear, but there was a new moon, so I could hardly see in front of me. Then suddenly I *tripped*, and fell right into a ditch on the side of the road."

Some of the other boys laughed, but not one interrupted the wild tale.

"I twisted my ankle—"

"Yeah, right, Ross," a boy called out.

Ross rolled his eyes. "Well, it's not like it was an official diagnosis or anything, but my ankle hurt, all right?"

Everyone laughed, and it was clear this boy was a favorite among the Exceptionals. It made sense—he was upbeat and charismatic, bringing the sort of unbridled joy and energy that the Olum seemed to suck out of us. I couldn't help but smile along as the boy continued.

"...and before I could get up, the boy caught up with me. So there I was, lying in the ditch, but very heroically, might I add. The guy was leaning over me, but I couldn't see what he looked like, because it was dark. And then the cloud drifted away, uncovering the moon—"

"I thought you just said there was a new moon!" one of the girls piped up.

Several people snickered, but Ross just waved them off. "Just roll with it, guys, okay?"

There were a few more chuckles, but Ross continued on, undeterred. "So the moon broke through, lighting up his entire body, and then I saw it. The *mark*. He was an *Exceptional!*"

The whole table roared with laughter, and I chuckled along. Of course back then—if this story was true—Ross would've been terrified to see an Exceptional. Now, however, we all knew that Exceptionals weren't the terrible people we'd thought them to be.

And not for the first time, I wondered why the rest of the world was taught to fear us.

"I don't think he realized he was an Exceptional, because he got all shocked when he saw his hand. Now, a normal person would've screamed," Ross said, giving the others a pointed look, "but *I* jumped up and singlehandedly tackled him to the ground, then shouted for someone to get the Expos. Luckily, a person who had been walking along the road heard us, and soon he was gone, and I was a hero."

Ross struck a pose, and the entire table burst into applause and laughter.

"But why was the boy chasing you, Rossy? Tell us that!" someone called out.

"Yeah, were you stealing or something?" another girl challenged.

"I can't believe you all think so little of me," Ross said, shaking his head and pressing a hand to his heart.

"That doesn't answer the question," the girl pressed, and Ross quickly switched the subject.

"Alright, who's talking next?" he called, raising his hands for silence. "Landis?"

"I spoke last night," the boy on the other side of June responded.

"Cora?"

"Stop calling on the same people, Ross!" someone protested from further down the table.

"Fine, fine, someone new," Ross agreed. His eyes traveled across the table until they locked on me. I started to shake my head, but it was too late. Ross lifted his arm and pointed. "How about you?"

Sixteen heads swiveled in my direction.

My heart skipped a beat. "What?"

"You're new, right? What's your name?"

"Aila," I said, glaring at him and hoping he would get the message and leave me alone.

He didn't. "Great. Now, Aila, why don't you tell us your story?"

"My...story?" I wished this would end. I did not do well as the center of attention.

"Yeah," Ross said, nodding. "Did you encounter an Exceptional before, and if so, what was it like?"

I immediately stiffened. Of course. *Of course* this was the one question they would ask me, on my first night here. An image of Chase flickered through my head. I took a deep, steadying breath and forced an innocent expression. "I never met one."

Everyone looked at June, who glanced at me apologetically before saying, "That's a lie."

I sucked in a breath, shooting her a startled look. June dropped her gaze. "I manifested my power a little while ago. I can tell truth from lies." She nodded at Ross. "For example, half of his story was a lie, especially the part where he said he wasn't scared."

Everyone laughed, but Ross rolled his eyes and directed the attention back toward me with a wave of his hand. "Come on," he urged. "Just tell the story. No one will judge."

Yes, they would. I knew they would. But everyone else started chipping in, encouraging me to speak, and finally, just to get them to back off, I jerked my head in a nod.

The table erupted in cheers, but everyone quickly fell silent as Ross sat down, waiting for me to continue.

I cleared my throat. I didn't know what to say. I didn't know how to start. Finally, I whispered, "His name was Chase Kader."

I saw the smiles drop off faces like flies as everyone realized this wasn't going to be a good-natured tale, like the one Ross had spun.

"He is my best friend," I said, "or, he was, until one day when we were eight years old."

No one was laughing anymore. Not even Ross.

"We were walking home from school when I saw the mark," I said quietly, dropping my gaze and staring at my plate. The food had

49

suddenly lost its appeal. "I reported him, and then the Expos came and took him away."

The atmosphere of the table had transformed completely, the boisterous laughter swallowed by a thick, solemn silence. I kept my eyes fixed on my plate, refusing to meet the gazes of those around me.

Finally, June said, "If he was taken by the Expos, he has to be here somewhere."

The others nodded, but I had already thought through the possibility countless times.

"Chase isn't here. I would've seen him by now."

"The Olum is a big place," Ross said. "Maybe you just missed him—"

"We were all given a decision." I lifted my head and met Ross's gaze head on. "We might not talk about it, but every single person sitting at this table decided to join the Expos."

Several of the Exceptionals shifted uncomfortably and dropped their gazes. Clearly, this topic wasn't discussed often.

"I knew Chase as well as I knew my own brother," I continued, although that wasn't really true. I hadn't known Warren enough to realize he would turn me in.

I shoved that thought away. "Chase is the kindest, most loving person I've ever known. He would sacrifice his life to save another like *that.*" I snapped my fingers, and Ross flinched. "He would rather die than capture Exceptionals. If Chase had to make the same decision as the rest of us, there's no doubt that he's…" I swallowed, unable to continue.

Suddenly, I couldn't bear it any longer: the sympathetic expressions of the others, the thought of Chase's kind, innocent face, the burden of what I had done pressing down on my shoulders…

I stood up abruptly and swung my leg over the bench. "I have to go."

June shot to her feet. "Aila, wait—"

Ignoring her, I turned my back on the table and hurried out of the Common Area and down the corridor.

And yet, even as I walked, there was no denying the truth: I could never escape my past.

But that didn't mean I had to face it.

"I hope we didn't get off on the wrong foot."

I spun around in alarm. Ross stood a few feet away from me, his hands shoved deep in his pockets. Despite the noise of the training room, I had receded so far into my thoughts I hadn't even heard him approach. A cocky grin split his face when he realized that he had startled me.

I glared at him, annoyed that he'd surprised me and annoyed by the reminder of the previous day's lunch. I'd hoped everyone had forgotten my story, although I supposed skipping breakfast this morning hadn't helped things.

"I mean, you've been avoiding me, so I'm scared that you think it's my fault," Ross continued, oblivious to my irritation as I turned away from him to face the training room's wall of weapons. "But it's not. I mean, I didn't *force* you to tell that story or anything."

I snorted. "You kind of did."

I really wasn't in the mood for Ross, whether he was teasing or joking or…failing terribly at apologizing, if that's what was going on right now. My new instructor had informed me today that an important part of moving on to Level Three included learning how to handle a sword efficiently, but I'd been avoiding the weapon at all costs after a disastrous training session a few days earlier.

"You could've left," Ross said as I reached up and warily picked a sword from where it hung on the wall. "Or told a lie, or screamed at us, or blown everyone up with your power—oh wait, I forgot you didn't have one."

I slowly turned around. "Was that supposed to be funny?"

Ross laughed weakly, his gaze dropping to where I clutched the sword in my hand. His eyebrows drew together. "Wow, no need to be so apprehensive. You attack *with* the sword, it doesn't attack you."

I was holding the sword away from my body, the point angled toward the floor, trying to distance myself from it as much as possible. "Be quiet," I snapped, quickly readjusting my grip so I held the sword upright. Ross raised an eyebrow. "What?" I asked defensively.

"It's a sword, Aila, not an ax."

I glowered at him and tried to adjust my grip again, but every way I held it just seemed plain wrong. Ross seemed to agree.

"Have you ever touched a sword before?"

"Yes."

"*Not* including the mandatory Level One training session?"

I hesitated, but for Ross that was clearly answer enough. "You know you have to be able to handle a sword before moving to the next training level."

"I am aware," I bit out. I might've been holding the sword wrong, but that didn't mean it wouldn't hurt if I hit him.

"Aila, I've noticed how well you perform in training," Ross said, spreading his hands out placatingly. "You pick up skills pretty quickly, and I must say, that was a clever trick you pulled on the rock wall yesterday."

I raised an eyebrow. "Jealous?"

"No," Ross said quickly, but I suspected otherwise.

He didn't just put all his effort into every activity because he was a hard worker. I had noticed Ross in training, too, especially the pride on his face when he beat someone in a challenge and the frustration in his gaze when he didn't.

"What I'm saying is you can't be the best at everything right away," Ross said. I frowned. That was the last message I'd been getting from him. "Maybe you just need some extra practice with the sword."

"If you're done insulting me, I'd like to get back to what I was doing," I snapped.

There was a beat of silence, during which Ross rolled his eyes up to the ceiling, like I was the one being difficult, and then he said, "That's my way of saying I'll help train you."

I almost laughed. "I don't think so."

"Is this because of yesterday? Because I really don't think—"

"Look, this conversation has been nothing but annoying. No offense, but I'm not exactly eager to sign myself up for *more* time with you."

"But it'll help you move on to Level Three!" Ross protested.

"Or it will make you look good for helping someone like me pick up a new skill. I guess it all depends on how you look at it."

"Would it help if June comes?" Ross offered desperately.

I hesitated. I *did* need help with the sword, and June seemed like she could be a good mediator.

Ross grinned at my contemplative expression. "So it's a yes then?"

"I didn't—"

"Great!" Ross patted me on the arm. "We'll meet you over here tomorrow during afternoon training for your first lesson: How to hold a sword."

He strode away, whistling happily, leaving me to stare after him and wonder what exactly had just happened.

7

STORM

Chase had been gone from my cell for no more than four seconds when I leapt off my bed and barreled into the hall after him.

"Chase!"

He spun around, but before either of us could speak, four guards surged in from the edges of the hallway, ripping their swords from their scabbards. In the blink of an eye, they surrounded me, trapping me with the points of their swords. Stunned, I raised my hands slowly in surrender.

Chase took a few steps toward me. "Stand down! He wasn't trying to escape," he said, giving me a look that said, *You'd better not be trying to escape.*

"I just want to talk, I promise," I said, and when the guards still looked dubious, I added, "If I take even one step out of line, then you guys can drag me back to my cell."

"It's not a cell, it's a private room," one of the guards snapped.

"Sure, if that's what you want to call it."

The guard glared, but then grumbled something to the others, and the four of them drew back to the fringes of the hallway. I noticed that they kept their swords in hand.

"What did you want to say?" Chase asked, drawing my attention back to him.

I hesitated, and Chase stared at me, his hazel eyes a mixture of wariness and hope.

Finally, I muttered, "I'll join."

54

Chase's face lit up. "Really?"

"Yes," I snapped, "but I don't want to get knocked unconscious anymore, okay?"

Chase laughed and stepped forward, clapping me on the back. "Follow your orders, and you won't have to worry about anything," he assured me.

That would have been much more comforting if my orders didn't involve being confined to this building. I would either be following them and worrying about Jon, or not following them and worrying about the Insurgence. I flinched at the thought.

"You made the right choice, Storm," Chase said. "Trust me. Now let's go tell Commander White."

When Chase and I exited Commander White's office nearly an hour later, our faces were split with relieved grins. However, I couldn't help but feel a pit of disappointment in my stomach. Commander White had informed me that only certain trainees were chosen to participate in Mission Week each month, and she'd made it clear it would take extra effort on my part to prove I was trustworthy enough to participate.

And yet, as Commander White explained the training program, I found myself growing excited. Not only would we train to use our powers once we manifested them, but we would also undergo a physical training regime to prepare us for potential obstacles during Mission Week. Each Exceptional had the chance to choose an additional supplementary class to take. She explained the paintings and tapestries on the walls were created by Exceptionals taking the artistry course. It hadn't been a hard decision for me—I eagerly signed up for a defense class.

I started to head down the hall to my right, the one that led back to my "private room," but Chase grabbed my arm to stop me.

"We don't have a reason to keep you isolated if you're part of the Insurgence," he said, turning around and starting in the other direction. "Male trainees sleep over here."

Chase and I walked in silence as he led me through the corridors. The quiet suited me just fine; my mind was spinning as I tried to sort out my thoughts. From what Commander White had said, the Insurgence sent out squads of three or more people to every major town and city, where they would wait in case an Exceptional was reported during Mission Week. If I could just convince her to let me join a squad that went to Ferrol...

The Insurgence halls were surprisingly busy at this time of night. Every few seconds we passed an Insurgence member, or sometimes an entire group, hurrying through the halls, stepping through doors, or holding brief conversations at the corners. But what surprised me most was how many people acknowledged Chase. Almost everyone that passed paused to say hello, and those who didn't at least spared a nod and a smile. Once again, I got the impression that Chase had been here for a long time.

"When did you become an Exceptional?" I asked as we stepped into a smaller hall, this one empty and lit only by a few flickering lanterns.

"I was eight."

I blinked in surprise. "You've been an Exceptional for..." I trailed off, struggling to do the math in my head.

Chase smirked. "Eight years."

"Leave me alone, I was pulled out of school when I was seven." Which I now realized was about the same age Chase had been when he was reported. I had felt like my life had hardly even begun when I turned eight, but for Chase his would have already been over. "That's a long time," I murmured.

"Believe me, I know. That's why I'm out of training. I was one of the quickest Exceptionals to move through the program, and Commander White found me trustworthy enough to promote very early on."

I nodded, still slightly stunned. Chase had spent half of his life here at the Insurgence. He hadn't even had a chance to grow up, to have a childhood. It all seemed so...cruel.

"Who reported you?" I asked, my voice darkening with anger. Leave it to someone in the Stone Cities to turn in an innocent eight-year-old boy.

Chase dropped his gaze, studying his boots. "My best friend."

I snorted. "Some best friend."

Chase whipped his head to the side, and I was surprised by the annoyance in his gaze. "She was scared, Storm. What else was she supposed to do? Help me go into hiding?" He shook his head. "We were *eight*. For all I know, she had no idea Exceptionals were supposed to be killed. She's probably spent her entire life regretting it."

I shoved my hands into my pockets. "Serves her right." Even an eight-year-old should've had enough sense to realize she was ruining her best friend's life.

"She made a mistake, Storm, and so have the rest of us," Chase snapped. "I've forgiven her, and my one regret is that she has no way of knowing that."

"She *betrayed* you," I said incredulously.

"Look," Chase said, stopping short and turning to face me. "If you can't forgive, then why should you ever expect forgiveness?"

I didn't have an answer for that. Chase just shook his head again and continued down the hall. We stopped in front of a wooden door labeled *Male Trainee's Dormitory*, and Chase bid me goodnight as I stepped inside.

The second I did, seventeen heads collectively swiveled to stare at me. Hesitantly, I closed the door behind me, then turned to face them. When nobody moved, I decided to break the silence by saying, "Hi."

Everyone promptly went back to what they had been doing, and I stood awkwardly at the door, studying the room before me.

I'd never been inside a room so nice. Five sets of bunk beds were pushed up against both sides of the wall. At the far end, a lush rug was spread before a crackling fire, and several boys reclined nearby on the plush chairs. Two large tables with lamps and chairs were in the corner on either side of the fireplace. I let out a disbelieving breath. It was hard to believe that I was going to spend the rest of my life here. Even if I had to sleep on the rug, I'd be more comfortable than I ever was in Ferrol.

I stood there uncomfortably until one of the older boys tossed me a look and said, "You'll bunk with Aris in the back."

I groaned inwardly. Of course I would get stuck with the exact person I wanted to avoid. I immediately made my way between the rows of bunks to where Aris was standing, his arms crossed, a scowl plastered on his face.

"You get the top bunk," he growled. "That's so when we're sore from training, you have to put in all the extra work to get into bed."

I shrugged. Top or bottom didn't matter; I was just excited to actually have a bed. I tried to step around Aris to reach the bunk, but he moved to block my path.

"What?" I snapped.

"You think that just because they aren't keeping you locked up, you can waltz around like you own the place?" Aris demanded.

"I don't own the place. I'm just trying to get to my bed."

I tried to move around Aris again, but he once more countered my step. "I'm surprised they trust you after that little stunt you tried after lunch—and again during our meeting with the commander. She might've forgiven you, but it will take longer for the rest of us to do the same."

I rolled my eyes. "Why do you even care?"

"Why do I care?" Aris growled. "You've tainted our whole group's reputation. When they look at us, all they'll see is your mistakes, you filthy, thieving—"

"Aris."

We both spun around aggressively to see one of the new Exceptionals had approached us. He was short and stocky and probably as old as Jon. The reminder of my brother sent a fresh pang of worry shooting through me, and I felt my anger deflate. The boy obviously wasn't from the Stone Cities, but he looked strong and healthy and carried himself with an easy confidence. He was probably the son of a merchant, trained to deal with customers from an early age.

"Let's swap places. You go bunk with Nico," he said, pointing to where an eighteen-year-old Exceptional, the oldest of us newcomers, was climbing into a bottom bunk.

"We can't just V" Aris began, but the boy promptly stepped around him and sat down on the edge of the lower bunk.

Aris glared at him for a moment, then glowered at me like it was all my fault before storming to the other bunk. I turned away and leaned against the bed frame, staring at the ground.

"I'm Arden." My attention snapped back to the boy. "From Tieran."

I was right once again. Tieran was full of merchants that specialized in certain trades. It was one of the business towns, and although the people who lived there weren't nearly as wealthy as the people in the Stone Cities, they didn't live in poverty, either.

"I'm—"

"Storm, right?" Arden interrupted. "That was the name everyone was yelling during your failed escape attempt."

I couldn't help but chuckle as Arden continued right on talking.

"I didn't switch bunks with Aris just because I wanted to be nice," he continued. "I did it because now you owe me a favor. But I'll consider it paid if you let me get the bottom bunk."

"Sure," I said, momentarily distracted by the argument Aris was having with Nico across the room. He just couldn't stop. "Whatever you want."

Arden beamed and climbed into the lower bunk, then poked his head out to add, "I also didn't want you and Aris to kill each other the first night, considering, you know, that you'll be living together for the rest of your lives."

Training started the next day, and it was somehow the best and the worst thing that had ever happened to me.

It was the best because it felt like I'd been preparing my whole life to show everyone up. Instead of running from the Securities, I was racing people across the courtyard. Instead of darting nimbly between crowds and across roofs, I was speeding through an obstacle course set up in the training room. And every time, I beat my peers with flying colors. Not only that, but for the first time in my life, I never had to worry about being hungry.

Training took place in one of two locations. Inside the building, there was a large room with decorative tapestries and tall windows that allowed light to pour in. Every day the place was set up differently. One day there was an elaborate obstacle course meant to test our strength and agility; the next, there were rows of desks where we sat to learn about basic Rosan geography.

Other days, we went outside. The building had a large cobblestone courtyard where most of my defense class and other active competitions were held. It was nice to get fresh air and feel the sun, but the stone walls towered so high it was impossible to catch a glimpse of the outside world, except for the occasional bough of a tree that swung over the edge of the wall.

But training was also the worst, because about four days in, I was pulled out of Defense Class and told that Commander White wanted to meet with me in her office.

"Do you know why I've called you in here today?" she asked, gazing down at me with her perpetually belittling expression.

There were many possible reasons, really: Because I'd accidentally punched Aris in Defense Class, because I'd snuck out of geography class the other day, or because she simply hated me. But I wasn't about to tell her any of this, so I just shook my head.

Commander White went on to list how I was doing well in all of my courses, but before I had the chance to get too excited about finally being celebrated for something, she said, "And then comes the issue of reading. Mr. Dawson, it is clear that you don't remember how to read."

And that's how I ended up having one-on-one tutoring lessons with Chase.

At first, they were horrendous. I didn't have the will, or to be honest, the skill, to learn how to read. So the second week of training ended with me returning to the dormitory, exhausted, frustrated, and missing Jon.

The next day, on the walk to the classroom Chase and I used for our lessons, I devised a plan to get out of it, at least for the day. By the time I entered the classroom, I had schooled my expression into one of distress.

"I can't do this today," I said, practically falling into the chair across from Chase. I rubbed my eyes. "I feel terrible. I think I'm coming down with something."

Chase blinked at me. "Yeah," he said, unconvinced.

"No, seriously," I insisted. Would it be too much to start tearing up? "My head hurts so much I can hardly even stand looking at the words."

"Maybe it has something to do with the shouting match you had with Aris the other day."

Wow, Chase was difficult. "Commander White doesn't understand," I insisted. "Reading just isn't good for me. It's making me sick."

"I can't begin to imagine," Chase said flatly. "Your life is very difficult, Storm."

My shoulders sagged. "You don't believe me."

"Were you trying to earn my *pity*?"

"I mean, come on, was I at least a bit convincing?"

"No!" Chase shook his head. "What were you even *doing*?"

"I don't know." I dropped my head, only to jerk it up a second later. "Are you...*laughing*?"

Chase nodded. "You're ridiculous," he said, and I couldn't help but crack a tiny smile. I didn't even know why I tried to be offended at him anymore.

"*This* is ridiculous," I muttered. "I don't know why I haven't discovered my power yet. That would fix half my problems."

"Powers don't fix as much as you think," Chase warned. "But don't worry. It'll come soon."

"Do you have yours yet?"

Chase suddenly broke eye contact. "Yes."

"What is it?"

He smirked. "Falling into the company of liars."

"Oh, come on. I wasn't lying. I was...acting."

"If that's what acting has stooped to these days, we might as well burn all the theaters."

I let out a dry chuckle that petered out as my eyes dropped to the textbooks before me. I felt the familiar bubble of worry in my stomach. "I can't do this." I shoved the book away, thrusting my chair away from the table as a sudden crippling need to be *doing something* caught hold of me. I let out a humorless laugh. "I'm sitting here learning to *read* while my brother is back in Ferrol, probably starving to death. It's just *wrong*."

All my life, I had thought all I needed to do was get out of Ferrol, and then my life would mean something, then I could finally live. But here I was, in a clean mansion with an endless supply of food and a soft bed, yet somehow I was just as trapped as I had been in Ferrol for all those years.

Chase watched me for a second, a thousand thoughts hidden behind his eyes. "You're talking about Jon, right?"

I dropped my gaze to the desk and nodded.

"Why don't you tell me about him?"

So I did, hesitantly at first, but picking up speed the more I talked. I told him about how Jon and I used to play games when we were little, hiding something in a tall field of corn and then seeing how long it would take for the other person to find it. How we would fight with stick swords behind our house as the sun went down, painting the sky in reds and pinks and purples, a rare stroke of beauty in an otherwise desperate town. I told him about how Jon had gotten sick, and how he was so stubborn that he fought his way through it, when even the strongest didn't survive. I told him how I'd begun to steal, and the late night conversations Jon and I would share over a piece of stolen fruit.

In return, Chase described to me the city of Bedrock. The Stone Cities were aptly named—stone streets, stone buildings, stone walls running between everything in a meticulous grid. But he remembered the beautiful hints of life that one could find almost anywhere. The brightly colored flowers spilling out of a window box attached to a house. The little hand-sewn flags that crisscrossed between the roofs of the buildings around the school. The fluttering birds that would flock students when they threw seeds in the town square.

"Sometimes, in the height of all their prestige, I think the Stone Cities can forget the beauties of normal life," Chase said.

I had never thought of it that way, that Ferrol had something the Stone Cities did not.

At the end of our lesson, when Chase convinced me to try reading just one short paragraph, my mind finally felt clear enough to comply. For the first time in a long while, I felt that I could breathe again, just a little bit.

The next day when I reached the classroom, the reading textbooks were nowhere in sight. Instead, Chase led me to the big training room, providing no explanation until he retrieved two swords from a closet. The training room was bustling with activity, trainees in various locations going through the day's activities, but Chase and I found a quiet corner underneath one of the large windows.

He passed me a sword, grinning at my surprised expression. "Let's see if you really are the top of your class."

I wasn't, at least, not to Chase's standards. He won our first two duels with ease, but after giving me a few pointers on how to attack and counterattack, I was able to hold my own against him as we started our third duel.

The sound of steel on steel rang through the room, and I was surprised at the strength of the blades. It was a far cry from the branches Jon and I had played with as kids, but even the weapons I'd gotten my hands on briefly from unattended stands in Carsley seemed weak in comparison to these.

"These blades are from the Stone Cities, aren't they?" I asked as I brought my sword up to block one of Chase's blows. Our blades ground against each other for one tense moment, then slid apart with a *shiiing*.

"They are." Chase attacked again, but I twisted away, bringing my sword down on his.

Of course they were. The Stone Cities had the best of the best; the best swords, the best homes, the best lives. Meanwhile, they just sat back and watched as small towns like Ferrol crumbled away into dust.

I swung my weapon at Chase with a renewed ferocity, and he just barely blocked it in time. Our blades locked, and his eyes searched mine. "What are you thinking about?"

We drew apart, breathing heavily. "The plague," I responded honestly. I couldn't help but sound accusatory when I added, "You probably don't even know what that is."

"The plague hit Bedrock too."

"Yeah, for about a week." I lashed out again with a flurry of swings, all of which were expertly deflected by Chase. "I would hardly call it a *hit* compared to what happened in the poorer towns," I grunted between strikes. "The Stone Cities took a year off to recover without offering assistance to anyone else, but they still expected the rest of the Empire to pick themselves up within a day and keep working."

Chase didn't object. We sprung apart.

"Sometimes...sometimes I feel like the Stone Cities are just like the Insurgence. They sat around and did nothing while the rest of Rosan suffered, just like the Insurgence isn't doing anything to help the Exceptionals."

"We are helping, Storm."

"Are you?" I lifted my sword and stepped in with another attack. "You're rescuing—what? Five Exceptionals a week? Good for you. Who cares if the other ten get sent off to their deaths. At least the Insurgence saved a *few*."

Chase's blade rang against mine. "Exactly—"

"But if they can rescue some Exceptionals, why not rescue more?" My blade crashed against Chase's as he swung forward. "The Insurgence has the element of surprise—no one knows that it exists, and if they do, they have no idea how organized the group is. The Insurgence needs to strike out, hit them harder, give the Exceptionals *real* help."

Sweat was beading on my brow. Chase swung again, and again, each attack faster than the last. My arms burned from the force of his hits.

"You think the Insurgence doesn't know what they can and can't do?" Chase said over the ring of the weapons. I gritted my teeth and slashed with my sword. Our blades locked, pinning us in place as our eyes found each other, each one daring the other to be the first to back down.

Chase's voice was quiet. "It's hard," he said, "and it's dangerous. One wrong move, and the Insurgence will be over. We can't risk destroying ourselves—"

"And *that's* the problem!" I jerked my blade away from Chase, stumbling back and letting my sword fall to my side. I was shouting, I realized, and had drawn the attention from the other Exceptionals in the room. I couldn't bring myself to care. "That's why the Stone Cities and the Insurgence are the same—*they put themselves first.* They don't care about the cause, about the greater good; they see themselves as more important!"

I flung my blade onto the floor with a clatter. The noise echoed in the otherwise silent room. When had everyone else stopped talking? All eyes were on Chase and me, waiting to see what he would say.

"You don't do the same?" Chase said quietly. "You don't put yourself first? You don't place your priorities over those of others?" He knelt down and scooped up my blade from the ground. "Sometimes, we're more like our enemies than we think," he said, then walked away, leaving me to stand alone in the corner of the room.

Slowly, the volume level of the room began to rise again as trainees returned to their previous activities. I felt a prickling on my neck and turned just in time to see Commander White sweep away through one of the side doors. She disappeared before I could speak, but not before I caught the look of disappointment in her pale green gaze.

65

8

AILA

I hated swords, and I never wanted to touch—scratch that, *see*—a sword again in my life.

But sadly, that didn't appear to be possible. My instructor made it clear that, without my power, I needed to obtain proficiency with a sword to advance to Level Three. He also didn't hesitate to point out that mine were more than lacking. So I found myself showing up to Ross's first training session, June in tow.

"He isn't a bad person, you know," June said as we crossed the training room toward the weapons corner. "He may be a *little* egotistical—"

I snorted, glancing ahead to where Ross was exaggeratedly swinging a fifteen pound mace, putting on a show for absolutely nobody.

"—but he's loyal, and he has a good heart and a lot of determination," June added. "Teasing is just his way of…reaching out to people. He makes a great friend once you get to know him."

When I gave her a dubious look, she added, "And he's great with swords. You could use his help."

I sighed and reluctantly kept moving toward Ross.

"Glad you decided to show up," Ross said, grinning broadly as I approached. "I was afraid you were still in self-denial about your talent with a sword—or lack thereof."

I shot June an exasperated look, and she quickly gained control of the situation. "I think we should start you off with a training sword," she said, pointing to a rack of wooden swords beneath the ones mounted on the wall. "It's lighter, so it'll be easier to handle." She picked one off the rack and tossed it in my direction. I caught it easily and was glad I could do at least one thing right.

"Let's go through the basic motions first," Ross said as June passed him a sword and chose one for herself.

"I already learned those—"

"Look, Aila, you have a sword prodigy offering you *free lessons*. To take full advantage of my talents, you're gonna have to trust me. What better place to start than the beginning?"

So Ross started with the basics, leading us through various exercises and pausing periodically to give me tips. I would never admit it to him, but his pointers did help. By the time an hour had passed, I was completing the moves as well as Ross himself.

"Told you I was a good teacher," he said smugly when we stopped, all three of us breathing heavily. "Now let's try some sparring."

That's when things started to go downhill. Ross and I faced off, swords in hand, and June counted down from three to start the match. Ross swept forward, swinging his wooden sword toward my midsection, and I brought mine up quickly for a block. The force knocked him off balance, and I knew this was my chance to act and disable him. But I found myself hesitating, unsure of whether to use an uppercut or a thrust. Ross regained his balance and feigned left before jabbing the point of his sword into my right side, landing the first blow and ending the match.

I threw down my sword in frustration. "I'm terrible."

"You hesitated," June said, her face creased in a frown. "Why did you hesitate? He was off balance. You could've ended the match right there."

"I don't know." I was irritated, but at myself more than Ross. "I couldn't choose which attack to use."

"You don't have to stop and think about it," June said. "Duels are quick. You need to commit to your actions, give yourself over to instinct. There's no time to think."

"I can't just do that." How was I supposed to make a split-second decision without knowing what consequences it would bring?

"Then learn how," June insisted. "That's the trick to sword fighting."

Ross bent down and picked up my sword, throwing a look at June. "I'm a little concerned that June's trying to usurp my position as teacher, but she *is* right." He offered me the weapon. "Let's try again."

But I'd had enough sword fighting for one day. Letting out a huff of frustration, I turned and stalked off across the training room.

"Okay, I'm getting your message!" Ross called after me. "See you tomorrow, same time, same place!"

Despite my frustration, I did show up the next day, and the next, and for the entire week after that. I realized that June had been right. Ross *was* growing on me. He had a joke for every situation and never failed to make me laugh, although I usually restrained myself and just cracked a smile. I didn't want him to get *too* cocky. As our number of training sessions and lunches together grew, I found myself turn from being annoyed at Ross to tolerating him to actually enjoying his presence.

That is, until a training session a few days before the start of Recruitment Week, when tensions were running particularly high for everyone in the Olum. I had dueled with both Ross and June several times, trying in vain to let my thoughts go and give myself over to instinct, but things had been going steadily downhill since the beginning of the lesson. All of Ross's lighthearted jokes were hitting too close to home, sounding more like insults then playful jibes. And he just *didn't know when to stop.*

"Remember the time that Aila was lightning fast in a duel and did that really cool sword move that defeated June?" he asked after a particularly frustrating training session. When June and I shot him confused looks, he smirked and said, "Yeah, me neither."

I didn't know whether to cry or hit him with my sword until I learned how to use it properly.

"You're getting better," June encouraged when I opted to just stare at him in utter distress.

"Am I?" I asked Ross. He shook his head.

For all of his maddening traits, at least he was honest. Sometimes brutally so.

"You'll get better soon," he encouraged. "After all, you have me as a teacher. Ross Erland: The man, the myth, the legend." He struck a pose.

"Ross, we've been doing this for eight days," I said flatly. "I'm losing every single duel."

Ross frowned. "You really are." He glanced over at June. "Maybe she just doesn't have the heart to stab people."

"Do you want to test that theory? Because I'm feeling a pretty strong urge to stab you right about now," I snapped.

Ross chuckled nervously. "Nope. Nope, sure don't."

I let my sword drop to my side. "This is useless."

"No, it's not," June insisted.

Ross nodded. "She's right. Just keep practicing. It's not like we're running out of time—"

"Oh really?" I snapped. "Easy for you to say, you're already in Level Three."

Ross's face paled. "No, I didn't mean—"

"You're probably *trying* to hold me back, aren't you? Because the sooner these lessons stop, the sooner *you'll* stop benefitting."

"Aila," June warned.

"You're probably not even in it to help me, you're just in it for yourself."

"What are you even talking about?" For the first time, Ross's grin dropped off his face. "I'm trying to *help* you, Aila!"

"Yeah, and that's doing me a whole lot of good, isn't it?"

Before Ross could respond, a bell rang throughout the room, signaling the end of the training session and our transition to dinner. I shoved my sword on the rack and started toward the door without looking back.

June caught up with me in the hall. "Don't give up, Aila," she said. "You'll get it after a little more practice."

"I don't have *time*," I snapped as we joined the flow of traffic heading for the Common Area.

"Aila, you haven't even been here for *four weeks*, and you're already at the top of Level Two. I was an Exceptional for half a year before I reached that point. So what if you're not in Level Three?"

"If I'm not in Level Three, I can't participate in Recruitment Week," I said. "Brone won't trust me if I can't participate."

June frowned. "That's what this is all about? You're scared of Brone?"

I gritted my teeth. I wasn't just scared of Brone; I was scared of what would happen if I was forced to continue sleeping in my tiny cell, stumbling through mindless days of meals and training. I was afraid that if I had any more time alone, any more time to think, the truth of the decision I'd made would catch up with me.

If I stopped long enough to think about what joining the Expos really meant, and who I was turning into, it would be too much.

The crowd drew to a near standstill as we funneled through the doors into the Common Area. June and I paused on the fringe of the crowd, and I began to think about which seat at the table was furthest away from Ross. I felt bad for yelling at him, but my spark of anger was still there, and I didn't need to hear a vivid retelling of how he bested me in our duel.

"Oh no," I muttered, noticing that Ross had just turned the corner and was heading toward us. "Hide me."

But there was nowhere to go. The crowd was still too thick for me to shove my way through, and Ross was determinedly making his way toward us, blocking my escape in the opposite direction. I stepped behind June and ducked my head, overcome with the sudden urge to disappear.

"Where's Aila?" Ross said as he approached.

I rolled my eyes. We all knew he had enhanced eyesight, so I didn't believe for a second that he'd gone blind. June looked confused, too, and turned her head in my direction. Her brows drew together as she looked at me.

"I don't know, she was here a second ago."

I chuckled drily. "Good one. Pretending I'm invisible. What a classic."

Ross and June both jumped, their eyes darting wildly around the corridor. "Where are you?" Ross demanded in a panicked voice.

The last of the Exceptionals had finally trickled into the Common Area, leaving the doorway open.

"Drop the joke," I said. I was grateful that Ross hadn't brought up our argument, but really wasn't in the mood for his humor. "Come on, let's go eat."

"Aila, what happened to you?" June said, staring at me.

But then I realized she wasn't staring *at* me. She seemed to be staring...*through* me.

My jaw dropped. "You're not joking?"

"Um, no," Ross squeaked. "Trust me, if I wanted to play a practical joke on you, it would be *much* cleverer."

"You seriously can't see me?"

"Can you see yourself?" June asked.

"Y-yes," I said. I glanced down, then inhaled sharply. "No."

The three of us stood there, staring at where my body should've been, then Ross's face split with a grin.

"You're invisible!" he said with a woop. "You got your power!"

"How do I go back?" Fear seized me, and suddenly the inability to see my feet made me stumble forward. I knocked into June, who recoiled in shock.

I held up my hands in front of me, but I saw nothing but the stone wall beyond. My chest tightened, and I sucked in a horrified breath. June looked around disconcertingly, and Ross continued to beam.

"Guys!" My voice was shrill with worry. "Is this permanent? Is that my power? Permanent invisibility?"

"Calm down!" June stepped forward, looking hard in the wrong direction.

"A little to the left," I said, and she adjusted to face me.

"What did you do to make yourself invisible?"

"I saw Ross coming toward me and wished I could turn invisible to avoid him."

71

Ross looked insulted. "Greater people fall over themselves trying to gain my attention."

"Do that again," June said. "Try to imagine yourself visible. Try it."

I squeezed my eyes shut and concentrated, imagining me standing fully visible before my friends. Ross let out a sudden cheer. My eyes flew open, and I released breath when I saw my blessedly visible hands before me.

"Can you go back?" Ross asked eagerly. "Turn yourself invisible again."

I wasn't exactly excited to risk trapping myself in invisibility again, but at Ross and June's encouragement, I reluctantly concentrated, picturing how it had been to see nothing, not my feet or legs or my torso. I kept my eyes open this time and gasped as my body faded out of view before my very eyes.

June grinned. "Aila, I can still see your head."

I grabbed a strand of brown hair and drew it in front of me, sagging in disappointment. I carefully concentrated, and slowly the rest of my body became visible once more.

"I guess I need some practice."

"Who cares if you need practice?" June said, grinning giddily. "You have your power, Aila. *You can turn invisible!*"

A smile slowly spread across my face; this meant I was one step closer to Level Three.

We never ended up making it to dinner. Ross, June, and I continued to test the limits of my power, and before we knew it, the Exceptionals were flooding back into the hallway, and Jax approached, ready to lead me back to my room.

As he closed the door behind me, I sank down onto my bed with an uncontrollable grin on my face. Finally, I had my power.

No sooner did the thought crossed my mind then realization struck me, stealing the very breath from my lungs. I had my power...and it wasn't dangerous at all.

In fact, the more I thought about it, most of the Exceptionals I had met didn't have dangerous powers, and if they did, they didn't seem corrupted or tempted to misuse them. But wasn't that the whole reason we were taken away? Because our powers were dangerous, otherworldly, and corrupting?

I leaned back against the stone wall of my cell, staring across the dark room in shock. For some reason, Brone was lying to us, which meant the Earl was lying to all of Rosan.

The entire world had been tricked into believing Exceptionals were dangerous, when in reality, there was no reason to fear us at all.

The next morning, Jax knocked on my door earlier than usual. As we left my cell, I started left, toward the training room, but he directed me instead to the right.

"Brone requested a meeting with you. I am to take you to his office."

I swallowed, my heart pounding as I followed Jax through the halls. I hadn't been to Brone's office before, but I wasn't surprised to find it was the only door in a short, broad, well-lit hall, save for one that was cracked open to reveal a utility room.

The door was made of dark oak, a shade darker than the rest of the doors in the Olum, and the handle was made of silver instead of brass. The guard pushed open the door to reveal an empty office. The first thing I noticed was the coldness of the air inside the room, as if Brone's chilly demeanor had infected the very temperature. My eyes briefly scanned the rest of the office. It was a quiet room with a single desk and four chairs. A bookshelf stood in one corner, a second door in the other. The desk was bare, except for a pen and a glass case holding a dagger that was engraved out of ice. An interesting choice of decoration, but it did match Brone's coldness.

But what caught my eye the most were the maps. They were tacked on the walls, piled on the shelves, spilling out of the open drawer of the desk, all a stark contrast to the otherwise meticulous tidiness of the room. There were sprawling maps of Rosan, more specific ones picturing certain regions, and even a few small maps of individual towns. Every single one was marked, the parchment scribbled over with a pen. X's were scrawled everywhere, and in some cases entire towns were scratched out.

"Take a seat," the guard said, gesturing to a chair on the closest side of the desk and interrupting my thoughts. "Brone will be with you shortly."

I obeyed, and moments later the guard was gone. My eyes immediately landed on the ice dagger. I wondered where Brone had gotten it, and if he kept the room so cold to keep it from melting.

The door across the room swung open. I immediately straightened as Brone stepped through, striding to take a seat in the chair on the opposite side of the desk. He folded his hands in front of him and, without any sort of welcome or preamble, said, "You will be participating in Recruitment Week in a few days."

My gut clenched. I had expected to feel a surge of joy at his words, but instead I felt a sudden pang of unease as the reality of what this meant settled over me.

But then I realized that he was choosing me to participate in Recruitment Week, even though I wasn't yet in Level Three. That meant Brone trusted me. That meant I was safe.

"Before you participate, however, I must share something I only tell the Exceptionals I trust enough to take part in Recruitment Week." He paused, then looked me in the eye and said, "Not all Exceptionals are brought to the Olum."

I grew still, Brone's words hanging in the air.

"There is a group of rebels working against us. We don't know how big they are, when it started, or if they have a name. All we know is that they disguise themselves as Exceptional Police during Recruitment Week in an attempt to rescue the Exceptionals before we get to them."

I felt a sudden surge of hope. The Olum wasn't the only option of survival. There was another group, another way. But I caught myself before I got too carried away. I didn't know anything about these rebels, and trying to find any information would be too risky.

"The rebels don't understand how dangerous the Exceptionals are," Brone added.

I thought about the revelation that had hit me like a battering ram last night. Exceptionals weren't dangerous at all—we were just gifted. And yet, here Brone was, speaking of us like *we* were the bad guys.

And at the same time brainwashing everyone here into thinking the same thing.

"They think they are doing what is right." Brone's voice suddenly sharpened, filling with an anger I had never heard him possess before. "But by saving Exceptionals, they are condemning others. What's going to happen if those Exceptionals escape? They must not be allowed to roam free with their powers." He leaned forward, his normally impassive gaze cutting into me. "If you ever see any members of this rebel group, report it to your squad leader immediately. If you ever learn of a possible location from which they operate, report it to your squad leader immediately. If you so much as *hear* any word of the rebels, report it to your squad leader immediately. Understand?"

I nodded, startled by the urgency in Brone's usually emotionless tone. I wondered if the Earl knew about this rebel group. Maybe Brone was worried because he knew how the rebels could ruin his reputation.

Brone leaned back in his chair, collecting himself into the man he was before. However, his voice still trembled slightly when he said, "I've seen firsthand the horrors an Exceptional can commit on innocent people. We must not allow it to happen again."

What horrors? Suddenly, I wanted nothing more than to know why Brone hated Exceptionals, what exactly had turned him into the man that sat stone-cold in the chair across from me.

"Jax is waiting outside, and will escort you to your training," Brone said, standing abruptly. "Tomorrow, you'll be sent to the seaside town of Biron for your mission. Good luck."

I hadn't been to the sea since Chase became an Exceptional. Perched on a hill overlooking Biron, all I could focus on was the water. A brisk breeze wafted strongly off the water, carrying with it the invigorating scent of salty sea spray. The sun sliced through the clear sky, and the ocean glittered like thousands of little diamonds. It would've been a perfect day if it wasn't Recruitment Week.

I had woken up at five o'clock sharp and reported to the Common Area to meet my squad, a group of three or for Expos that traveled out together. June and I were ecstatic to learn I was joining her group. We'd spent the entire ride talking, more than we ever had. There was a certain sense of liberty that came with being out of the Olum.

Stepping out of the Olum and breathing fresh air for the first time since becoming an Exceptional had been indescribably wonderful. The sun had just begun to inch over the horizon, casting beams of light across the empty fields that stretched in every direction.

I was confused. I'd always thought the Olum would be hidden deep within a thick forest, not out in the middle of the open. "The Olum is so easy to see," I said to June. "How come nobody has noticed it before?"

"Laster is the nearest town, and you can't even see it," June said, pointing off into the distance. "All the fields here have rocky soil, terrible for growing or raising animals, so there aren't even any roads in this direction. No one ever travels past Laster."

My eyes widened in understanding. We were in the Barrens, a place I'd only heard stories about. It was a strip of unforgiving land in eastern Rosan that was not good for anything and was known to have harsh, unexpected weather. For the first time, I noticed the coarseness of the grass beneath my feet and the brittle wind sweeping across the dry ground. But I still wondered how much of the rumors had been made up just to keep people away from the Olum, to keep Brone's secrets hidden.

The rest of the Olum was as I expected: a stone building, all sharp angles and exact proportions. But then I noticed how tall it was, tall enough for a second story, maybe even a third. I didn't recall ever seeing any stairs.

The Olum was a flurry of activity that morning, full of people mounting horses and preparing to leave. It felt more alive than I'd ever seen it, but my mood was dampened by the knowledge of what I was setting out to do. I was relieved when we finally rode away, leaving the ominous building behind.

Now, the four of us in my squad paused on the crest of a hill overlooking the bustling seaside town of Biron. The town started on the side of the hill and spilled down toward the ocean in a wave of color and life, crashing to a halt at the sea's edge. Stone and wood cottages lined the crooked cobblestone streets, smoke twirling out of their chimneys in an intricate dance. Although the sun had just barely cleared the horizon, shoppers were awake and weaving through the market of brightly colored tents. Children played at the bubbling fountain in the market's center.

Men were at work on the docks, the early risers already pushing off in their boats, the night fishers hoisting nets filled with the evening's catch onto the stones. I wanted nothing more than to be a part of this simple world, but the second we entered the town, people seemed to trip over themselves to clear the way.

Kala was the leader of our squad and set a straight, unflinching path for the Security Station. She was an older woman who didn't speak more than necessary and had barely finished introducing herself to me in the morning before she put on her helmet, instructing the rest of us to do the same. Her voice had left no room for argument. On the way to Biron, June had informed me that she was one of Brone's closest advisors.

Trav was the fourth member of our group, a young man with a kind smile who had taken off his Expo glove to show me the X on his hand. "I was originally from Kryon," he told me.

I was surprised. Even though Kryon wasn't far from the Stone City of Arkose, it was one of the poor farming towns. I hadn't expected people from Kryon to be nice like Trav, or trustworthy enough for Brone to send them on Recruitment Week. I'd always thought people from farming towns would be rough and rude, hardened from years of work. But there Trav was, proving me wrong.

We tied our horses to the post in front of the Security Station, and Kala promptly led us inside to a small room dedicated to Expo use. I immediately positioned myself in the chair facing the window, where I could just catch a glimpse of the sea between two tall buildings.

I saw some children playing on the pebbly shore and felt my heart clench as memories of similar days spent by the water swept in. When I was young, my family would travel to the shore with the Kader's every year. But it all stopped after Chase had been taken away. Back then, I'd told myself it was for the best; it wouldn't have felt the same with my best friend gone and my brother ignoring me. But it had been one of many changes in our home. My father had spent longer hours at work, and my mother didn't seem as eager to let Warren and I play in the streets. It was like fear had taken hold of my family, trapping us in a fist. All I had wanted was to go back to the sea, the place where all my worries seemed to wash away with the tide.

But now that I had finally returned, I felt as though my worries were only building. I spent the entire morning hoping with all my might that there wouldn't be a report of an Exceptional. Ever since Brone had told me about the rebels, I'd spent hours dreaming of defying the Expos and running away to find them. Despite this, I knew that if a report came today, there would be no choice but for me to put on my helmet and step into the role of a faceless Exceptional Police.

The thought left me sick to my stomach as June and I played a few rounds of chess to pass the time. I could hardly focus, and June easily trumped me three straight games, so easily that she noticed my distraction.

"The first week is always the hardest," she said sympathetically as we set up our pieces for a fourth round. "Just remember that they're given the chance to live, and many take it."

My pawn clattered onto the board, and I lifted my head to stare at her. "Are you serious?" I hissed. June looked up in surprise. "It doesn't matter if they're given the chance to live! Knowing that I'm ripping them away from their family is bad enough."

"Aila." June's gaze darted warningly to where Kala was sitting at a desk, bent over a pile of papers. Trav sat even closer, his nose buried in a historic book on the first Earl of Rosan. But neither of them seemed to have heard my words.

"Becoming an Expo isn't *living*, June," I said, and she pursed her lips. "How can you not see it? Exceptionals aren't dangerous. How can you *not* feel guilt about taking them from their normal lives? How can everyone just go along with this? How can Brone ruin so many people's lives?"

Too late, I realized my voice had escalated with anger. Trav glanced up from his book to stare at me, and though Kala's back was still turned, her pen had stilled, hovering motionlessly over the page.

My heart began to beat furiously as I took a deep, unsteady breath. It was one thing questioning Brone's motives in front of my closest friends, and something completely different to do so in front of Kala, Brone's trusted advisor. Fear began to claw at me, and I turned numbly back to the chess board.

"Brone wasn't always this way."

I startled, twisting in my chair to stare at Kala. She was still sitting at her desk, backlit by the light filtering through the window.

"He was a child once, just like you," she continued, her voice strangely soft. "But just like you, one event in his life forced him to grow up faster than he should've."

There was a personal note in Kala's tone, one that surprised me. I knew she wasn't an Exceptional—I had seen her unmarked hand before she pulled her gloves on. But she was too old to be Brone's childhood friend. What bond had they formed that made her become an Expo under him?

"Brone didn't always believe Exceptionals were dangerous, and I assure you he has reasons why he changed. They may not be clear, but Brone has experienced a lot of hardship in this world. He is doing what he can to make things right."

Right? Did he really think it was right that Exceptionals were feared, hated, and reported on sight, just because of a mark on their hand?

But I didn't say this out loud. Instead, I said, "I don't want to seem disloyal." At last, Kala turned to fix me with a sharp stare. I swallowed. "I wasn't questioning Brone, I was just…confused."

"I will speak to Brone about this incident, but he'll be less disappointed than you think," Kala responded. "He appreciates someone who can think for themselves, someone who doesn't devote themselves blindly to a cause while neglecting everything else. He's seen what can happen when someone becomes too obsessed with one thing."

Kala's words surprised me. What could've happened to Brone to make him feel that way, to make him hardly feel at all?

The door to the room banged open, and a man rushed in, startling us all. He clung to the door frame, gasping for breath until he managed to wheeze, "There's an Exceptional. Down by the docks."

No, I thought wildly, but Kala was already moving, stuffing her helmet onto her head and leaving me no choice but to do the same. She stopped me as we rushed out of the Security Station, pausing just long enough to give me a significant look through her visor. I understood it perfectly. This was the first time I would participate in recruiting an Exceptional.

And this was the perfect chance to prove the depth of my loyalty to Brone.

9

STORM

Anticipation hung in the air, as thick as the heat in Ferrol fields on late summer afternoons. If everything today went well, I would be able to feel that heat for the first time in a month tomorrow morning.

It was the day before the start of Mission Week, and I stood shoulder-to-shoulder with my fellow trainees as we waited for Commander White. Once she arrived, she would announce which of us were going to participate, and which of us would have to wait another agonizing month.

I still could plainly see Commander White's expression from the day I had dueled with Chase, her lips pursed in disapproval. I'd messed up that day, let my anger get the best of me, and I'd been throwing myself into every assignment since to make up for it. On a more encouraging note, I had been showing promise in my tutoring sessions with Chase. He seemed to understand that mastery was not achieved by cramming all the information into the student's head as quickly as possible, but by taking things slowly and only moving on once the previous subject was learned.

Chase and I also continued to practice with the sword, and as the days passed, I began to think of him more as a friend. I never had many friends back in Ferrol, and that had suited me just fine. I didn't need anyone else to worry about, and I didn't need anyone to help me. However, Chase didn't try to do either of those things. He was someone I could laugh with, someone I could talk to, someone I could trust with my life.

To my relief, he hadn't brought up our conversation during our duel the other day. It was clear he disagreed, but he didn't press it. Maybe that's why I trusted him so much; he was patient and understanding.

I rolled my shoulders, my gaze darting toward the closed doors on the other side of the room. I wasn't exactly worried. There were countless reasons for Commander White to pick me. What scared me more was what would happen after she did.

The door on the far end of the training room swung open, and silence wrapped around the room like a blanket. Commander White strode through the doorway, her boots clicking on the stone floor, her posture straight and businesslike as always. A group of nearly a dozen other people—including our trainers and a handful of other Insurgents—filed in behind her, and I spotted Chase among them.

Commander White stopped in front of us, her final footstep echoing off the walls. With meticulous movements that seemed unnecessarily slow, she drew a piece of paper from her pocket and unfolded it.

"I hold here a list of those who will be joining us on Mission Week." Her voice bounced off the walls in such a commanding way that it made us all straighten with attention. "There are twenty-two of you in this program, but not everyone will be going. And remember, just because you are participating in Mission Week does not mean you are out of the training program."

We all nodded emphatically, but I doubted any of us were really listening. My eyes were trained on the paper in her hand.

"The names are: Gale Rios. Harlow Browning. Wells Chapman."

With each name called, some trainees sagged in relief, while others looked increasingly anxious. I waited with anticipation, but as Commander White continued further down the list, I heard more and more names that were not my own. She was reaching the final names when I felt the first twinge of anxiety.

"...Lena Burke and Aris Castillo. That is all."

Further down the row, Aris let out a breath, and the room immediately filled with chatter of relief and disappointment. But I was frozen in place, certain I had heard incorrectly, certain there had been some sort of mistake. I stood still, waiting for her to realize her error and read out my name.

But Commander White simply folded up the paper, slipped it into her pocket, and turned to exit the room.

"Wait!" I shouted.

The whole room fell silent. Commander White drew to an abrupt halt.

Her back still turned, she said in a slow, deliberate voice, "Is something wrong, Mr. Dawson?"

I hurried up to her side. "My name wasn't on the list."

"You are correct. Your name was not on the list," Commander White said, "which means you are not invited to participate in Mission Week this month."

I stared at her. "You can't be serious!" I let out a bark of disbelieving laughter that seemed to echo in the quiet of the room. "I've done the best in all the training exercises, and *everyone* knows I'm the most athletic person in this room."

For the first time, Commander White turned to face me, her pale green eyes boring into mine. I sucked in a breath as they once more reminded of her authority. "Athleticism is only part of it, Mr. Dawson. Your agility means nothing to me if you can't follow orders."

With that, she turned on her heel and strode away, leaving me to stare after her in stunned outrage. I huffed indignantly and started to follow when I locked eyes with Chase across the room. He gave a tiny, barely perceptible shake of his head. I hesitated, glared after Commander White, then spun around and stalked out of the room in the other direction.

Chase caught up with me moments later. I heard him approaching long before he actually reached me, so I was ready when he did.

"I can't believe she isn't letting me go on missions!" I burst out angrily. "Can't she see how big of a help I'd be?"

Chase licked his lips, and to my annoyance, he seemed to be fighting a smile. "No offense, Storm, but the Insurgence has been doing just fine for many years without you."

I tore my gaze away with a frustrated shake of my head. "That's not the point."

"Then what is the point?"

I spun around and pointed furiously back down the hall. "I've beaten every single trainee in that room at nearly every exercise we do. I can outrun all of them. I complete obstacle courses with a solid minute lead. And yet she chooses *them* to go on the missions, not me!"

"And?"

"It's unfair!" I tore my fingers through my hair and started back down the hall, away from the training room. "It's all because she doesn't trust me."

"Exactly," Chase said, jogging to catch up. "She said it herself: Agility means nothing if you can't follow orders. So why are you upset?"

I was upset because I would have to wait another month before getting out of this place. I was upset because Commander White had just said in front of everyone that she didn't trust me. I was upset because I had been stupid enough to announce to the entire room that I thought I was better than them—which was true, but it wouldn't help my reputation.

"I don't understand," I muttered. "Why doesn't she trust me?"

Chase gave me an incredulous look. "Storm, you've only been here a *month*, and already you tried to run away three times, you skipped out on tutoring twice, and you basically told everyone that when you were home, you used to skip work in the fields and go rob people instead."

"Okay, that last one was Aris."

"But is it true?"

I paused, then insisted, "I've changed!"

"On the outside, maybe," Chase said, "but who's to say you're not still the same on the inside? Sure, behaved well enough for the past couple of weeks, but for all Commander White knows, you have some ulterior plan you're waiting to put into action until you're outside. She doesn't trust you, and she's waiting for you to prove she can before she chooses you for Mission Week."

I looked away, annoyed that Chase seemed to have everything figured out, from me to Commander White to all the mess in between.

"Is she right?" he said quietly after a moment. "*Do* you have another plan?"

"I thought I've proved otherwise the past three weeks," I snapped.

"Don't you see?" Chase said in exasperation. When I frowned, he gestured back down the hall toward the training room. "Back there, that was all a test. She wanted to see how you would react when your name wasn't called, and what you did proved her *right*."

My heart dropped to my feet as I turned my gaze skyward with a groan. Why hadn't I just kept my mouth shut? But when I looked back at Chase, it was with a fresh glint of determination in my gaze.

"What?" he asked warily.

"If she was willing to change her mind today, she probably still is. I'm going on a mission this week, even if it's just the last day."

Chase shook his head, a small smile playing on his lips. "You know what you are?"

"What?"

"Stubborn. You're stubborn."

"Ouch."

"Infuriatingly so."

Then Chase threw an arm around me, and we started down the hall toward our rooms. If it had been anyone but Chase to lay out my flaws so bluntly, I probably would've pickpocketed them or shouted at them or stormed off, likely a combination of all three.

Chase saw all my mistakes so clearly, and didn't hesitate to point them out, but the thing was...he didn't think any less of me for them. He still wanted to be my friend. Maybe one day, if I was lucky, I would be half the person he was.

I could tell something was wrong with Chase the second I spotted him in the training room the last day of Mission Week.

Throughout the week, those of us not participating had been given a break from training, but our trainers liked to assign menial tasks to keep us busy throughout the day. One Insurgent had given me a pile of fresh Expo uniforms last night and asked me to fold and drop them off before everyone left for their mission. Despite the fact that this meant getting up long before dawn, I agreed before he even finished asking. If I was lucky, he would report my readiness to help to Commander White. Time was running out before the end of Mission Week, and I was beginning to grow desperate.

Judging by the look on Chase's face when I spotted him across the room, I wasn't the only one riddled with worry.

"What's the matter?" I asked after dropping the uniforms by the door and weaving my way through the crowd to find him. The whole room was filled with an air of anxiety, and I felt like I was missing something.

Chase's voice was taut with worry. "A bunch of group leaders have caught some sort of sickness."

I paled, a memory of Jon flashing before my eyes. He was small, weak, shivering under a thin blanket in the thick of winter, coughing up a storm larger than the one that had raged outside. No one had expected him to survive.

Chase saw the panic in my eyes and rushed to reassure me. "It's just a cold, but it means we won't be able to have as many groups as normal."

I clenched my jaw. "So you won't be able to reach as many towns?"

Chase nodded, looking lost. "We've only rescued two Exceptionals so far this week, and if we operate like we are now, I doubt we'll find any more. I've been trying to convince the commander to let groups go without leaders, but she won't do it."

"Why not?"

Chase shrugged, and I glared around the room in search of her. He caught a glimpse of my expression and grabbed my arm.

"Calm down, Storm. She must have a good reason."

"Yeah, and what reason is that?" I scoffed.

"It's not my place to ask."

"*Lives* are at *risk*." I ripped my arm from his grasp. "I don't care what our place is. I'm talking to Commander White." I turned around and strode toward the exit of the training room before Chase could say a word to stop me.

Commander White was already on her feet when I pushed open the door to her office, bent over a map of Rosan that was spread across her desk. She jerked her head up in surprise as I strode directly toward her.

"Mr. Dawson." Her voice lacked its usual commanding air. She swept the map off her desk and began to roll it up. "I cannot speak right now. I have to get down to the training room and assign new groups, but—"

"Commander, I think you should listen to Chase."

Her hands paused. "What?"

"He's right. You should let some groups go without leaders. Have someone responsible head each group, and send them to a small town. We *need* to reach as many towns as possible."

Commander White opened her mouth but didn't quite seem to know what to say, so I continued.

"If this was last month, *I* could've been one of those Exceptionals that wasn't rescued because of the lack of groups. And I know that would've made your life a whole lot easier, but it would've meant the end of mine. It's our responsibility to do everything we can to save these Exceptionals. We *need* to try our best."

I thudded my fist down on the desk and fell silent. Commander White was quiet for so long that I began to think she was trying to hold back the impulse to yell at me. I dropped my gaze to my feet, breathing rapidly.

And then she said, "I'm impressed, Mr. Dawson." I jerked my head up, but there was no sarcasm in her gaze. Just grudging admiration. "And maybe just a little bit inspired."

"What's the catch?" I asked warily.

"There is none. I'll admit, it wasn't what I was expecting, but finally you seem to have the Insurgence's best interest at heart: protecting Exceptionals." She rolled up the rest of the map then cracked a smile. "And for the first time you referred to the Insurgence as *we*, not you."

I blinked. I hadn't even noticed that.

"I'm not saying I trust you fully, Storm, but you have spirit and dedication. Maybe one day, you'll be able to channel that into the Insurgence. As for today…I suppose we could use you on Mission Week."

My next breath sounded more like a laugh. Of course the one time I wasn't trying to trick the commander into trusting me was the time she finally did trust me. I was finally able to participate in Mission Week. My mind began to race.

"Thank you, Commander," I mumbled, turning numbly toward the door.

Commander White dipped her head in acknowledgement, stepping around her desk to join me. "Thank *you*. You and Mr. Kader may be on to something."

However, she didn't make her decision as we walked down the hall toward the training room. Instead, she gave me a brief rundown of what to expect on my first mission.

"The Expos station themselves in the Security Stations. We roam the surrounding streets, so when a messenger is sent with word of the Exceptional, we can intercept them before they reach the Expos. If things go smoothly, the Expos never realize there was an Exceptional. But sometimes, the messenger slips past us and gets to the Expos."

Commander White turned her head in my direction, her green eyes piercing. "That is why I must be able to trust everyone on the missions. In the event that Expos do receive the call, it is not time for heroics. You must not—I repeat, *must not*—interfere. The Expos *cannot* be made aware of your presence. Let it go, forget it, and move on. That is what we must do, every time."

I frowned. "But what if—"

"*No*," Commander White snapped, and I fell silent. "No exceptions. If the Expos are at the scene, you must leave immediately. Do you understand?"

I hesitated.

"*Mr. Dawson.*"

"Yes," I relented, gritting my teeth. "I will let it go, forget it, and move on."

The commander still looked unsatisfied, but she dropped the subject, instructing me to find a uniform and helmet that fit and change in the bunk room.

When I exited the room five minutes later, I saw Chase hurrying down the hall in my direction. He grinned when he saw me decked out in the uniform with the helmet tucked beneath my arm.

"You did it, Storm!" he said, spreading his arms wide before slapping me on the back. "I'm glad she's letting you join."

I grinned back at him. "So what's going on?"

"Do you want the good news or the bad news?"

"Good news."

"We're in the same group."

My smile widened. I couldn't imagine a better day; not only was I able to go outside, but I was doing it with my best friend. "And the bad news?"

Chase beamed. "Thanks for talking to Commander White. She agreed that we can still operate the same number of groups, even without some of the leaders."

"That's not bad news."

Chase's smile fell a bit. "The groups are smaller, and she assigned new team leaders."

"What's the bad news?"

Chase's entire expression had morphed into a frown. "Please promise me you won't be angry and reckless."

I knew the answer to my question before I asked it. "Who is our team leader, Chase?"

At that exact moment, Aris Castillo rounded the corner, looking thoroughly annoyed. "Are you two about ready to go? Half the groups have left already!"

I turned to Chase and groaned. "Seriously?"

"Storm," he said warningly. He gave me a look, then started after Aris, who was already turning around to start down the hall.

I rolled my eyes and followed. "Why'd she choose *him*? Couldn't it have at least been you? You're more experienced, and you're not as rude. Or as cocky. Or as all-around insufferable."

Aris scowled. "Are you quite done insulting me yet?"

I glared at him.

"His power is more important than mine," Chase said as we wove our way through the corridors.

"Really? I wouldn't know, you've never bothered to tell me what yours is."

"You're just upset because you don't have one," Aris sneered.

"He can hear well," I said, ignoring Aris. "So what?"

"No, I can make inanimate objects amplify sound," Aris snapped. "Give me your helmet."

He ripped it from under my arm before I could even comply, then stopped in the center of the hallway. Closing his eyes, he grasped both sides of the helmet. After a moment, he tossed it back and kept moving forward. "As long as we all have our helmets on, we'll be able to hear each other clearly, even if it's a whisper."

"What if I don't want to hear you?"

Aris began to turn around, but Chase pushed him forward. "Just keep walking." He then shot me an irritated glance. "Storm, just be happy you get to go outside."

After a few more minutes of tense silence, Aris stopped in front of a nondescript wooden door and shoved it open. It swung forward to reveal the stables.

I gawked. "*This* is the door to the outside?" It looked like every other door in the hall, and in fact the entire Base.

Aris smirked. "You could've tried to escape a thousand times, and you never would've guessed, huh, Dawson?"

I was barely paying attention. Elation filled me like a fountain as we crossed through the wooden stables and stepped out the door into the sunlight. Fields stretched before me, rolling hills in every direction. I saw a cluster of trees marking the beginning of a forest on one side, and I could hear the rush of a stream on the other. I hadn't realized how much I'd missed being outside with no walls keeping me back.

I turned around to look at the Base. It was a large, intricate stone building with meticulous masonry and beautiful arching windows. I started in surprise. Even though the inside of the Base was huge, I had always thought the outside of the building would be something simple that wouldn't raise the suspicions of any passersby. But this...this was an *estate*.

"Where are we?" I said, twisting to face Chase.

Chase looked up from where he was untying a horse's reins from a post. "We're southeast of Norite."

"Norite?" It was one of the Stone Cities, and I had known there were fields nearby, but they were populated. How had no one noticed and questioned the huge, obvious building? "Is this Duke Leighton's estate?"

He nodded, and I let out a disbelieving chuckle.

"The duke died right when the Insurgence was starting," Chase said. "They spread rumors that he had grown sick and didn't like to travel, and everyone bought them because of the plague."

"And Earl Nicolin doesn't visit?" I knew the brothers weren't especially close, Nicolin being a decade older, but how hadn't he noticed his brother had just stopped communicating?

"The earl never really trusted Leighton and only ever gave him inconsequential tasks. The Insurgence responds to any letters sent our way, but for the most part, everyone thinks Leighton just likes to stay holed up in his estate."

I glanced back toward the building with a half grin on my face. I had been spending the last month sleeping under Duke Leighton's roof without even knowing it. I couldn't wait to tell Jon when I saw him today.

A thought struck me, and I turned back to Chase. "Wait. Is our training room supposed to be...a *ballroom?*"

Chase laughed, but Aris cleared his throat, drawing me back to the task at hand. I stepped up to one of the few remaining horses. I had only ridden a horse a few times before—no one in Ferrol was rich enough to afford a riding horse—and I mounted the animal with some difficulty. Aris snickered.

"Where are we going?" I asked, not even sparing Aris a glance.

Chase looked at me warningly.

"What?" I demanded. I hadn't done anything wrong, unless struggling to mount a horse was suddenly a crime.

Then Chase said, "We're heading to Ferrol."

I tried to conceal my excitement with a look of intense focus, but inside, I silently rejoiced. *Ferrol.* It was like Commander White knew the plan that had been forming in my head ever since I agreed to join the Insurgence and decided to help me along with it. To get to Ferrol, we would have to pass through Carsley, and all I had to do was create a minor diversion, slip away, and find Jon at the schoolhouse.

It wouldn't matter, really, if we got to Ferrol long after the Expos. What were the chances of there being another Exceptional, only a month after I had been taken away? Finding Jon was far more important.

We rode hard and fast, reaching Carsley only an hour after sunrise. Already, the streets were packed with vendors and customers. I couldn't help but break into a grin as we wove our way between the jostling crowds and packed vending stands. It wasn't until I was immersed in the light, laughter, and color of Carsley Market that I realized how deeply I'd missed it. The place just felt so *alive*, a feeling the stone walls of the Insurgence Base lacked.

As we traveled deeper into the town, the streets quickly grew too full to maneuver on horseback. That suited me just fine; it gave me more time to relish the taste of my past and lose myself in the memories that flashed before my eyes with each street corner.

"We need to water our horses and then be right on our way," Aris said as he directed us toward a water trough outside of a stable. "We can't waste any more time because—What are you smiling at?" he demanded, catching sight of my eager expression.

"Nothing," I said innocently, and as I averted my gaze, I caught sight of none other than Omar.

For a moment, my grin widened as I wondered how the merchant was doing now that he didn't have me stealing from his stands. Then I realized he might recognize me and quickly jammed my helmet onto my head.

Aris noticed this gesture, and a look of realization dawned on him. "You said you're from Ferrol," he said slowly, turning to face me, "but you also said you stole. Which means you came to *this* dirt pit to get your food!"

I glared at him through my visor. "Carsley is not a dirt pit."

"Hey," Chase said, a warning edge to his tone.

"I can see why you liked it here," Aris sneered. "It's just *crawling* with street rats and thieves like you."

"Aris, stop."

"Is that a challenge?" I stepped right up to him. "Do you want to see how well *you* can steal from a stand? Go on, try him over there." I pointed to Omar.

Aris snorted. "I am never going to *steal*, Dawson, not even for a challenge. I'd rather lose my honor than stoop that low."

"I know you're blind to anything beyond your own privilege, but that's what I had to do to *eat*."

"Did your parents hate you that much?"

For a moment, I was no longer standing across from Aris in Carsley. I was crying, staring at the receding back of a woman as Tritan Dawson tried to drag me inside a house. Then, I snapped back to reality and lunged forward. Chase shoved me back before I could reach Aris.

"Stop it!" he snapped. "Calm down, Storm, okay?" He swung around to face Aris. "You too! Quit arguing and water your horses!"

93

I glanced at Omar, then ripped off my helmet and dropped it to the ground. "My horse is hungry," I said abruptly. "I'm going to get him an apple."

Without waiting for a response, I darted off into the crowd.

"What? Storm, stop!" Chase's cries faded into the distance as I was swallowed by the crowd. I knew he'd try to follow, but I cut across the street and slipped down a familiar alleyway, losing him on the other side of the stands. At least for now.

I passed a stand packed with fresh apples but pressed on, making a beeline for the schoolhouse. I kept my head low as I wove my way through street vendors and shoppers, dodging the children that darted between the adult's legs. I spotted a familiar face and changed course, hurrying down a narrow street before stepping onto the shriveled grass lawn of the schoolyard.

The long, stone building stretched before me as if it were a painting, unchanged from when I came here as a kid. Windows dotted either side, one for each classroom, but I didn't know which one Jon was in. I chose the right side of the building and curled my fingers around the wood of the windowsill, my fingernails scraping off flakes of paint and sending them spiraling to the ground like snow. I doubted schools in the Stone Cities had crumbling stone sides and windows that needed a new paint job. I hoisted myself up and peered through the dirt-stained panes and into the classroom.

A teacher stood in front of the room, trying to get a bunch of five- or six-year-olds to settle down. I dropped back onto the ground with a flicker of impatience and moved to the next window.

The next classroom looked like it belonged to seven- and eight-year-olds, and the next held kids only a year older. I rounded the back of the building and pulled myself up by the sill of the next window.

Now I was gazing into a classroom with about four teens. I fell back onto the ground, my heart thudding in my chest. I worked my way down the building, peering into classroom after classroom until I reached the last window. With some difficulty, I climbed up to peer inside. Here, at last, were the eleven-year-olds.

My stomach dropped. My eyes desperately roved the faces of the few students I could see. But I knew it was no use.

Jon was not in the classroom.

Footsteps came from behind, startling me. My grip on the windowsill slipped, and I dropped back to the ground with a thud.

I turned around, and Chase was there, jaw clenched, looking simultaneously worried and annoyed. "What are you *doing*, Storm? I've been looking for you everywhere!"

I didn't respond. I was still confused by the fact that Jon was not in school. Had my parents stopped sending him, so he could replace me in the fields despite his weakness? Or had he voluntarily stopped going? My heart skipped a beat as I wondered if he dropped out of school to steal because he needed more food.

"Storm, I'm talking to you!" Chase exclaimed. His eyes darted around the small, dilapidated yard. "What is this place anyway? A...a school?" I watched as realization dawned upon him. He groaned. "Oh no. Please tell me you weren't looking for your brother."

I ignored him and instead started back toward the street from which I had come. My brain was full of warring emotions, and I felt suddenly sick. "Let's find Aris. He's probably angry."

"He's not the only one!" Chase snapped. "Storm, you said you'd stop! You said you wouldn't go back."

I shook my head.

"You promised, but you lied," Chase said, pacing after me. "You *lied* to me."

"Stop."

"Now I'm going to have to tell Commander White that you betrayed her trust again, and—"

"*Chase.*" I spun around to face him. "Jon wasn't there. He wasn't in the school."

Chase stopped short, his mouth forming the beginnings of several different sentences, but all that came out was, "Oh." After several tense seconds, he murmured, "Where is he, then?"

"I...I don't know." Admitting it aloud made it real, and my stomach began to twist.

We stood there in silence, then Chase said, "We'd better get back to Aris, or you'll be in more trouble."

I trailed after Chase as he started back into the Market. After what I'd seen at the schoolhouse—or, more accurately, *not* seen—I couldn't help but think that I wasn't the only one in trouble.

But that Jon was, too.

10

AILA

We reached the docks in five minutes.

I followed the messenger blindly, still struggling to wrap my mind around what was happening. We flew down the streets, past the market with all of its awnings, past the fountain that seemed to bubble less happily than before. I wasn't ready to be an Expo. I wasn't ready to do my job.

But I didn't have a choice. We reached the crowd that had gathered by the docks and shoved our way through. I immediately stopped in my tracks.

Rolling waves slapped against the seawall, sending spray arcing into the air and water splashing onto the stones. The fishermen had stopped their work, pausing with hands half wrapped in nets. The shoppers and children in the streets had gathered together, uncertain as to whether they should push forward to get a better view or move as far from the Exceptional as possible.

The Exceptional was kneeling in a puddle on the cobblestones, bent over his marked hand and shaking in horror. He was small and trembling, and seemingly ignorant of the crowd that had just gathered around him. The four of us drew close, and when he lifted his head, his face drained of all its blood at the sight of our uniforms.

All the joy and spirit of the town seemed to have disappeared, washed away like dirt in the rain. Trav opened a little pouch at his belt and pulled out a folded cloth, clutching it in his gloved hand as he stepped toward the boy.

"No, wait!" A scream tore itself from the crowd, and I whirled to see a woman rip her arm out of another woman's hand. She stumbled forward, two small children clinging to her skirts. "Let my son go!" Her voice was raw with terror. "He's done nothing wrong!"

The crowd suddenly surged forward with her, trying to get closer to the action. Kala and June rushed to meet them, yelling and gesturing wildly, trying to force them back. But the mother continued forward, fearful yet undeterred, her piercing shouts slicing through the air.

This is my chance to prove myself. The thought flashed briefly across my mind, and before I knew what was happening, I had intercepted her. I grabbed her shoulders and held her back, stopping her advance.

"Step back, ma'am." The voice that came out of my mouth startled me. It was foreign, sharp and commanding. It was not my voice at all.

It was the voice of an Expo.

"He could be dangerous," I continued, my voice still unfamiliarly cold and detached. The lie slipped easily from my mouth as the woman's face crumbled in fear and grief.

"Torias!" she screamed, straining against me. I held her back. "Torias!"

I flinched. I did not want to know the boy's name. I did not want to know that he had an identity, a life, friends, a family. It was easier to avoid thinking of everything we were ripping away from him.

Behind me, the boy started to cry. His mother still shrieked his name. Her two young children wailed in desperation. I continued to restrain the woman. Kala and June kept the crowd at bay. I spared a glance behind me just in time to see Trav cover the boy's mouth with the cloth. He crumpled unceremoniously into Trav's arms, and Kala gestured for us to move out.

And just like that, it was over.

I stepped away from the woman, and she collapsed to the ground, sobbing. But her cries weren't the worst part. Neither were the faces of the other children as they saw their brother being carried away, or the fact that everyone was staring at me like I was just another faceless Expo.

No, the worst thing was the expression on the boy's face right before the sedative took over. It was the exact same expression Chase had worn, an expression I had probably worn, too.

An expression I would have to get used to now that I was an Expo.

I proved that I was trustworthy. I proved that I was trustworthy. These words cycled through my head like a chant as we rode back to the Olum that afternoon. And yet, however hard I tried to convince myself, the guilt stayed there, poking and prodding at my consciousness as I guided my horse into the Olum's stables.

I felt numb as I dismounted. I watched as two men unloaded the Exceptional from a wagon Trav had retrieved at the Security Station. He looked so young and peaceful, and I had to look away as they carried him past me.

I'd clearly surprised everyone today. June had congratulated me profusely on our way out of Biron, and Trav had given me a proud smile. Kala even spared a curt, "Well done," and I could tell from June's expression that those words were high praise coming from her.

Despite all the praise, the internal chant in my mind slowly transformed. *I proved that I was trustworthy* was now intermingled with a much deeper question. *What have I done?* I didn't even feel regret as we stepped back into the Olum, the door slamming closed behind us, cutting off the fresh air. I was just glad to see them shut out the horrors of the day.

"What happens next?" I asked June as we followed Kala and Trav down the main hall. My voice sounded strained in my ears, but at least it was my own again.

"You three have the rest of the day free. I'll bring a report of the day to Brone," Kala said, overhearing my question. She made eye contact with me over her shoulder. "I'll be sure to mention your contribution."

I proved that I was trustworthy, I told myself again. But again, my conscience asked, *What have I done?*

When we reached the intersection of halls, Kala started toward Brone's office, and the rest of us drew to a halt beneath one of the flickering torches of the corridor. Trav gave me an approving look.

"You did *very* well today, Aila," he said. "The first time I helped recruit an Exceptional, I seized up and was practically useless. Just knowing that what we're doing is right doesn't mean it isn't overwhelming." June nodded in agreement.

I stared at him. "What did Brone do?"

"Nothing. Kala yelled at me for a hot minute," he said with a chuckle, "but Brone doesn't care. It happens to every new Expo. I mean, he understands that not everyone is as emotionless as he is." Trav congratulated me again, then continued down the hall.

I stared after him in surprise, then turned to follow June toward the Common Area where we would wait for Ross. So what I had done was abnormal. I had kept my wits, stuck to the job, when most Expos froze up. But why?

It wasn't really a question. After my slip up in the Security building, the only thing on my mind was keeping myself from facing Brone's wrath. And I had done what I had to ensure I stayed safe. That's what I had always done.

I proved that I was trustworthy. That's what it took to keep me moving forward.

The next day, Jax informed me that I would be moved from my cell to the girl's dormitory. June had been ecstatic and eagerly gave me a tour of the room. And yet, I wasn't really listening, the chant in my head as unstoppable as the day before, but twice more deafening.

I proved that I was trustworthy. What have I done?

This time, though, I knew the answer: I had become an Expo.

The second call came on the fifth day of Recruitment Week.

Brone changed the squad location assignments based on where the most recent Exceptionals had been reported. When I learned where my group was stationed for the day, I had considered feigning sickness or bailing entirely. And yet, as the midmorning sun began to peek over the edge of the smooth stone buildings, I found myself guiding my horse into the city of Bedrock.

I clung to the faint hope that the chances were slim of an Exceptional being reported in Bedrock two months in a row, but it was no use. The messenger arrived mid-afternoon, her eyes shot wide as she shouted, "There's an Exceptional, on the east side of town!"

My breath caught in my throat. *The east side.* That's where I lived, before I became an Exceptional. A sudden, horrifying realization swept through me. *It could be Warren.*

What if it was? What would I do then? As we thudded down the stairs and rushed through the broad, tidy streets of Bedrock, I realized I knew the answer. I would do exactly as I had done during my first Exceptional recruitment: Step into my role as an Expo.

The second we passed into the east side of the city, I became a kid again, trotting through the streets with Warren and Chase, instead of running along with fellow Expos. There was the blacksmith shop where we'd always stop and watch tools being made. I spotted the peaked roof of the library Warren had gotten kicked out of for trying to climb up the shelves, instead of using the ladder. I could still remember how Chase and I had teased him the entire way home, doubled over with laughter.

It was like walking into a living memory.

At every intersection, I instinctively leaned toward the turn I would take to go to my home, and my heart pounded with increased intensity when the messenger took that turn too. When she rounded the final corner and led us onto my old street, I almost couldn't bear to follow.

But it was immediately clear that the Exceptional was not Warren. Unlike the crowd in Biron that had pressed forward with an uncertain eagerness to get closer to the action, everyone on the street had withdrawn to the doorsteps of houses and the narrow alleyways, leaving the Exceptional alone in the center of the street, restrained only by a single Security.

She was a girl, likely older than me, and her eyes were darting around in wild disbelief.

Kala and Trav swept forward, and I moved to follow them, but someone caught my arm. I spun around, wrenching my elbow from the man's grasp. No, not a man, I realized as I froze in shock. A boy.

Warren stood there, staring straight at me.

It took me a moment to realize he didn't recognize me. Of course he didn't; the helmet covered my face, and I was dressed in my Expo uniform.

And, of course, Warren thought I was dead.

I caught my breath and tried to step away, but Warren reached out to stop me.

"Do you have to take her?" he asked, his voice filled with desperation. "Is there any way you can save her?"

I stopped short. Surprise hit me, followed by a wave of pain. He had reported me, his own sister, without blinking, but now he had sudden concern for someone else?

"Please," Warren begged. "I can't see this happen again. I can't—" His voice broke, and he looked away.

For a moment, I couldn't speak. This entire time I had been blaming my brother, thinking the worst of him. But by reporting me, Warren was left to suffer with guilt, just like when I reported Chase. And now, like me, he was doing everything he could to try to make that guilt disappear, even if it meant daring to approach an Expo.

"I'm sorry." My voice slipped back into its harsh, commanding tone like it was second nature. I spotted Kala shoot me an impatient look from where she stood near the stunned Exceptional. "I'm going to have to ask you to move out of the way."

"Save her," Warren said again, but I just pulled away.

I did not recognize the Exceptional, and I doubted Warren did, either. But I was too numb to care, moving through the motions robotically and helping June hold the Exceptional still as Trav covered her mouth with the cloth.

102

The crowd dispersed almost immediately, and I found myself searching the receding backs for Warren as we carried the Exceptional down the street. But he was already gone, disappeared into our house. I lingered for a moment, staring at the plain wooden door cut into the stone face. The lilies in the flower box looked like they hadn't been watered in a long time. The window was dark, a curtain drawn over it. I felt an overwhelming urge to run up to the door and knock, to hug my mother again and talk to my father. But then I caught a glimpse of June, pausing on the corner of the street and watching me with a questioning look on her face, and I turned away from my old life toward the future I had chosen.

A future with the Exceptional Police.

Kala shot me a critical look as she helped Trav situate the Exceptional in the wagon. "Try to avoid conversing with random citizens in the future," she said coldly.

"That boy wasn't a random citizen, was he?" June asked before I could respond. "You're from Bedrock."

Kala glanced at me sharply, and I nodded slowly.

"You look just like him," she continued, staring at me. "Aila, was that your brother?"

I gave another slow nod, and Kala narrowed her eyes.

"Did he recognize you?" she asked, a warning edge to her tone.

"No. He just wanted me to rescue the Exceptional. To save her." I glanced at the limp girl in the wagon. "I said I couldn't, and I asked him to get out of the way."

Kala gave a curt nod. "Well done, Aila," she said briskly. "Brone was wondering what you'd do when sent to your hometown, and he'll be impressed to hear how you handled facing your own brother."

I jerked my head up. "Brone planned this?"

Kala didn't respond and instead turned and mounted her horse. Trav and June did the same, and I had no choice but to follow suit.

My eyes landed on the girl in the wagon as we pulled away, and I quickly averted my gaze. Only five days of being a true Expo, and I was already wondering if I would be able to finish out the week.

The girl's dormitory was much louder than the solitude of my cell. I laid awake on the top bunk, staring at the ceiling, listening to the breathing and sleepy mumbles of the girls around me. But that wasn't the only reason I was still awake. Warren's desperate face was etched in my brain, his pleading words echoing in my head. I'd pushed him aside, moving on with my duty, dismissing him like he was a stranger.

What have I done?

I sat up abruptly, swinging my legs out of bed and springing nimbly to the floor. I needed to take a walk, to clear my head, to shove all the distractions away and focus on what mattered: Taking each day one at a time and continuing to move forward.

As far as I knew, Brone had never enforced any type of curfew, but I still turned myself invisible as I stepped into the deserted, shadowed halls of the Olum. It was eerier at night, dark and silent save for the occasional flickering flame of a lantern or torch. As I slipped through the empty halls, halls that looked nearly identical in the dim light, I thought about the mysterious second floor, but I saw no hints of a staircase. I was just about to return to the dormitories when I realized I was in the hall where Brone's office was located.

To my surprise, the door was open just a crack, lamplight streaming into the otherwise dark hall. I heard voices inside, two familiar, one belonging to a stranger. I moved closer to make out the words.

"...quite concerning," a man was saying as I neared the door. I quickly recognized the distinct, hoarse rasp of his voice. It was Merrick. He, along with Kala, was one of Brone's second-in-commands. I'd only ever caught glimpses of him, in the hall between meals or during training. What was he doing in Brone's office, this late at night? For a terrified moment, I wondered if they were talking about me. Deciding that I didn't want to find out, I turned to go.

Then Brone's voice drifted into the hall. "There have been three more cases of Exceptionals using their powers dangerously since your last visit."

The blatant lie stopped me in my tacks. No Exceptionals had ever used their powers dangerously in the time I'd been at the Olum. I'd never even heard of that happening here ever.

"You're right, this is very concerning," the unfamiliar voice responded, "and unexpected. Earl Nicolin thought you would have gained control of the situation."

Earl Nicolin? This stranger must've been some kind of messenger, sent from Earl Nicolin to get an in-person update from Brone.

And Brone was lying to him, saying that three Exceptionals had acted up.

"The Earl should not be worried. The Exceptionals were dealt with, and no one was hurt," Merrick said.

"Yes, but what have you done to prevent future outbursts like this?" the other man responded, his tone taking on a challenging note. "You are still keeping the Exceptionals alive, which leads to these incidents."

"Just because these *incidents* aren't preventable doesn't mean they're dangerous," Merrick rasped. "The only way we can grow in numbers is by keeping the Exceptionals alive, because your precious *Earl* has done nothing to provide us with the help we need."

"You'd be wise to watch your tongue," the stranger snapped. "You are speaking of the leader of our country."

There was a beat of tense silence, then Brone's impassive voice cut in. "All of these outbursts are safely contained in the Olum. As Merrick has said, no one is even remotely in harm's way. Exceptionals should be feared, but not while they are in the Olum."

"Very well." The stranger still sounded skeptical, but it was clear he knew it was useless to argue. "Any more news you wish for me to report to the Earl?"

"Nothing of importance," Brone responded. "Thank you for your time."

Recognizing the clear end of the conversation, I spun around and backtracked down the hall, disappearing around the corner long before the door opened. As I made my way back toward the dormitories, my heart pounded and my mind raced. Brone was lying to the Earl's official about the Exceptionals, but why? The lie seemed like it would do nothing but jeopardize his job. If an outburst had occurred, I would've thought that he would hide it. Unless…

I inhaled sharply. If the Earl realized the Exceptionals weren't dangerous, he might call off the weekly roundups. For some reason, Brone didn't want that to happen. He was trying to keep the Earl afraid and believing that Exceptionals needed to be collected. He was scaring the government into thinking Exceptionals were dangerous.

Since I became an Exceptional, I'd been living a lie. Longer than that, even. Everyone thought Exceptionals were killed, instead of recruited as Expos, and that was the ultimate lie. Yet as I slipped back into the girl's dormitory, I realized the network of lies and deception the Olum was founded on ran deeper than just a common misconception. No, they were rooted deep in the heart of the government.

I didn't know why Brone was lying. I didn't know what he was planning to achieve. But for the first time, I felt a waver of confidence, felt the urge to prove myself trustworthy slip just the tiniest bit. There was something going on at the Olum, something much bigger than I had ever anticipated.

And I knew it was something I did not want to be involved in.

11

STORM

As expected, Aris was furious when Chase and I returned to where we had left our horses.

"What were you doing?" he spat, stalking up to me with my helmet clutched in his hands. "And *don't* say getting an apple for your horse. I know that was a filthy lie."

I had in fact snagged an apple from an unattended stand as Chase and I passed through the market, which I now dropped in front of my horse before crossing my arms. "I haven't been in Carsley for a month. Don't I have the right to look around?"

"No, you do *not*," Aris snapped. "We are on a *mission*, Storm. You can't just do whatever you want whenever you feel like it. You're jeopardizing all of us!"

"Oh, calm down. No one even noticed me."

"Are you sure?"

I hesitated. Aris thrusted my helmet into my gut, knocking the wind out of me. He turned and began to untie the reins of his horse with furious, jerky movements. "Let's just get out of this grimy town."

If he thought Carsley was grimy, he would get a kick out of Ferrol.

"So you're saying if you were in Travertine, you wouldn't take time to look around?" I said, taking a step toward him.

Aris thrust his face near mine, his eyes ablaze. "I don't know what you were doing, Dawson, but I know you weren't just looking around for the fun of it," he hissed. "You're up to something, and I'm telling you now that Commander White is going to hear about it."

Chase shoved his way between us. "Stop arguing!"

"I'm not arguing," I grumbled, folding my arms. "I'm just explaining why I'm right. In a loud voice."

"We need to go," Chase said to Aris. "The longer we stay here, the more chance there is that the Expos could beat us to an Exceptional."

"I'm not the one you need to tell that to," Aris growled.

But Chase hardly even acknowledged me as he moved to untether his horse. I turned to mount my own when he grabbed my arm.

"Don't go looking for Jon, okay? We're on a mission here. We need to stay focused."

I yanked my arm away and hopped on my horse without responding.

I wasn't going to make any promises.

The journey from Carsley to Ferrol was an uncomfortable one. Aris rode in front, refusing to speak to either of us unless he was barking an order. I rode next to Chase in tense silence. He never quite looked at me, his expression distant and troubled, but I had the feeling he was staying close to make sure I didn't run away.

We tied our horses to a post outside the town and began our trek toward the Security Station. Unlike Carsley, my homecoming to Ferrol was one I would've liked to skip. The second the road leading out of town disappeared behind us, I felt that familiar sense of being trapped. It wasn't helped by the fact that Chase was so close I didn't have the chance to slip away and find Jon.

Aris, who seemed intent on making sure he was always several strides ahead of us, stopped short near the center of town. "Is that normal?" he asked, pointing.

I stepped up next to him, following his gesture to find a large crowd of people had gathered in the center of the street. They were facing away from us, blocking the view of whatever had caught their attention.

"No, all those people should be in the fields or in their homes. I haven't seen a gathering of this many people since—" I abruptly fell silent as realization swept over me, followed by a wave of horror. "Oh, no."

Chase's eyes widened. "They found an Exceptional. We're too late."

"We're too late," Aris repeated in a hushed tone. We all stood there, staring at the scene, until he rounded on me in fury. "This is all your fault!"

"Don't start," Chase said, stepping in front of me before I could respond. "Aris, what are your instructions?"

Aris stared down the street for a moment longer, and I could see the trepidation in his gaze. Finally, he murmured, "We need to follow orders. Let's get out of here before anyone sees us."

"No!" I blurted before anyone could take a step in the opposite direction. Aris and Chase turned to stare at me, and I fumbled for words. "We have to at least scout out the scene first. What if it isn't an Exceptional? It could be something else."

Aris scowled. "You *just* said—"

"But how could I know for sure? Maybe someone got kicked by a horse or…something."

"No." He shook his head, stepping away from me. "We're told to let it go."

"You think it's my fault that we arrived here late, but if we leave and it turns out it wasn't an Exceptional, or the Expos hadn't yet reached the scene, that's on you."

"But what if the Expos are there?" Aris said.

"Then we shouldn't just let them take that Exceptional away," I said fiercely. "What's the point of the Insurgence if all we do is wait for things to be easy? This isn't going to end unless we stand up to the Expos."

Aris stared at me for a moment, then glanced at Chase, then finally stuffed his helmet onto his head.

"I'm not doing this because it might be an Exceptional, I'm doing this because it might not be," he snapped. "Let's split up and see if we can catch a glimpse through the crowd. I'll go to the far side. Chase, you take left, Storm takes right. Don't forget, if you say anything—even a whisper—our helmets will pick it up, and we can talk back. Got it?"

"Got it," Chase and I echoed. My heart began to pound.

"Try to stay unnoticed," Aris added. "If the Expos are there, we get out right away. Understand?"

I shot off down a side street without response and then took a sharp turn into the alleyway that would lead me to my house. I knew Aris would hate me for this, but if I was lucky, I would never see him again anyway.

The end of the alleyway was clogged by the crowd. I grunted in frustration as I was forced further down the street. The next alley was similarly jammed, and the next, and the next. I gritted my teeth. I needed to cross the street to get back home. I needed to find Jon.

I was passing the opening of the next alley when the crowd suddenly began to shift. The spectators started to disperse, and people streamed in my direction. I darted toward a pile of broken crates that had carried goods from Carsley, pressing myself back against the wall until the small road was empty. I moved forward cautiously, not wanting to be seen by citizens or Chase. I peered around the corner of the crumbling building next to me and onto the main street.

A Security had been the one to break up the crowd, and when I saw why, my heart sank. There was indeed an Exceptional, but it looked like the Expos had forced him to inhale their sedative already. Shame clutched me like a suffocating fist. Aris was right. It was my fault. For the first time, I forgot my mission to find Jon and crept closer, desperate to identify the Exceptional I had just failed. Further down the street, I spotted Chase peering around the corner of another building.

Then, to my horror, one of the Expos glanced in Chase's direction. Chase darted out of view, but it was too late. The Expo leaned toward the person next to her and muttered something through her helmet.

The second Expo nodded and barked a command. Immediately, the squad dispersed and moved up the street, one of them supporting the unconscious Exceptional. I leaned forward just as one of the Expos twisted, giving me my first clear look of the Exceptional. Blood drained from my face as my heart stopped beating.

We had been told that, when we arrived late, we should let it go. Forget it. Move on.

But there was no way I was going to be able to forget the face I had just seen. I stared, the breath stolen from my lungs as the Expos moved further up the street and closer to the Security Station. I couldn't breathe, couldn't think, couldn't feel anything past the stark terror consuming me. My hands began to shake.

"That's my brother," I managed to choke out into my helmet. Then, louder because I wasn't sure if they had heard, "That's Jon."

I was seriously beginning to doubt whether Aris's power actually worked when I heard Chase say, "Storm."

That was enough to snap me out of my trance. I tore out onto the street, a cry ripping itself from my throat as I chased after the receding forms of the Expos. As I chased after my little brother. I was dimly aware of Aris's voice in my ear, screaming at me to fall back. But I barely made it more than a few yards before Chase appeared out of nowhere and, in one vicious motion, dragged me into the cover of an alleyway and slammed me against the wall.

"Let me go!" I screamed, punching and kicking at him. "That's Jon! I need to get to Jon!"

"Storm," Chase growled as he fought against me. "Stop. Struggling."

"That's Jon! That's Jon!"

"Aris told you to fall back!"

"They're taking him away!" My voice was raw, my eyes wild.

"Calm down!" Chase gave my shoulders a jerk. "What are you going to do? Chase after him, then get yourself captured? Think about it for a second, Storm!"

111

Suddenly, all the fight drained out of me. I sagged against the wall, Chase's grip the only thing keeping me upright. Tears started coming, and I ripped off my helmet and threw it to the ground.

"They have Jon," I whispered. No matter how many times I said it, I was still hit with a fresh wave of terror. "They captured…they got him…"

Chase still held me against the wall, as if uncertain whether I would run, but his grip loosened slightly. "It's okay, Storm," Chase said. "We'll get him back. We will."

I jerked my head up. "How?"

"It doesn't matter," he said fiercely. "We'll find a way. We'll sneak out of the Insurgence Base, find the Expos, something. Anything. Whatever it takes."

"Whatever it takes," I repeated numbly.

And then Aris was there, chucking his helmet on the ground and shoving Chase aside to take his place.

"What was *that*?" he snarled, slamming me back against the wall.

My head cracked into the stone, but Aris didn't seem to care. "I told you to fall back! Were you *trying* to get yourself killed?" he seethed. "It was obvious from day one that you were reckless and had terrible judgment, but I never thought you were *that* stupid." His face was inches from mine as he all but spat in my face. "You risked the entire existence of the Insurgence!"

Anger flowed in, harsh and hot as I shoved Aris away. I caught him off guard, and he stumbled back.

"That was my *brother*," I snapped back, advancing toward him. "How would you feel if you just watched someone you loved be dragged away to their death? Huh?"

Aris stared at me.

"Oh, that's right," I said, my voice dripping with venom. "Your heart is too hard to love."

Aris's face twisted. "You—"

"Stop!" Chase ripped off his helmet and stepped between us, arms wide. Something inside all of us had snapped, and now Chase's voice was brimming with an anger I never thought he could have. "Just

112

stop arguing for *one second*, will you?" He rounded on me. "Aris is right. You put the entire Insurgence in danger by running after the Expos."

Aris shot me a smug look until Chase rounded on face him. "And you! You're supposed to be our leader, and yet you can't take one step without provoking or arguing with Storm!"

Aris recoiled, clearly stunned by Chase's outburst. Sighing, Chase dropped his arms. "Let's get back to the Base," he muttered. "Commander White will want an update."

He retrieved his helmet and disappeared down the alleyway, leaving Aris and I standing there, chests heaving, eyeing each other warily. Then, to my surprise, Aris stepped forward and patted me awkwardly on the shoulder.

"I'm sorry," he said, "about your brother."

For a moment, I wondered if there was some part of Aris deep down that wasn't touched by his foul mood and arrogance, but then he added, "It must be hard, knowing it was all your fault."

I didn't even have the energy to fight back as he snatched up his helmet and followed after Chase. He was right. It was my fault we had arrived late, my fault Jon was captured. My fault that I'd left him alone this long in the first place.

All of a sudden, every bit of horror, grief, and helplessness I had been feeling was replaced by a sudden, piercing determination. All of this had happened because of me, and I realized that Chase had been right. I was willing to do whatever it took to get Jon back.

12

AILA

I paced back and forth in front of Brone's office, my mind swirling. I had thought that when Brone assigned us to Ferrol, we'd finally get an easy day. Kala had been sick, leaving Trav in charge, and we had all thought Ferrol was too small to have an Exceptional. I was relieved. After realizing the lies Brone was telling, I didn't think I'd have the heart to capture another Exceptional.

But we had hardly been there for more than an hour when the messenger came. My heart dropped. Trav had assigned me to handle the cloth, and my hands shook as the young man led us to the scene.

The entire street was in chaos. People were rushing to gather near, chattering wildly. I overheard snippets of their conversations.

"Another Exceptional? We just had one last month!"

"And he's from the same family, too!"

"What are the chances? This must be genetic."

I shut out the conversations and tried to block up the pity that was threatening to spill over, but the second I spotted the Exceptional, all my walls came crashing down. He was small and thin, only about ten or eleven. He stood there, not even bothering to run or hide the X on his left hand. Instead, he just watched us approach with an expression of resignation.

At that moment, several teenage boys managed to shove their way through the crowd, dropping to their knees in front of the boy. I could see the resemblance in their faces and knew they were brothers.

The oldest spotted the boy's hand and recoiled. "No...Jon, no..."

Trav stepped forward. "We're going to have to ask you to move back," he said in a firm tone. The Securities had already moved forward and were trying to disperse the crowd.

With a few last regretful looks at their brother, the boys quickly stood and stepped back. Trav nodded to me, and I moved in, retrieving the cloth from its pouch and unfolding it slowly. The boy took a deep, shuddering breath, then closed his defeat-filled eyes. He didn't even flinch as I pressed the cloth over his mouth until he took a breath of the sedative. The boy crumpled unceremoniously into Trav's arms. One of the Securities shouted at the crowd to disperse, and just like that we were done.

And then I saw him. Someone wearing the outfit of an Expo was peering around the corner of an alleyway and in our direction. He was part of the rebels, I realized with a start, and he'd arrived at the scene just moments too late. I found myself staring, and that's how I realized something about him I hadn't noticed before. There was something about the way he leaned against the wall, something about the way he cocked his head, so that even with the helmet covering his head, I knew his eyes were lasering in on the scene. My breath caught in my throat.

He must've seen me, because he suddenly recoiled, disappearing around the corner of the building. I stared after him for a second longer, then before either of them could notice, turned to Trav. "Let's go." My voice was firm, even though I could feel my knees buckling, even though I could feel my hands shaking slightly and my heart beating faster.

"Move out!" Trav barked, and he and June started down the street, both unaware of what I had seen, oblivious to the shock coursing through me. Because just that brief glimpse was enough.

Somehow, Chase Kader was alive.

On the way back to the Olum, it took Trav three tries to get my attention long enough for him to congratulate me on a successful day and ask me to give the report to Brone. I hadn't even responded, and I felt as though I was floating on my way to Brone's office.

The image of Chase, peering from around the corner of a Ferrol building, haunted me as much as that image of him eight years ago.

The door to Brone's office opened, startling me out of my thoughts. Another Expo stepped from the room, nodding curtly to me as he strode past. Taking a deep breath, I stepped forward and pushed open the door.

Brone was sitting at his desk, bent over an unrolled map. He looked up as I entered, sweeping it to the side and gesturing for me to take a seat. I did, my fingers curling around the edges of the wooden armrests.

Brone folded his hands on the desk. "How did the mission go today?"

"It went well. We successfully capt—*recruited*—an Exceptional. A boy, probably around ten or eleven years old." I paused, uncertain as to how much information he wanted. This was usually Kala's job.

Brone nodded slowly, his expression betraying neither displeasure nor satisfaction. "You were in Ferrol, correct? At what time did this occur?"

"We arrived just shy of midmorning and were notified of the Exceptional almost immediately. He was found just down the street from the Security Station." If the run-down, tiny wooden building could even be called that.

"Good." Brone bent over a piece of paper and scribbled something while I watched apprehensively. When he looked up, he fixed me with a stare. "Tell me, Aila, were there any sightings of the rebels today?"

My grip on the armrests tightened. Did he know? Was this a test? My thoughts began to spiral, but I forced my tone to remain steady. "No. We didn't see the rebels."

Brone studied me, and for a moment I thought he was going to call my bluff, but he merely said, "Good job, Aila Vinn. I knew there was a reason to trust you."

I frowned.

Brone continued, "I must say, there are usually reasons to *doubt* an Expo's loyalty during the first Recruitment Week, yet you stepped into

116

the role—three times—without hesitation. Kala was less certain, so I suggested a little test. I wanted to see how you would do with more responsibility, so we put Trav in charge, and you had the duty of handling the sedative. I wasn't expecting there to be an Exceptional; I simply wanted to see your reaction to your new assignment. You performed better than I could have hoped."

I opened my mouth, struggling to comprehend his words. "Kala faked sickness?"

Brone nodded.

"Does Trav know?" I didn't have to ask about June; she would've picked out the lie the second it was uttered. Brone had probably told her ahead of time to keep the secret. A part of me felt betrayed at the thought.

"He does," Brone said. "After all, I needed someone to watch your behavior. By sending you to deliver the report, Trav has communicated that you performed admirably."

My mind spun. Right when I was starting to doubt if I trusted Brone, I had succeeded in proving myself trustworthy to him. Suddenly, I wasn't sure if I wanted his trust.

"I was right about you. You are a survivor, and you do what needs to be done." Brone leaned forward. "I'm impressed, Miss Vinn. I'm impressed, and I don't say that to just anyone."

I dropped my eyes, busying myself with studying the ice dagger. I was no longer sure if a compliment from Brone was a good thing.

He leaned back, his hand drifting toward the map once more. But he seemed to catch himself, wrapping his gloved hand into a fist before dropping it onto the table. "I have a meeting with one of the Earl's officials at midnight. I need time to rest and prepare."

I knew a dismissal when I heard one and wasted no time escaping the room and Brone's icy gaze.

My mind was still wrapped around my conversation with Brone as I slid into my normal seat next to June at dinner. I passed the test. Brone trusted me. A few days ago, I would've been relieved to hear this. But now, after hearing Brone lie to Earl Nicolin's *official*, I didn't know what to think.

I stared at my plate in frustration. Everything was so complicated now.

"I know that look," Ross said, dropping into a seat across from me with his perpetual grin already spreading across his face. "It's the look of someone who has been trying to master a skill, but can't seem to get it."

"You see that in the mirror often, don't you?" I asked flatly.

Ross's smile dropped. "Not funny."

"So you can give, but you can't take, is that it?" June challenged. I laughed, feeling my mood lift a little. This was what I needed in this place: Friends that could make me laugh, not problems around every corner.

This meal was one of celebration. Everyone was in high spirits, exhausted but happy after the long, hard work of Recruitment Week. Each person had stories, which they eagerly shared without needing Ross to call on them. I couldn't tell if everyone was celebrating a job well done, or the fact that, for the next three weeks, we could go back to pretending we weren't Expos.

Ross soon gained the attention of the entire table and started calling on people, boisterously asking them to display their power. One boy created a ball of light that was so blinding it was as if the sun was cupped in his hand. Another girl picked out a word Ross said to a nearby boy, despite being on the other side of the room. June entertained everyone by easily winning a game of two truths and a lie, and even called Ross out when he threw a loop by giving two lies.

When Ross turned to me, I was glad that I could contribute without having to relive any of the worst moments of my life. With his prompting, I focused and slowly faded my body from view. My act was met by a smattering of applause, and Ross chipped in to point out that he had been the first to witness my power.

118

Laughter filled the halls as we returned to the dormitories, but my mood grew solemn as I prepared for bed. I couldn't erase the image of the young Exceptional from my mind. He had looked so small, standing there in the center of the crowd, already resigned to his fate. My mind turned to my meeting with Brone, and I was just beginning to drift off to sleep when I jerked upright.

Until now, I hadn't processed the words he had used to dismiss me from his office. *I have a meeting with one of the Earl's officials at midnight tonight.* It had to be midnight soon, which meant the meeting would start any minute. And for the first time since I heard Brone and Merrick speaking with the official two nights ago, I knew exactly what I had to do.

I entered Brone's hall several minutes later, cloaked in invisibility. I'd nearly bumped into the Earl's official on the way over, and had been trailing him silently ever since. Brone was mid-sentence as I came within earshot, pressing myself against the wall next to his door.

"...to see you again, Dion," he was saying.

"Likewise," a now-familiar voice responded, accompanied by the sound of a chair scraping against the ground as he took his seat. So Dion was the name of the Earl's official.

I heard Merrick mumble a greeting, but then to my surprise, a third voice spoke.

"Is there a reason you pushed the meeting back so late?" It was Kala. My heart sank to learn that even she was in on Brone's lies. She was often harsh, but I'd hoped she was trustworthy too.

"I apologize. There was much going on at Adwick Palace today. It seems like there was a disturbance this morning involving Expos." Dion paused, then added, "In Ferrol."

I inhaled slowly, waiting for someone to respond, but all three were silent. After a pause, Dion continued.

"It is my understanding that an Exceptional was reported in Ferrol this morning."

"Yes, and we took him into custody," Kala said, her voice taking on a hard edge. "He was collected by the group I usually lead, but unfortunately I was unable to do so today."

"A citizen in town said that after the Exceptional had been taken care of, she noticed the arrival of another Expo. Instead of joining the main group, he hid behind a pile of crates. No other citizens reported seeing the same thing, but it is concerning." There was another pause, then Dion said in a low voice, "Why was the Expo hiding?"

"Is the citizen reliable?" Brone sounded entirely calm, as if the Earl's official wasn't on the verge of discovering the rebels. "She is from Ferrol, after all. Perhaps she was just making something up for an excuse to visit Adwick Palace."

"If she is from Ferrol, she doesn't have time to waste taking a joyride across Rosan to go *sightseeing*," Dion said scornfully. "I trust the accuracy of her witness, and it's not the first report of suspicious activity. We have not had many reports, but enough that the Earl thinks it is time to bring them to your attention. What has been going on with your Expos, Brone?"

"Are you accusing us of lying?" Merrick rasped.

"Whatever I am accusing you of is not without reason," Dion snapped.

"All Expos have promised to report any suspicious activity as soon as they see it," Brone said swiftly. "If that Expo was one of ours, he has been reported and dealt with. If he was merely someone mistaken for an Expo, then we have nothing to worry about."

Dion's voice hardened. "So was it one of your Expos or not?"

I heard the sound of a chair scraping back as someone stood. "Brone said everything was dealt with." Merrick's voice was low and dangerous. "Thank you for bringing this to our attention. Please tell the Earl there is nothing to worry about."

Dion stood, too, his chair raking against the floor. "I will report every word of this conversation to the Earl, and if he finds it even half as suspicious as I do, I'll see you *much* sooner than next week."

Dion crossed to the door and flung it open, stalking out of the office and straight past me. I heard footsteps of someone crossing the room to close the door, and without thinking, I darted inside, folding myself into a corner as Kala shut the door.

My heart thudded in my chest as Kala, Brone, and Merrick all sank into their seats. What had I just done? Now I was not only eavesdropping on a conversation, but I was doing it *in Brone's office*. Every inch of my body screamed at me to escape, but I was trapped. I couldn't get out of here without them noticing me opening the door.

All three were arranged around the desk, facing the chair that Dion had left empty. Kala folded her hands tightly on the desk and watched Brone with a cautious expression, but his gaze was fixed on the closed door, his eyes betraying nothing. Merrick stood up abruptly and began to pace back and forth, tugging his hands through his dark hair, his golden eyes burning.

"Who was the one that gave the report from Ferrol today?" Kala asked after a moment of tense silence. Her voice was tight, as if she already suspected the answer.

Brone let out a slow breath. "It was Aila."

I stiffened, feeling a rush of panic as Kala's lips twisted into a frown. She shook her head. "Brone—"

"I know what you're going to say, and I disagree," Brone said coldly, snapping his gaze away from the door to look at Kala. "Aila has shown herself to be a survivor, and she's proven herself trustworthy this past week."

"Be wary of trusting someone too quickly, Brone," Merrick rasped.

Brone's fists tightened around the armrests of his chair. "You think that I, of all people, need to be reminded of that?" His voice was dangerously smooth. Merick averted his gaze.

"We know you don't," Kala said quickly. "But either way, Aila could have hidden motives."

"Aila is not what I'm worried about." Each of Brone's words were ground out with a surprising mixture of anger and worry. As I watched, he drew out a small wooden pendant with an X carved into its center from beneath the collar of his shirt. He ran a gloved thumb over the carving, his gaze growing distant. When he glanced back up at Kala and Merrick, his expression was troubled.

"If that was the rebels today, the Earl hears about them—" He wrapped his gloved fist around the amulet before letting it drop back beneath his shirt.

Then, before I could wrap my head around the fact that Brone looked *worried*, Kala reached out and laid a hand on his arm.

"It does not seem like the Earl shares as strong convictions as Dion," she said, her voice startlingly gentle. I almost fell over. She sounded concerned. About *Brone*. And he wasn't doing anything to push her away. Was it possible that Kala and Brone were siblings? She seemed too old to be his sister, but I couldn't think of another explanation.

I was still reeling from shock when Brone said, "If Dion's concerns do spread to the Earl, the Olum will be shut down. The Expos could be disbanded. Then it will be impossible to overthrow Earl Nicolin."

The entire world seemed to tilt. I sucked in a breath, pressing my palms against the cold stone wall in a desperate effort to ground myself. Brone's words rang in my ears, loud and undeniable. *Overthrow Earl Nicolin.*

When I first came to the Olum, I had thought Brone was capturing Exceptionals out of fear. Even later, when I realized he knew Exceptionals weren't as dangerous as the rest of Rosan believed, I'd been certain there was a justifiable reason behind his actions.

And now, finally, I knew his motivation, but it was far from justifiable.

I was so startled, so shaken, that I didn't hear the next several sentences of the conversation and nearly missed my opportunity to slip out the office door after Kala and Merrick. I stole through the dark corridors back toward the dormitory, my heart thudding in horror. We were not just being trained to become Expos. No, Brone was working toward something else entirely.

He was building an army.

He was working toward something more sinister and destructive than I could've imagined, with motives that I couldn't understand. Soon, he would be the head of a mutiny, possibly a war.

And as an Exceptional and Expo, I was going to be caught in the middle of it.

13

STORM

Aris slammed his plate down on the table across from me. I glanced up from where I had been silently pushing my dinner around my plate and straight into his raging gaze. So, he was still angry at me for what I'd done today. I shouldn't have been surprised; today had been Aris's first day leading a mission group, his first chance to truly prove himself to Commander White, and I had ruined everything.

Well, that was one thing I didn't regret.

Every table in the Refectory was occupied, filling the room with celebratory chatter and laughter. It reminded me of the time Earl Nicolin had passed through Carsley. The minute he left, everyone wanted to share their stories about how he personally stopped to tell them how amazing they were. Except now, everyone wanted to brag about how they were the heroes of the Insurgence.

I'd spent the whole meal waiting for Commander White to storm into the room and sentence me to death, or at least give me some sort of miserable punishment. I was pretty sure having to eat the rest of my meal next to Aris was worse.

"What did you tell her?" I asked after a moment, dropping my gaze to the juicy plum and nut pastry I hadn't even touched.

Aris's voice was taut with anger. "Nothing," he snarled. "Chase managed to convince me to let him be the bearer of bad news. I only agreed because she'd trust him to give all the right details."

Chase. I hadn't seen him since we had arrived back at the Base. Just like before, he'd ridden next to me on the journey home, which only made me more aware of the stony silence that sat between us. At one point, he had picked up the pace and shared a whispered conversation with Aris, which I guessed was when they arranged for Chase to report the failed mission. When we arrived at the Base, he'd disappeared inside the building without even sparing me a glance.

I had messed up in a lot of ways, but my biggest mistake was losing Chase's trust.

Whatever it takes, he'd told me in the alleyway, when it seemed like my world was crumbling into dust. Now I was beginning to wonder if he meant a word he'd said.

A pit of dread had lodged itself in my stomach hours ago, and it was still there, so intense I felt like I was about to be sick. Commander White's punishment was the least of my worries. Jon was an *Exceptional*, and every time I remembered, it was like being stabbed in the gut all over again.

For the first time since Jon had first contracted the plague, I felt completely and utterly helpless.

I continued to stare silently at my food, waiting for Aris to go away, but he remained stubbornly rooted to his spot. I'd been told squads ate together on the last day of Mission Week as a sort of celebration, but I hadn't expected Aris to actually follow through.

After a few minutes, I realized he was staring at me expectantly, as if he was waiting for something. A reaction, maybe, or an apology, or a plea for forgiveness. In that moment, I decided I would not give him the satisfaction of seeing how worried I was. I stabbed at a corner of the nut pastry and popped it into my mouth.

Aris's expression darkened.

"Look," he said irritably, "I don't even know half the stuff you did, since you *ran away* in the middle of the mission, but if I were you, I'd start putting my affairs in order, because—"

Across the room, the door to the Refectory swung open. I jerked my head up, expecting to see Commander White, but instead Chase stalked into the room, his expression hidden behind an impassive mask.

My heart thudded frantically again as he filled a plate with food and turned around, pinpointing Aris and me from across the room. To

125

my surprise, he decided to sit next to Aris, which hurt more than I wanted to admit, even though I deserved it.

Chase didn't speak as he arranged the food on his plate, and the three of us lapsed into a strained silence. We picked at our plates, avoiding each others' gazes like the plague. The tension hanging over our table was a stark contrast to the celebrations going on around the room.

When I couldn't stand it anymore, I cleared my throat. "Let's lighten up a little. We've all earned a bit of—"

"Stop."

Chase spoke the word so quietly I almost didn't hear him. I immediately fell silent.

"Don't say we've earned celebration," Chase continued, his eyes still fixed on his plate. "You've done nothing to earn any kind of reward."

I swallowed. "I didn't do anything *that* bad—"

"You lied about going after Jon, you ran away to the schoolhouse in Carsley," Chase said, ticking off his fingers, "you constantly challenged Aris's authority, you convinced us to stay back when we saw the crowd instead of *forgetting* and *moving on* like we're supposed to, you tried to directly confront the Expos, and...Am I missing anything?" Chase's gaze snapped up. "Oh, yeah. You jeopardized the entire *existence* of the Insurgence all because you couldn't think about anyone but yourself for one second."

I stared at Chase, stunned. When he put it that way, I began to wonder why I hadn't been locked up in a cell ages ago.

"Look, I'm sorry—"

"That's what you said last time," Chase said, "right before you betrayed everyone's trust."

I looked away. Chase's voice was hollow with disappointment, and I was beginning to wonder if our friendship would ever be the same.

After a long pause, I muttered, "What did Commander White say when you talked to her?"

Chase didn't respond for several seconds, then said, "Aris, can you leave?"

Aris's chest puffed out as he opened his mouth to speak, but Chase interrupted him.

"I know you've done nothing wrong, but I need to speak to Storm." When Aris still didn't move, he added, "Alone."

Glaring at me like I was somehow the one who was booting him from the table, Aris seized his plate and stalked off, leaving Chase and I alone and out of earshot from the surrounding high-spirited tables.

"I lied to Commander White."

He said it without prelude, and so matter-of-factly that I nearly fell off the bench. "*What?*"

"You heard me. I'm not saying it again."

I stared at him, trying to comprehend the fact that Chase had said the words *I* and *lied* in the same sentence. "Wh-why?"

"We can't rescue Jon if you're locked up in a cell, no matter how much you deserve it."

I gawked, hardly daring to believe him. "You're not angry at me?"

"I'm furious," Chase said, "but we can save the cell for after Jon is safe."

I wasn't sure if I should be happy or worried, so I just said, "What about Aris?"

"By the time he figures out something is wrong, we'll be long gone."

I leaned back, unable to suppress a grin. From the second I had spotted Jon crumpled in the Expo's arm, I'd known I wasn't going to stop searching for him until he was safe. With Chase helping me, I would be able to rescue Jon even faster.

"Why are you doing this?"

"You were right before. It's time for the Insurgence to act up. Maybe if we rescue Jon, we can show Commander White that we're capable of so much more than what we're already doing."

I nodded, and for the first time I felt like I could breathe through the panic that had been suffocating me. Chase sounded so confident in our ability to rescue Jon that the task we were about to tackle didn't seem so impossible anymore.

I poked at the meal still sitting on my plate. "No one's ever tried this before." Not only did we have to make it out of the Insurgence Base, but we had to find where the Expos operated, break in, and find Jon.

If he was still alive.

My grip tightened on my fork as I refused to even consider that option. We would get to him before it was too late. I just *knew*.

Chase grinned. "Then they'll never see us coming." He leaned forward and extended his hand. "We'll do this. Whatever it takes."

I reached out and we shook, sealing the decision. Sealing our fate. "Whatever it takes."

To my surprise, Chase seemed confident that Exceptionals weren't killed immediately after their capture. I would've questioned his conviction if I wasn't so eager to believe it. However, Chase also insisted that we wait one more day before making a move. I disagreed, and loudly. I'd waited too long getting back to Jon the first time. I wasn't going to wait again.

"Think for a second, Storm," Chase said as we exited the Refectory and headed toward our rooms. "We don't have a plan—"

"We don't need a plan."

"What, you're going to walk out of the Insurgence Base, show up wherever the Expos are, and just ask to see Jon?"

"Yes," I said immediately.

Chase stared. "It's too dangerous to wing this whole thing." I opened my mouth to argue, but he didn't give me a chance. "We're not stealing a piece of bread, we're breaking into a government building. There are bigger stakes and bigger consequences, so we have to take bigger precautions. Just one day. Please."

"What about Aris? You think he's just going to sit around and let me roam free?"

"I can hold him off for another twenty-four hours," Chase said. "Just keep your head low and your mouth shut, and I promise we'll be out of here by tomorrow night."

I grudgingly agreed, bidding Chase goodnight at the hall where our paths parted. When I started toward the bunk room, it was with an extra spring in my step and a relieved smile on my face.

The second I entered the bunk room, Aris was there, standing in front of me with his arms crossed over his chest.

"What do you look so happy about?" he growled.

My smile fell as I remembered Chase's words. "What are you talking about?"

"Shouldn't you have been locked up in a cell by now?"

"And shouldn't you have stopped being so annoying?" I shrugged. "Yet here we are."

Aris stared at me through slitted eyes. "Why aren't you locked up?" Each word was enunciated slowly and with rage.

I couldn't stop myself. He was too easy to goad. Smirking innocently, I said, "Locked up? What for?"

Aris darted a glance toward our roommates before grabbing my arm and dragging me to a quiet corner of the room. He confronted me there, his eyes burning. "Don't pretend like everything you did this morning didn't happen, Dawson."

I made a show of furrowing my brows and looking around in confusion. "I have no idea what you're talking about, and I'm sure no one else does, either."

Aris's glare could've withered all my family's crops. "Why aren't you in trouble yet?"

I shrugged, basking in his irritation. "I guess Commander White didn't think my actions were punishable."

Aris narrowed his eyes, searched my face, then took a step back in realization. "Chase didn't tell the truth."

My heart dropped. Not two minutes ago, Chase had warned me to keep my head low and my mouth shut, but here I was, doing everything but that. A sick feeling of worry rolled in once more, so fresh and sudden that it nearly knocked me off my feet.

"What are you talking about?" I said, a snappish edge to my voice that I hoped hid the panic coursing through me. But I could already feel everything spiraling out of control. It was all my fault. *Again.*

"Don't play innocent. If Commander White knew what you did today, you would not be standing in front of me right now. The only question is, why did Chase lie?"

For once, I kept my mouth shut and hoped that Aris wouldn't stumble across the truth. But after several seconds of an intense staredown, he said, "It has to do with what he was telling you in the alley earlier, doesn't it?"

"No." The word came out as a strangled croak.

The noise in the room had dropped from lively chatter to muted murmurs as the other boys climbed into their bunks, but I'd abandoned all hope that Aris would follow suit.

"You're planning something," Aris said, "and it has to do with your brother. Am I right?"

How had this all fallen apart so quickly? I opened my mouth to respond, but no words came out. Aris and I stood there, staring at each other. I could see the confusion in his eyes, the doubt that Chase was actually part of a plan that went against the rules of the Insurgence. I saw the hesitation to report me, knowing that it would also hurt Chase.

Aris stared at me for a beat longer, then stalked toward the door. "I'm telling Commander White."

"Aris—"

"No!" he shouted, spinning around. "I'm not listening to your excuses. I don't care what you're doing, and I don't care why. You've been allowed to make enough mistakes today, Dawson, and I'm not going to let you make another one."

The boys turned to watch us, eyes wide and curious. I saw Arden peering at me apprehensively from around the banister of our bunk. I felt as though I couldn't take a breath, my eyes darting from one concerned face to the next.

Aris seized the moment and whirled around, sweeping out of the room, the door banging closed behind him. Everyone in the room froze, their eyes snapping between me and the door. I didn't know how much they knew, but there was no doubt they'd heard Aris's last words. Before anyone could react, I spun and sprinted into the hall, veering left toward Chase's private quarters.

I skidded to a halt and pounded on Chase's door, the wood rattling beneath the force of my fist. The door swung open and with one quick sweep of his gaze, Chase took in my panicked expression.

"Storm, what—"

I pushed past him and entered the room, shoving the door closed behind me. "We have to go."

"What?" Chase shook his head. "No. No, you said you'd give me twenty-four hours—"

"Change of plans. We have to leave. *Now.*" I spotted two packs Chase had been preparing, half-filled with supplies and sitting on his bed. It would have to do. I grabbed one and tossed the other across the room toward Chase. "Come on."

Chase stared at the bag at his feet. "I told you we'd leave tomorrow." He gave me an exhausted look. "What did you do?"

I gritted my teeth, my eyes searching the rest of the room for supplies. The bedroom was the size of the one I shared with my brothers in Ferrol and had a window high above an ornate wardrobe. The flickering lanterns would've added a warm feel if it weren't for the tension coursing through me. "Aris wondered why I hadn't gotten in trouble, and..." I trailed off, and Chase groaned.

"I told you to keep your mouth shut!"

"Turns out I'm bad at following instructions." I spotted some apples and pears laid out on Chase's desk and shoved them into my pack. "Aris left to find Commander White a couple minutes ago."

Chase's eyes widened. He snatched up his pack, throwing it over his shoulder before moving toward the door. "We have to go."

"That's what I just—"

Chase silenced me with a look and flung open the door. The hallway beyond was empty, but I knew it wouldn't be long until Commander White sent someone to find us.

"Here's the plan," Chase muttered as we started down the hall at a brisk clip. "We'll use the smaller halls to reach the commander's office. Hopefully by the time we get there, she'll be out looking for us, so stealing her key will be easy. As soon as we find it we'll head toward the door leading to the stables."

"And then what?"

"I don't know, steal some horses or something," Chase grumbled. "Be grateful I came up with that much. I was expecting to have twenty-four hours, not twenty-four *seconds*."

We made it the rest of the way to Commander White's office without encountering any Insurgents. Chase took a path down several narrow halls I'd never seen before and through doors that revealed hidden corridors he explained had once been servant's passages. We paused when we reached Commander White's door. It was closed, but no voices were coming from inside. Chase warily reached to test the handle. The door swung open easily to reveal an empty room.

We tumbled into the office with sighs of relief.

"Keep watch," Chase said, pointing at the open door as he strode across the room toward her desk.

I pushed the door nearly all the way closed, leaving a crack just large enough for me to see the hall beyond. Behind me, Chase was moving quickly, yanking open desk drawers and rifling through stacks of paper.

"Do you know what you're looking for?" I asked over my shoulder. Chase was bent over, digging through a drawer full of folders with a concentrated expression.

"I was with the commander when she unlocked the door one week," Chase responded. "I know what the key looks like, but I don't know where she keeps it." He looked up and noticed that I had turned my back to the door. "Keep watching!"

I faced the door once more as Chase pulled open yet another drawer. The seconds ticked by, and my tension rose with each passing minute. I was just about to tell Chase to hurry up when he triumphantly proclaimed, "Found it!"

I abandoned my post and rushed to his side as he pulled a key out of the false bottom of a drawer. I took the key from his hands and turned it over in mine as he replaced the wooden bottom and the papers he had disrupted.

The key was made of brass, matching the handle and lock of the door that led to the stables. I quickly pocketed it and started for the door. I was halfway across the room before I realized Chase wasn't following.

"Come on, we have to go."

"Wait," Chase said, and I turned toward him impatiently. "I found some—"

The door to the office banged open. I spun around. Commander White marched into the room, Aris filling the doorway behind her. Chase and I both froze, facing her with a mixture of shock and guilt.

Well, only Chase looked guilty. I had no regrets.

"I thought I told you to keep watch," Chase hissed.

"I was. Earlier."

Commander White pinned us with a withering glare. My chest tightened as I scanned the room, but Aris was blocking the only exit, and I'd be more likely to convince a Security to let me through than him.

"You were right," Commander White said, turning her head just barely in Aris's direction. "They were heading to my office for the key. It was a perfect trap."

Chase stepped forward. "Commander."

"Mr. Kader." Her voice was like ice. "I would never have thought you, of all people, would assist this...this renegade." She gestured dismissively to me. "I almost didn't believe Aris when he told me." Her voice faltered, and for a moment, her tone filled with regret. "I trusted you, Chase."

Chase's eyes were wide with confliction. "Commander, I—"

"*Silence.*"

Chase recoiled like a scolded dog. I felt a flare of anger and shoved myself in front of him. "So Aris is the one who gave you all this information, huh? Well, did he tell you that the Exceptional the Expos dragged away was my *brother?*"

Commander White's eyes widened just a fraction, but that was enough to tell me he'd conveniently left that detail out.

"I don't care about the rules or the consequences," I continued, growing louder and more confident with each word. "If the Insurgence isn't going to work against the Expos, if they aren't going to do *anything else* to help the Exceptionals, then I'm out. I can't watch them take away more and more innocent kids while I sit here waiting for you guys to actually *do* something."

Commander White stared at me. My heart thudded erratically, and I couldn't help but feel a twinge of satisfaction. It felt good to finally speak my opinion of the Insurgence straight to her face. We stood there, facing each other for long enough that I began to wonder what was going to happen next. I realized Commander White was stalling, trying to keep Chase and me here until reinforcements arrived. Things were only going to get worse. If we were going to get out of here, it was now or never.

I heard Chase shifting behind me and hoped he was ready to run. I lifted my chin and stared straight at Commander White. "The Insurgence could've rescued my brother, but they didn't. If you aren't going to act, then I will."

Commander White's eyes widened, and I felt a flicker of pride that my words had shocked her. At the exact moment I realized she was looking at something behind me, the whole world exploded in a cloud of dust.

14

AILA

I was so preoccupied that I didn't notice my invisibility had dropped until it was too late.

Darkness shrouded the silent halls, broken only by the flicker of an occasional torch. The pounding of my heart seemed to echo in the empty corridors. I wished I hadn't overheard that conversation. I wished I didn't know that Brone was trying to overthrow the Earl.

I hurried past the main hall, a broad corridor stretching from the Common Area at the back of the Olum to the main entrance. I cast a glance down toward the looming front doors, now reduced to two hulking black shadows in the darkness of the night. Movement caught my eye, and I stopped short.

A small figure was creeping along the edge of the hall, clinging to the shadows cast by the lights in the wall sconces. A pack was slung over one shoulder, and although I could tell it was a boy—and a fellow Exceptional—the darkness hid his identity.

As I watched, he crept along the edge of the corridor, running his fingers along the stone wall to his right, moving carefully to avoid the ring of light cast by the flame. I would've missed him if I hadn't been studying the corridor to make sure Dion was gone.

The first thought that struck me was that this boy did not know how to sneak around and would've truly benefited from the power of invisibility.

The second was that the boy was clearly trying to sneak out of the Olum.

The third was that this boy wasn't thinking logically. There was no way he would make it past the guards Brone had undoubtedly posted on the other side of the doors. I was caught between the choice to warn him against trying to escape and the choice to return to my room, avoiding the risk of being caught and accused of trying to escape.

I groaned inwardly. Why was it that my life seemed to be a knot of lies and difficult decisions?

The boy darted to the next clump of shadows, once more feeling carefully along the wall. I took a step in his direction, then gritted my teeth and turned away. It was better if only one of us got caught. But as I continued across the hall, the flame in the wall sconce closest to me flickered and died. Alerted by the sudden change in lighting, the boy spun around and froze. That's when I realized, with a wave of horror, that I'd been so distracted my invisibility had slipped.

Now I *had* to do something.

The light from one of the torches fell on the boy's face, and I recognized him instantly. It was Landis, one of the boys that I ate dinner with. I had spoken to him for the first time a few days ago, and he had admitted that he hadn't yet manifested his power. Now, our gazes locked for a brief moment, Landis's eyes green pools of fear.

I moved first, rushing down the hall and grabbing his arm before he could run. He fought against me instantly, and I struggled to keep my grip.

"Stop. Landis, stop!" I hissed, giving him a little jerk. "I'm not—" His foot caught me in the shin, and I sucked in a pained breath, my grip slackening. "Stop! I'm not going to turn you in!"

Landis paused, just long enough for me to regain a tight grip on his forearm and clasp my other hand around his pack. He glanced down at the hand on his arm then back up at me, his gaze a mixture of terror and anger.

"It sure seems like you are," he spat, giving his arm another jerk. But we both knew he wasn't going anywhere until I released him.

"No, I promise!" I glanced around, then leaned closer. "What do you think you're doing?"

136

"What does it look like I'm doing?" Landis said, the fear in his gaze contradicting the courage he was trying to muster in his tone.

"You can't try to escape. You'll get caught."

"No, I won't."

"Do you think Brone is stupid enough to make it possible for people to escape through the *front door*? You know the only reason the halls are empty is because the exits are heavily guarded."

Landis tried to pull away again. "Let go of me," he spat.

"Stop *fighting*!" I gave his arm another jerk. "I'm here to help."

"Well, you're doing a terrible job!"

"This isn't going to work. Just listen to me and *think* for a second how stupid this idea—"

"Aila."

Landis had stopped fighting against me, so I fell still and looked at him. His gaze was sharp with determination. "I've been planning this for months, almost for a year. I know how to get past the guards." He leaned forward, his eyes glittering in the light of the nearest torch. "I know how to escape."

His words were heavy with significance. With a start, I realized he wasn't planning on going through the front doors at all. I sucked in a breath. "You—"

"Hey!"

I whipped around and gasped. Brone had rounded the corner and was striding down the hall toward us. His expression was grim, and I fought the urge to take off in the opposite direction.

"Explain yourselves," he said, his voice eerily calm. "Now."

I froze, my heart pounding in my chest. *So this is what happens when you try to help*, I thought fiercely. *You get caught, and it seems like you're the one trying to escape.*

I took a shaky breath. "I wasn't..."

Brone's gaze jumped from where I was gripping Landis's arm to where I was clasping the strap of his pack. Realization dawned on him the same time it struck me, and I shoved Landis away.

He thought I was trying to stop Landis—not to rescue him, but to turn him in.

Landis realized this, too, and before Brone could say another word, he twisted around and bolted down the hall. What happened next occurred so fast it was no more than a blur. Brone shouted for guards, and five Expos appeared out of nowhere, pouring into the hall. One of them drove a shoulder into Landis's side, pinning him against the wall. The other ripped Landis's pack from his shoulders and tossed it to the ground as a third guard bound his hands with a cord of rope. The final two men stepped forward, each grabbing one of Landis's arms. Before he could even scream, they pulled him from the wall and started dragging him down the corridor.

Landis finally came to his senses. He began to punch and kick, fighting wildly like a trapped animal.

It was no use. The guards yanked him forward, and I got one last glimpse of his angry green eyes before he disappeared around the corner. The remaining Expos melted back into the shadows, returning to their posts. Only Brone and I were left, staring into the darkness.

"It appears I have underestimated you," he said calmly, folding his hands behind his back and gazing off in the direction Landis and the guards had disappeared. "The boy would've been caught either way, but I see you wanted to do your part to ensure he did not escape. That is brave, stopping one of your own, especially when they are a friend. I am impressed."

With that, Brone spun around and stalked off down the hall, his boots echoing off the empty walls.

I don't know how long I stood there, staring after him with a dumbfounded expression, but when I finally turned to go I spotted Landis's pack, discarded in the middle of the hall. My heart wrenched with guilt. Recruitment Week was over, and yet here I was, still betraying the lives of innocents. I reached down and, without thinking, picked up Landis's pack and slung it over my shoulder. With an extra weight in my step, I continued back to my room, leaving the hall dark and silent as if nothing had ever happened.

No one seemed concerned by Landis's absence at breakfast the next morning, and I forced myself to adopt an unworried expression. But inside, I felt empty, still stunned by last night's events. In trying to help Landis, I had only succeeded in getting him captured. Maybe he would've made it if I hadn't stopped him. Maybe if I'd come up with an explanation, instead of going along with what Brone said, I could've rescued both of us. But instead Landis was gone, and Brone thought I was even more trustworthy than before.

Despite my best efforts, I could tell June knew something was wrong as we filed out of the Common Area and started toward training. She and Ross were making their way through the crowd in my direction—and I was making up a cover story in my head—when Jax intercepted me. Ross and June paused to watch, clearly as surprised to see him as me. Jax had stopped escorting me around the Olum when I was moved to the female barracks. I'd assumed he'd been assigned to a new Exceptional.

If Brone had sent him back to watch me, it couldn't mean anything good.

"Jax," I stammered out. "What…what are you doing here?"

Jax's expression gave away nothing. "Brone requests your presence in his office."

I dug my nails into my palm. He must've figured out that I hadn't been trying to turn Landis in.

Unless he wanted to reward me, which was somehow worse.

Then, to my surprise, Jax turned and flitted off down a side hallway, leaving me alone. If Brone hadn't instructed him to guide me, clearly I still held his trust.

Ross and June shot me questioning looks, but I forced a smile and gestured at them to keep walking as I started toward Brone's office. I was halfway there when I decided I had to tell the truth. I would tell Brone the whole story—leaving out the part where I eavesdropped on his conversation, of course—and make it clear that the reason I'd been talking to Landis was to dissuade him from trying to escape. It would be risky, and there was a possibility that I'd end up in a cell right next to

Landis, but it was better than living with the shame of ruining yet another person's life.

I reached Brone's door and knocked.

"Come in." His calm voice contrasted the raging storm within me. I took a deep breath, steeled myself, then opened the door.

Brone was sitting with his hands folded on his desk. He looked up when I entered and smiled.

I did a double take. Except for during his conversation with Merrick and Kala last night, I had never seen any sort of emotion on Brone's stoic face. I hadn't even realized he knew what smiling *was*.

I was thrown, and the words I'd died on my lips.

"It's good to see you, Aila," Brone said, the smile dropping from his face and his expression returning to normal. I felt myself relax. It was unnerving to see this man, this *villain*, smile. "Please, sit down."

It was now or never. I wrapped my hands around the back of the chair in front of me. "Brone, I wanted to say—"

"No words are necessary," Brone interrupted. "All offenses for being out so late are forgiven."

I blinked. "That's not what I—"

"However, it is not the reason I called you to my office today," Brone continued smoothly, as if I had never spoken.

"Brone—"

"Please," he said firmly. "Have a seat."

I clenched my teeth and dropped into the chair. "Listen," I began, but Brone silenced me with a wave of his hand.

"Let me speak first," he said. "Aila, as I said last night, I seem to have underestimated you." I desperately opened my mouth to speak, but I didn't have the chance to get a word in. "Your loyalty was questionable at first, but it is now clear that you have strong devotion to the Exceptional Police."

I gaped at Brone, all the words disappearing from my mind as shock flooded in. He thought I had a *strong devotion* to the Expos? The thought filled me with horror. It couldn't be further from the truth. The only thing keeping me from setting the whole Olum on fire was my concern for what would happen to me if I did.

"Although you may not have noticed, we are a little short on staff here at the Olum," Brone said. "We do have an abundance of young Exceptionals like you, but not all of them have gained my trust." He looked at me, his brows raised like he was expecting a response.

"I…don't understand," I said slowly.

Brone let out a breath. Rearranged some of the papers on his desk. Finally, he met my gaze, his dark gray eyes chilling me to the bone. "I am promoting you, Miss Vinn. To the position of an officer."

Oh. I sucked in a breath. I had no clue what officers were, but I knew with sudden certainty that I didn't want to be one.

Brone continued, oblivious to the desperation coursing through me. "Of course, you will still participate in training, as your sword skills are…less than admirable." I winced. "But you will experience privileges that haven't been available to you before. You will be moved from the female barracks into a more comfortable, private room. The curfew will no longer apply to you, and you have the option to eat in the officer's Common Area if you so desire."

I opened my mouth, then closed it again, unable to form words.

"We need more leadership during Recruitment Week as well," Brone went on. "I will most likely reassign you to a new squad as a second-in-command, similar to Trav's position."

I forced myself to speak. "Brone, I don't…" *I don't think I want this. I don't deserve this. I don't have the amount of loyalty you think I do.* The half-finished sentence died on my lips.

"Aila." Brone fixed me with a piercing stare. "I know it sounds overwhelming, but you will be supported. This promotion is an honor that others would kill to have. You'd be wise to accept it."

I tried to swallow, but my throat had gone dry. Brone finally fell silent, and I knew this was my chance to speak up, to decline the offer, to tell him the truth.

But the words had become stuck in my throat, unwilling to be spoken into existence. When I opened my mouth, what came out was the complete opposite of what I wanted to say. "Thank you for this opportunity. I look forward to my new position."

My Expo voice. I was speaking in my Expo voice again, a voice that didn't belong to me. Brone looked almost proud as he dismissed me from his office, instructing me to pack up my things and wait for someone to escort me to my new quarters.

As I numbly passed through the empty halls, I tried to convince myself that it was for the best, that speaking up would just get me in trouble.

But I was beginning to wonder how long I could keep doing this, how long I could keep working at the Olum before it broke me.

How long I could keep faking my loyalty to an organization toward which I felt nothing but hate.

"Hey, where were you during training this morning?"

I spun around to see June approaching me, Ross on her heels. I had been trying to convey my hatred for swords by glaring at the weapons rack, all the while hoping my friends would miraculously forget about our training lesson.

Of course, they didn't.

"You were missing at lunch, too," Ross said, and I was surprised by his concern. "Did the meeting with Brone go okay? I mean, obviously you're still alive, which is good and all, but it's not like you to miss a meal."

"No, Ross, it's not like *you* to miss a meal, and you just can't comprehend the fact that someone else would do it," June said. She and Ross laughed, but when I didn't join in, their smiles fell.

"How was the meeting?" June tried again, more cautiously than Ross.

"It was fine." I turned away, back toward the swords. I picked up my usual one, which was beginning to feel more comfortable in my hand. At least something in this horrid situation was going right.

"This is Brone we're talking about," Ross said, and I swiped the weapon through the air a few times. "Anything that involves him is *not* 'fine'."

I spun around and attacked the air in front of me with a series of aggressive cuts, then dropped the sword to my side with a frustrated breath. June raised her eyebrows, and Ross let out a low whistle.

"It was that bad, huh?"

June's eyes searched my face, her brows creased. "Are you in trouble?"

Yes, I was in trouble. Everyone here who was following Brone was in trouble, and we had been ever since we had agreed to join the Expos. But I couldn't tell my friends any of that.

"Do you guys know about the rebels?"

The entire air around me seemed to change. Ross and June exchanged glances, and Ross shrugged with a wary smile.

"Yeah, of course, everyone who's allowed to participate in Recruitment Week does." He hesitated, then asked almost nervously, "What about them?"

"Have you ever thought…thought about…joining them?"

It was like I'd expressed my intention to kill someone. June recoiled, almost reflexively, and Ross's expression closed up like shutters covering a window.

"Well," June said carefully, her voice crackling with sudden tension, "the thought has crossed my mind before, yes." Ross jerked his head in mute agreement.

"Just crossed your mind?" I pressed.

"Aila—"

"You can trust me," I insisted. Ross and June exchanged glances again.

"Exceptionals are dangerous," Ross said at last, not quite meeting my gaze. "We're doing the right thing by helping Brone."

"They're dangerous? Are you serious right now?" I snorted in derision. "You think *we're* dangerous?"

"Well, I'd prefer the term handsome, but—"

"Look, I don't care if you aren't going to admit it out loud, but we can all agree that Brone is lying about Exceptionals. But Brone works for the Earl, and do you really think the Earl would lie to the entire country, if he knew the truth?"

"Aila!" June hissed, throwing a panicked glance over her shoulder. "You can't just say that!"

Ross lifted his gaze, looking at me for the first time. "Are you accusing us of being brainwashed?" The humor had drained from his face, and his blue eyes were suddenly flinty.

"That's not what I'm saying," I insisted. "Come on, you can't honestly think—"

"What else do you want us to think?" June interrupted. "That Exceptionals are good? That the government is lying to us? Those thoughts will bring us nothing but trouble." She shook her head, turning away. "I'm not having this conversation."

"The Earl sends an official to the Olum for updates every week," I said suddenly, the words spilling out of my mouth before I could consider the consequences. "He meets with Brone and—and I've listened in on some of their conversations."

June and Ross fell still. My eyes flitted around the room, but there was no one in earshot. The closest teens seemed to currently be having a battle of who could scream the loudest in frustration when they kept missing the archery target.

Ross was the first to break his silence. "You eavesdropped on Brone?"

"I was invisible," I said quickly.

June broke from her trance, stepping away with a furious shake of her head. "No. No, I did not want to hear that."

"I was invisible," I said again, more desperately this time. "He had no idea I was there!"

"You eavesdropped on *Brone?*" Ross looked at June in disbelief. "She eavesdropped. On *Brone.*"

"I didn't try, I just happened to overhear him talking about—"

"What were you thinking?" June asked, spinning angrily back in my direction.

"I was invisible." I felt a flicker of frustration. "I knew what I was getting into."

"No, what were you thinking telling *us* about it?" June laughed desperately. "We've told you, Aila, following Brone is the right thing to do."

"I—"

"Do you see what you just did?" She let out a breath, seeming to deflate, and I saw the fear in her gaze. "You told us something that could get you in trouble. Big trouble."

"You're my friends," I said, suddenly uncertain. "I don't believe you'd turn me in."

"Aila, we can get in trouble for just knowing. We're putting our lives at risk by keeping your secret." A dry laugh seemed to force its way from her throat. "You can't trust anyone at the Olum. Not even us."

I glanced over at Ross, but he was staring at the ground. Now that he wasn't putting on a show with his big persona, he seemed smaller. Younger. Scared.

"Will you really tell?" I asked after a moment. "Are you really going to go to Brone?"

June dropped her gaze. "I have one goal here, Aila, and that goal is to survive and live as normal a life as possible."

That had been my goal, too, until I heard too much to keep believing that would be possible.

"But I won't say anything. I'll keep your secret."

I let out a relieved breath, and looked at Ross.

"I won't turn you in now, Aila, but..." He shook his head ruefully. "If the situation gets risky, I can't...I can't say what I'll do. I have a family in Carsley, and maybe if I become an officer, Brone will let me visit them. Let them know I'm okay. But I can't do any of that if I'm dead."

I nodded, feeling hollow and numb. I'd expected my friends to be there to lean on, to support me. But the fear that seemed to live and breathe in the walls of the Olum had caught even them in a viselike grip.

145

"I'm sorry, Aila," June said quietly, "but we all knew what we were getting into when we decided to join the Expos. There's no going back."

I nodded again. I'd been the same way, and I couldn't blame them. I still felt the pressing weight on my shoulders of the knowledge of Brone's lies and deceptions, and I wanted nothing more than to blurt it all out anyway. But they were risking themselves to protect me, and it was the least I could do to protect them from the difficulties of the truth.

However, even as we slowly fell back into the comfortableness of the sword lessons, I couldn't help but hear June's words still ringing in my ears. *You can't trust anyone at the Olum.*

15

AILA

It took me twenty minutes of wandering through narrow, dimly lit halls before I found the staircase leading down to the dungeons.

The broad steps were wrapped in shadows, leading to a corridor that snaked around the corner and out of sight. Despite the eerie glow of the lanterns and the cold, clammy feeling of the air, I much preferred this place to the officer's Common Area, or worse, my brand new, personal officer's quarters. A few weeks ago, I would've been ecstatic to have a room like the one I had now. It was surprisingly spacious, despite the large bed, the red velvet chair, and the mahogany desk and dresser. It reminded me of my room at home, except for the lack of windows.

But now, every second I spent in that room was a reminder that I was an officer, a position that bound me even more to the lies of the Olum. It made me feel sick, which was what led me to walk through the dark halls of the Olum, wondering if I was breaking any rules by doing so.

I rounded the corner and found myself in another hall, this one just as dark and just as deserted. When I stepped around the final bend, two guards came into view, leaning lazily against opposite sides of the wall. Beyond them stretched a corridor lined on both sides with iron bars. The dungeon. I sucked in a breath of the stale, damp air and forced myself to stride up to the guards confidently.

They straightened as I approached, sharing skeptical glances with each other before stepping to block my path.

"You're not allowed down here, trainee," one of the guards snapped as I drew near. His hand dropped to the sword at his waist.

I fumbled for my officer's badge, a curved metal medallion with an intricately carved X in its center that reminded me of the wooden pendant I'd seen Brone wearing the night before. He had told me to wear it around my neck, but I did not yet have the heart to keep it anywhere but hidden in my pocket.

"I'm not a trainee," I said, lifting the necklace, allowing it to dangle from my fingers. The cool metal seemed to burn my fingers, and I hastily dropped it back into my pocket and out of sight. Lifting my chin, I added, "I'm here to talk to a prisoner."

The guards exchanged glances again.

My confidence faltered. "Is that allowed?"

"It is, for officers," the first guard relented after a moment. He was an older man with a rigid face and a pointed glare to rival Kala's. "You'd better hope you're telling the truth, because Brone will hear about this."

"Brone is the one who gave me this badge. I'm allowed to be down here."

The guards exchanged looks again, then the second one, a young woman, relented and said, "Who is it you want to see?"

"Landis." I paused when I realized I didn't know his last name. I hardly knew him at all. "He was brought here last night."

Realization swept over the woman's face. "You're the girl who turned him in when he was trying to escape," she said, nodding. "I have to say, it takes guts to report a friend."

I opened my mouth to correct her, to say that Landis and I weren't really friends and I *hadn't* turned him in, but she was already turning to lead me down the hall.

The cells ranged in size and cleanliness, but as far as I could tell, most were empty. I didn't look too hard. After seeing two Exceptionals folded up on their beds in the far corner of their cells, I turned my face resolutely forward, focusing on the wall at the corridor's end.

Landis's cell was over halfway down the hall, far enough that when the guard returned to her post after informing me I had five minutes, I knew we could talk without worrying about being overheard. I waited until she was out of earshot before turning to Landis. I sucked in a breath.

He looked terrible. He had only been here for a day, but already looked so worn and beaten that it'd be easy to assume he'd spent most of his life here. His eye was black and blue and nearly swollen shut, and he had an ugly bruise on his shin. He looked exhausted and terrified at the same time, but when he registered who I was he scrambled off his pitiful bed and stumbled to grab the bars.

"Please tell me you're here to break me out of this place," he begged, wrapping his filthy fingers around the iron bars.

I shook my head. "I…"

Landis's face was etched with hurt. "You promised that you wouldn't turn me in," he said desperately. "You said you were just helping. You *promised!*" His voice hardened suddenly, as if he was beginning to doubt the truth to my words.

"I know, and I wasn't lying!" I said quickly when he released the bars and took a step back. "It was an accident! Brone…he just *assumed* I was trying to stop you and turn you in. I didn't say anything, remember?"

"Oh, I remember," Landis said coldly, his fear momentarily shadowed by his anger. "He trusted you, but you didn't say *anything.* Nothing against me, sure, but nothing in my defense either."

My shoulders sagged. "Landis, I'm sorry. Brone called me to his office today and I tried—"

"How'd you even get down here?" Landis interrupted, glancing down the hall, toward where the guards had gone back to reclining against the walls.

My fingers involuntarily clenched around the officer's badge in my pocket. The movement drew Landis's attention, and he glared at my concealed hand until I drew the medallion out of my pocket, unfurling my fingers to reveal the badge.

Landis's eyes widened. "He made you an officer." His voice shook with disbelief and fury.

I shoved the badge back into my pocket like it had stung my hand. "No—"

"He *rewarded* you, for doing *nothing!*"

"Look—"

"Did you even *try* to set him straight? Did it even cross your mind to come clean? Or does it not bother you at all to bask in praise that comes at the expense of another?"

"I tried, I promise!" I said. Now it was my turn to grip the bars, leaning in, begging for him to understand.

But Landis pulled away. "Your word means nothing to me."

"Brone *made* me take the position! If I had told him the truth, I-I…"

"Would be right here in the cell next to me." Landis snorted and looked away. "That's what you deserve."

"I didn't do anything wrong!"

"Not to Brone," Landis agreed, "but betrayal is the worst kind of crime."

I thought of Chase and inhaled shakily. I felt bare, as though Landis could see straight into my soul. "I tried to help you," I whispered.

Huffing, he turned away and stalked to the back of his cell, placing his hands on either side of the little sink in the corner and leaning into it. He looked even more exhausted than when I first saw him.

"Landis. Please." My tone broke with regret. "I'm not here to argue or to gloat or anything like that. I came here because…because I…"

"Spit it out," Landis snapped from the sink.

I huffed a breath. "I feel guilty, alright?" Landis's head snapped up. He didn't turn, but he didn't yell at me either. "I couldn't sit in my nice room with my officer's badge and know you were down here. Because of me."

Landis stood very still, but I saw his grip on the sink loosen, very slightly.

"I am guilty," I said again, "and I…I don't know what to do."

I had never known what to do with the guilt. Not after I had betrayed Chase, not after I had joined the Expos, not now. Landis was silent for so long, I considered walking away instead of wasting more of my time, but then, so softly I almost didn't hear him, he murmured, "I didn't, either."

"What?"

"The guilt," he said, his back still turned. "The guilt that came with knowing after each successful mission, another Exceptional's life had been ripped away, and I had helped. Knowing that I was one of those Expos every child feared, but also knowing I wouldn't stop because the consequences were too great if I did. You know what it's like, don't you?"

I stared at Landis. He was putting the mess and chaos swirling inside of me into words so perfectly. Slowly, I nodded.

"The guilt ruins you," he whispered, dropping his head. "It's like a monster that claws at your insides, shredding you up until there's nothing left, threatening to consume you whole. And the worst part is, you don't know how to defeat the monster. Even if you did know, you aren't strong enough to risk being destroyed to get rid of it."

I felt something warm built in my chest. The warmth of connection, of understanding.

"What changed?" I asked after a moment. "What gave you the strength to try and defeat the monster?"

Landis stared down at the sink and didn't respond. His face was still turned, his expression hidden.

"I'm on your side," I said quietly.

Landis didn't quite seem to agree. "I realized that the Expos weren't the same people I first thought they were," he said guardedly.

I startled at his words and opened my mouth, eager words ready to pour out of my lips. *You know about Brone's deception, too? You know about the lies?* But something made me hesitate. I couldn't be sure he wouldn't use the information against me. *You can't trust anyone at the Olum,* June had said.

But just as quickly as the thought sprung into my mind, I felt a spark of shame and shoved it away. Landis couldn't do anything—he was locked in a cell, desperate for help. *He* was the one who shouldn't be trusting *me*, not the other way around.

So I said, "You figured out that Brone has been lying to the Earl in order to build an army."

Landis spun around, his good eye growing wide with alarm. "How do you know that?" he demanded, lurching toward the bars separating us. "Did Brone tell you? Aila, you said you were—"

"Brone didn't tell me. I figured it out for myself."

Landis's wide eyes searched my face. "So you know about his plan too?"

I nodded.

"*That's* why I decided to leave," he said fiercely. "I always knew there was something off about what was going on here. When I uncovered the truth, I knew I couldn't stay. If Brone's plan crashed and burned, I didn't want to burn with it. But to get out of the Olum, I had to do it without anyone noticing."

"That's impossible."

"No, it isn't." Landis stepped closer to me. "I know a way. I know how to escape from the Olum."

That's impossible, I almost said again. But the way Landis stood there, a half smile on his face, his eyes glowing with the weight of a secret…I felt a flicker of hope. "How?" I breathed. He paused again, and I felt a surge in irritation. "If it's a plan that will work, I can break you out of here, and we can—"

"No," he interrupted, turning away from me once more. He tore his fingers through his hair, then dropped his hands to his side in defeat. "It won't work."

"You just said—"

"I know how to escape the Olum just fine, but escaping from a cell is a whole different problem."

I glanced down the hall and noticed that the female guard had turned from her post and was walking toward me. Five minutes were up. "We can figure out a way."

"No, we can't." Landis spun around, furious and desperate. "I don't have enough time."

"I'm an officer now," I hissed, aware of the approaching guard. "I can—"

"Aila, please." Landis's voice broke, and he hung his head. "Please don't give me false hope."

152

I fell into a despairing silence. The guard was nearly a quarter way down the hall. Finally, I murmured, "Tell me."

"What?"

"If you believe there truly is a way out of here, at least one of us can escape."

It was a horrible thing to ask a boy who was facing death, but I couldn't let this chance pass me by. Landis glanced down the corridor, conscious of the approaching guard. When he looked back at me, his expression was still hesitant.

"I want to find the rebels." The words tumbled out of my mouth in a rush. "I want to tell them the secrets of the Olum, help them attack the Expos. I-I want to destroy the monster as much as you do."

Landis stared at me for a long moment, his expression wavering between distrust and hope. Finally, he muttered, "The air ducts."

I blinked. "The what?"

"You know, the vents that allow fresh air from the outside into the Olum." Landis rolled his eyes and began to turn away. "Forget it. I'm not telling my escape plan to an idiot."

"No, I know what air ducts are!" I said impatiently. "But those lead up to the roof. I can't escape from the roof. I can't *fly*." The guard was nearly upon us. I didn't have time for this.

"The ones on the ground floor lead to the roof," Landis agreed, "but the ones from the second floor lead down and come out on the side of the building."

"The...second floor?" I remembered how surprised I'd been when I first stepped out of the Olum and realized there was a second story. I'd still never seen a staircase leading upward.

Landis eyed the guard and leaned even closer, his voice a hushed whisper, the words flying from his mouth so fast I almost didn't register them. "There is a secret door in the wall of the corridor leading to the exit. It's hidden beyond the light's reach of the third torch on the right. Press the stones—you'll have to find which one, it's hard to tell—and it'll open to a passage leading upstairs. Find the nearest air duct, and crawl through it until the vent drops off. I hid a rope in the secret passage that you can use to lower yourself down. Once you reach the bottom of the vent, you're free."

"Your time is up."

The guard's voice startled me. I stumbled away from Landis, my mind swirling with questions. But the information he had given me was enough. Landis knew how to escape the Olum, and now, so did I.

"Destroy the monster," Landis said, anger dripping from his words for the benefit of the guard.

She banged her sword against the iron bars of the cell. "Shut your mouth, boy."

As she led me away, I glanced back at Landis, hoping my eyes conveyed my gratitude and sympathy. Landis lifted his hand, but whether it was a gesture of longing or farwell, I could not tell.

16

STORM

I threw myself flat on the ground, flinging an arm over my face. It was no use. Thick dust exploded everywhere, filling the room, coating every surface. I tried to breathe, but only succeeded in inhaling mouthfuls of dust. My brain screamed in confusion, but I didn't dare open my eyes to assess the situation.

Then I felt a hand snatch me by the shirt, and someone began to drag me across the room. *No.* I lashed out with my foot and heard a pained grunt as I made contact with someone's leg, but then I heard Chase hiss, "It's me."

I finally opened my eyes to see he had dragged me out into the hall. I scrambled to my feet, gulping in breaths of fresh air and wiping at the dirt that coated my sweat-slicked skin. I blinked the remaining dust out of my eyes and tripped down the hall after Chase.

"What was that?" I gasped between coughs.

"Dust bomb." He plowed down the hall without sparing a backwards glance. "We weren't going to make it out of there without a distraction."

"I—thanks," I said, still stunned. Chase was right: If he hadn't thought fast and thrown the dust bomb, we never would've made it out of that room, let alone the Insurgence Base.

I recollected my wits by the time Chase and I reached the exit. We had a close call with a patrol guard, and I'd been tempted to turn and sprint in the other direction, but he only gave our dust-caked clothes an odd look as we passed.

155

Clearly, word of our insubordination had not yet spread.

We skidded to a halt in front of the door. The stables were just on the other side; I could practically hear the horses snorting and stomping, just waiting to be used. I dug the key from my pocket and tossed it to Chase. He thrust it into the keyhole and wrenched it to the side.

The key didn't budge.

Chase looked at me, eyes wide, then tried again, once more with no avail. Shouts came from down the hall. He began to frantically rattle the doorknob.

I pushed Chase out of the way and grabbed the key, jamming it back into the lock. However, instead of turning it left or right, I jerked it upward and then to the side. The lock gave a satisfying click.

"Trick locks," I said breathlessly. "Some of the merchants in Carsley use them to lock their buildings because they're harder to pick."

I felt a swell of pride at the impressed look on Chase's face as he said, "Let's go."

We burst into the stables, and I kicked the door closed behind us.

"Lock it," Chase commanded. "If they don't have another key on them, it'll buy us some extra time. I'll get the horses."

I shoved the door closed the rest of the way, locked it, then pocketed the key. I didn't see myself returning anytime soon—or ever—but after we rescued Jon, Chase would probably want a way back into the building. He had more of a life here than I ever would.

As I turned toward Chase, who was leading two horses from one of the stalls, I saw a flash of movement from outside the stables. I could've kicked myself. Of *course* there was someone guarding the entrance to the Base. He probably had no idea what we were doing, but he would know enough to realize we weren't supposed to be out here.

Before Chase even noticed what was going on, I darted out into the sunlight. The guard's eyes widened in surprise—he hadn't noticed me in the shadows at the back of the stables. He barely had time to react before I swung at him, my fist cracking into his temple. He crumpled, and as I lowered him to the ground, I recognized him as the man who'd tried to stop me from escaping Commander White's office.

"How does it feel?" I sneered, but of course he didn't respond as I propped him up against one of the posts.

Chase took one glance at the guard then handed me the reins of a horse. We simultaneously swung ourselves into the saddles. For a moment, our gazes connected as we realized what we had just succeeded in doing. Then, Chase kicked his horse into motion, and I spurred mine to follow. Wind roared in my ears and fresh air filled my lungs. I crowed in triumph as our horses galloped off, leaving the Insurgence Base behind.

We stopped for the night in a secluded spot along the Hastcola River. It was the same river that ran across Rosan and fed the irrigation canals for Ferrol. Chase attempted to start a fire with the small kindling he'd gathered, leaving me to collect more sticks from the nearby forest.

As I gathered pieces of wood into my arms, I realized I'd never been as free as I was in this moment. Whether it was the prospect of having to provide for Jon or the locked doors of the Insurgence Base, there'd always been something tying me down.

Several summers ago, during our rare breaks from the fields and school, Jon and I would travel down to the Hastcola to swim. We would meet my friend Dustin and spend the entire day playing in the water, imagining what it would be like to build a raft and float down the river, dreaming of all the places we could go. I smiled at the memory. I could do that now. There was nothing left holding me back. No one would notice my absence but Chase.

My smile fell as I remembered the events that happened at the end of that summer. Dustin's father had been suffering lasting effects of the plague, and eventually the combination of overworking himself in the fields and the lack of food overcame him. He died, and not more than a week later, Dustin's family left, disappearing like we'd dreamed of doing on our raft.

That's when I started stealing, terrified that Jon would meet the same fate and determined to keep him from the clutches of death. Even now, I realized I didn't have complete freedom. Jon still needed to be rescued, and no one was going to do that but me.

When I returned back to our camp, Chase was carefully feeding a flickering flame with small pieces of bark.

"So why are you really helping me?" I asked, dropping a pile of sticks next to the fire. I'd asked him the question before, but I felt like there was more to the answer.

Chase glanced up at me. "Well, why are you going after Jon?"

"He's my brother. I'll do anything for him."

"And you're my friend," he said with a shrug, adding a few crooked branches to the growing fire. "Besides, it's the right thing to do."

"No, really." I crossed my arms. "You said it yourself: This is dangerous. Why would you risk your life, your reputation, just so I can get my brother back?"

"Because you'll die if you try alone," Chase said. "Like I said, you're my friend. I don't want that to happen to you."

I knew it wasn't the truth, but Chase never pressed me for my secrets, so I decided to let him have his. I dropped to a crouch before the fire, grabbing one of the sticks. The silence stretched as I jabbed it into the hot coals.

"I understand how you feel."

"What?" I jerked my head up, my gaze meeting Chase's across the fire.

He quickly dropped his eyes to his lap. "I've rescued countless Exceptionals over the years," he said quietly, "but the ones that stick out to me are the ones that remind me of my childhood, of what it was like to be free and make choices."

I wondered if that's why he befriended me, wondered if the fact that I dared to defy Commander White reminded him of what it felt like to stand up for something. I nudged at a burning log with my stick, waiting for him to continue.

"I was twelve when I went on my first mission. I pestered Commander White until she let me go to a small town that wasn't

158

supposed to have much uproar. That day we rescued a little girl who had turned eight only a month before. When we were back at the base, I met her formally and…and I was startled, because it was like I was talking to my best friend again."

The one who betrayed you? I thought coldly, but I shut my mouth on the words.

"Her name was Erin." I heard a hitch in Chase's breathing, and I stirred around the burning coals as he continued. "She became my best friend. She was like a little sister to me." His voice was quiet, no more than a whisper, but he had caught my attention. "That year, I devoted myself and everything in me into helping the Insurgence. I realized if there was a chance at making the world a place where Erin could live a happy life, then it was worth putting all my time into fighting for. All I wanted was a safe world where Erin could grow up like a normal girl." Chase took a deep, trembling breath. "That was before the second wave hit."

My fingers tightened around the stick. I remembered the second wave of the plague much clearer than the first, probably because the same fear for Jon that had seized me then was still haunting me today. I jabbed at a log that was propped up against two others. The log slipped, crashing into the fire with a shower of sparks. Embers danced into the air, momentarily illuminating Chase's face, and I saw his eyes were glistening. I quickly pulled my stick from the fire, clenching it in my hands.

"The Insurgence doesn't have limited money and supplies," he said, his voice strained. "We tried everything we could, but the herbal remedies were just too expensive, and too many people were sick—" Chase sucked in a shaky breath and fell silent.

I didn't need him to continue. The fact that I'd never met—or even heard of—Erin told me enough. I felt sick, remembering with a pang of shame how I had accused people from the Stone Cities of not feeling the effects of the plague. Chase had just calmly corrected me. He hadn't even hinted that he'd lost someone as close as a sister.

I didn't realize I had been bending the stick in my hands until it snapped, the crack slicing through the silence that had settled over us.

"So I understand how you feel, because even now, years later, I would do anything to get her back." Chase lifted his head, his wistful hazel eyes meeting mine across the fire. "That's why I'm helping you. I know what it's like to feel helpless, and if this was Erin, I'd want someone to help me."

"Thank you," I whispered. The words failed to express the grief and gratitude churning inside of me. So I just leaned back, lying on the soft grass and staring up at the sparks spiraling into the moonlight.

Chase did the same, and after a moment I murmured, "So what are you planning to do after we rescue Jon? Go back to the Insurgence?"

Chase's eyes were fixed upon the stars. "I don't think things will ever be the same if I go back. Commander White needs people she can fully trust, and I'm not one of those people anymore."

I clenched my jaw. It was unfair that Chase would lose the position he'd worked so hard to gain, just because he wanted to help out a friend. The Insurgents were supposed to be the good guys, but even they had glaring flaws.

"Maybe I'll start my own group, one that more directly hurts the Expos," Chase said.

"And if you could go anywhere? Do anything?" *If we weren't Exceptionals?* I left that part unsaid. Maybe someday it'd become a possibility to be free again.

"I would find Aila," Chase said without hesitation. "I would forgive her for turning me in, I would go back to Bedrock and live with my parents, and I would start a school."

"A school."

Chase looked over at me, mock annoyance on his face. "Yeah, for Exceptionals to go and feel like they belong. And if that didn't work out, I'd just be a regular teacher."

"In Bedrock?"

Chase smirked. "Wherever I can make the biggest difference in the lives of troubled teens like you."

"Troubled teens?" I protested, pushing myself up with my elbows. "Well, then I'd start a school in the Stone Cities trying to get the snob out of kids like you."

160

"What did I ever do to you?"

"Okay, fine. Kids like Aris."

"Storm, you are telling yourself one big lie if you think you'd have the patience to deal with a classroom full of kids."

I laughed, pushing myself into a sitting position and reaching toward my pack for a blanket as Chase moved to extinguish the fire. He paused, glancing over his shoulder at me.

"This is going to be difficult, Storm, and we're going to have to trust each other. But I want you to know that whatever happens, I trust you."

He splashed water over the flames and the camp went dark, leaving me to drift off to sleep feeling as though a weight had been lifted from my shoulders.

The complete exhilaration that had filled me the day before had since crashed and burned, leaving behind ashes of resentment as Chase and I rode into the town of Tagna the following evening. Chase's eyes were dull, exhaustion written across his face.

I wasn't nearly as tired, having spent the day sitting on a stone bench in the stupidly perfect town of Norite.

When Chase and I had packed up camp this morning at the Hastcola River, I'd asked him about his plan. When he reluctantly told me we were heading in the direction of one of the Stone Cities, I had pulled my horse to an abrupt stop.

"We're not going to the Stone Cities," I snapped, my voice leaving no room for argument.

Chase argued anyway. "They'll search for us in the other towns. Norite is far enough away that they won't think that's where we're headed."

"I don't know where the Expos operate, but I am positive it's not from Norite."

"What do you care about more, holding onto some ridiculous grudge or rescuing Jon?" Chase had demanded. "A ton of government workers live in Norite. If anyone has information, it's them. I promise, we'll only be there for a day."

I had hated everything about the town, from the clean streets to the large houses to the smiles on the faces of passing families. Everything was so easy for them. Too easy. They had more than enough to spare for the suffering citizens of Ferrol.

Chase had gone off on his own to collect information, and as soon as he returned, I had demanded an update. "Let's just keep moving," he'd said. "I'll let you know when we stop for a break."

As we rode into the quaint riverside town of Tagna, I found my patience wearing thin. We had traveled through the night, and now the edges of the horizon were beginning to glow with the promise of dawn. The town was quiet, the windows of the two-story wood buildings tightly shuttered. Chase and I wore riding gloves to cover our Exceptional marks even though the streets were empty.

Although our wandering seemed aimless, I had a hunch Chase was looking for something as we rode through the small town. Maybe he was seeking a place to eat. We hadn't had time to pack much food, and the little we did was running low. Soon, he spotted a stable that still appeared to be open and directed his horse toward it. I wasn't exactly sure why we were stopping here, but Chase seemed confident as he dismounted his horse, so I followed suit.

As we knotted the reins of our horse to a post, Chase said, "Where's the money?"

"What money?"

"If you think I'll believe for one second that you actually had the self-control to sit calmly on that bench all day, then we should probably just give up this entire plan because you have no brain cells left," Chase said flatly.

I was actually pretty proud of the coins I had scraped up while only pickpocketing a small amount from each person. "It's in my pack. Why?"

Chase ignored my question, and as he dug through my pack a stablehand holding a broom stepped out of one of the empty stalls and gave us a suspicious look.

"You're up early for a bunch of kids," he said belittlingly, side-eyeing us as he leaned the broom on one of the wooden posts.

"Oh come on, you're literally as old as we are," I snapped.

Chase silenced me with a look. "We were traveling during the night. Do you have two empty stalls that we can use for the next few hours? We're going to sleep at the inn across the street."

I threw a panicked glance across the street, and noticed there indeed was a small inn with candlelight still glowing in the front windows. I rounded on Chase. "No, we've got to keep mov—"

"We can pay," Chase added when the stablehand frowned.

"Chase—"

"We have two open stalls," the stablehand responded, then named the price.

"It's okay," I told him, trying to step in front of Chase. "We actually don't need them. We're leaving."

"Sounds good," Chase told the stablehand. He counted through the coins in his palm.

My eyes widened. "Don't you dare—"

Chase dropped the coins into the boy's hand, and they both nodded, as if a deal had been made.

And I suppose it had, so quickly that I hadn't been able to stop it.

"The money is good for the next six hours if you're staying at the inn. I'll take your horses. You two can grab your packs and head directly over there."

Chase nodded and snatched up his pack, but I blocked his path before he could start toward the inn.

"What are you doing?" I hissed.

"What does it look like?" he asked, sidestepping me and continuing across the street. "I'm heading directly over there."

For several seconds, I stared at him disbelievingly, then understanding dawned on me.

"We're throwing them off," I said, grinning at Chase's brilliance. "When the Insurgence shows up looking for two boys and two horses, they'll find our horses and think we're sleeping at the inn. But we won't be. We'll have bought two horses from another man and be halfway across Rosan."

"No, we'll be in the inn, sleeping."

My smile fell. "You're joking."

"Storm, I'm tired. We just rode through the night, and however much you're trying to deny it, we'll fall asleep on our horses if we keep going."

"I'm fine."

"Sure." Chase pulled open the door to the inn, stepping inside. I followed him with furious strides.

"We're not doing this! We have to rescue Jon!" My voice was angry but hushed. The warm, wooden lobby we entered was empty, but I could see shadows as a person in the room behind the desk periodically blocked the light of the lamp.

Chase rounded on me, pausing halfway to the front counter. "Do you have a better plan?"

"My plan was to follow your plan."

"Exactly." Chase turned away, as if the conversation was over.

"This is not a plan! This...this is a waste of time!"

"It's just a *nap*, Storm, not the end of the world."

"It might not be for you, but my brother has been captured by *the Expos*. As far as I know, he could be—"

I stopped short. The innkeeper must've heard our voices because he whirled out from behind the wall and bustled to the counter, apologizing profusely for not noticing us earlier.

Chase assured him it was no trouble. "We'll take a room for two, the cheapest one you have."

The innkeeper nodded, accepting the coins from Chase. He disappeared once more into the back to collect our blankets.

Chase leaned against the counter and dropped his head, but I grabbed his arm and jerked him to face me.

"Why are we stopping?" I demanded, my voice low. "Did you find something important in Norite?"

Chase immediately stilled. His expression was blank, but his eyes darted briefly to the side, and that was indication enough.

"You found something out in Norite," I said slowly, dangerously, "*right?*"

"Storm, I tried—"

He must've seen something dark in my gaze because he fell silent. I stared at him, stunned and betrayed, then spun around without a word and stalked out of the inn, letting the door slam close behind me.

Chase found me sometime later on the roof. It had been surprisingly easy to find my way up there. I'd discovered a staircase in the back of the inn that led up to a wooden balcony facing a river. A ladder had been resting against the wall, and after climbing it I was able to reach the edge of the roof and hoist my way up. The building was a story taller than most of the surrounding structures and had been built on a small hill, giving a beautiful view of the water below. The river was much larger than the Hastcola, and multiple sturdy, wooden bridges stretched across. The water swirled with colors of red and purple as it reflected the vibrant sunrise.

I didn't speak until Chase dropped down next to me. He had changed out of his earlier clothes, which were still dusty from our escape, and now wore a jacket that protected him against the bitter dawn cold. It was a stark contrast to the heat in Ferrol, but I hardly even noticed.

"I'm sorry for getting upset at you," I muttered into the silence. "It's not your fault that people in the Stone Cities are rude and never talk to anyone."

"It's okay," Chase said, lifting his gaze to look at the sky. "I know it's hard, knowing your brother is in danger."

I nodded, dropping my gaze to the street below. I could see the stablehand standing in one of the stalls, brushing down Chase's horse.

"Storm," Chase said carefully after a moment. "Why do you hate the Stone Cities so much?"

I pressed my palms flat onto the roof next to me, nearly cutting my hands on the sharp shingles. "No one good ever comes from there."

"I came from there, and you don't hate me."

"I chalk it up to the fact that you spent a large portion of your life with the Insurgence," I said, still not quite meeting his gaze. I took a breath. "We should brainstorm where to head tomorrow."

I could feel Chase's gaze on my back as I stood, sliding to the edge of the roof and descending the ladder. He wasn't satisfied with my answer, but everyone had secrets, and I wasn't going to let him blame me for wanting to keep mine.

Instead of continuing down the stairs, I stepped up to the balcony railing, digging my fingernails into the soft wood. The sky was brighter now, the slashes of red and purple slowly softening into swaths orange and pink. I heard Chase start down the ladder and felt a wave of guilt. *We're going to have to trust each other,* he'd said last night. And he had, sharing with me the darkest moments of his life.

I spun around abruptly. "I'm adopted."

Chase dropped onto the balcony and stood there, watching me as if he was trying to predict what rash thing I would do next. Slowly, he nodded. "I assumed so," he said. "You looked nothing like Jon—or anyone in Ferrol, for that matter."

I dropped my gaze to the worn floor of the balcony, years of footsteps having worn the rough wood smooth. "I was four, when they adopted me." I paused and swallowed. This was harder than I thought; I hadn't spoken to anyone but Jon about my adoption, and even that had been difficult. "My mother was the one who brought me to the Dawson's house. I...I don't really remember it."

That wasn't entirely true. I could still clearly picture her receding back as she hurried off down the road, not turning around even as I screamed at her to come back. I could still feel Tritan's iron grip on my forearm as he wrenched me inside the house, closing the wooden door on my old life. I could hear the older boys' curious questions, intermingled with Jon's hungry cries. Each question had seemed innocent on the outside, but even at four years old I could detect the unwelcoming undertone that laced each word. Those undertones had never quite gone away.

For a while, I had thought the only other memory I had of my mother was of her eyes, twin sapphires glittering with love as she gazed down at me. Then I realized that these eyes could not have belonged to the woman that gave me up when I was almost too young to remember.

I spun desperately back toward the river, my eyes searching the waters. "She was from the Stone Cities." The words were hard to say. I had not admitted this to anyone, not even to Jon. Not even to myself. My parents knew, of course, but they never mentioned it, and that made it easy to pretend it wasn't true.

I turned toward Chase, meeting his wide hazel eyes. My anger sparked suddenly as I thought of my mother walking away from the Dawson household, probably relieved to get rid of me.

"My mother was from the Stone Cities and had all the money in the world. She didn't even need to work. It would've been easy for her to provide for me. She could've gone as far as walking me to school each day if she really wanted to. She could've raised me to be another one of those spoiled brats who would never know what it's like to need something. She could've even paid to ship me off to a boarding school when she got tired of me." My voice trembled, my vision growing hazy on the edges.

"But she didn't. Instead she dropped me at the doorstep of a family who could barely even keep a roof over their heads. She left me in a place where she knew I had no future. The Dawson's didn't even want me—she probably bribed them with money." I had never given voice to that thought before, but now that I had, my anger only increased. "*That's* why I hate the Stone Cities," I spat. "They're rightfully named. Everyone there has a heart of stone and never cared for anyone but themselves."

My chest heaved and I clamped my mouth closed, as stunned at my sudden outburst as Chase seemed to be. I felt a flicker of embarrassment mix with my anger and turned back around, gripping the railing.

I let out a long, furious breath. "So. Now you know."

I felt Chase move to stand up next to me, but I didn't dare turn my head, fearing that he would see the brokenness in my gaze.

When he finally spoke, his voice was soft. "I'm not saying what your mother did was right, but not everyone from the Stone Cities is the same."

I let out a bark of laughter. "She betrayed me, just like your friend betrayed you, just like Aris betrayed us yesterday. I think that's all the evidence we need."

Chase shot me a look of regret and opened his mouth, but I cut him off. "Can we please just talk about where to look for Jon?"

He must've heard something break in my voice because he nodded, his eyes dropping to the street below. "I'm sorry, Storm. I tried, I really did, but I have no idea where the Expos operate from."

I took a deep breath and nodded, the wheels in my head beginning to turn. It felt good to do this, to focus on making plans and outsmarting the enemy instead of getting caught up in my emotions. I spun and began to pace across the balcony. "We need to think about this," I said, reaching the top of the stairs and spinning around to start in the other direction. "Where is the logical place to center the operation? The Capital?"

"No," Chase said after a moment. "No, the Expos' work is not exactly honorable. The Earl would want to disassociate himself from it as much as possible."

I nodded. "So somewhere far away then. Like a rural town."

"There are a lot of Expos," Chase said. "Unless they go home each night, the place is going to have to be big enough to accommodate them, and the captured Exceptionals, too."

"But how come no one's seen it before?" I said, my boots digging into the wood as I paced past him. "No one ever talks about the building where the Exceptionals are taken. Is it hidden in another dead duke's estate?"

"There's only one dead duke."

I stopped at the edge of the balcony, resting my arms on the railing and dropping my head, feeling that churning sea of hopelessness rise again. But then my head snapped up, my gaze connecting with Chase's as realization sparked.

"The Barrens," I whispered.

"What?"

"The Barrens," I repeated excitedly, rushing toward him. "No one has any reason to go there. It'd be the perfect place to hide a giant building, and it's far away from the earl."

Chase grinned, his eyes brightening with amazement. "Storm, that's brilliant!"

I grinned back, my pulse racing. "I know, I'm a genius."

He elbowed me in the ribs. "Now, let's not get cocky."

"What's the closest town to the Barrens?" I said, pushing him away and spinning toward the stairs before turning back to Chase. The balcony was too small to contain my excitement.

"Did you ever pay attention in geography class?" I shot Chase an impatient, giddy look, and he said, "It's Laster."

I exhaled slowly, my face still split with a smile as I started toward the stairs.

"Wait, Storm." I stopped at the sound of Chase's voice, turning impatiently toward him. "Let's wait for a few hours. We'll leave as soon as we wake up, okay? I promise. But we need rest first."

I clenched my jaw and nodded, but I couldn't help but feel a flicker of worry. This was the second night since Jon's capture.

And I knew we were running out of time.

17

AILA

I never thought I would be claustrophobic. I knelt before the entrance to the air vent and peered into the darkness, wondering if now was the right time to find out.

I shook the thoughts from my head. It was too late to go back now. After a day and a half of being plagued with indecision, eating meals alone in the Officer Common Area, and avoiding Ross and June, I finally gave in. I retrieved Landis's pack from the night of his capture and added a few items to what was already there. As soon as night began to fall, I snuck out of my room and into the dark halls of the Olum. I needed to defeat the monster, and this was the only way I knew how.

I would use Landis's route to escape. I would go to the nearest town and collect food and supplies. And then I would find the rebels.

To my surprise, the hardest challenge had been finding the hidden latch to activate the opening of the secret staircase. Once inside, I collected the coil of rope Landis had hidden in the shadows of the stairwell and ascended the stairs to the floor above without incident.

Now, I stood in a hall that was nearly an exact replica of the one below me, consulting the open air vent. The dark shaft stretched out of sight and hardly looked large enough for me to fit through.

But really, I didn't have a choice or time to hesitate. With some difficulty, I clambered into the tiny opening and pulled the metal grate closed behind me.

The further I crawled into the dark, narrow space, the greater my urge to turn around grew. The darkness was suffocating, and the stone walls pressed in around me. I placed each hand in front of the other with care, worried that the floor would drop off suddenly.

It did, but I managed to catch myself before I went tumbling over the edge. I located a hook attached to the stone above me and firmly knotted one end of the rope around it. Landis must've drilled it there in preparation for his escape. An escape that would never happen. Gritting my teeth, I tossed the free end of the rope into the black abyss below me. I wrapped my hands around the coarse rope, braced my feet against the stone walls on either side of me, and began to descend.

As I slid down the rope, the air grew less stuffy, and I felt the occasional breeze of fresh air brush against my face. The rope slipped suddenly in my hands, and my boots scraped desperately against the rough stone as I fought to slow my descent. Finally, my feet hit the ground, and I saw a glimmer of light coming through another metal grate. I clenched my jaw and kicked at it furiously, again and again, until it finally came loose and fell onto the grass.

Fresh air flowed into the stuffy space more freely than before, crisp and invigorating. My heart began to pound. I abandoned the rope and crawled forward, peering out of the small opening.

The sun had just dipped below the horizon, and the first stars were beginning to glitter in the night sky. But there was still enough lingering light to illuminate my surroundings. A field stretched before me as far as I could see, absolutely empty and leading directly to Laster.

There was no sign of any Olum guards. The coast was clear. I slipped through the opening and wedged the grate back into place. Then, finally, I turned around.

A crazed laugh bubbled in my throat. I curled my fingers around the straps of my backpack and took off, my feet flying over the hard ground, never looking back. I had just escaped the Olum.

I was free.

The lights of Laster beckoned me as the last glow of the sun leaked from the sky, but they still seemed little more than dots in the distance. I had long since slowed to a jog, and eventually a walk. My adrenaline was the only thing pushing me forward. As long as Landis kept quiet, no one would know that I had escaped, and no one would discover I was missing until the morning. I didn't have forever, but at least for now, I had some time.

When I finally crept into Laster using the narrow paths between buildings, I had made up my mind to steal a horse and move on to the next town before trying to find more supplies. Laster lay on the outskirts of Rosan, so far removed that it was nearly forgotten. Because of that, the town had become largely self-sufficient. Most of the citizens made their living by growing and harvesting fig trees, the only crop that seemed to survive the tough, sandy soil.

The town had clean cobblestone streets and well-built stone buildings. Its apparent largeness was mostly due to the groves of fig trees that stretched out from the northern and eastern ends of town. It didn't take me long to spot the hulking wooden structure of the stables at the corner of one street.

A startlingly cold wind snaked between the buildings, swinging the wooden sign and flickering lantern that hung outside the house of the stable owner. To my relief, I didn't hear any noise or activity as I crept around the back of the stables. I didn't have an excuse for the clear X mark on my hand, and I definitely didn't need any witnesses when I stole the horse.

I sat on a rickety bench pushed up against the back wall of the hut, shielding myself from the wind and trying to work up the nerve to break a horse out of its stall. I wasn't one for stealing, or for horses, for that matter. I sat there for nearly an hour, shivering and debating, until I decided I might as well go back to the Olum if I wasn't going to make a move. Clenching my jaw, I stood up and started toward the adjacent stables.

Then, between the horses' snorts and the stamping hooves, I heard a whisper come from the other side of the stables.

"No one's here."

172

I froze, jerking to a halt. Had someone seen me? Were they talking *to* me? I was beginning to hope I'd just imagined the voice when I heard a second murmur, this one thick with sarcasm.

"I hadn't noticed."

There was a pause, then the first voice suggested, "If we just wait—"

"No," the second voice interrupted flatly. "I'm not wasting more time."

"We need to talk to someone, and I'm not trying to lead my horse around the whole town before we—"

"*No*," the second person repeated, louder this time.

By now, I'd concluded that the voices belonged to two boys, probably around my age. I found it strange that two teenage boys had shown up alone in this town in the middle of the night, and I crept closer to the corner of the stables, so I could hear their conversation better.

Irritation laced the first boy's voice. "Well, what do you suggest, then?"

"I don't know," the second boy responded grouchily. "Don't you have an idea?"

"Yes."

"*Another* idea?"

"Why do I have to be the one to come up with all the ideas?"

"You've been controlling everything we've done since we left," the second boy snapped back.

"We're *not* having this argument again—"

As the boys dissolved into bickering, I noticed that I had caught the attention of one of the horses in the stall closest to me. It swung its head in my direction and looked straight at me with big, brown eyes. I froze. I couldn't do anything but stare, silently begging it not to make a noise. In response, it snorted and looked at me like it was considering eating my hair.

Chase and Warren had always mocked me for my fear of horses. I often corrected them, claiming it was only an *apprehension*. But now, I was seriously considering running all the way back to the Olum when the horse thrust its nose toward me. Startled, I stumbled back and knocked into a pail. It tipped and fell onto the cobblestones with a loud *clatter*. My back hit the side of the stone hut.

The arguing on the other side of the stables stopped. I froze, knowing I should run, but I found myself unable to do anything but stare helplessly at the corner of the wooden stables. Then a boy appeared, little more than a shadow outlined against the looming stables.

I was still deciding whether I should run or play it off when a gust of wind whirled around the corner. The lantern swayed and cast a ray of light directly onto me.

The boy's face was momentarily illuminated, too, and I saw his eyes drop to the mark on my left hand. We sucked in a simultaneous breath.

Then I turned and fled.

"Wait!" the boy cried, but I did the exact opposite, careening around the corner of the hut and bolting down the street.

I heard boots pound against the cobblestone behind me and my heart sank. The boy was chasing me. He'd probably sent his companion to notify the Securities.

I raced through the quiet town, the boy in hot pursuit. He yelled at me to stop, but I only picked up speed, darting around the side of a tavern and down the narrow alley between two buildings. Two torches were mounted at the corners of the buildings, illuminating the edge of the fig orchard just ahead.

But I had taken no more than one stride into the orchard when someone stepped out from between the trees and blocked my path. I skidded to a stop. He must've been the other boy from the stables, because he held the reins of two horses. I glanced down the row of fig trees to my right, but before I could start running again a hand grabbed my arm, wrenching me around.

"Stop!" I screamed, fighting against his grip. I couldn't go back to the Olum. Not like this.

"Wait, I just want to—" The boy froze. I froze. The torchlight jumped, flickered in the wind, then settled just enough to illuminate our faces.

174

I found myself staring into kind eyes. Hazel eyes. Familiar eyes, ones that had been burned into my memory from the day I'd first seen them, seared with pain from the day I'd sent him to his death. Eyes that had once been so full of fear, but were now filled with something else, something I couldn't quite place. I had never thought I'd see these eyes again. I had never thought anyone would.

We stood there, trapped in a silence, the kind that even a quick breath might shatter into a million pieces.

I didn't know what to do. I didn't know what to feel. I didn't know how to handle the fact that he was standing right there. Right in front of me.

"Aila," he breathed at last, his eyes filled with uncertainty.

With that word, the dam broke, and a thousand emotions came flooding in. "Chase, you're..." *Alive.* But I'd already known that, from that day in Ferrol. *Here. You're here. After all these years, I never thought... I'm sorry. I'm sorry. I'm so sorry.* But I couldn't bring myself to say any of those things. There were no words to express the mix of joy and regret churning within me.

"Aila," Chase said again, his voice firmer but still stunned. I took an uncertain step back. Chase's hand, which he'd used to grab me and pull me to a halt, dropped quickly away.

"Hold on," a new voice interrupted. I twisted around in surprise. I'd nearly forgotten about the other boy until he shoved his way between us. A cold, stinging wind seemed to follow him, and I snapped back to reality. "You two," he said, waving his free hand between us, "know each other?" He shot Chase a questioning look.

Chase was shaking his head slowly, as though he couldn't quite believe what was happening. Then, the strangest thing happened; his face lit up in a brilliant smile. That's when I knew he hadn't recognized me that day in Ferrol. He must've forgotten that I'd reported him, too, because there was no way he would be smiling if he remembered what I'd done. I felt a flicker of hope.

"Storm, this is Aila," Chase said, his hazel eyes glowing. "I told you about her, remember? She's my—"

"Friend who turned you in when you became an Exceptional," Storm interrupted coldly. "Yeah, I recall."

My hopes dissipated immediately. Chase did remember.

Storm turned to Chase, their expressions as different as night and day. "Why are you smiling?"

"Are you kidding? This is...I can't..." He let out a disbelieving laugh, a grin still stretched across his face. Then his eyes dropped to my hand, and his brows drew together in sympathy.

Storm followed his gaze, and his expression flooded with horror. "It's a trap!" he shouted, his alarmed voice splitting through the quiet orchard. "Chase, we need to go."

I jolted, finally finding my voice. "What? No!" I'd only known this Storm person for about two minutes, and already he'd reminded me of the worst moment of my life, expressed open hatred, and now he was accusing me of something so ridiculous I wasn't sure whether to laugh or cry. He sure fit his name well.

"What are you even talking about?" Chase said, throwing a startled glance toward Storm. "Calm down."

"We've never seen her with the Insurgence, so that meant she was taken by the government," Storm said frantically. "She should be dead, but instead she's wandering freely, which means she must work with—"

"The Expos," Chase finished at the same moment Storm launched himself into the saddle of one of the horses.

"No, I don't! I don't!" I said, lurching forward. "I just escaped from them tonight, I promise!"

To my surprise, Chase didn't seem fazed by the fact that I was an Exceptional walking free. "I believe you," he said simply.

Storm stared. "What? Chase, do you remember what she did to you?"

Chase's tone sharpened. "I remember, but like I told you, I've forgiven her." He took a deep breath, his gaze dropping to the ground. "And...I believe her. She isn't an Expo."

With a sinking feeling, I realized I had spoken too quickly. I *had* been an Expo—an officer, in fact—it's just that I had run away when given the chance. But Storm still looked ready to bolt, so I just said, "I was a prisoner at the Olum. I just barely escaped tonight."

Storm leaned forward. "The Olum? What's that?"

I was startled by the sudden intensity of his gaze. "It's…where the Expos work—"

"You were a prisoner?" he demanded. "They didn't kill you?"

"Does it look like they killed me?"

Storm didn't seem to hear me. "They don't kill Exceptionals?" he whispered, his voice trembling with hope.

I hesitated. If I told them that they only kept Exceptionals alive if they agreed to become Expos, they would know who I really was. And I didn't know what these two boys were doing in Laster, but the fact that Chase was an Exceptional and was still alive told me enough. They were part of the rebels, and if I wanted to join them, I would have to keep my decision to work for Brone a secret.

Then, very quietly, Storm murmured, "Jon is still alive?"

Jon. With that name, everything clicked, and all my hopes came crashing down.

Chase had been in Ferrol that day, and had told Storm about Jon's capture. That's why they were here. They were trying to rescue Jon, who had been captured and taken to the Olum.

And I had been one of the Expos who helped with his capture.

18

STORM

My heart pounded in my chest. I felt detached, like I was watching the conversation from above instead of being in it. Jon was still alive. He was *alive*. And depending on how long it had been since Aila became an Exceptional, it was possible that he would stay alive long enough for us to rescue him.

"Let me get something straight," Chase said, pulling me back to reality. He was standing next to my horse, his eyes fixed on Aila. "When you became an Exceptional, the Expos took you away to the Olum, correct?"

"Yes, they said we could stay alive as long as we agreed to join the Expos." When I tightened my grip on the horse's reins, she quickly added, "But I didn't!"

I met her wide eyes with a glare. I didn't trust her, and I wanted to make sure she knew it. There had to be a reason the first thing she'd done was run when Chase had confronted her at the stables. She was scared. Or hiding something. Maybe even both. The fact that she betrayed Chase when she was only eight didn't add much to her credibility. Just because she was also an Exceptional didn't mean I forgave her, even if Chase did.

"When did you become an Exceptional?" Chase still sounded stunned, but his voice brimmed with wonder and joy. "Just recently?"

"No, I—" Aila broke off and bit her lip, casting me a sideways glance. I narrowed my eyes at her until she murmured, "I became an Exceptional last month, but Brone thought...he thought I'd make a good

Expo. He gave me more time to make my choice. But I promise, I was still a prisoner."

I snorted. I thought she'd make a good Expo, too. Clearly she didn't mind ripping innocent children away from their happy lives.

"Brone? Who's Brone?" Chase asked.

"He's the one who founded the Exceptional Police. He's the one behind all of this."

"He's the one who took my brother," I growled. Aila nodded. "So if Jon became an Exceptional two days ago, how much longer would he have?"

"He has until the end of this week." Aila spoke cautiously, as if unsure how I would respond to the information. "Unless he decides to join the Expos before then."

Jon wouldn't join the Expos. This wasn't the first life-or-death situation he'd faced, and I knew he'd keep his chin held high and refuse to join forces with Brone. That gave me all the more reason to go after him, although for a moment, I couldn't help but feel an elating joy that I had five more days to rescue my brother.

Chase, who had been staring at Aila intensely for several seconds, suddenly spoke. "You said you figured out a way to escape the Olum. Do you know a way to get back in?"

Aila frowned, thinking. "If I had to, I could probably get in the way I got out, but I don't know why I'd ever—" She stopped short, and realization struck us at the same time.

"No," we both said in unison.

"We're not relying on her," I told Chase.

"I am *not* going back to the Olum," Aila insisted.

"Let's get out of here. We don't need her help—!"

"I just got out of there. Do you really think I'll be able to do it again—?"

"Don't you remember what she *did*? We can't trust her!"

Aila glared at me.

"Yes, we can," Chase said calmly. "If Aila was on the Expo's side, she wouldn't be standing here, would she?" I found that to be an extremely weak argument, but he was already turning back to her. "Please, we need your help."

Aila took a step back, shaking her head frantically. Her brown eyes were suddenly wild. "I can't go back there. You don't understand, I can't. I—" She broke off and swallowed hard, pressing a hand against the trunk of the nearest tree to steady herself. "I didn't escape the Olum just to turn around and go back. I escaped to join the rebels."

"The Insurgence," Chase said immediately. I frowned down at him. For someone who was so protective of the Insurgence, he seemed a bit too willing to spill all its secrets to this girl with questionable loyalties.

"The Insurgence," Aila repeated with a sort of reverence. Her eyes darted between us with a sudden excitement. "Are you part of the Insurgence? Can you take me to them?"

"You think the Insurgence is going to accept you?" I scoffed.

"I lived in the Olum for a month. I have information they need!"

"Yeah, sure." I was done with her facade. I'd waited days to get this far, and now that I was almost at the Olum, she seemed determined to stand in our way. "You lived at the Olum for a month when you *should have been dead*, and you turned Chase in when he became an Exceptional. Not something to brag about."

"I was *eight*!" Aila said, and we both looked to Chase to back us up.

Chase gave me a look that said, *Why do you keep putting me in these situations?*, then turned to Aila. "Storm and I can't go back to the Insurgence Base until we rescue Jon. We'll take you to them right after, okay? Storm's right, the Insurgence might not trust you, but they will if you help us save Jon."

"We don't need her help!" I shouted.

Chase spun around and gave me an agitated look. We stared each other down for several seconds, then he said, "Why are you still on the horse?"

I swung myself out of the saddle, my boots hitting the ground with an aggressive thud. Chase jerked his head, and I grudgingly followed him out of earshot of Aila.

180

"I know what you're going to say," he said before I could even take a breath. "And I understand. You don't want to trust her with Jon's life. Fine. But if you can't trust her, trust me. I know you don't like it, but Aila's our only hope of getting into the Olum and finding Jon."

I gritted my teeth, glancing back to where Aila was pretending not to listen in. "How do we know she isn't lying?"

"Sometimes, we have to give people the benefit of the doubt," Chase said. "You haven't always made the best decisions, either, and yet I trusted you enough to join this ridiculous mission."

"That's different."

"Is it?"

"I…" He'd backed me into the corner, but I refused to admit it. I kicked at the ground with the toe of my boot before mumbling, "You really trust her?"

"With my life."

I paused. Glanced back in her direction. Rolled my eyes and sighed. "She reminds me of Aris."

I would never agree with Chase about Aila, but he knew that—for the time being—I would trust him. His face split with a grin, and he clapped me on the shoulder. "You'll learn to get along."

As he started back toward Aila, I sucked in a deep breath, turning my eyes to the sky. The edges of the horizon were beginning to brighten. The orchard was slowly coming alive. Fewer crickets were buzzing, and a shrill call of a mockingbird sliced suddenly through the trees. Five more days. Five short, short days left to rescue Jon. We could do it. We didn't have a choice.

Chase turned and beckoned me toward him and Aila. "She agreed to help."

"Great," I said unenthusiastically.

Aila leveled a stare at me. "I'll help on one condition," she said. "You have to promise to take me to the Insurgence Base after all this is over, and help me become a member."

Chase and I exchanged glances, and Aila's eyes narrowed.

"What? I thought you knew where their base was!"

"We do," Chase said slowly, "but this mission isn't exactly for the Insurgence."

"What?"

I mumbled something under my breath.

"*What?*" Aila said more sharply, shooting me a piercing glare.

"What he said was that we ran away from the Insurgence Base to rescue his brother because they weren't doing anything about it," Chase translated, although in reality I had said something more along the lines of how pushy she was being.

Aila stared at us. "So when we get back to the Insurgence..."

"We might be in a lot of trouble," Chase said, his shoulders sagging. "They might not trust me anymore. And because of that...they might not trust you."

Aila's face fell, her eyes dropping to the ground in defeat, a thousand emotions flickering across her face. Finally, she said, "We could lie."

Chase and I exchanged glances.

"Tell them that you broke me out, too," she said, her voice growing eager. "We were friends, Chase, so it would make sense. Just don't mention anything about my past, and they won't be able to turn me away."

Chase gave me another wary look, but I shrugged. "Lying to the Insurgence seems like a win to me."

Another bird began to sing, a sweet, lilting sound that reminded me of a lullaby I used to know. Aila's head jerked up in alarm.

"You should get back to the Olum," Chase said, stepping back and reaching for his horse's reins, which I still clutched in my hands. "You can take my horse, if you want."

"No. No, it'll draw too much attention." Aila's expression had suddenly changed, fear crawling over her face. I felt a stab of panic. Jon was trapped in the exact place that was causing Aila so much worry. She closed her eyes and took a steadying breath before glancing back at Chase. "Should we meet tomorrow?"

"Yes," I said before he could respond. "We don't have time today, but if you get here a bit earlier tomorrow, you can show us to the Olum and we can break in."

Aila gave me a startled look. "That's too soon."

"She's right," Chase jumped in. "We need a plan."

"Then we'll make a plan," I said, shrugging, "and put it into action tomorrow night."

"We can't just jump into this, Storm—"

"Jon's *life* is on the line. I don't think not jumping is an option here."

"We've talked about this already! We all want to rescue Jon, but we're not going to be reckless." Chase's voice rose in irritation. "Things could go wrong if we rush."

"And things *will* go wrong if we don't!"

"Chase is right, we need to think this through," Aila said.

I spun to face her. "Did I ask?"

"Fine, fine, you're right!" Chase nearly shouted before Aila could respond. "We'll plan to break Jon out tomorrow, okay? We're doing it tomorrow."

I nodded, and the three of us drew still, chest heaving, breaths puffing out in little clouds. A fragile silence stretched over us, a precious moment of peace before the storm.

"Aila," Chase said at last, breaking the quiet, "you know the Olum the best. Can you try to come up with an idea on how to get us in there?"

"I-I guess so," Aila said anxiously. "Do either of you have powers I can work with?"

I crossed my arms. "Do you?"

In the blink of an eye, Aila disappeared, and before I knew what was happening I felt something jab me in the small of my back. I yelped and spun around as Aila flickered back into sight, holding a stick she'd retrieved from beneath one of the fig trees.

I glowered at her. She crossed her arms smugly. "Do you have a power?"

I twisted my horse's reins in my fingers. "Chase does," I offered, pointing.

Chase shot me an annoyed look and folded his arms. "My power is not important. It won't help us with the plan."

I rolled my eyes. Even in the urgency of the situation, he was still guarding his secret.

"Fine. I'll figure something out by tomorrow. Maybe," she added, throwing me an irritated look. I met it with a glare.

"Thank you, Aila," Chase said. He let out a breath and gave her a crooked grin. "You have no idea what it means to us that you're helping."

"I can't believe it. After that day, I thought…" Aila swallowed, suddenly unable to continue. Chase dropped his gaze, his eyes glassy. I felt an uncontrollable longing for the day when I would have this type of reunion with Jon.

"I'll meet you here, tomorrow after the sun goes down," Aila said. She turned to go, but not before catching my gaze. "This will work, Storm. Promise."

I gave her a jerky nod as she disappeared between the buildings. I felt a tug on the reins and turned to see my horse had dropped its head and was now scavenging among the grass and leaves for fallen figs, clearly done with waiting. I could understand. I was impatient and exhausted. I just wanted to be done running, done worrying, but that didn't feel like an option when we had just partnered with a girl who had questionable motives.

"I trust her," Chase said, reading my expression.

"You think she knows what she's doing?"

Chase hesitated. "Well, I wouldn't go that far."

I frowned as I watched the first rays of sunlight slant through the low-hanging boughs of the trees.

"Hey, cheer up," Chase said, grinning. "You'll get to see Jon tomorrow. Now let's go get a stall for our horses."

I jerked my horse's reins and followed Chase into town, pausing only to glance in the direction Aila had disappeared. *I'm coming, Jon,* I thought silently, my grip tightening on the reins. *You'll be out of there before you can even blink.*

19

AILA

It had only been two days since I'd last talked to Ross and June, but our friendship seemed like it was from another lifetime. I should've been in training, chatting with June and tolerating Ross, but instead I was standing in front of Brone's office, rapping my knuckles against the door for the fifth time in a row.

I stepped back and waited, anxiety coursing through me. I felt like I was toying with danger, walking straight up to Brone just hours after running away from the Olum. I wanted nothing more than to spin around and return to my old life, a life of innocent sword lessons and friendships. But when no response came, I forced myself to step up to the door and knock one last time.

The office on the other side of the door was silent. I glanced up and down the hall, half expecting Brone to stride around a corner with a stoic expression on his face, but the corridor remained empty. I turned back to the door and stared at it, tempted to spin around and hurry back down the hall. Then, before I could second guess my decision, I wrapped my hand around the cold doorknob and pushed the door open.

I wasn't expecting it to be unlocked, but I was even more surprised to see Brone sitting at his desk, head bent, focused on something that rested on the desktop. His head snapped up when I entered. Alarm flashed briefly through his eyes, but he quickly shifted his gaze back into impassivity as he shoved the object into a drawer. Before he slammed the drawer shut, I caught a glimpse of something that looked like an icicle. Or maybe it was a sword.

"Why did you enter without knocking?" Brone's voice was sharp like broken ice.

I froze, his unusually furious gaze pinning me to the spot. "I...did."

A flicker of confusion crossed Brone's face, but it was gone as quickly as it came. When he spoke next, his voice had smoothed out. "Why aren't you in training? Do you need something?"

I took a deep breath, rolling back my shoulders and smoothing my face into what I hoped was a passive expression. "I had a request. I want to speak with the new Exceptionals."

One of Brone's eyebrows lifted.

"I know I haven't been here for long, but that means I can relate to them more than anyone else here at the Olum. I want to try to convince them to join the Expos." The words tasted sour on my lips, but Brone didn't interrupt, so my act must've been working. "I know I am an officer now, but I wanted to ask your permission."

Several long, agonizing seconds passed during which I held my breath and wondered if I should've just kept my mouth shut. But then Brone gave a barely perceptible nod. "Permission granted," he said slowly. His eyes locked with mine. "You never fail to surprise me, Miss Vinn."

Just wait until Jon and I break out of this place. "Thank you, sir."

I turned and hurried out of the room, closing the door behind me for what I hoped would be the last time.

Only when I had put several long corridors and sharp turns between me and Brone's office did I allow myself to relax, my shoulders drooping as tension flowed out of me. I couldn't shake the feeling that he would figure out what I had done. I had expected him to demand to know why I had snuck out of the Olum, or reveal that he was aware of our plans. After returning to my room last night, I'd spent until dawn pacing and worrying. But now that our conversation was over, I was finally able to turn my mind to how I would notify Jon of our plan.

I reached the hall with Exceptional cells and strode up to the closest guard, a middle-aged woman who regarded me with a wary expression.

"I'm here to speak to the Exceptionals," I said. "Brone gave me permission."

The woman's lips pinched together, so I dug my officer's badge out of my pocket and held it up. It felt less painful to hold, knowing that I was finally making an effort to step out of this life.

She inspected the badge with narrowed eyes, as if suspecting forgery, then gestured to her comrade,who was patrolling up and down the hall. He strode to her side, and they proceeded to hold a conversation full of harsh whispers and furtive glances in my direction. I rolled my eyes. Clearly, they were desperate for any kind of excitement, even if that meant making an issue out of nothing.

They finally broke apart, and the woman reapproached me as the other guard resumed his patrol. At the other end of the corridor I spotted a third guard, leaning against the wall and gazing across at us with disinterest.

"You are allowed to speak with the Exceptionals," the woman said in a tone that suggested she was giving me a great gift. "Call for Valen—" she gestured to the guard ambling lazily down the hall "—if you need any help. Slide open the panel on the doors to speak with the Exceptional inside the room."

I nodded. My eyes scanned the hall once more, and I took a mental note of the guards' positions before starting for the first iron door. The hall that intersected this one was narrow and ran along the outside of the Olum. If I remembered correctly, that same hall led to a heavily guarded door attached to the stables. It would be the perfect place for Chase to sneak in and make a diversion while Storm and I approached from the other direction.

I studied the hall as I walked, quickly counting the doors that lined the walls. There were ten on each side, although I suspected many of them were empty or holding Exceptionals from past weeks who had not yet gained Brone's trust. I spotted the door leading to my old cell and flinched away, deciding to start with one on the other side of the hall.

I dropped to my knees and forced the metal panel open with some difficulty before peering inside. A girl probably a year younger than me sat on the bed in the far corner, her legs pulled tight to her chest, her face buried in her arms. Not Jon. I was about to move on when I caught a glimpse of the female guard at the other end of the hall, watching me out of the corner of her eye. She would certainly find it suspicious if I didn't make a show of trying to talk to each Exceptional. So, although she was out of earshot, I began to speak.

"Hi. How are you?" The words came out of my mouth before I could stop them, and I winced. The answer should've been obvious. Her life as she knew it had just been upended.

The girl's head snapped up, and with a start I realized that her face was streaked with tears, her eyes red and puffy. I felt a stab of pity.

"You're not an Expo," she said, swiping the back of her hand across her face.

I frowned. That had definitely not been the first thing I expected her to say. "Um...I actually am."

"What are you doing here, then?" she asked, her voice hardening. "Shouldn't you be out there, capturing Exceptionals and ruining their lives?"

"No. No, I only have to do that during Recruitment Week."

"Like that makes you any less of a monster," the girl spat. "If you're here to try and convince me to join you, don't. I'm not doing it."

I bit my lip. I didn't want these kids to become Expos, but I didn't want them to experience the alternative, either. I must've hesitated too long, because the girl looked away and pulled her knees up to her chin once more. I stared at her for a moment longer, then checked over my shoulder to make sure no guards were in earshot. "I know it's a hard decision to make, and I'm not saying what the Expos do is good, but just because you choose to join the Expos doesn't mean you're a bad person."

I thought of Ross, whose only goal was to see his family one more time. I thought of June, who was so thoughtful and encouraging despite the decision she made.

The girl let out a derisive snort. "Don't lie to make it seem like you aren't a murderer. Did they brainwash you or something?"

"What? No, I'm on your side! I..." The girl turned her back to me, and I trailed off, wanting to say more but knowing I didn't have the time. I gave her a regretful look, then pushed the panel closed with a *clang* and moved on to the next cell.

Two empty cells, five full ones, and three difficult conversations later, I pulled open the metal panel and felt my heart stutter in relief.

"Jon!" The name sprung from my lips before I could stop it, and I snapped my mouth closed, casting a panicked glance at the guards.

Valen was on the far side of the hall with the other male guard, and the female guard had finally turned her attention away from me. When I glanced back to Jon, I felt my heart skip for an entirely different reason. He had the same hopeless look he'd had the day of his capture, and he stared at the ceiling with a vacant gaze. It was clear that, although he had not made his decision, Jon had given up.

"I still have five more days to live," Jon said flatly. "Leave me alone."

His voice was hollow, lacking any true conviction. A lump formed in my throat. "I'm not here to talk about that," I whispered.

Jon's eyes shifted to me for a moment, but he looked away just as quickly. My chest squeezed in pity.

"I don't care what you have to say," he stated.

"Yes, you do." I glanced over my shoulder, but Valen was still chatting with the other guard. I leaned forward, my voice trembling eagerly. "I met your brother. Storm."

Jon's head snapped up. It was like someone had struck a match. Emotions flooded his face, one after another. Surprise. Regret. Grief. And then, finally, hope. "Storm?" he whispered. "Is he...is he alive?" He scrambled to his feet, and for the first time I noticed how thin and pale he looked. His eyes were wild. "I'll join the Expos if he's here."

189

I shook my head, and Jon's shoulders sagged. He fell back onto the bed, his expression crumbling. "Of course he didn't," he whispered, and I had the sudden feeling that he'd forgotten I was there.

With a start, I remembered Jon had no idea that the Insurgence existed. He had no idea that his brother had been rescued. I leaned forward, planting my hands on either side of the metal slot.

"Jon," I said. He stopped and looked at me, blinking away grief. "I talked to your brother yesterday. Storm is *alive*."

"Wh-what?" Jon's voice sounded small. He shook his head. "No. You just said—"

"Storm wasn't taken by the Expos," I said in a rush. "The Insurgence saved him first."

"The Insurgence?" Jon's eyes were filled with tears.

"They're a group of rebels who try to rescue Exceptionals before the Expos can take them away. Storm was rescued, and he's here. He's going to get you out."

"What? Storm is here?" He was on his feet in an instant, lurching toward the door.

"No, no, not *here!*" My gaze darted around, conscious of the fact that Vinson had left his post and was starting back down the hall. My voice dropped. "He's in a town nearby, waiting with…his friend."

I almost said *my friend*, but stopped myself at the last moment. I didn't deserve Chase's friendship, not when I was lying to him about who I really was.

"He's alive," Jon whispered, his voice still trembling with shock. He made a disbelieving sound that was halfway between a laugh and a sob.

"That's right." My heart swelled. It felt good, bearing good news for a change. "We're going to break you out of here, tonight after everyone is asleep."

Jon backed up until his back was against the wall, his eyes glistening, his face filled with wonder. "You're telling the truth?" he asked after a moment. "It's actually happening?"

"It's happening, Jon." My heart pounded loudly at the words. "It's happening tonight."

190

The boys were parked within the first line of fig trees outside of Laster, ready to leave. Storm was already on his horse, and I fought the urge to throw him a glare. I had skipped dinner to rest, but I'd only been able to get an hour of sleep before I was awake again, anxiously running through the plan in my mind. It felt like there was an endless list of things that could go wrong, and I needed more time to be able to think it all through. But of course, Storm wouldn't see this as a valid reason to put things off until tomorrow.

"Good news," I said, striding up to Chase and ignoring the insufferable boy beside him. "I overheard Brone speaking to Merrick on my way out of the Olum. He's traveling to the palace to meet with Earl Nicolin. He'll be gone by the time we get to the Olum and isn't returning until tomorrow night."

"That's great." Chase visibly sagged, and I realized he was just as anxious as I was.

"Do you have a plan?" Storm asked, and I finally acknowledged his presence with an irritated stare. His horse stamped at the ground and trotted in place, mirroring Storm's impatience.

"Of course I have a plan. Isn't that what you told me to do?" I snapped.

Storm narrowed his eyes at my sharp tone, but Chase interrupted him with a sigh. "She's been here for two seconds. Can you at least try to get along?"

Storm scowled. "Let's just focus on the mission."

"I'd be more than happy to," I muttered back.

"So what's your plan?" Chase asked, his voice as steady as ever.

"Well I was able to speak to Jon—"

"You were?" Storm interrupted. He leaned so far forward he almost fell off his horse. "What did he say? Is he okay? Have they hurt him? If they hurt him, I promise I'll—"

"He's fine," I said. "He's been struggling, but once I told him you were alive, it was like the life came back to him."

191

For the first time, Storm didn't look angry or worried or impatient. His eyes filled with emotion, and he looked away.

"Great, so Jon's aware of the plan," Chase said with a nod. "What do you need us to do?"

"Storm and I will enter the Olum through the air vents. That's how I snuck out the past two nights. Chase, you'll use the door around the right side of the building. With Brone gone, the security won't be as tight, because he won't be around to enforce it. The door is locked, though, so you'll have to break it down or something."

Storm snorted. "Yeah. Very discreet."

"Chase isn't trying to be discreet, we are," I snapped. "His job is to get in there and create a diversion to draw the guards away from Jon. Then we'll sneak in, free your brother, and sneak out." I fell silent, realizing just how bare bones this plan truly was. Chase and Storm must've noticed the same thing, because they exchanged glances.

Storm frowned at me. "Sounds less like we're following a plan and more like we're winging it."

I spun to face him. "Yeah, and whose fault is that?"

"What are you talking about? I'm not the one who was supposed to figure it out!"

"And I'm supposed to just come up with a detailed plan in *one day*?"

"Oh, I'm sorry, is that too much to ask?"

"Yes, actually, it is. But maybe if I had *more time*—"

"More time that we can't spare?"

"We can—"

"Guys!"

Storm and I both fell silent. He glared at me, fuming, and I suddenly wished I hadn't partnered with us for the plan. But he was too reckless to be left alone, especially when his brother's life was on the line.

Chase rolled his eyes. "If we're going to do this, we need to be a team, okay? Can you do that for just a few hours? Please?"

Storm and I nodded, but I could tell Chase was still skeptical. Finally, I said, "We need to figure out what you're doing for a diversion."

Chase grinned. "Don't worry, I've come prepared."

He slipped his arms out of the straps of his pack and swung it to the ground. He dug inside for a few moments, then drew out two cylindrical canisters, both about the size of his palm.

Storm's eyes widened in admiration. "Dust bombs."

Chase stood up, swinging his pack back onto his shoulder. "They've helped Storm and me once before, and I have no doubt they'll help again."

I nodded, a slow smile coming to my face. Yes, we hardly had a plan, and yes, there were an innumerable amount of things that could go wrong, but the Expos had no idea what was coming. For the first time, I began to think that our plan might actually work.

Two minutes into our journey, Storm grew impatient and suggested we run the rest of the way to the Olum.

"Absolutely not," I snapped. "We have all night, and it's stupid to waste our energy now."

Two minutes later, Storm decided he would run whether we liked it or not, and because he had absolutely no idea where he was heading, Chase and I were forced to keep up with him.

We reached the Olum out of breath and trembling with nerves. It would've been easier to give into Storm and let us take the horses, but it would've drawn too much attention. I directed Chase to the side of the building where the door was located and told him to give Storm and me fifteen minutes before making his move. He nodded and disappeared around the corner without hesitation.

I couldn't help but stare after him. Why was he helping Storm in this reckless plan? Storm and I both had our own motives, but what were his?

I pried off the grate with some difficulty and made Storm go up the rope first. Halfway through the ventilation shaft, I realized my mistake. Having someone crawling slowly in front of me, blocking the faint light up ahead, only intensified my feeling of claustrophobia. It didn't help that Storm spent the entire crawl grumbling so loud I was sure the whole Olum could hear him.

I was half expecting there to be a barrage of guards waiting for us at the other end of the shaft, having heard Storm's complaints from the second we left Laster, but we slipped through the opening and into the stairwell without problem. For the second time that night, I felt my heart begin to beat faster with hope. Maybe this plan would go our way after all.

We were in the bottom of the dark, hidden stairwell when everything went wrong. Time was already running short, thanks to the hour-long pace Storm had set for us on our crawl through the shaft, so I wasted no time striding from the bottom of the stairs and shoving up the lever next to the hidden door.

By the time I realized the lever was supposed to be pulled down, not pushed up, it was too late. The door emitted a horrible sound, metal grinding against metal, stone scraping against stone. I sucked in a breath. The door slid open the barest sliver of an inch, then it shuddered, made a low screeching sound, and stopped moving entirely.

I heard Storm draw up next to me. He was breathing heavily from adrenaline. Or maybe I'd been right, and he *had* wasted all his energy on the run to the Olum. I knew if I hesitated too long, he'd catch his breath and start making more snappy remarks, so I stepped forward and yanked the lever down.

The door didn't budge.

I shoved it up, and to my horror the door only succeeded in sliding nearly all the way shut, leaving no more than a finger's width between the door and the wall. I knew Chase would be making his move any minute now. My brain began to spin, and I took a panicked step toward the door.

I fit my fingers in the crack and pulled, trying to force it open.

"Excellent." Storm's insufferable drawl came from behind me. "The whole plan is going to fail because you broke a door."

I shushed him through clenched teeth, refusing to rise to the bait.

"Or maybe you meant for it to be this way," Storm continued. His voice was a harsh whisper in the darkness of the room. "Maybe I was right all along. You're trying to sabotage our plan."

My jaw tightened as I continued to pull, unsure how much more taunting I could take without a response. *Stay calm, Aila.*

For a second, I thought Storm was done talking and let out a breath before putting renewed efforts into prying open the door.

But then he hissed, "You think you've earned our trust, you think that Chase forgives you, but the truth is, no one will be able to overlook who you really are."

Please be quiet, I silently begged, but I didn't dare let him see how his words were affecting me.

"Even you know that, deep down, you're nothing but a liar and a *traitor.*"

"No I'm *not!*" I shouted, spinning to face him.

Storm stared at me, startled, and I quickly lowered my voice to a furious hiss.

"I never betrayed *anyone.*"

"Really? Then what do you call turning in your best friend? Let me guess, *serving the greater community?*"

My chest heaved. A thousand bitter comments swirled through my head, landing on the tip of my tongue. But I locked my jaw, aware of the ticking clock, aware of the prospect of guards waiting for us on the other side of this door. I forced my voice to lower as I gestured to the door and snapped, "What makes you think you'd do any better?"

I couldn't make out Storm's expression in the darkness, but after a moment of hesitation, he muttered, "Move."

I obliged, and he set to work trying to pull the door open wider. I heard the stone rake back a bit, but Storm only succeeded in forcing it another inch open. His teeth were gritted, and even in the darkness I could see his muscles straining. I couldn't help but feel a flicker of satisfaction.

But then Chase's words from earlier entered my thoughts. *If we're going to do this, we need to do it as a team.* The door would not move without our combined effort. For a moment, I had the irrational desire to wait a

195

few seconds and relish Storm's struggle. But I felt a stab of guilt and reluctantly stepped up next to him, wrapping my hands around the door.

Together, we were able to force it open just wide enough to fit through. We released the door and stumbled into the dark hall beyond.

I gasped for breath, my heart beating wildly. Storm's chest was heaving, too, and his eyes darted around the wide hall as if he would find Jon waiting at the corner. We needed to move, but I couldn't, not with Storm's stinging words still echoing in my ears.

I released a breath. "I didn't know they were supposed to die."

Storm's head whipped around. His dark blue eyes flashed as he studied me. "What do you mean?"

"Exceptionals," I said, panting. "I didn't know they were taken away to die. I thought they were just repaired and sent back to their normal lives. I thought..." I took a deep, trembling breath. "I thought I was helping Chase by turning him in."

For once, Storm was silent, his burning blue eyes reflecting the flame of the closest torch.

"I know what you're going to say," I said at last, starting down the hall, "so I'll say it first. I was stupid to think things would be that easy."

Storm and I did not say a word to each other as we rushed through the halls of the Olum, darting from corner to corner, peering ahead to make sure the coast was clear before making another move. I told myself we were quiet out of necessity, trying to avoid being overheard and discovered, but I knew that wasn't the only reason. I could still feel anger rolling off of Storm in waves, and every time I turned around to make sure he was still following, his baleful blue gaze met mine unflinchingly.

He despised me. He despised me, and he wanted me to know it.

Finally, it became too much. The pressure of the situation, the unwarranted hate, his gaze pressing into my back. I spun around halfway down a hall, suddenly not caring if anyone heard us.

"You would've done the same thing," I snapped.

Storm's eyes flashed with warning.

"Admit it. You would've turned someone in, if it meant saving Jon. Am I wrong?" Storm inhaled sharply. Glared at me. "*Am I wrong?*"

"*Stop it!*" Storm snarled suddenly. "You're guilty and you're looking for someone to blame! Well, you won't find it, because no one has ever dared to stoop as low as you did, you—"

I turned my back on him, unable to bear another word, and that's when I realized someone else had rounded the corner.

I froze, so abruptly that Storm crashed into my back.

"Aila, what—?"

He spotted the figure and immediately fell silent, the protest dropping from his lips as I met the all-too-familiar impassive gaze of the man striding toward us.

20

STORM

Say something! I mentally screamed at Aila. My fury dissipated as if it had never existed, allowing torrents of fear to come flooding in. My eyes darted between Aila and the man. *Stop standing there suspiciously and say something!*

But all Aila did was stand and stare as the man—who I assumed was an Expo—drew closer and finally stopped in front of us. I couldn't blame her. My own heart was thundering loudly in my chest. There was something about his tall figure, his commanding stride, that seemed to steal my ability to move.

Finally, Aila choked out, "Brone."

My whole world screeched to a halt. *No*, I thought. *No, no, no, no, no.*

But I shouldn't have been surprised. The man in front of us had the face I'd expect the leader of the Expos to have. His gaze was stone-cold and dispassionate, the exact expression of a person who had spent his life ripping children away from their homes.

It was the face of the man who had captured my brother.

"What are you doing here?" Aila managed, her voice thick with fear.

"I could ask you the same thing," Brone said. His eyes drifted to me, and my heart stilled. He knew that I wasn't supposed to be here; I was certain of it.

Aila had betrayed us. I was certain of it.

"But...the Palace—"

"I pushed back my departure time," Brone said, "and it's a good thing I did, because right as I was saddling my horse, a guard came running to inform me of a disruption out front." Brone's gaze swept across us, making me want to run, to hide, to do *something* to escape his presence. "He said he had spotted something suspicious out front. Three teens arrived at the Olum. One of them went around the side of the building while the other two climbed into an air vent."

Aila's eyes were wide, and I began to rethink my initial judgment. She didn't look like someone who'd planned this. She looked just as scared as I was. Maybe she *was* on our side after all.

But in this case, it wasn't a good thing. They had figured out our plan, a plan that had been doomed to fail from the very beginning.

"One of the teens," Brone continued, "was you, Miss Vinn. And I supposed the second was this scrawny street rat next to you."

I had the strength to shoot him an indignant look, but his eyes were trained on Aila. Seizing the opportunity, I glanced around, scanning for a way to escape. But there was no point. I had no way of communicating with Aila, and I couldn't leave her behind; Chase would never forgive me. Out of the corner of my eye, I saw Aila's expression. I could tell the wheels in her head were also turning as she struggled to put together a coherent sentence.

What she finally settled on startled me. "Did you capture the other teen?"

As the words came out of her mouth, a change seemed to sweep through her. Aila drew herself up, rolled back her shoulders, and lifted her chin. Her voice sounded…different. The words were filled with determination and a hint of the coldness in Brone's voice. Something was very wrong.

Brone frowned, too. "We have men waiting to capture him the moment he enters the building."

Aila nodded. "I apologize. I hadn't expected to carry out the plan tonight. If I'd known things would move so quickly, I would've notified you beforehand."

Brone's brows creased slightly. "Excuse me?"

"Aila, what are you talking about?" I demanded, finally finding my voice, terrified of the answer.

"When I met the boys, I knew immediately that I had to lure them into a trap," Aila said, her gaze fixed resolutely on Brone. "I wanted to bring them here tomorrow night, but Storm insisted we rescue his brother tonight. I didn't have time to warn you."

My world, which had been spiraling downward for the past several minutes, finally crashed to the ground and shattered into a million pieces. I reeled backward, shock, horror, and betrayal washing over me with the pain of a thousand shards of glass.

"You're about to capture the first boy," Aila said, not even sparing me a backwards glance, "and here is the second."

Brone's lips were pressed into a tight line. "My sources informed me that you appeared to be working with the boys, Miss Vinn."

"Of course that's how I appeared. I needed them to trust me," Aila said. She still sounded completely collected, but I noticed her eyes vegan to dart again. "But you see, I was the one who captured this boy's brother. Would I really turn around and help him after doing that?"

"*What?*" I spoke before I even had the chance to think. Aila finally turned to me, although she didn't quite meet my gaze.

"You didn't know?" Brone asked, his attention shifting to me. "Aila has recruited quite a few Exceptionals herself."

"No," I said, shaking my head and backing away. "No, that's not true. She would've told me." But she wouldn't have. Hadn't I known that, all along?

Aila suddenly looked uncertain. "Storm," she whispered.

"She's a prisoner," I insisted, looking back at Brone. "She's a captive."

"If she is, then why isn't she in a cell?"

My head whipped back in Aila's direction. For the first time since Brone's arrival, our gazes locked, and I saw her suck in a breath. My chest heaved, my panic mounted, my heart beat wildly in my chest.

Thump. Thump. Thump.

"Is it true?" I said between ragged breaths.

200

For a moment, I thought I saw distress flash in her gaze, but she didn't deny it. *Thump. Thump.*

"Are you one of them?" *Thump.*

"Storm—" *Thump.*

"*Is it true?!*" I screamed.

Thump. Thump. Thump.

Aila's face twisted slowly into a grim smile. "You were right, Storm. You shouldn't have trusted me. I'm not just an Expo. I'm an *officer.*"

I couldn't do anything but stare. If this revelation had come a few hours earlier, I would've felt satisfaction, but now I just felt empty. I was alone. Aila had betrayed me, Jon was still imprisoned—by Aila's own hand—and if I didn't act now, Chase would soon be captured. I needed to go, to get him out of here before things got worse.

But I couldn't move, not when Aila was still standing there, that smug smile on her face, triumph at her betrayal scrawled across her expression. I felt something hot and dangerous boil inside of me.

"I did capture your brother, Storm, and I took joy in every second. You should've been there to see it: the tears in his eyes, your family's fear. It was all worth it, knowing that it was for the greater good."

Something inside of me snapped.

"*Traitor!*" The word tore itself from my mouth in a frenzied rage. "We trusted you! You promised to help us!"

Aila shrugged, indifferent. "I did what it took to get you to walk right into Brone's arms."

I backed away, as if distancing myself from her and Brone could save me. My entire body shook. "You've been lying this whole time, haven't you?" I spat. "I bet you lied about what you thought happened to Exceptionals. I bet you knew you were sending Chase to his death."

Aila's face flickered with sudden emotion. Was it guilt? Regret? I couldn't quite tell, and I honestly didn't care. She didn't deserve sympathy. She deserved whatever she was putting Jon through. But I didn't have the time to give her that right now.

My hand dropped into my pocket, my fingers slipping around an object I had hidden there, just in case.

"We trusted you!" My voice was raw with fury, but my eyes burned with tears. It was all too much. The betrayal, Chase's imminent capture, my failure to rescue Jon…I could hardly breathe. "Chase *forgave* you!"

For the first time, Aila's eyes widened, distress shooting through her. But Brone's gaze darkened. "That is *enough*. Guards!"

Three guards flooded into the hall from behind him and started toward me, but I had no intention of letting them get any nearer. I yanked the dust bomb from my pocket and chucked it onto the ground.

Time seemed to slow. Brone's eyes widened in shock and Aila's widened in realization. She threw herself to the ground and flung one arm over her face as the dust bomb exploded.

The world snapped back into speed. Dust rained everywhere, and I heard shouts of alarm and startled cries from Brone and the Expos. But I felt no satisfaction. I only felt sick, crippled with remorse. *I should've left earlier.* If my anger hadn't gotten the better of me, if I had just let it go and run, I might've been able to rescue Chase. Then the two of us could've still rescued Jon.

I had been stupid to trust Aila, stupid to think we'd succeed, and stupid to keep standing there. But now I knew it was stupid to stay here a minute longer. Choking on more than just dust, I drew the hem of my shirt over my nose and fled down the hall.

I reached the Insurgence Base the next evening. I had pushed my horse into a gallop and ridden nearly the whole day, only stopping twice for no more than five minutes. Everything felt surreal. The events back at the Olum, the fields and towns flying past us, the weight of my mistakes…it all felt like a dream.

A horrible, terrifying, too-bad-to-be-true dream.

I reached the Base and slid clumsily from the back of my horse, delirious from my lack of sleep and from the slew of emotions that were tormenting me. I didn't bother unsaddling my horse. I barely even guided it into one of the stalls before I pulled the key from my pack and stumbled through the stables.

I fell on my knees in front of the lock, but my hands were trembling so violently it took several tries for me to slip the key in. *Get yourself together, Storm,* I told myself sharply. I needed my wits about me if I was going to convince the Insurgence to help rescue Chase and Jon.

But how could I recover when the hope I'd so tenuously built up had come crashing down?

I finally got the door open, and I forced myself to bury my exhaustion, guilt, and fear as I tripped into the Base. I made a beeline for Commander White's office, focusing on nothing but the hall ahead. Hopefully, if anyone saw me, they would miraculously forget that I had been the one to run away from the Insurgence and let me pass. I just needed to reach the commander's office.

But of course, everything went wrong. I was halfway down a broad hall that passed the Refectory when a group of chatting Insurgents rounded the corner and nearly collided with me. There were five of them, all adults who ranked high in the Insurgence hierarchy. I knew it was useless to run, so I ducked my head and attempted to slip past unnoticed.

A strong hand caught me by the arm, twisting me around before I could slip past. I found myself face-to-face with one of the men, and he studied me scrutinizingly. His eyes widened. "You're Storm Dawson."

My mouth went dry, words tumbling from my lips in desperation. "I need to speak with the commander—"

The man shoved me against the wall. I tried to fight but only landed two kicks when my limbs suddenly went limp. I crumpled, but the man was ready and caught me before I hit the ground. No matter how hard I tried to twist out of his arms, my limbs refused to move. Something about his power had paralyzed me.

Panic bubbled inside of me, but I couldn't do anything but scream internally as he carried me through the halls. We started down a flight of steps, but it wasn't until we reached the bottom and I caught a glimpse of a wall of bars that I realized where we were.

The man shoved me unceremoniously into a cell. At his final touch, I was able to move just in time to catch myself before hitting the floor. He slammed the cell door closed and walked away.

"Wait!" My voice cracked in desperation. I stumbled, catching myself on the bars. "I need to speak with Commander White!"

The man turned around and gave me an incredulous look. "You're in big trouble, kid. You don't get to choose what to do."

"It's important!" I shouted, but my pleas fell on deaf ears. I couldn't do anything but watch as he disappeared down the end of the hallway.

For the first time, the weight of what Aila had done—of what *I'd* done—settled fully over me. Aila was a traitor. Jon was imprisoned. Chase was captured. And here I was, safe from the Expos yet locked up all the same. My chest tightened. Suddenly, I couldn't take a breath. I wanted to yell, but I couldn't make a sound. I gripped the bars, released them and spun around, then dropped onto the narrow pallet that served as a bed.

Despite my fear and hopelessness, my exhaustion finally overcame me, and I fell asleep.

I jolted upright in bed, my forehead slick with sweat, my chest heaving with each ragged breath. I wasn't sure what had woken me. I couldn't even tell how long I'd been asleep, but I was happy to be awake. Jon, Aila, Brone, and Chase had wandered in and out of my dreams, haunting me all night long. I'd had the worst nightmare just moments before, but now that I was awake, I remembered nothing.

All that remained was my wildly pounding heart.

"Mr. Dawson."

I jerked my head in the direction of the voice. Commander White had appeared like a ghost on the other side of the bars, her hands clasped behind her back, her expression pinched with disapproval. Despite this, I felt a cool wave of relief wash over me.

"Commander." I scrambled off the bed and toward the bars. My legs felt weak, aching from my ride across Rosan the night before. "I've been waiting to talk to you."

"So Chadrick said," the commander responded, "but I want to make it clear that I did not come here upon your request."

My throat went dry, and I felt a wave of dread.

"Disobeying a direct order, escaping from the Insurgence Base after several attempts, endangering the members of the Insurgence, engaging in reckless activity…" I was reminded of how Chase had listed my crimes in a similar manner at dinner not long ago. It seemed like another lifetime. "The list goes on and on. You have wandered into dangerous territory before, but this time, you have crossed a line."

"Commander—"

"We can no longer trust you, Mr. Dawson," she interrupted. "You are reckless, impulsive, and think only of yourself when making decisions instead of the consequences. And yet, there *are* consequences."

I dropped my chin. I understood that more than she could imagine.

"In this case, your consequence is being here, locked in your cell until further notice."

My head snapped up. "What? No, I can't be here right now."

"Then it is a shame you made those decisions, isn't it?" Commander White said coolly. "You will receive three meals a day, and Chadwick will supervise you on a fifteen minute walk around the building. He will not hesitate to use his ability if you misbehave. I hope you use this time to reflect on your mistakes, and maybe we can come to an agreement in the future."

Commander White turned and began to walk away, and with a start I realized she thought the conversation was over.

"Wait!" I cried, rushing to the bars.

She continued to walk, not even sparing me a glance.

"Please, listen to me! Please!"

Commander White ignored me. I shook my head desperately. If I let her walk away, it was over. It would all be over.

"Chase is in trouble!" I shouted at last.

205

She stopped dead in her tracks. Several seconds passed, but Commander White didn't turn. She just stood there, staring off in the opposite direction.

Then she spun around and strode back to my cell.

"You went to rescue your brother, and Chase did not return." She spoke quickly now, but her voice was cold as ice. "How miserably did you fail?"

"We were working with a girl, and she…she betrayed us." My voice felt suddenly thick, and I gritted my teeth. I wasn't about to break down in front of the commander. "Chase was captured, and I was just barely able to escape. They imprisoned him at the Olum, and I don't know how much time he and my brother have left."

Commander White studied me, as if trying to measure the truth of my words. She gave a slow nod. "Thank you for telling me," she said, then turned on her heel and started down the hall again.

I stared after her. "What are you going to do?" I called out.

Commander White stopped, but she didn't turn to face me. "I will share this information with those I trust."

"That's all? You're just going to talk about it?"

"It's none of your business anymore," she snapped. She started striding away again, this time at a brisk pace, as if she were eager to escape my presence.

"We're talking about Chase's *life*! Of course it's my business!" I shouted after her. "How can you just *talk* about it? That's all you ever do—that's all anybody here ever does! Talk, talk, talk, but no action. What's the point of the Insurgence if we're just going to hide here and watch the world burn? Rescuing a couple of kids means nothing if we're not doing anything to stop those kids from having to be rescued!"

Commander White didn't stop, didn't acknowledge me, but I knew she heard every word. I hoped it cut right to her heart.

And then she disappeared around the corner, leaving me with an overwhelming sense of powerlessness. Chase and I had been willing to do whatever it took to rescue Jon from the Olum.

But I was afraid we had taken things too far.

The next twenty-four hours were the worst moments of my life. As Commander White promised, I was fed three times a day and allowed a short walk through the Base under Chadwick's supervision. But other than that, I was stuck in the cell, and without fail hot anger came seeping in.

I spent the first chunk of the day screaming at the Insurgence for being cowards, yelling at them to come let me out so we could talk like civilized people, shouting all sorts of things that I hoped they heard through the stone ceiling. When my voice went hoarse, I began stalking around the tiny cell, kicking the wall and beating the thin pillow against the bars until it exploded into a feathery cloud. It looked like this dungeon hadn't been touched since the days of Duke Leighton, and I doubted many Insurgents did anything bad enough to end up down here. The furniture was decades old, and everything broke easily beneath my anger.

Once all the furniture was either shattered or overturned, I paced back and forth across the cell, my strides eating up ground but getting me nowhere.

But the worst part was the long, empty hours of solitude with only my thoughts to occupy me. Ideas formed in my head, criticizing lists of every simple thing I should've done to keep the plan from going so horribly wrong. Each revelation sent me spiraling back into another furious cycle of shouting and kicking.

As the daylight faded, my fury dissolved into hopelessness. I stopped pacing and fell onto my bed, dropping my face in my hands.

Inevitably, Jon's face drifted through my mind. Jon, who I had fought so hard to protect. Jon, who had lost all chance of survival because of my failures. Jon, who would have to suffer because I couldn't control my anger.

I clenched my hands into fists, my nails digging into my palms as I tried to shake the thoughts from my head. They were quickly replaced by a memory of Chase, peering at me in the Ferrol alleyway with an expression of confidence and compassion that could be found in no one else. His voice echoed hauntingly in my mind.

"We'll get him back. Whatever it takes."

He had put all his trust in me, throwing away his work, his friends, and everything he'd built just so he could get my brother back. In the end, it *had* taken everything. And now it was about to take his life.

I buried my face into my hands, then jerked my head up. My palms were scalding hot. I stared down at my hands in shock. They tingled fiercely. I clenched and unclenched my fists, and even shook out my hands a few times, but the stinging didn't stop.

I stared blankly out of the bars of my cell, struggling to understand what was happening. My hands had been covering my face, and it felt as though my face were burning. I glanced back down at my palms.

Then, impulsively, I flipped one of my hands over and placed the palm flat on the pale bedsheet underneath me. I let it rest there for a moment, then tentatively lifted my hand. I caught my breath.

A charred outline of my hand lay pressed into the surface of the otherwise white sheet.

My hands began to sting even more, and I stood up, shaking them wildly, trying to get the pain to go away. Was I manifesting my power? Was it supposed to hurt this much? Both hands felt as though they were on fire, and no matter how hard I clenched my fists, it wouldn't stop. Sweat broke out of my forehead, and pain lanced up my arms.

What happened next was almost instinctive. The pain became too much to bear, and with a cry of agony, I threw my arms up, palms out.

A pillar of fire exploded from my hands.

21

AILA

The dust settled, coating the ground the same way guilt coated my heart.

Brone and the Expos began to pick themselves up, brushing off their uniforms and climbing slowly to their feet. Brone was the first to come to his senses.

"After him!" he barked, jerking his hand sharply in the direction Storm had disappeared.

The Expos scrambled to their feet and down the hall, but I knew they wouldn't catch Storm. He had spent his entire life escaping dangerous situations. He knew how to run away.

If only I could say the same.

I heard Brone moving behind me as he continued to brush himself off. I knew he would interrogate me about my motives, but for now, I couldn't care less. I was trembling, the realization of what I'd just done threatening to send me to my knees.

I had proven that every horrible thing Storm had ever said about me was absolutely true.

"Who was that?"

I blinked. I had not expected that to be the first question out of Brone's mouth. I turned to face him, surprised to find that he looked as off-balanced as I did. Brone, who never showed emotion, whose features were harder than the stone walls of the Olum, seemed *shaken* as he stared off after Storm.

"Storm Dawson," I said. "From Ferrol."

"Storm Dawson." Brone repeated the name in almost a whisper. His gaze cut to mine. "No, he doesn't look like he's from Ferrol at all."

"He was adopted," I explained. This much I had learned during our run to the Olum only an hour earlier. As Storm had raced ahead, I'd questioned Chase about him, about his motives.

"*It's for his brother,*" Chase had said. "*He does everything for his brother. Even the stupid things.*"

My heart ached to think of Chase's fate now. *Because of me.*

"Adopted," Brone said absentmindedly, although I'd never before dared to think of Brone as absentminded. He continued to gaze down the hall, even though both Storm and the Expos were long gone. "I can't believe... All this time I thought..."

I never got to figure out what he was going to say. Brone inhaled sharply, then turned away, his stoic mask sliding back into place as if it had never disappeared. "Why didn't you tell me?"

I opened his mouth. I wanted to tell the truth. I wanted to tell him that I *had* been conspiring with Chase and Storm, and that I felt nothing but horror at what I'd just done.

But all that came out was, "I'm sorry. I wanted to prove I was trustworthy. I was afraid I wasn't doing enough as an officer, and I thought if I made this easier for you, you'd be happy." More lies, slipping out of my mouth more easily than the truth ever had. The lies made my insides twist, but I had no other choice.

Brone gazed stonily down at me. "I understand that you want to prove yourself worthy, but the best way to prove that is to follow instructions."

I nodded and dropped my gaze to the ground, waiting for him to yell at me, to summon the guards, to issue the punishment I deserved.

But when he spoke, his voice was surprisingly tender. "You must wonder why I chose you to be an officer."

I had, many times, but that didn't mean I wanted to have this conversation. Not now, when what I had done was tearing me up. Not now, when I was trying as hard as I could to keep from collapsing to the floor and crying.

But Brone was unaware of my internal turmoil. "The truth is, you remind me of myself."

He likely intended the words as praise, but they hit me like a slap in the face, only adding to the pain that was already consuming me. But the worst part wasn't the words. It was the fact that they rang true.

"You do what it takes to survive. You do what you know must be done, even if others don't understand it."

My throat was dry. I wanted him to stop talking. I didn't want to hear him voice the truths I'd been trying so hard to ignore.

"I have always done the same thing, ever since I was young. That's why I decided to found the Exceptional Police."

Somewhere in the middle of the numbness, I felt a flicker of surprise. I had thought the Expos stretched back further than just one man's lifetime. But maybe it was just the fear that had always been there.

Brone noticed my reaction. "I am older than you might think. The current Earl wasn't even born when I created the Olum. People didn't always see Exceptionals as dangerous, but they at least knew they were different. Exceptionals were taken away to schools where they were trained to grow in using their powers." He let out a mirthless laugh. "My family ran the school for generations. I grew up around Exceptionals, and I was the one who finally saw them for what they truly were. I was the one who formed the Exceptional Police and the Olum.

"And that, Miss Vinn, is how we are similar. Not many people saw Exceptionals the same way I did, the same way you do. My parents were the first to object to the thought of killing them, but they were foolish and blind. They were willing to overlook the truth and the hurt the Exceptionals caused for the benefits of running the school."

I was surprised by the anger scrawled across Brone's face. I had seen flickers of emotion before, but this was different. It made me think of the way Storm had looked at me, right before he threw the dust bomb. The uncontained fury in Brone's expression was worse than no expression at all. But as I watched, it crumbled away into something that resembled...*sadness*.

"What hurt did the Exceptionals cause?" I knew asking the question was a risk, but I had lost so much today already. "What made you form the Expos?"

For a moment, I didn't think he would answer. Brone's eyes searched the hall once more, landing on the corner where Storm had disappeared.

"Her name was Mila."

He said the words so quickly, so quietly, that I almost thought I'd imagined his response.

But then he said, "We were young, around your age, when she was killed by an Exceptional. She was my best friend, and the day of her murder, I vowed to never forget her. I made it my mission to avenge her, to tear down everything my parents had built and give the Exceptionals what they truly deserved. It took sacrifices, but I was willing to make them if it meant protecting innocent lives like Mila's."

Brone's gaze was distant as he pulled on the leather cord around his neck and wrapped his fist around the carved X pendant. I couldn't help but stare. All along, I had thought that Brone was evil. Heartless. Yet, the pain in his voice when he spoke of Mila proved otherwise.

Just as quickly, I clenched my teeth. I had to remember that this was the man who sent children to their deaths because they refused to work for him, the man who was willing to mercilessly punish those who dared defy him, the man who was building an army and plotting against the Earl. Brone was a coldhearted liar constructing an empire founded on revenge, and nothing would excuse the crimes he'd committed. I shoved all remaining pity aside.

Brone dropped his necklace back beneath his shirt, his gaze clearing. "I know you understand pain and anger. Don't forget those emotions, Miss Vinn. They may seem horrible in the moment, but they will be what drives you to powerful places. Hold on to that pain, cherish that anger, and one day, you may end up like me."

I shuddered. He didn't understand how horrifying his words were. Guilt pierced me once more, emotion welling up within me.

Brone cleared his throat, his eyes darting away from me and down the hall. "I must see if the boys have been apprehended."

I mumbled something that resembled an agreement and watched as he strode away. It took all my strength to wait until he turned the corner before I slid to the ground, buried my head in my arms, and began to cry.

I woke up late the following morning, my body screaming with exhaustion. I staggered out of my room and down the hall, struggling to put even two thoughts together.

Maybe that's why I ended up pushing open the door to the trainee's Common Area instead of continuing on to the one for officers.

That would've been the safer option.

Ross and June sat at the end of one of the long wooden tables, separated from the rest of the group by a few empty benches. Their heads were bent together, and they were deep in whispered conversation. June noticed me first. Her eyes widened slightly, and Ross turned to follow her gaze as I approached.

"Nice of you to finally join us," he said, unsuccessfully trying to conceal his injured tone. "Seems like a lot more important things have been taking up your time recently."

June tossed Ross a warning glance, which I ignored as I practically fell onto the bench beside him. I began to eat the pile of food on my plate. Hopefully, eating would rejuvenate me. Maybe it would even numb some of the pain. "I'm sorry I haven't been at training. A lot has been going on."

"Not just training." June spoke up from across the table as I busied myself with peeling an orange. "Aila, we haven't seen you in the past *two days*, and you haven't been coming back to the room at night."

I dropped a chunk of peel onto my plate. "A lot has been going on," I repeated. I quickly peeled the rest of the fruit and dropped a slice into my mouth to avoid elaborating. A pang of hunger shot through my stomach, and I realized just how little I'd been eating recently.

Ross and June exchanged glances, and out of the corner of my eye I saw Ross give her the tiniest of nods. When I spotted the betrayal in June's eyes as she turned to me, the orange in my mouth immediately soured.

"We know you're an officer," she said. "Brone announced it at lunch yesterday."

I swallowed my piece of orange, but it was like swallowing a piece of dry parchment. "I was going to tell you—"

"Were you?" June sounded more hurt than angry. "We gave you three chances in the past thirty seconds alone."

I fell silent, guilt clawing at me. I didn't deserve these friends. Even after they realized I was lying, they gave me the opportunity to tell them myself.

"I...I didn't know how to bring it up," I said at last. "A lot—"

"—has been going on. So you've said," Ross spat. I whipped my head around to look at him, startled by his venomous tone.

"I'm sorry I kept a secret," I muttered, finally finding my voice again. "But face it, everyone has secrets at the Olum." *More than the two of you will ever know.*

"So what are your secrets, then?" Ross said, his blue eyes sparking. "Do tell. What made Brone choose *you*, of all people, to become an officer when there are two dozen other Exceptionals who have been working their fingers to the bone trying to get there? What's up with that?"

I was speechless, shocked at the rage in his voice. And then, with a sinking feeling, I remember what Ross had said a few days earlier. *I have family in Carsley, and maybe if I become an officer, I'll be able to visit them.*

Of course Ross was upset. He had thrown himself tirelessly into every exercise, mastered his power, and even used his sword skills to give me lessons. Meanwhile, I was the one who reaped the benefits while Ross was pushed to the sidelines. Ross lived for glory, but he also lived to become an officer in order to see his family. Both of those things had been given to me.

Little did he know it was because I had the same qualities of a villain.

214

"I don't want to be an officer," I muttered, then immediately regretted it.

Ross slammed his hands down on the table and stood up so abruptly that his plate tipped over, roasted potatoes rolling across the wood. "Oh, is that *right?*" he practically snarled. "You don't want to be an officer? Wow, don't you deserve *so much sympathy.*" He spun to face the rest of the table, who had caught wind of our conversation and had fallen silent. "Did you hear that everyone? Poor Aila doesn't *like* being an officer. Doesn't she have *such a hard life?*"

No one responded. They all just stared at Ross and me with wide eyes. He threw me a disgusted look. "I'm done here." His angry gaze swept across the rest of the table, and everyone quickly returned their eyes to their plates as Ross stepped over the bench.

I suddenly remembered all the things I had trusted to Ross, all the secrets he knew about me, and I panicked, jolting to my feet. "Wait—"

"Oh, don't worry," Ross said, his voice dripping with contempt. "I won't spill your little secrets. Trust me, I know guilt is a worse punishment than anything Brone could do to you."

I knew that, too, more than he could understand.

"So I'll leave you with this." He leaned forward, dropping his voice so only I could hear his next words. "As of this morning, mine isn't the only life you've ruined."

I grew very still. *Ross knew about Landis.* There was no other explanation.

"Brone made an announcement right before you came." Ross's voice was trembling, and with dread I realized it wasn't because of anger. "Landis is dead."

It felt like someone had punched me in the gut, knocking all the air from my lungs. No wonder Ross was so angry. He had lost the position of glory, the position he had worked so hard for, but he had also lost a friend, a boy who he had eaten lunch with, a roommate, maybe even a bunkmate.

And all of this was because of me.

"No." The word slipped between my lips as a strangled gasp.

215

No. I couldn't do this. Not today, not after last night, not when everything in my world was already fading to dust. My gaze flicked to June, who was watching us with an unreadable expression.

"She doesn't know, but she'll find out," Ross spat. "I guess it just depends from who."

He leaned back, and for a moment, I saw past the armor of glory and bluster to the broken boy underneath. Then he turned around and stalked away, leaving me to stare after him in horror.

Ross had lost one friend and broken ties with another. And just like him, I had seen the last real thing I had shatter into pieces right before my eyes.

He was right. Guilt was the worst punishment one could ever have.

22

AILA

When I reached Jon's cell door, I hesitated before sliding the panel open. I couldn't help it. The prospect of facing the boy I'd given so much hope to, only to steal it away selfishly, left me sick with dread. But I owed Jon an explanation, even if I didn't share the entire truth.

I didn't have anything better to do. The second Ross had disappeared, stalking through the doors of the Common Area without a backwards glance, I'd hurried off in the opposite direction. I didn't have the courage to face June and the questions that she was clearly waiting to ask. After wandering aimlessly through the halls, I worked up the nerve to turn in the direction of the Exceptional cells.

But the second I slid open the panel covering the metal slot, I regretted my decision. Jon's eyes widened in recognition, and he shot off his bed toward the door.

"You're here! What happened? Is Storm okay? Why didn't you rescue me?"

I opened my mouth to respond, but the words were stuck in my throat as more and more frantic questions poured from Jon's mouth.

"Did you guys give up? Did your plan fail? Where's Storm?" His eyes widened with horror. "Wait—what happened to him? Is he captured? Is he okay? Is he—"

"Jon," I interrupted. He fell silent, staring at me with wide, anxious eyes. "Storm is okay. He...he was able to escape."

That much Brone had told me when I stopped by his office during my aimless wandering earlier today. I had asked him which of the boys were captured, and the answer left a pit in my stomach. Chase was imprisoned in the basement of the Olum, all because of me.

"Wait, what?" Jon's voice pulled me back to the present. "What do you mean, escape?"

"Things didn't go according to plan last night," I said, my voice quavering. "We were discovered. Storm managed to get away, but Chase—his friend—was captured."

Jon sank onto the floor, his gaze hollow. "What about you?" His eyes narrowed as he realized the validity of his question. "Why aren't you in a cell?"

My voice caught in my throat. "I—"

"If you were discovered, the Expos should've figured out that you were working against them," Jon continued, his voice rising. "Why are you able to walk free?"

Automatic suspicion must've run in the family. Except this time, I deserved every ounce of skepticism he was throwing at me.

"What happened?" Jon demanded. "What did you do?"

I thought of Storm's furious, broken, betrayed expression. I leaned away, tears of guilt pricking my eyes. "I'm sorry," I said, the words coming out as barely more than a whisper.

"What did you do to them?" Jon shouted.

"I didn't want this to happen," I insisted. "I'm sorry, please understand—"

"What happened?" Jon's voice was wild with panic. "*What did you do?*"

I couldn't bear it. I slammed the panel closed on his questions and retreated down the hall, trying to escape my shame.

I would've rather faced Brone with all my lies laid bare than face Chase in the dungeons, and yet I somehow managed to muster the courage to visit him. I spent the entire descent down the stairs and the corridor trying to convince myself that it needed to be done. But the second I rounded the corner and caught the glimpse of the row of cells, reminding me of my conversation with Landis just a few days prior, I got cold feet.

Before I could turn around, one of the guards spotted me and shot me a questioning look. She was the same one from a few days before. "Landis isn't here."

She said it flippantly, like he was out spending the day at the market. I had to swallow the lump that formed in my throat before I could speak. "I know. I'm here to talk to the boy who was captured yesterday." It hurt, the reminder that Chase was yet another prisoner locked up so I could stay safe.

Yet another reminder of my selfishness.

The guard exchanged a word with her partner, probably explaining that I was an officer with authorization, before she started down the hall and beckoned for me to follow. My limbs locked. This was my last chance to leave before I would be forced into a conversation with Chase.

But I couldn't do it. I had to let him know what I'd done, the truth behind why he was locked up. And maybe if he wasn't too angry, I'd be able to convince him to join the Expos and spare his life.

The guard glanced over her shoulder to make sure I was following, and I hurried to catch up. We stopped in front of a cell in the middle of the hall, not far from where they had kept Landis. The guard looked back at me.

"He's asleep."

I peered through the bars at Chase, who was curled into a ball on top of what could hardly pass as a bed, even in the Olum. He looked almost peaceful lying there, as if he wasn't sleeping in a prison cell during one of the darkest moments of his life. That's one of the things I remembered about Chase from our childhood: his ability to make the best out of any situation.

My gaze flicked back to the guard. Maybe it was a sign that this conversation wasn't meant to take place. "That's okay, I can just come back late—"

219

The guard yanked her sword out of its scabbard and banged it on the metal bars three times, so hard that the sound rang throughout the entire floor.

"Oh, you didn't have to—" I started guiltily, but Chase was already stirring. The guard nodded at me curtly and started off down the hall, back to her regular post.

So maybe this conversation was supposed to happen after all.

I glanced back at Chase apprehensively, just in time to see his head snap up and his eyes fly to me.

"Aila?" he asked, his voice thick with confusion.

I sucked in a horrified breath. There was a large cut on his forehead, just above his right eye, and dried blood crusted his face around the wound. I reached out, as if to touch it, but of course he was on the other side of the cell, so I settled for wrapping my fingers around the bars.

"Chase, you're hurt."

"Am I really?" Chase smirked, lifting a hand to feel the edges of the wound with gentle fingers. "Hey, it isn't bleeding anymore. That's...nice."

I swallowed. There wasn't anything *nice* about this situation, and we both knew it. "They didn't give you a bandage?"

Chase laughed, but the sound was hollow. "Of course not. I'm in a dungeon, not a top-rate medical center. And I'm probably going to end up dead anyway. I don't think the Expos care whether it's from blood loss or...something else."

My hands tightened around the bars.

"It doesn't hurt anymore, anyway," Chase said, standing. I didn't need June to tell that he was lying; his wince gave it away. "Hey, I got to sleep last night. Haven't been doing much of that recently."

It was a feeble attempt to make me feel better, and it failed utterly. Instead, I was just left to wonder why Chase wasn't asking me where Storm was, or why I wasn't behind bars like him.

Suddenly, I couldn't hold it in any longer. "Chase, I'm sorry."

Chase met my gaze, but I couldn't look into his hazel eyes for long. I dropped my head, my eyes watering.

"I came here to tell you that it's all my fault," I said, my voice trembling. "All of it. Brone saw us entering the Olum, and Storm and I ran into him, and then I-I—"

"I know."

My head jerked up. "What?"

"I know what happened," Chase said slowly. "When suddenly put into a risky situation, you gave in and pretended to be on the Expos' side. Storm just barely managed to escape, and the entire plan was ruined."

A thousand questions flooded my thoughts. If he knew, why hadn't he said something before? Why was he still talking to me? Why wasn't he looking at me the way Storm did last night, with an expression so full of hate?

But instead, what came out was, "How?"

Chase let out a breath, rolling a loose stone around the floor with the toe of his boot. "I don't tell many people about my power," he said at last. "They know I have one, but barely anyone knows what it is. I don't...I don't want people to feel like they can use me."

I remained silent. I didn't want to break this moment with my words, which seemed to be getting me into nothing but trouble.

"The thing is, I...I can sense stuff."

"What?"

"I know, it sounds stupid, but I don't know how else to put it. I can sort of...tell when something is wrong, or when someone is lying, or when something bad is going to happen." Chase shrugged almost bashfully. "It's like intuition, but..."

"It's always right," I finished quietly. Chase nodded.

I released the bars and stepped away, my mind spinning. I opened my mouth, then shut it before trying again. "So—" I struggled for words. "You knew all along the plan was going to fail, and you didn't tell us?" The words sounded more accusatory than I intended them to be, but I had to know.

When Chase shook his head, I breathed a sigh of relief. "It's not like that. I knew something would go wrong, but I didn't know what." He dropped his head, but not before I caught a glimpse of regret on his face. "I thought that, whatever it was, we'd be able to push through it. But as soon as I stepped through the door and was caught by the Expos, I knew I'd made a mistake. I knew you and Storm had run into trouble, and I knew Storm had somehow escaped." Chase glanced quickly up at me. "And I knew you were feeling guilty, like you'd just done something terrible."

I swallowed, my throat dry as I struggled to make sense of what he was saying. "And you could tell that Storm was okay?" Chase nodded. "And that Jon wasn't free?" Another nod. "That's why you were always making the decisions, why you rose up in the ranks of the Insurgence, isn't it? You could tell what would work, what would make people happy, if you would be able to reach the Exceptional before the Expos did—" I stopped short as an impossible thought jumped into my mind. I stared at Chase.

He stared back, waiting.

Finally, I whispered, "You knew it was me."

Chase didn't need any more clarification. He nodded.

I elaborated anyway, needing to be certain it was true. "The day we captured Jon in Ferrol. You knew I was one of the Expos. You knew I was lying when I told you and Storm I was a prisoner. You knew all along." Chase held my gaze for several seconds, then I whispered, "And you still trusted me."

"Aila," Chase said fiercely. He stepped up to the bars and wrapped his fingers around them tightly. "I don't regret a single decision I made when it comes to you. I don't regret still considering you my friend, I don't regret trusting you, and I will *never* regret forgiving you. Do you understand? You don't have to feel guilty anymore."

I shook my head, backing away. I didn't deserve an ounce of his forgiveness, and yet he kept giving it to me without hesitation. Without regret.

"You wouldn't even *be* here if it weren't for me," I whispered.

"And if it weren't for you, I never would've been taken away to the Insurgence Base. I never would've been able to rescue all of the Exceptionals. I never would've met Storm or been able to help him."

I fell silent. His words rang true, but they did nothing to excuse my mistakes.

222

"You should hate me." My voice was hollow. "I messed up *everything*."

"We all make mistakes, Aila," Chase responded quietly. "Everyone makes mistakes."

Yes, but not everyone's mistakes landed their friends in prison. Repeatedly. I opened my mouth to tell him so, but he continued before I could speak.

"It's not about the mistakes we make, but about what each person does about them."

I met Chase's sincere hazel eyes through the bars, and in that exact moment, I knew I didn't have to bother telling Chase he should join the Expos. He would never take me up on the offer.

Chase's fingers dropped from the bars and took a step back. "What are you going to do about your mistakes?"

Footsteps came from the far end of the corridor, and one glance confirmed that the guard was coming to retrieve me. I looked back at Chase, whose calm expression was a stark contrast to the emotions warring within me.

I shook my head frantically. "I-I can't do anything."

Remorse flashed through Chase's eyes before he took a step back, dropping his gaze. "Goodbye, Aila." His voice held no distaste, just a warmth that I didn't deserve.

"Chase—" I lurched toward him.

"I'm glad…" He trailed off, lifting his gaze to meet mine. His eyes welled with gratitude. "I'm glad I got to see you again, to forgive you in person. Did you know that was the one thing I wanted most in life? To tell you that I didn't blame you?"

I shook my head. I couldn't speak. I could hardly even see Chase past the tears that had sprung suddenly to my eyes.

Chase smiled sadly. "You should probably go now."

This was goodbye. Not the kind of goodbye we from two nights ago, a goodbye filled with hope and wonder and possibilities. This goodbye felt forced. Final. I knew I should say something, knew I should do something, but I found myself tearing my gaze away from Chase's hazel eyes and hurrying down the corridor with nothing but a whispered farewell.

I couldn't sleep that night, despite the softness of my bed and the press of exhaustion behind my eyes. My conversation with Chase kept rolling through my head, his final question echoing loudest of all. *What are you going to do about your mistakes?* I'd told him that I couldn't do anything, and that was true. I couldn't break him and Jon out of the Olum, and even if I did, where would I go? The Insurgence would never accept me after what I did, and it wasn't like I could roam free with the Exceptional mark so obvious on my hand.

It was ironic. The only place I would be accepted was here, at the Olum, right with all the other liars and villains. I was a traitor, and not even Chase with his connections to the Insurgence could prove otherwise. Even if he tried, he'd said himself that his words might mean nothing because of his choice to run away and rescue Jon.

My thoughts screeched to a stop.

When Chase left the Insurgence, he did so knowing that he was throwing all of the trust he had built out the window. But he did it anyway, for Storm. Not because it benefitted him in any way, not because he would experience any type of glory. In fact, quite the opposite was true.

He did it simply because he unselfishly wanted to help a friend in need.

I sat up and leaned against the wall, stunned. Here I was, getting people into trouble and refusing to help them so I could save myself. And then there was Chase, who was willing to be locked in a cell if it meant he could help a friend in need.

In that moment, I knew I couldn't keep sitting around. I jumped to my feet and yanked an empty pack from beneath my bed. I began to shove it full with clothes, shoes, the journal I'd found in my desk drawer but hadn't even opened. I filled it with anything of value I could find in my small room, because this time, when I left the Olum, I wouldn't be coming back to stay.

I thought of Landis and our conversation about guilt. All this time, I hadn't been defeating the monster at all. I'd just been trying to run from it. As I stood there in the darkness of my room, tightening the straps on my pack and forming the shaky outline of a plan, I decided that was going to change.

Once more, Chase's question rang through my head. *What are you going to do about your mistakes?*

This time, I knew the answer.

23

STORM

Fire shot from my hands and slammed into the wall with such force that I launched backward. I crashed into the opposite wall, the pillar of fire disappearing as quickly as it had come.

An ominous silence settled over the cell, broken only by my ragged breaths. I would've thought I had imagined the whole incident if it wasn't for the two identical scorch marks on the wall across from me. My hands no longer tingled, and when I looked at them, there appeared no logical way that a pillar of fire could have possibly exploded from my hands.

No logical way, unless I had just manifested my power.

For the first time since I'd returned to the Base, I felt a flicker of something other than defeat. I pushed myself off the wall and strode into the center of the cell, facing the bars. Across the corridor and through another wall of bars, I could see the back wall of the cell across from mine. *My next target.* I shook out my hands and planted my feet.

My eyes dropped closed. I wrapped my hands into fists. Sucked in a breath. Concentrated. My palms began to tingle painfully again, like they were burning.

Then I planted one foot forward and threw out my arms, palms out. There was a roar like a thundering waterfall, and my eyes flew open just in time to see two columns of fire burst from my hands. I was ready this time, and when the constant streams of flame hit the opposite wall, I leaned into the force. I didn't feel pain anymore. I just felt power.

I wrapped my hands back into fists, and the flame stopped, leaving a smattering of scorch marks on the hard stone wall.

I couldn't help but laugh. Aris would be so jealous when I told him.

I spent the next hour experimenting with my new ability. When I shot out a constant stream of flame, it seemed to have a range of about fifteen feet. By clenching and unclenching my fists, I could send short jets of fire bursting from my hands. If I held my hand palm up and cupped it, a swirling, sparking ball of fire would form, and I spent way longer than necessary making targets for myself by scorching a wall and then practicing my aim with the balls of fire.

But my elation only lasted so long before I remembered Chase, and Jon, and Aila's betrayal. I scowled and kicked at the bars, as if that would somehow free me. I had my power, but I was still trapped.

Footsteps strode down the hall, and I quickly shoved my hands into my pockets. Moments later, Chadrick swept around the corner carrying a plate of food, which he kicked through a slot at the bottom of the bars.

"Eat quickly," he said gruffly. "It's late, and I still have to supervise you on your walk after this."

I glared at him and proceeded to eat as slowly as I could, which was pretty impressive given how badly my stomach was growling. Although it was hard to get a sense of time in the windowless dungeon, I had a feeling Chadrick had conveniently skipped a few meals.

Chadrick paced back and forth on the other side of the bars as I ate. He probably wished anyone else in the estate would take his job right now, and I couldn't blame him. I supposed that's what he got for having such a good power. Not that his power was anything compared to mine.

I opened my mouth to tell him so, then froze as realization dawned on me. Chadrick didn't know about my power. No one did. And that meant I had an element of surprise. Sure, he could still render me motionless with a single touch, but if I could catch him off guard while we were in a deserted hall...

"What?" Chadrick snapped, catching a glimpse of me.

I realized my mouth was still open, my fork hanging in the air, and I quickly finished the last bite before standing. "I'm done."

Chadrick didn't need to be told twice. He set my plate aside and unlocked my cell. The door swung open, and I considered lunging for him right then. But I hardly had time to process the thought before Chadrick stepped forward and grabbed my arm. I scowled. By keeping constant contact, he would be able to use his ability whenever necessary. He was too good at this job.

Commander White had said I could have a fifteen minute walk. That would be more than enough time for Chadrick to let his guard down. Until then, I would have to remain on perfect behavior.

The first five minutes of the walk were spent in a stony silence, and as each agonizing second passed, I inwardly urged Chadrick to loosen his clutch. But he insisted on keeping an iron grip on my arm, occasionally giving it a sharp tug to direct me around a corner. It was becoming abundantly clear that he wasn't about to just let go. I was going to have to make the first move. Slowly, I curled my hands into fist and felt them begin to burn.

I waited until we were down a quiet hall, one that was lined with classrooms that would be empty at this late hour. I dropped back, so I was a fraction of a step behind Chadrick, then tripped and stumbled into him. He was thrown off balance and released my arm to steady himself against the wall.

I was free. Chadrick's eyes widened, and he lunged for me, but I dodged his hands and planted my hot palms on his shoulders, shoving him back.

Pain and confusion flashed across his face as my power seared him. I didn't give him time to process what was happening. I drew back a fist and punched him directly in the side of his head. He crumpled, and I caught him just in time, lowering him gently to the floor.

I brushed off my hands and looked down at Chadrick with a grim smile. Who said you could only use your power to get things done? I had plenty of skills from my life spent stealing and escaping that had helped me come out on top once again.

I started down the hall at a brisk, quiet jog, slipping past the Refectory and through the deserted corridors. My heart began to pound, excitement shooting through my veins like bolts of electricity. The closer the exit became, the faster I ran, until I was flat-out sprinting, my boots slapping against the ground.

Three halls left. Two halls.

One.

My eyes locked on the door. On freedom.

Something slammed into my chest, shoving me into the wall of the corridor. Air flew out my lungs, and I was silenced mid-shout as a cloth smothered my mouth.

Suddenly, the world around me disappeared. The stone walls faded away, replaced by an image of Chase in an Expo uniform, his hazel eyes telling me everything would be fine as he covered my mouth with the same type of cloth.

I snapped back to reality and sucked in a wheezing breath. This time, it was Aris holding the cloth, and instead of blacking out, my limbs went slack. Aris stumbled to catch me, but did little to stop my rough fall to the floor. I tried desperately to jerk away from him, but my body refused to respond.

The startled confusion in my gaze must've been obvious, because Aris dropped to a crouch next to me. "After you and Chase escaped, Commander White started posting guards at the door each night with instructions to disable anyone who tried to run away." He waved the cloth in front of my face, then pocketed it. "It has a concoction of gelsemium plant, and works exactly like Chadrick's power."

I glared at Aris, my hatred so strong that I couldn't even muster the words to respond. I should've known he'd be the last thing standing between me and my freedom. Between me and *Jon's* freedom. My jaw clenched in fury.

"How did you get away from Chadrick, anyway?" Aris frowned down at me, his tone casual, as if we were just making pleasant conversation over the breakfast table.

Not that we'd ever had a pleasant conversation.

229

"Get away from me," I bit out, my voice quivering with rage. "You don't even know how big of a mistake you're making."

"Commander White assigned him to watch you because of his power," Aris continued, as if I had never spoken. "He should've been able to stop you before you got away. How'd you do it?"

I hesitated, anger rolling through me, but what did it matter? The news would be out the second Chadrick woke up anyway. "I manifested my power," I growled.

Aris's eyebrows shot up. "Really?"

"It's a fire power," I muttered. "Chadrick didn't know, so I thought..." The fight drained out of me as I released a breath. "I should've planned on you being here to ruin my life, as always."

My anger at the situation suddenly clashed with the realization of what this meant. I was out of secrets, out of tricks. This was it. The Insurgence would never trust me again. I would spend the rest of my life locked in a cell, alone with my guilt and the knowledge of what I could've done differently.

My gaze traveled to the door, just a few feet away. I was so close. *So close.*

I'm sorry, Jon.

Aris rocked back on his heels, studying me with a surprisingly placid expression. In a normal situation, I would be disappointed by his lack of jealousy toward my power, but tonight was different. Something seemed...off. There was something wrong about the fact that Aris wasn't filling every spare second by bragging about my capture or spitting out condescending comments. He opened his mouth to say something, then seemed to think better of it and looked away.

I blinked in surprise. Aris *never* held his tongue. That was the one thing we had in common.

After a moment, Aris stood, darting a glance down the empty corridor. "The guard I'm working with went to circle through the other halls, but he should be back in five minutes. By then, the herb will have worn off, and we'll take you to Commander White."

I didn't bother giving him a response, and instead shifted my gaze to the ceiling. I wondered what Chase was doing now, what Jon was doing. I'd never gotten the chance to give either of them a proper goodbye, all because I wasn't smart enough to anticipate the fact that Commander White would set up guards.

"Storm?" Aris's voice startled me from my thoughts. I couldn't remember ever hearing him refer to me by my first name, especially not in such a calm tone.

"What?" I muttered, not even looking at him.

Aris took a deep, shaky breath and dropped to his knees next to me. "What happened to Chase?"

"Why, your precious commander didn't tell you?" I snapped.

Aris didn't rise to the bait, just shook his head once. "All we know is that you and Chase ran away, and a few nights later, you came back…alone. No one knows what happened, why you left, or…or if Chase is—" Aris abruptly fell silent, and I was startled by the worry lacing his tone. I had thought him incapable of feeling anything but superior.

"Chase is alive." *For now*, I thought, but I left that part unsaid. I was about to leave it at that but was once again struck with the realization that it didn't matter anymore, and the words came spilling out. "We went to the Olum to rescue my brother. We met up with Chase's childhood friend, and he said we should trust her, but she—she betrayed us. Chase was captured, and I just barely escaped."

It wasn't the whole story, but I couldn't bring myself to admit to Aris that I shared part of the blame for the failed mission. Aris just stared at me with wide eyes, seeming to understand what I had been unable to say. Chase was alive, but he might not be for long.

Minutes ticked by in silence, and with a start, I realized I could move my fingers and toes. Aris must've seen my thumbs twitching because he stood up and offered me a hand. A thousand ideas flashed through my head, most of them involving me yanking Aris to the ground before making a break for it. The Insurgence Base key was still tucked away in my pocket.

But something in me let him help me up, and kept me standing there in front of him. "Are you going to turn me in?"

Confliction crossed Aris's expression. "What are you planning to do?"

"I'm going back to the Olum," I said, my voice hardening with determination. "I messed up, and I need to fix my mistakes. I need to rescue Chase and my brother, whatever it takes."

An agonizing second scraped by, then Aris shook his head. "No, I won't turn you in," he responded slowly, like each word was a struggle to force past his lips. "You're doing the right thing. Chase needs to be rescued."

"I...thanks." I stared at Aris for a moment longer before withdrawing my hidden key and unlocking the door. Out of the corner of my eye, I saw Aris roll his eyes, a bit of his true character creeping back in.

The lock clicked, and I reached to open the door, but a thought struck me. "What will you say, once they learn I've escaped?"

Aris patted the pouch containing the cloth. "I'll say you stole this and used it on me, and by the time I recovered, you were long gone."

A shout came from several corridors away. "Aris! Quick, Chadrick's unconscious!"

"You should go." Aris all but pushed me forward.

"Wait." I quickly turned to face him. "I know it might be a lot to ask, but...now's as good a time as any to convince the Insurgence to attack the Expos." Aris frowned but remained silent as I gave him directions to the Olum. "Think about it," I said.

"I'll try," he responded uncertainly.

I smirked. "Try hard."

I didn't waste any more time throwing open the door and leading my horse out of the stables. I needed every spare second I could get.

Because the biggest thing between me and my mission was time.

24

AILA

Night was falling upon Laster, and I was growing worried.

I had been leaning against an abandoned stone building, staring down the dusty path that cut through the corner of the orchard and away from Laster, and waiting for the past twelve hours.

I'd easily slipped out of the Olum and had reached Laster not long after dawn. At first, I was fully prepared to continue through the town and across Rosan in search of the Insurgence, despite having a plan that no one but Storm would approve of. Then I realized that, after Storm told the Insurgence of Chase's capture, they would waste any time setting out for the Olum to rescue him. All I had to do was wait at the entrance of Laster and join them when they passed.

But I had been sitting here vigilantly for the entire day, only taking a break at midday to grab a bite for lunch, and I had seen no trace of the Insurgence. A few hours ago, I'd resorted to stopping those entering the town and asking if they had seen a large group of people traveling in this direction. Everyone had met my question with confusion, and as dusk fell and the streets grew empty, I felt anxiety begin to claw at my stomach.

It had been a few days since our failed mission, and I was sure Storm would've been able to reach the Insurgence by now, especially since—according to a stablehand—he had retrieved his horse from the stables. If the Insurgence wasn't at the Olum already, they should've been nearby. But maybe they weren't going to show up at all. Or maybe Storm hadn't made it back. Maybe he was injured and passed out in some ditch on the side of the road, or maybe the Expos had caught him after all and thrown him in a cell right next to Chase.

I gritted my teeth and forced myself to reign in my thoughts. If I went down the rabbit hole of worry any further, I'd be too crippled with anxiety to do anything. Blinking rapidly to ward off exhaustion, I stood up and moved to sit in the grass at the base of a fig tree. Then I fixed my attention once more on the road ahead of me. Storm was on his way, and the Insurgence army behind him. I had to believe it.

Because when it was me against the Expos, I needed all the hope I could get.

I snapped awake with a gasp. I hadn't meant to fall asleep, just lean my back against the tree to get more comfortable. But the stillness of the dark orchard and the exhaustion of many sleepless nights had lulled me under against my will.

For one wild second as my eyes adjusted to the bright morning light, I feared I'd missed Storm and the Insurgence entirely. But then the world slid into focus, and I realized I was completely wrong. Storm was towering over me, his palms pointed directly at my face.

And he looked livid.

A thousand questions stampeded through my head at once, but they were all silenced by the heat of Storm's glare. Something was wrong. Slowly, I pushed myself to my feet. Storm tracked my movement, lifting his arms to keep his palms directed at me.

"Storm, what are you—?" Something in his gaze made me stop, and without thinking, I twisted to the side just as a jet of fire exploded from his hands.

"*Traitor!*" Storm screamed, his voice raw with fury. The flames slammed into the ground where I had been standing moments before.

I froze. Had the fire just come from his *hands*?

Storm spun to face me, and I quickly came to my senses. I dove out of the way, narrowly avoiding a ball of fire. I hit the ground hard and rolled onto my back, gasping for air. Storm was already advancing toward me, the glowing orbs of fire cupped in his hands a stark contrast to his dark expression. The weight of the situation hit me like a speeding wagon.

"*Stop!*" I choked out, scrambling to avoid the ball of flame he threw in my direction.

But Storm continued to advance with slow, determined steps, throwing ball after sparking ball of fire in my direction. I was forced to roll and scramble on the ground to avoid his attacks. Panic clawed at my stomach, but I had the sense that Storm was holding back. If he really wanted to set me on fire, he would've done so already. He was taunting me.

Focus, Aila, focus! a voice screamed in the back of my head. I mustered up my strength and, as Storm launched the next blazing orb in my direction, leapt to my feet and spun out of the way. Storm growled something angrily, then froze.

I let out a breath of relief, my chest still heaving from the frantic scramble for survival. He couldn't see me. Yes, he apparently could now shoot fire from his hands, but that power had little effect if he couldn't see his target.

"Oh, so you're not just a traitor, but you're a coward now too?" Storm sneered. I remained silent as he furiously threw one of his balls of flame into the orchard.

It missed me by a mile, and I sagged with relief. He had no idea where I was.

But a grove of trees wasn't a place for him to be recklessly using his powers. I needed to draw him back into the open.

"You're worse than Brone!" he shouted. "At least everyone knows where his loyalties lie."

I gritted my teeth and took several steps backward until I cleared the orchard and crossed the dirt path to the empty strip of grass on the other side. Storm was still wandering through the fig trees, so I picked up a stone and lobbed it in his direction. His head jerked around, his eyes narrowing like an animal zeroing in on its prey.

"You ruined everything, Aila!" Storm yelled. He stepped out onto the road, punctuating his words by chucking another fireball in the direction from which I'd thrown the stone. But I was already moving, quietly circling toward him. His voice shook with rage. "You ruined *everything*. Our plan, Chase's future, my brother's life. All of it! People will die because of you, and it's *all your fault!*"

I clenched my jaw and lunged. Before Storm could react, I tackled him to the ground. His startled shout was muffled by the dirt as I not-so-gently planted my knee in the center of his back and pinned his wrists, palms down, to the ground. Storm writhed beneath my grip, but I dug my knee further into his back until he fell still, his chest heaving furiously. I let myself become visible again.

"I hate you," Storm spat, venom dripping from his voice.

"*You're* the one trying to kill me," I ground out.

"Don't you *dare* make this my fault." Storm began to fight again, twisting in my grasp.

"Stop it!" I yelled at him. "Just relax for one minute and *listen*, okay?"

Storm, of course, ignored my pleas and continued to try to jerk his hands out of my grasp. I gritted my teeth and fought back, straining to keep his palms face-down.

"You'll have to let up eventually," he said bitterly. "When you do, you'd better hope that you can run fast."

My blood ran cold at his words. Storm had always been insufferable, constantly complaining and quick to accuse, but now...he was different. He had let his hatred overcome him. The boy I'd pinned to the ground was different from the desperate brother I'd met in Laster.

"You can't stay angry at me forever," I said.

Storm fell still and barked out a humorless laugh. "Actually, I'm pretty sure I can."

"I know you're upset—"

"*Upset?*" Storm scoffed.

"—and I understand, but you and I both know anger won't rescue Chase and Jon. I was waiting here because I hoped we could work together to get them out of the Olum."

236

For the first time, Storm didn't clap back with a biting remark. When he spoke, some of the anger seemed to have disappeared from his voice. "I'm not stupid enough to believe your lies anymore." His voice shook. "I've learned from my mistakes."

"So have I!" I insisted desperately. "I want to fix my mistakes. But I need your help."

Storm was quiet again, and I hoped that meant he was considering my offer. But then he clenched his jaw, his head dropping back to the ground.

"I was scared, Storm," I said, frustrated. "I thought I was going to die."

"So you figured it's better Chase dies than you, is that it?" Storm snapped. "You haven't changed a bit since you were eight."

I felt panic begin to bubble in me. I was a fool to believe that Storm would help me. I should've expected this. "I lied to Brone," I said. "I lied to Brone, and I've spent every second since regretting it. But if you hurt me now and try to do this on your own, you'll spend the rest of your life regretting it. I don't care what happens after we rescue Chase. You can set me on fire all you want, but right now people are going to start dying if you don't calm down and work with me." I let out a breath, then said in a trembling voice, "Please."

Storm was silent for so long that I wondered if he'd fallen asleep, his head pressed against the rough grass on the ground. Then, he growled, "Fine."

My heart leapt. "What?"

"I said fine," he snapped. "I'll go with you. I'll stop trying to light you on fire, at least for now. Can you let me up?"

I hesitated, my eyes darting uncertainly to his hands, which I was still holding palm-down.

"I'm not lying, you know," he said irritably. "Unlike you, I don't go back on my word."

I gritted my teeth and shoved myself away from him, pacing back a few cautious yards as he stood and brushed himself off. Although Storm's gaze was still hard, I noticed the burning hatred in his eyes had subsided. Only then did I allow myself to breathe.

237

"Where's the rest of the Insurgence?" I said, my eyes darting around. The orchard and the road were as empty as they had been the entire day prior.

Storm let out a derisive laugh. "They're almost as bad as you," he muttered, although I didn't miss the hurt hidden underneath his sharp words. "They threw me in a cell as soon as I got back. Didn't even bother asking what happened to Chase. If I hadn't discovered my power, I would still be locked up in a prison by the people I used to trust."

So the Insurgence had turned their backs on Chase after all. Suddenly, they no longer seemed like the heroes I'd made them out to be. "That's terrible."

Storm's dark blue eyes met mine. "Seems like the world is full of liars and cheats these days, huh?"

I tore my gaze away. His words stung, because they were true.

"I don't need them," Storm continued, although his indifference was clearly forced. "I have my power now. I'm stronger than I was before. This time..." He chuckled, but it was a dark, mirthless sound. "This time I'll be able to stop anyone who gets in my way."

I found myself shaking as I crawled through the dark, narrow air shaft. Every time I returned to the Olum, it was like stepping back into a nightmare. Hopefully when I left later today, I would leave for good.

The shaft was as suffocating as the silence that had settled over Storm and me on our trip to the Olum. Tension hung over us like a thick cloud, and we'd moved toward our destination without a word. I'd attempted to break the silence once, sharing with him what Brone had told me about his past and Mila, but Storm snapped, "You know, I honestly don't care if some girl he knew died. It doesn't excuse what he did. He probably deserved it," and we lapsed back into silence.

Angry Storm was bad enough, and I was just grateful I didn't have to deal with Angry Storm in an air vent. He'd gone to search for another way into the Olum, an entrance that would be closer to the dungeons. He hadn't liked the idea of going after Chase and leaving me to rescue Jon, but when I pointed out he'd get nowhere near his brother without my power of invisibility, he grudgingly relented. But I could still tell he didn't trust me. He probably thought I was going to do something sadistic, like trap Jon in the air shaft instead of rescuing him.

I pressed on through the vent despite the tightness in my chest, knowing that if I stopped for even a second to catch my breath, it would risk the entire mission. We were playing it simple this time. No tricks, no diversions. Just get in, rescue Chase and Jon, and get out. I just hoped Storm wouldn't waste time attacking random Expos for revenge. It was the two of us in a sea of enemies, and we needed to be careful.

Finally, I reached the end of the shaft. After peering through the slots in the grate to make sure the coast was clear, I turned invisible and slipped toward the stairs leading to the lower level.

I was halfway to Jon's cell when I whipped around a corner and almost ran straight into Kala.

I bit back an instinctive shout of alarm and flattened myself to the wall, my heart thudding so loudly I was sure Kala would hear. But she brushed by, her attention completely fixed on the person she was talking to. I sucked in a breath. June.

Under normal circumstances, I would've let them pass and gone on my way, but something in June's expression made me pause. Something was wrong, and that's what caused me to peel off the wall and silently fall into step behind them.

Kala spoke first, her voice full of suspicion. "You're absolutely certain she said nothing to you? You're clearly her best friend here."

"I wouldn't lie to you." June's tone was etched with worry. "Aila's been avoiding me lately. She said nothing about escaping."

The hurt in her voice stabbed me harder than Ross's training sword ever could.

"Nothing at all?" Kala pressed, almost desperately. "Not even a mention of a location, or what she might be doing?"

A fresh pang of guilt shot through me. I understood now why June looked so anxious. I had never thought that when my disappearance was discovered, the weight of my actions would fall on the shoulders of my friends. I continued to follow them, waiting for June to admit the interest I had expressed in finding the rebels.

But June just slowed to a halt and turned to face Kala, her expression sincere. "I promise, I don't know where she is. I never thought Aila would do something like this. She's an *officer*. Are you sure she didn't just get lost or captured?"

I didn't need June's power to tell she was lying, and I felt a warm wave of gratitude. Tears pricked my eyes. June owed me absolutely nothing, and yet there she was, standing strong as ever, withholding information just to keep me safe. If only I had half her bravery.

Kala clenched her jaw in frustration, but it was clear she believed June. After several tense seconds, she drew herself up with a huff and said, "If you remember *anything*, anything at all, you'd be wise to bring that information to Brone's attention as quickly as possible. I'm sure you know what will happen if we discover you are keeping secrets from us."

June didn't even flinch as Kala spun around and stalked off down the corridor in the opposite direction from where I was standing. June stared until Kala disappeared around the corner, then turned in the opposite direction.

She froze. "Aila?"

No longer invisible, I took a step forward. June countered it with a step back, her eyes wide, and then she turned to run. I threw my arms out in panic. If she ran to tell Kala, the whole mission would be over.

"Wait! June, please."

June stopped, but her eyes still darted around wildly. Then, without warning, she grabbed my arm and pulled me through the closest door.

We found ourselves in a small, empty room that had probably been a storage closet once.

"What are you *doing* here?" June hissed. "If Brone catches you—"

"He won't," I said before she could voice my fears. "I'll be invisible. He'll have no idea."

"Not unless I tell him." There was a challenge in June's voice.

"We both know you're not going to," I responded, "because when you realized I ran away, you wished you had come with me." It was a gamble, but I saw surprise flash in June's eyes. "I just told the truth, didn't I?"

June let out an agitated sigh, her shoulders drooping. "Fine. But what difference does it make? We've got no more future out there than in here. We're *Exceptionals.*"

"We're not the only ones," I whispered eagerly. "I met people who are part of the Insurgence."

I didn't know what I expected. Surprise, or maybe even excitement, but what I got instead was a blank, utterly disappointing stare.

"The what?" June said, unimpressed.

"The-the Insurgence," I said, slightly dumbfounded. "You know, the rebels Brone warns everyone about before we start going on missions?"

Recognition flashed across June's gaze. "They have a name? Sounds a little ambitious for a small group of renegades."

"Not small," I said. "Big. Way bigger than Brone let on. Or so Chase and Storm told me."

June frowned. "Are those the boys who broke into the Olum with you the other night?"

"You know about that?"

"I'm not supposed to," June said, "but what can I say? Word gets around." Suddenly, understanding dawned on her. "That's why you're here. You're back to rescue the one who got captured, aren't you? And if you succeed, they'll let you join the Insurgence."

There were a few more complications than that, namely one called Storm, but I didn't feel the need to get into the specifics.

"Yeah, I'm here with the other boy, Storm, and we're trying to break his younger brother and Chase out." With a start, I realized just how long this conversation was taking. I didn't have more time to waste. "Storm is heading to the dungeons right now. Do you know where those are?"

I had surprised June, but little by little I saw her confidence creeping back, until she was the girl I had first met on the rock wall all

241

those days ago. She knew what I was asking of her, but when she spoke, her voice was hardened with resolve. "Tell me what I need to do."

25

STORM

I didn't feel good about my plan.

I hurried through the halls of the Olum, Aila's brief directions echoing in my head. *Take the first left. Then another left. Then the second right after the double doors.* The moment I spotted a staircase leading down, lit only by a few flickering lanterns, I knew with certainty I'd found my way to the dungeons. It hadn't been hard, but I knew things could only get worse from here. My plan had been to just walk up to the guards and attack them with fire until they handed over the keys, but the further I strode down the corridor, the more I began to question this method of attack. Aila had said there were two guards, and I didn't know if I could fight both at once. My power didn't solve every problem; I hadn't even been able to defeat Aila.

I was still trying to come up with a better idea when I heard footsteps traveling rapidly from the direction of the stairs. My heart leapt in my chest, and I lunged toward a door embedded in the stone wall. Throwing myself inside, I pulled the door closed just as two men rounded the corner. I dropped into a crouch and peered through the keyhole, forcing myself to breathe steadily, so I could hear what they were saying.

"...hate having guard duty in the afternoon," one of the men was saying in irritation. "Think we can bribe the others into a double shift?"

I let out a frustrated breath. It sounded like they were switching shifts, which meant I would have to wait for the other guards to be relieved of their positions and pass me before I could move from my hiding place.

"We've tried that before," the other guard muttered exasperatedly as they approached my limited view through the keyhole. "Get over it and do your job."

I caught a glimpse of the lower halves of the guards as they passed and continued down the hall, one striding briskly, the other strolling lazily behind.

"I just really wanted to be in on the action in case Brone sent groups to search for that Aila girl," the first guard complained. "How can I help when I'm stuck guarding a single prisoner? He's going to be dead tomorrow anyway."

I sucked in a breath. *Dead tomorrow.* The words hit me with a spear of panic.

"Grow up," the second guard snapped back.

The first began to respond, but his voice faded away as they disappeared around another corner. My heart was still pounding, and I sucked in anxious breaths. Brone knew of Aila's escape. Chase would be dead tomorrow. We were all nearly out of time.

I stood up and twisted around, taking stock of the room I was in for the first time. At first glance, I thought it was a closet. Various items were arranged neatly on shelves that stretched across three walls of the little room. A coil of rope lay on one shelf. A pile of what looked like clothes sat on the shelf below. My eyes skipped to the next shelf and froze when I saw the leather pack that had been dropped there. I recognized that pack.

It belonged to Chase.

I darted across the room and snatched it up, clutching it in my hands. My throat tightened, and I saw a memory of Chase standing in his room, exasperatedly questioning why I hadn't kept my head down as I shoved last minute items into our packs. I had ruined the plan even then, but he still stuck with me. In the end, it had landed him here, in a jail cell in the basement of the Olum.

I let out my breath and flipped open the pack. Everything lay in there, untouched. I pushed aside Chase's spare pair of clothes and multiple dust bombs, then sucked in a breath. A dagger with a gleaming gold hilt lay at the bottom, encased in a smooth leather sheath. I didn't know when Chase got it. Maybe he'd stolen it from Commander White's office, along with the key and the dust bombs. Whatever it was, he had probably been saving it for if he got in a sticky situation at the Olum. In the end, it hadn't made a difference the day Chase was captured, but it could make one now. I tucked the dagger into my pocket.

I slipped a dust bomb in my pocket as well before flipping closed the flap and swinging the pack onto my shoulders. I turned around and scanned the room again. This must've been where they kept prisoners' belongings after they were arrested. Once more, my eyes landed on the coil of rope, but this time an idea sprung into my head.

When I moved out into the hall again, it was with a fully formed plan and a renewed sense of confidence.

I peered around the final corner of the corridor before flattening myself back against the wall as one of the guards' eyes traveled lazily in my direction. I couldn't get caught now. Too much rested on the success of this mission. I waited several seconds before looking again. To my relief, the guards had shifted in the opposite direction, giving me a chance to size them up.

The younger guard one slouched against the wall, kicking at the ground and muttering to himself in obvious discontent. The older one's hand rested on his sword, and he stood upright and alert even as the minutes dragged on. His eyes swept in a constant circle, and as they turned in my direction once more, I whipped my head back around the corner.

Pressing myself back against the cool stone wall, I let out a slow breath. One hand curled around the dust bomb in my pocket, and I used my free hand to pull a piece of fabric up over my mouth. I had torn it from one of the shirts in the closet. I bent down and snatched up part of the coil of rope, which I had sawed into a smaller piece using Chase's dagger. I inhaled one last time, cocked my arm, then spun around the corner and lobbed two dust bombs toward the guards as hard as I could.

I caught them completely by surprise. The older one noticed first, and opened his mouth to call out a warning, but instead inhaled a mouthful of dust as the bombs exploded. Both men cried out and shielded themselves from the dust, but I just darted through the cloud, narrowing my eyes and breathing through my mask.

I was in position in five seconds flat.

The cloud settled, and the older guard hacked up dust, wiping at the dirt that now coated his face. He blinked several times, unsheathed his sword, then darted a glance toward the younger guard. He froze at the sight that greeted him.

I had one arm wrapped around the younger guard's neck, holding a dagger to his throat.

With my free hand, I reached up and pulled down my mask. "Don't move," I commanded. The guard instinctively took a step closer, and I barked, "Don't! Or he gets hurt."

My hostage whimpered at my words, and I smothered a smirk. Brone needed a better screening process for his guards; he hadn't even put up a fight.

"You won't kill him," the older guard shouted, although he had frozen in place at my warning. His eyes darted down the corridor from which I had come, as if seeking help.

The guard was right, but he didn't need him to know that. "Are you sure?" I pressed the dagger harder against my captive's throat, not enough to draw blood, but enough to force out another scared whimper.

"You're outnumbered," the older guard said, turning back to me with a glare. He was clearly furious that this had happened on his shift.

"Am I?"

My rhetorical questions weren't amusing him. "It's two to one."

"You don't know who you're dealing with."

The guard let out a dry, condescending chuckle. "You're just a boy."

The words had barely left his mouth when I jerked my free hand up. A ball of fire exploded from my palm, missing him by inches and leaving a scorch mark on the wall. His eyes shot wide, a terrified understanding spreading across his face.

"Drop your sword," I told him.

The weapon clattered to the ground.

I let out a breath of relief. *I'm coming, Chase*, I called silently.

"I'm going to tie you up, and if either of you move, I'll use my power again. Next time, I won't miss."

I kept my eyes trained on the older guard as I bent to pick up one of the lengths of rope I had dropped on the ground. I pulled the dagger from the younger man's throat and couldn't help but feel a twinge of guilt as he sagged in visible relief. Hastily, I bound his feet together and tied his hands behind his back before pulling a strip of cloth from my back pocket. My fingers fumbled as I tied the gag into a knot at the back of his head. I couldn't seem to move fast enough as I snatched up the remaining pieces of rope and bound the older guard.

I grabbed both of their swords from their scabbards and tossed them off to the side, out of reach from the guards. I snatched the ring of keys from the older guard's pocket and sprinted off down the hall.

I passed empty cell after empty cell, and was beginning to feel a wave of sickening dread when I spotted an unmoving figure curled up on one of the cots.

"*Chase*," I choked out. My throat tightened suddenly with a mixture of relief and regret. I rushed up to the bars and, in a louder voice, repeated, "Chase!"

No response. I stepped closer, fumbling with the key ring when noise down the hall caught my attention.

Somehow, the younger guard had maneuvered to where I'd deposited his sword just a few feet away. He had managed to use the edge of the blade to slice through the ropes binding his feet and was now trying to cut off the ties of his hands by sliding the blade between his knees and his bonds. I guess I hadn't given him enough credit before.

"Hey!" I shouted, and started running down the hall in his direction. I clenched my hands into fists, and they began to burn.

The guard's eyes shot wide with terror, and with some difficulty he scrambled to his feet and took off down the hall, his hands still bound. Moments later, he disappeared around the corner.

I growled in frustration as I slowed to a stop in front of the remaining guard, a ball of fire swirling in my palm. I didn't have time to go after him, but at least I could keep from making the same mistake twice. I snatched up the two blades and hurried back to Chase's cell.

I dropped the swords to the ground and started sifting through the ring of keys again. There were at least thirty, maybe more, all of them different shapes and sizes. I chose one at random and fitted it into the lock, twisting it. The metal shrieked in protest, and I quickly pulled the key back out. Wrong one. I desperately chose the next key and shoved it into the lock, twisting furiously. The lock didn't budge. There were too many keys. I didn't have enough time—

I heard footsteps and spun around, expecting to find the older guard had miraculously escaped and was coming to attack me. Instead, a girl strode quickly down the corridor in my direction. Judging by the look on her face, she knew exactly who I was.

"Stop! Don't come any closer!" My voice cracked in panic as I balled my hands into fists. *I didn't have time.*

The girl stopped in her tracks, her eyes flitting warily to my hands. Somehow, she knew about my power. "You don't want to hurt me."

"But I will," I said, bending to reach one of the guard's swords. "I *will.*"

It wasn't exactly true, but I needed her to leave. I needed to get Chase out of here, and *now.* My heart thudded, and suddenly I found it difficult to take a deep breath.

She must've sensed the panic rising within me, because she rolled her eyes and said, "Relax." Suddenly I felt ridiculous, standing there with a sword clutched in one hand, the key ring dangling from the other. "I'm on your side, Storm. Aila sent me."

"Aila?" I tightened my grip on the sword. "She never told me about having an accomplice in the building."

248

"And she never told me that she was going to run away, or that she didn't trust Brone, or that she knew people who were part of the Insurgence. Yet here we are."

I winced. This girl sure knew a lot of things she shouldn't.

"Look, I'm here to help, so stop being stupid and put the sword down."

"The name-calling isn't making me want to trust you."

The girl let out an exasperated sigh and stepped forward. I tensed, but she just grabbed the keys from my hand and sifted through them before singling one out. She held it up for me to see. "This one will unlock the cell."

I narrowed my eyes. "Give me one good reason why I should believe you."

For the first time, the lighthearted annoyance in the girl's gaze was replaced by dead sincerity. "I promise, I'm here to help you." We locked eyes, and she added, "Whatever it takes."

I dropped the sword and extended a hand. "Give me the key."

The girl passed me the ring, and I immediately shoved the chosen key into the lock and turned it. I let out a breath when I heard a click.

I shoved the cell door open and strode to Chase. My stomach twisted as I dropped to my knees beside his bed. He looked thinner than the last time I had seen him, paler. The ugly gash above his brow made me wince. I grabbed his shoulders and gave him a shake. "Chase. Chase, wake up."

The girl watched silently from behind as I continued to jostle Chase's shoulder, but he remained still. I turned around, my eyes wide and anxious.

"He's not—" My breath caught as I tried to swallow my fear. "He's not waking up. What did they do to him?"

The girl only shook her head, her eyes reflecting my concern. I turned back to Chase. I could hardly carry him up and out of the Olum, but if we didn't get moving, we'd be trapped down here. I glanced back at the girl, desperate for ideas.

"Maybe he just needs something to jolt him awake." Her eyes dropped to my hands.

I clenched my fist, and my hand began to heat up. I sent a silent apology to Chase, then placed three fingers on his wrist and pushed the heat into his skin. Chase's eyes snapped open with a gasp of pain.

"Sorry!" I cried out, jerking back like I was the one who had been burned. "Sorry, I was just trying to—"

"Storm?" Chase's voice was filled with disbelief. His pained expression melted into a grin. "What are you doing here?"

I could've cried in relief, but I mustered a weak smile. "Saving you."

Chase sat up, rubbing his wrist and flinching. "Nice job."

I laughed, my heart beginning to beat again. "Let's go, we need to get out of here."

Chase's eyes darted over my shoulder to the girl behind me. "Who's that?" he asked, his gaze clouding with suspicion.

The girl stepped further into the cell. "I'm June. One of Aila's friends." Chase's expression cleared, and he swung his legs out of bed as she continued. "Storm's right, we need to get out of here. I passed the escaped guard on the way down here, and I untied his hands and gag. By now he'll have told Brone about you."

I narrowed my eyes. "I thought you said you were here to help."

"Yes, and it would really help us all if I gave away that I was working with you," June said drily. "Honestly. I can see why Aila can't stand you."

I scowled. "Aila said she can't—?"

"No, but it was heavily implied by her tone."

I made a mental note to tell Aila that the feeling was mutual the next time I saw her. I stood, offering Chase a hand and helping him to his feet. He swayed slightly, and his eyes fluttered closed.

"You alright?" He looked even paler than before.

Chase's eyes snapped open. "I'm fine," he said, releasing my hand and following June out of the cell. "Just tired."

I didn't quite believe him, but I knew it took more than a little cut to stop Chase. I stooped down, retrieving the guards' swords from the ground and passing one to June and the other to Chase. "Keep these. We might have to fight our way out of here."

He frowned. "What are you supposed to do? Fistfight?"

In response, I lifted my hands and blasted two pillars of fire out of my palms. They slammed into the opposite wall, leaving two identical streaks of soot. Chase and June both stumbled back a step, gawking.

I brushed my hands off on my pants and smirked at Chase's stunned expression. I then drew the dagger out of the side pocket of his pack, which was still on my back. "I will keep this, though. If you don't mind."

Chase grinned, then glanced around at the cells, his expression tightening in determination. "Come on. Let's get out of here."

26

AILA

My hand flexed around the handle of the broom. My eyes fluttered closed. *I can do this. I can do this.*

I'd always enjoyed being able to turn invisible, but now I was beginning to wish I had a more aggressive power. Invisibility didn't get me far when I had to knock out three guards. June had directed me to a cleaning closet to get a broom, but even though the broomstick was made of a stiff hazel wood, I wasn't sure if it was a worthy weapon to take on three guards at once. Especially when they were hand-picked by Brone to guard the Exceptional hallway.

You're invisible. They won't even see you coming, I told myself sharply. One guard, the only female, stood at the opposite end of the hall with her back to me. The two nearest guards leaned against the wall as they discussed the dinner menu, oblivious to my presence. All I had to do was disable them, steal the keys, and free Jon. It was simple. I shouldn't be hesitating.

I took a deep breath, gritted my teeth, and lifted the broomstick.

A man tumbled around the corner before I could make my move. A piece of rope was wrapped around his ankle, trailing behind him, but he didn't seem to notice.

"He's back!" he shouted, skidding to a halt right in front of where I stood against the wall. The two guards at the mouth of the hallway spun to face him, and I saw the one at the opposite end leave her post to draw closer.

I didn't hear his next words over the blood rushing in my ears, but I didn't have to. Storm was in trouble.

We all were.

I'd made a beeline for this hall the second June left to find Storm in the dungeons, but clearly I'd waited too long before attacking the guards. Now, everyone was about to learn that we were here.

"—here to break his friend out of the jail," the guard said, still gasping for breath. "He tied us up. I only escaped because I cut the rope with my sword and made a break for it."

I rolled my eyes. I didn't exactly have high expectations for Storm, but I thought he'd at least have the ability to keep a couple of people tied up.

By now, the third guard had reached the end of the hall. She immediately took charge. "Brone should be in his office. Fenner, take this information to him right away."

The guard with the rope still looped around his ankle nodded and continued past me, racing down the hall. The other guard turned to her comrades. She pointed to the youngest one. "Stay here and guard the Exceptionals. We'll find the boy in the dungeons. He'll wish he never set foot in the Olum." She unclipped a ring of keys from her belt and tossed them to the younger guard, who just barely caught them as the others peeled away in the direction of the dungeons.

I sagged in relief. It would be much easier to handle one guard than the whole group. Remaining invisible, I moved so my footsteps were soundless as I crept toward the younger guard. I lifted the broom handle once more, lining it up with his temple.

"It's the best place to hit if you want to knock someone out," Storm had instructed before he agreed to let me be the one to rescue Jon. *"Trust me. I know from experience."*

I pulled my arm back and swung as hard as I could.

The handle of the broom hit the side of his head with a *crack*. I gasped and jolted back in surprise. The guard's eyes shot wide open, then he dropped to the floor, his head thudding onto the ground. I winced guiltily. He'd have one terrible headache when he woke up.

253

I dropped the broom and fell on my knees next to the guard, yanking the key ring from his fingers. Then I darted to Jon's cell, silently hoping that he hadn't made his decision yet. I studied the size of the lock and sifted through the keys for one that looked like it would fit, but when I shoved it into the lock, it refused to turn. Frantically, I tried key after key. None of them worked. My palms began to sweat.

I was fumbling to lift the next key when I heard the release of a breath behind me.

The blood drained out of my face. The key ring fell limp in my hands. In my rush, I had lost my focus, and my invisibility had dropped. Heart pounding in my chest, I slowly stood and turned around. My stomach dropped.

Ross was facing me, his expression grim.

"You shouldn't be here," he said, looking not at all surprised to see me. He must've heard that Storm was in the building and had clearly realized we were working together

His expression was dark as he faced me. I hadn't realized how different he looked without the light of humor dancing in his eyes. It was unsettling, and I felt dread creep in even further.

"Ross," I began, but he silenced me with a sharp look.

"Do you understand how much danger you're in, coming back here?" he demanded. "When you left, June and I—" Ross's breath caught, and for a moment, I thought I saw a flicker of my old friend beneath the cold mask. But then the moment passed, and I found myself tightening my grip on the key ring, as if I could somehow use it as a weapon. Ross growled, "We hoped you had enough common sense to stay away, but clearly you just can't stop making mistakes."

I took a step forward, holding out my hands. "Look—"

"Stop!" Ross shouted, and I froze in my tracks. "Stop right there! Don't move, or I'll-I'll…" He broke off, his hand dropping to his side. I tracked the movement, and my eyes landed on a sword buckled to his belt. I jerked my gaze up in horror.

"As soon as Brone heard Storm was here, he sent me to look for you." Ross's voice shook. "He gave me this sword and told me to prove my loyalty."

My heart skipped a beat when I saw the determination sweep across Ross's face. My only consolation was the fact that he hadn't drawn his sword yet. He was hesitating. Giving me a chance.

"You won't hurt me," I said, hoping my voice didn't betray the fear coursing through my veins. "We're friends, Ross."

"Are we?" His hand descended on his sword, but it was trembling. "Friends don't keep secrets, Aila."

"I kept a secret because I was ashamed!"

Ross scoffed.

"I *was*," I insisted. "I was ashamed because I was only promoted because Brone trusted me. I was ashamed because I made a *murderer* proud. I didn't want to be an officer because I realized that meant spending my life working for a cause I know is wrong."

For a moment, I thought I saw a flicker of something other than anger in Ross's gaze, but it quickly disappeared. My face fell. He had too much to prove.

"Fine," he snapped. "You were ashamed. But that doesn't justify the fact that you didn't tell us. That you *ignored* us."

"That's not—"

In a flash, Ross unsheathed his sword. I stumbled away, my back colliding with the iron door. "You *knew* that's what I wanted!" he yelled. His face was red, his eyes wild. "You *knew*! It was all I wanted, and you *took it from me*!" The point of the sword trembled, inches from my face.

But his words hurt me more than the sword ever could. Ross thought he could find fulfillment in Brone's approval. I should've been angry, but all I felt was pity. Pain. The Olum was such a horrible place that it could change even the most lighthearted of boys into someone cruel and twisted.

"No," I said, shaking my head. "That's not all you wanted. You wanted two things: To see your family, and to get glory."

For the first time, Ross didn't seem to have a response, so I pushed ahead while I was still in one piece.

"Maybe becoming an officer seemed like the answer to those problems, but deep down, you know it's not. *I* know it's not. You can't try to get what you want by doing something you know is wrong, because in the end…" My voice broke, and a moment passed before I could continue. "In the end, when you do get what you want, you won't feel any satisfaction because of all the horrible things you did to get there. You'll just feel like a monster."

Ross was quiet for a long moment, the sword still grasped in his quivering hand, still pointed at my neck. His eyes had filled with tears. The keys rattled in my hand, and I realized I was shaking, too. But Ross didn't move, didn't speak, so I seized my chance again.

"Help me," I said. "Help me, and you can come back to the rebel base with us."

Ross shook his head sharply. "You and Storm are going to be killed, and so will anyone who works with you," he said, but I saw the point of his sword dip a few inches.

"How do you know?" I said. "Storm manifested his power, and June decided to work with us."

"June?" This, finally, cracked Ross's facade.

"She realized it's better to risk her life doing the right thing than blindly doing the wrong thing. You said so yourself. Guilt is worse than anything Brone can do."

Ross's eyes darted from his sword to the keys to the cell door behind me. Then, in one sharp motion, he sliced his sword through the air. I jerked away with a gasp.

But instead of cutting into me, the weapon slid neatly into its sheath, the glinting blade disappearing with a *shiiing*.

Ross took a deep breath, then held out his hand. "Give me the keys. Brone told me which one to use."

Relief rushed in, so powerful I almost sank to my knees. Ross singled out a key and fitted it into the lock.

The door swung open, and my eyes immediately landed on Jon. He was curled on top of his bed in the corner of the room, just like the last time we spoke. His knees were drawn to his chest, his gaze fixed blankly on the ground.

His head snapped up when I entered, and before I could react, he flew across the room and flung his arms around me. I stiffened in surprise.

"I thought you weren't gonna come." His voice broke, and I softened, wrapping my arms comfortingly around him. "I thought I was going to…" He trailed off and pulled away, dragging the back of his hand across his eyes to wipe his tears.

Once again, I was struck by how young he was. Far too young to have this choice weighing on his shoulders.

But then, weren't we all?

"We're here now," I said, "but we have to leave right away. Do you understand? Quickly and quietly."

Jon sniffed and nodded, his eyes darting past me to where Ross lingered in the hall. "Where's Storm?"

"He's rescuing a friend from the dungeons. We'll meet him on the way." I left out the fact that Storm was probably in trouble. We'd get to him before anything bad happened. I had to believe it.

"Okay," Jon said, his voice hardening with confidence. "Okay. Let's go."

He followed me into the hall, but I paused as we stepped past Ross. "Are you with us?"

Ross looked smaller than he ever had, his usual bluster gone. But his voice, though quiet, was strong when he said, "I'm with you."

I would've cried in relief if it wasn't for the urgency coursing through me. We still had the entire Olum to get through, and Storm, Chase, and June to find. I had a feeling everything wasn't about to go smoothly. My gaze dropped to Ross's sword. "Where'd you get that?"

"Brone gave it to me, but he got it from a storage room near the training areas," Ross responded, glancing down at the weapon. He looked up, and his old smirk crept onto his face. "I can get us two more, if you're up for braving it."

I rolled my eyes, but I felt a familiar flicker of dread at the thought of having to expose my lack of sword skills again. But there were more pressing matters. I lifted my chin and grinned back. "I'll brave it. Whatever it takes."

Ross caught me testing my sword's weight as he kicked closed the door to the weapons closet. "At least you're not holding it like an ax anymore," he teased, then easily dodged my attempt to hit him with the flat edge of the sword.

I tossed him an annoyed look, but I was glad to hear Ross joking again.

The sword was much heavier than the wooden training ones I'd been practicing with, and judging by the way the tip of Jon's sword dipped toward the ground, we weren't any better off with three swords than with one. Ross took the lead as we started through the halls, and I followed, silently hoping at each corner that there wouldn't be any Expos in the next corridor.

It wasn't until we passed through three main halls that I realized something was wrong.

I quickened my pace until I fell into step with Ross.

"Hey," I said as we stopped at the corner of the next hall. It led from the Common Areas to the Expo and officer sleeping areas, and was one of the busiest corridors in the Olum. If we were going to get caught, it would be in this hall. "Does anything seem...amiss?"

Ross, who had been peering around the corner, looked back at me. "Amiss as in, the next hall is always full of traffic, but today is completely empty?"

I stared at him, then stepped forward and poked my head around the corner.

It was completely deserted.

I recoiled in alarm. "We need to—"

A gasp from behind cut me off. Ross and I spun around, and I sucked in a horrified breath.

Merrick was standing several paces away with a knife to Jon's throat.

Jon's gaze collided with mine; I saw the terror scrawled across his face. His sword dropped out of his grip and crashed to the ground.

Behind Merrick stood several other officers and Expos, many of whom seemed to have emerged from the very walls. I heard footsteps and turned to see more Expos filing into the hall behind us. I stumbled

258

back a step and knocked into Ross. We exchanged wide-eyed glances as two terrifying thoughts flashed through my head. The first was that Storm was going to kill me if anything happened to his brother.

The second was that he would never get the chance, because I wasn't going to make it out of this hall alive.

27

STORM

We had just made it out of the dungeon, starting for the hidden staircase where we'd meet Aila, when June stopped so abruptly that I crashed into her.

"What?" I snapped, impatient.

Chase was free. One of Aila's friends was helping. We hadn't seen any Expos. Things were going smoothly, and I finally had the chance to turn my mind to Jon. What was I going to say when I saw him? Would I even be able to get words out? Would I ever let him out of my sight again? The anticipation of finally seeing my brother again was so strong I wanted to scream. I wanted to fight anything that got in my way, and right now, June's sudden refusal to move another step was treading a very thin line.

Letting out an irritated breath, I tried to step around her.

In the blink of an eye, June grabbed my arm and yanked me back, all but flinging me into the wall. She pressed a finger to her lips and gave me a sharp look, silencing the objection on the tip of my tongue. "*Listen.*"

I froze, straining to hear what had made June pause. For the first time, I heard several pairs of boots shuffling, as if the hall around the corner was filled with people. But other than that, all that met my ears was an eerie silence.

Until Aila's voice sliced through the quiet, loud but not enough to disguise its trembling. "Let him go."

My heart stopped. *Jon.* She couldn't be talking about anyone else. Blood drained from my face as I heard more shuffling, followed by a

260

strained grunt of pain. It was as if the person restraining my brother had tightened his grip, driving the breath from Jon's lungs.

I clenched my jaw and surged forward, but Chase intercepted me, grabbing my shoulders and trapping me against the wall.

"Let me go," I hissed as voices once more filtered around the corner. Aila, begging for Jon's captor to release him.

Chase shook his head once as a gravelly voice responded, "You thought it would be that easy? You *really* thought you could break an Exceptional and a prisoner out of the Olum?"

"Please, Chase," I begged in a hoarse whisper.

"Please, Merrick." Aila's words mirrored my own. I was shocked to hear the concern in her voice. It was so unlike the cold, calculating tone that had controlled her when we were confronted last time. "You don't understand. I don't know what you think we're doing, but—"

"Don't play dumb with me," Merrick rasped. "I know exactly what you're doing. And so does Brone."

Chase didn't budge. June took one look at my panicked expression and said, "I'll go."

"What?" Chase and I whispered in unison.

"Does Brone really want Jon hurt?" Aila said, changing tactics. "His only bargaining chip?"

"I have a plan, but it means you have to stay hidden here," June said. She looked from Chase to me.

"I don't think he cares what happens to the boy," Merrick was saying. "None of you are going to escape alive."

I stiffened as I heard another gasp from Jon. My eyes snapped to June's. "Go."

She needed no further prompting. With a courage I found impressive, she started down the hall at a brisk jog and careened around the corner.

"Merrick!" June shouted as she disappeared from sight. "Brone needs your help!"

A startled silence settled over the crowd, and I heard Aila gasp.

"What?" Merrick demanded finally. "What are you doing here?"

I broke away from Chase before he could react and darted down the hall to the corner. Chase caught up to me and seized my arm, but all I did was peer around the corner. Expos filled the hall, and Aila and Jon were trapped in their center. The only thing that surprised me was the boy standing shoulder-to-shoulder with Aila, his sword raised, his jaw set with determination. I'd never seen him before, but he faced the Expos with resolute confidence.

Then an Expo shifted, giving me a better glimpse of Jon. Time seemed to slow. A month had passed since I'd last seen him properly, and that month had changed him. He was thinner than before, and much paler, with dark circles under his eyes. But my heart still leapt at the sight of my little brother. *He was here.* My throat suddenly felt tight. I never thought I'd see him again.

But the thrill of joy only lasted so long as I took in the rest of the situation. A man—Merrick—had a dagger pressed against Jon's neck, and Jon's eyes were wide with fear. Anger flared within me.

"Storm attacked Brone and the others," June gasped, her voice trembling. "He-he lit the entire hall on fire! I just made it out."

I had to admit, June was playing the part of a hysterical girl well. She almost convinced *me* that I was attacking Brone and the Exceptionals.

"Please, come quick," she begged.

Merrick frowned, a look of uncertainty passing over his face. But before he could respond, three slow, loud claps came from the other side of the group. The claps were oddly muffled, as if the person were wearing gloves. I knew even before the crowd parted that Brone was not on fire, but right here with us.

Brone continued to clap as he strode through the group, stopping only when he was next to Merrick. His expression was stone cold.

"Very impressive, Miss Palmer," he said, his voice like ice. "I would've believed you, if it weren't for the fact that I am standing right here."

June's mouth dropped as fast as her charade. The false panic from moments before was replaced by very real fear, and her gaze flicked briefly to where Chase and I hid.

That gesture was all the prompting I needed. Ripping my arm from Chase's grasp, I lunged around the corner and threw out my arms. Two columns of fire exploded from my palms. The Expos shouted in alarm and scattered, but I hadn't been aiming for them.

The flames struck their mark, and the wooden beam supporting the ceiling burst into flame.

The beams were close enough together that the fire began to hungrily spread from one piece of wood to the next, all along the hall. Expos began to run in every direction, shouts and terrified wails rising from the chaos. The flame darted from ceiling beam to ceiling beam like a slithering snake. Smoke swirled into the air.

Chase grabbed my arm. "We need to get out of here!" he shouted, pointing. I followed his arm up to see one of the beams, weakened by the flame, had begun to splinter.

My eyes followed its imminent path, and I sucked in a breath. Aila, who had been shoved to the ground in the chaos, was just stumbling to her feet beneath the breaking beam.

I didn't think. As the air filled with the *crack* of snapping wood, I leapt forward, throwing myself into Aila and sending us both flying to the ground.

We hit the floor hard, just as the beam crashed to the ground with the thundering sound of wood breaking and scattering across the floor. It landed where Aila had been moments before, sending sparks flying in every direction. I threw an arm over my head to shield my face and quickly turned my back, blocking Aila from the embers as she struggled to make sense of what had just happened.

Aila came to her senses and stared at me, for once without irritation. "Thanks," she said hoarsely.

My mind flashed back to June's words. *I can see why Aila can't stand you.* "This doesn't mean we're friends," I told her, and rolled to the side.

Aila's body began to shake from a coughing fit, and I rose to my feet unsteadily, my eyes burning from the smoke and my arm stinging from the hot sparks. Smoke roiled through the hall, concealing everything but the flames that darted in every direction. One glance toward the flaming, fallen beam, and I felt my heart sink. The beam stretched from one wall of the corridor to the other. By pushing Aila out of the way, I had put us on the opposite side of the wood as our friends. We were trapped here in a hall with a flaming ceiling that was about to collapse, and Jon was…Jon was…

"Jon!" I screamed. Panic hit me harder than the fiery beam had hit the ground. All other concerns were forgotten. I took off into the wall of smoke, ignoring Aila's shouts for me to wait.

The further I ran, the more I realized the extent of the destruction. The flame had spread further than I thought, and more portions of wooden beams had fallen, a few trapping Expos beneath. Other Expos laid on the ground, gasping for breath, and still others had passed out from the smoke.

But everywhere I looked, I could only see more and more Expos. Jon was missing. Not just Jon but also, I soon realized, Brone and Merrick.

I burst out of the flaming hall and into an intersecting corridor. The smoke was thinner here, and I desperately scanned both directions for signs of my brother. One of them had taken him. I just knew it. One of them had grabbed Jon and made a run for it, knowing I would follow.

It was hard to see anything through the ever-shifting wall of smoke, but at the far end of the hall, I thought I spotted movement. Peering harder, I was able to make out Merrick's muscular form before he disappeared around the corner. I scooped up a dropped sword and took off, sprinting through the thinning smoke toward him, and hopefully, toward Jon.

I heard footsteps behind me and knew who it was without even turning.

"Go back!" I shouted at Aila, slowing just long enough to spin around and point back toward the flaming hall we had just escaped from. "Go find Chase and get him out of here. I have to save Jon from Merrick. I'll…I'll meet you in Laster."

Aila shook her head. "I'm coming with you."

"No, you're not," I snapped. I could practically hear the seconds ticking by as Merrick got further and further away. "The Expos will regroup any minute. You need to get out of here before they do. Don't wait for me." I reached in my pocket, where Chase's dagger was still hidden, and held it out to her. "Take it."

Aila hesitated, and I was struck with surprise. She really had changed. If we had been in this situation a couple of days ago, she would've run off down the hall without a second thought. But now, she truly wanted to help. She was willing to risk her *life* to help.

But in the end, logic won out, and Aila grabbed the weapon with resignation and hurried back down the hall. I didn't wait any longer. I sprinted off in the opposite direction. A single goal consumed my mind.

I would find Jon and get him out of here, even if it was the last thing I did.

I didn't know where Merrick was going, but it immediately became clear that he wanted me to follow. Every time I paused, uncertain of where to go next, I would see a flash of movement at the end of the hall, or the shadow of someone disappearing around a corner. And yet, no matter how hard I ran, I was never able to catch up. My panic had mounted to a point where I wanted to scream when I finally spotted a large, arched doorway with two wooden doors.

One of the doors had been left slightly ajar.

I yanked it open and burst inside. I was greeted by rows of long, wooden tables and benches. *Flammable* wooden tables and benches. Merrick was at the opposite end of the cavernous chamber, one arm locked tightly around Jon's chest, restraining him. I felt both paralyzing fear and overwhelming relief at the sight of my brother. Jon wasn't safe yet, but at least this time Merrick didn't have a weapon to his throat.

I clenched the fist of my left hand, then uncurled my fingers to reveal a spinning ball of flame. I started toward Merrick with slow, vicious steps, and he tracked my motions with a fearless gaze. I stopped halfway between Merrick and the doors.

"Let him go!" My voice echoed off the walls of the empty room, furious and determined.

To my complete shock, Merrick nodded and released his hold on Jon, stepping away. Jon was anything but free, with Merrick still hovering behind him, but for a moment, I let out a breath.

That's when I noticed Jon's hands had been tied behind his back. The other end of the rope was knotted firmly around the leg of a nearby table. Immediately, I realized what Merrick had done. If I lit even one table on fire, the flames would spread to the tables surrounding Jon, but he would be unable to run away. Yet I couldn't untie him without Merrick attacking me. I looked up, and saw an infuriatingly smug look on Merrick's face.

"Brone and I have no quarrel with your brother," Merrick said after I waited too long, trying to figure out what to do. My sword hung limply at my side, my other hand still cupping the flame. "Turn yourself over without a fight, and you will be unharmed."

"Don't do it!" Jon shouted suddenly, his shrill voice bouncing off the walls. "He's going to kill you!"

For a moment, the sound of my brother's voice triggered an overwhelming surge of love and protection, but it was quickly doused by fear.

"Quiet!" Merrick shouted. He drove his foot into the back of Jon's knee, and Jon's leg gave out. He collapsed to the ground, pain flashing across his face.

The ball of flame in my hand disappeared with a hiss as I lurched forward, but Merrick immediately countered the movement. He pulled Jon roughly to his feet and secured a tight hold on him once more, but this time he put a dagger to Jon's throat.

I stopped dead in my tracks. "Stop!"

Merrick only pressed the dagger harder against Jon's throat. There was no hesitation in his gaze, just cold ferocity. I didn't know what to do. I didn't have a plan, not even a stupid, reckless, half-formed one. A choking fear bubbled inside of me. "He hasn't done anything!"

Merrick didn't even flinch.

"We'll leave!" I begged, my voice cracking in desperation. "Just let us go! We never did anything to hurt you!"

At this, Merrick let loose a sharp, guttural laugh that reverberated eerily in the empty room. "This one might be innocent," he conceded, giving Jon a little jerk, "but you've done more than your fair share of hurt to Brone."

My eyes darted from Jon to Merrick. "I don't even know what you're talking about," I said desperately. Maybe I had humiliated Brone by breaking into his fortress, but that shouldn't have been enough to leave him bent on revenge.

Merrick's eyes narrowed. "Do you even know who you are?"

For a moment, I was at a loss for words, confusion rooting me to the spot. What did that even mean? Then Jon's pained gasp dragged me back into the present. The terror in my brother's eyes made the decision for me, although it wasn't much of a decision at all. I dropped my sword to the ground.

"What are your conditions?" I said, hating the tremble in my voice. "My life for his freedom?"

Jon suddenly jerked in Merrick's grasp. "No, Storm, please don't—"

His words were replaced by a cry of pain as Merrick pressed the dagger harder into his skin. Even from my distance, I could see the blood that began to trickle from the wound.

I stumbled forward in horror, but my movement was immediately met with a strangled shout from Jon. "No, stop! Stop!" I shouted, freezing in place. "I agree, okay? I agree to whatever your terms are. *Stop hurting him!*"

A slow smile formed on Merrick's face, and he finally pulled the dagger away. The room was silent, except for my pounding heart and Jon's ragged breaths. For a moment, I met his gaze, but the tears in his eyes made me look away.

"Excellent. I knew you'd make the right decision."

I nodded breathlessly, my heart thudding. Jon continued to stare at me, shaking his head, muttering, "No. No. *Don't do it.*"

"Jon," I said, unable to watch him crumble any further. "Jon, listen to me. Remember that day in Carsley Market? The day I became an Exceptional?"

267

Merrick frowned, but Jon nodded numbly, tears streaming down his face. I clenched my fists, giving Jon what I hoped was a significant look.

"Remember what I told you after you stole Omar's ring? Do you remember?"

It wasn't much, but it was enough for Jon to prepare. Understanding dawned on him, and he gave me a quick nod. Merrick opened his mouth, realizing too late what was happening."

"Don't—" he began, but was cut off as I roared, "*Now!*" and threw my hands out in front of me.

28

AILA

Smoke and fire still filled the hall that led back to my friends, so I was forced to take the long way around. I spent each step hoping I wouldn't run into an Expo, but they seemed to have been momentarily chased away by the flames. My lungs burned from the acrid smoke, and my eyes watered, but I pushed forward. We were so close. *We were almost free.* But I couldn't help but feel a twinge of worry for Storm. Facing Brone and Merrick alone, even with his power, was unlikely to end well.

The smoke-filled air thickened as I reached the other end of the corridor. I was almost there when I heard it: a deafening *boom* that seemed to shake the entire Olum. I barreled around the corner as a wave of roiling fire exploded from the hall, churning outwards. I was flung backward by the force, hitting the wall across from me with a *thud*. The sudden burst of flame died down just as quickly as it had come, but the hall Storm had lit on fire was now completely engulfed in flame.

Time slowed. I suddenly couldn't hear anything but the pounding of my heart and the blood rushing in my ears. My friends were in there. My friends were trapped in that hallway.

"No!" I screamed. "No, no, *no!*"

I fell to my knees, still screaming. *This was all Storm's fault.* He had been reckless enough to set an entire hallway on fire while we were still in it. They were trapped, because of him. They were...

"Aila!"

I spun around. Chase appeared through a haze of smoke, a tired grin on his face. His voice was hoarse, and his face was streaked with blood and soot, but he was alive.

I rushed forward and threw my arms around him. My fear slipped away, and so did my anger, leaving me with an emotion I couldn't quite understand. A hollowness that could only be explained by the fact that I had immediately jumped to accusing Storm of my friends' supposed deaths.

I stepped back from Chase as Ross and June stumbled into view. Ross's lips were pulled into a tight, agonized line, and that's when I noticed that he was leaning heavily on June for support.

"You okay?" I asked, stepping forward to help him as we moved down the hall, away from the heat and smoke.

"Yeah," Ross muttered between clenched teeth.

I glanced at June for clarification. "A beam of wood fell on his leg," she explained, her brow scrunched with effort as we lowered Ross heavily to the ground.

"Could've been worse," Ross said, forcing a smile. "It could've been on fire."

June blinked. "It was."

"Yeah, well, not the whole thing."

I shook my head. "I don't know what Storm was thinking, setting the whole hall on fire with us in it."

Chase's head jerked up. "Is he okay? Did he make it out?"

"Merrick and Brone disappeared with Jon, so Storm...went after them," I said, bracing myself.

"Alone?" Chase demanded, right on cue. I nodded, and he shook his head, muttering under his breath. Then he looked up at me. "You should've gone with him."

"He wouldn't let me," I said defensively, "and it wasn't like I was going to leave you behind. If Storm wants to make reckless decisions, that's his own fault."

"Storm is just trying to save his brother," Chase argued. "His reckless decisions have saved you, too."

270

I thought of Storm shoving me from beneath the path of the beam and felt a twinge of guilt. Afterwards, he had made it clear that it didn't mean things were fine between us. Still, he had saved me.

I dropped my gaze. "He told me to leave him. He told me we should meet him in Laster."

Chase barked a laugh, as if at the ridiculousness of Storm's request. "We're *not* leaving him. Which direction did Merrick go? We need to—"

"Guys," June said suddenly. The urgency in her tone cut Chase short, and we both followed her gaze. She was peering down the hall, into the smoke and toward the fire.

I squinted, unsure of what she was seeing. My eyes were still burning. But the moment Chase stiffened beside me, I saw him. Brone, a sword grasped in one hand, a cold grin on his face, stepped through the smoke to meet us. A dozen Expos filled the hall behind him. They looked exhausted, their faces and clothes streaked with soot, but it didn't matter. We were heavily outnumbered.

I saw Kala, her expression cold, and Trav, a sword gripped in his hand. Even Jax was there, the guard who'd escorted me to my training sessions. I'd once known these people. I'd even called some of them my friends.

And now, here I was, standing against them and everything they believed in.

"Anyone have a weapon?" Chase hissed.

June and I shook our heads. I had been more focused on staying alive in the flaming hall than keeping track of my sword. Ross struggled to sit up straighter. He unsheathed his sword and passed it to Chase, but I frowned. One boy holding one weapon wasn't going to get us very far.

"So...we run?" Ross suggested.

"I mean, go ahead," June said, pointing.

The rest of us turned to follow her gesture, and my jaw clenched. Several more Expos had stepped into the corridor behind us, blocking our escape. For the second time today, I had allowed myself to be trapped by the Expos. I looked instinctively at Chase for support, but all I found

271

was my own fear mirrored in his gaze. June had gone still, and even Ross had turned serious in the weight of the situation.

We were fools, I thought suddenly. Irrational fools who had made the mistake of thinking we could really defeat Brone.

"As you can see, you are outnumbered," Brone called to us. "If I were you, I'd recommend surrendering. It's the less painful option."

I grimaced. I had known all along that it could end like this, but I'd somehow managed to convince myself that everything would turn out okay. Not only that, but I had convinced Ross and June to join, too, but now we were standing side by side, staring our deaths in the face.

I took one last look at my friends. At Ross, who had been hesitant at first, but now glared at Brone with a fierce confidence. At June, who knew firsthand the dangers of crossing Brone, yet was loyal until the end. And at Chase, who had sacrificed everything only for it to end here. Out of everyone, he deserved this the least. He had been nothing but patient and selfless.

Selfless. The word flashed through my mind again, and I realized with sudden certainty what I had to do. I glanced at Chase, and determination stirred within me. Apparently, it showed, because he frowned, then opened his mouth to speak.

Before I could talk myself out of it, I wrenched the sword out of his grasp and threw it on the ground.

A sharp inhale seemed to rise from both parties, and Chase shot me a startled look. I didn't meet his gaze. I couldn't. I just took one step forward.

"Take me," I said, spreading out my arms. "I'll go with you willingly, as long as you promise to let the rest of them go free."

Out of the corner of my eye, I saw Chase do a double take. "Aila—"

Brone cut him off with a laugh. "Take just you, when I can easily have everyone? I'm disappointed. I thought you were smarter than that."

"I know things about the rebels," I said, trying my best to avoid the alarmed look Chase gave me and instead focus on the interest sparking in Brone's gaze. "I'll talk if you let them go."

Chase stared at me. "What? No—"

272

"Quiet!" Brone barked. Chase fell silent, but I could sense the shock rolling off of him in waves like the smoke that still poured from the burning corridor.

Brone's attention fixed on me once more. "What information?"

"Their name, for one." Each word was a challenge to force out. I was terrified that Brone would call my bluff. "How they've evaded you for so long. And…their location."

For a moment, Brone's gaze flicked to my friends, as if he was considering the offer. But then, just as quickly, his face hardened again. "I don't think that's going to happen."

My heart skipped a beat. "But-but if you capture us all, you won't get the information."

Brone's laugh chilled me to the bone. "When you see what I can do to your friends, you'll be more willing to talk."

The blood drained out of my face, and I stumbled back a step. I had failed. I'd *failed*. Brone began to speak, barking a command to the Expos, but his voice was suddenly drowned out by a distant, rumbling bang.

Everyone in the hallway froze. The Expos who had started forward at Brone's command stopped abruptly.

Another bang reverberated through the building, closer and louder. It was different from the explosion of fire in the hall. This sounded bigger.

I glanced sideways at Chase and saw a look of wonder cross over his face. His lips moved, but I couldn't hear his words over the next bang that echoed through the Olum, followed by another, and another. Alarm washed over the Expos' faces, and for the first time ever, Brone's confidence appeared to be waning as his eyes darted in every direction. Ross, June, and I had stiffened, too.

Chase was the only one who didn't seem frozen in fear.

"What's happening?" I shouted in panic.

Chase grinned back. "Ace!" he shouted, just as the wall next to us exploded.

29

STORM

Jon lurched to the side as best he could while still tied to the table, and flames burst from my palms. Merrick dropped to his stomach, but not fast enough. The pillars of fire shot over him, coming so close that the sparks sent his shirt bursting into flame. A panicked shout tore itself from Merrick's throat, and he began to roll wildly on the floor like a fish out of water.

I snatched up my sword and sprinted to Jon, dropping to my knees with a gasp of relief. I'd taken a risk, but we were both still alive. My hands trembled. I couldn't cut through Jon's ropes fast enough.

My sword finally found its mark, and the bonds dropped to the ground. I offered Jon a hand and pulled him to his feet. The second he was standing, I dropped my sword and threw my arms around him. Jon buried his face into my shirt, clinging to me as if he would crumble to dust if I stepped away.

"Storm," he sobbed. "I thought you were...I didn't think I'd ever..."

"Jon, I'm sorry." I felt his tears through my shirt and shut my eyes against my own. "I'm so, so sorry."

"It's not your fault, Storm," Jon responded, his voice muffled.

I shook my head. Jon wouldn't be hugging me if he knew all the things I'd done since becoming an Exceptional.

"Jon, listen—" I cut off abruptly as I saw a flash of movement out of the corner of my eye.

A few yards away, Merrick had finally beaten out the flames and was now pushing himself to his feet, his gaze dark with hatred. His shirt hung in charred tatters, and I could see his skin had begun to blister beneath.

Merrick unsheathed his sword, and I felt my confidence waver. He had much more experience with a sword, and although I was an Exceptional, I couldn't fight him without risking setting the whole room on fire. A quick burst of flame was one thing, but an entire duel was something else.

I pulled away from Jon and bent to pick up the sword, never taking my eyes off Merrick. I risked turning my head slightly in Jon's direction. "Get out of here."

"What?" Jon demanded.

For the time being, Merrick hesitated, but I knew the second he realized I wasn't going to use my power, he would attack.

"You need to hide," I told Jon. "Find…I don't know, a closet or something."

"I'm not leaving you." Even with the raw terror in his eyes, Jon managed to sound confident. I'd forgotten how stubborn he was.

He clearly took after me.

"Well I'm not letting you stay here," I said petulantly. "I'll come find you after this is over, I promise, but I can't fight him with you here."

Jon's voice turned suddenly sharp. "Is that how you see me?"

"No, that's not what I meant," I snapped, finally risking an angry glance toward him. Why couldn't he just see my logic and *leave* already?

"Then what do you mean?" When I didn't respond, he said, "Tell me, or I'm not leaving."

Merrick seemed to be coming to his senses. He lifted his sword. I raised my palm and sent another burst of flame, and he flinched back a step. It bought me time, but not much.

"Jon." My voice was rushed and ragged, but I refused to give into my anger. I'd made that mistake one too many times already. "I've almost lost you once. I need to know you're safe, okay?"

"But what about you?" Jon whispered. "What if you don't win?"

275

What if I don't win? I didn't dare consider the possibility. "I have to do this alone. I promise, I'll see you in a few minutes."

Jon's eyes brimmed with tears again, but this time he didn't look relieved, just scared. He stumbled back a step, then whirled and fled. My gut clenched, but at least whatever happened in this room, I could know Jon was safe.

I lifted my sword and turned to face Merrick.

A smirk sprang to his face when I saw I had chosen to fight him with a sword. "You and your brother aren't going to make it out of here alive," he taunted. "You might think you're safe because you're an Exceptional, but Brone has ten times more Exceptionals on his side than you have on yours."

If I had been any less stubborn, I probably would've attacked, but I refused to let him see how much he was getting to me. I rolled back my shoulders, forcing my chin up. "I'll give you one chance to lay down your weapon and leave this room alive."

"When I can win this little duel so easily? I don't think so."

"Easily? Please, you don't actually think the rebels like me sit around and *relax*, do you? They've trained me to beat their best swordsman in a fight."

Merrick hesitated, and I took a moment to wish that Chase was around to see my newfound acting skills. But just as quickly, Merrick's expression darkened.

"So maybe I'm not leaving alive," he said with a sneer, then pointed to the door, "but that boy isn't either."

My gaze tracked his gesture against my will, landing on the doors through which Jon had just disappeared. My breath caught.

"You might've noticed how quickly Brone disappeared from the fire. You might've hoped he'd just run away, but he was waiting this entire time. Waiting on the other side of the door, waiting for you to send your brother away, right into his open arms."

My blood ran cold; Merrick's mocking voice rang in my ears. "You really do hurt everyone around you, don't you?"

"*No!*" I screamed. I lunged for the door, but suddenly Merrick was in front of me, cutting off my escape with a raised blade.

"It's too late to rescue him now," he rasped.

I felt something strong roar to life inside of me. My hatred toward Brone, toward this man before me—and more importantly, toward everything they stood for—cast a shadow on my fear. Merrick's next words were lost in the ringing of my ears as I felt a sort of dangerous focus wash over me. Suddenly, I no longer cared if this entire room went up in flames. I just wanted to destroy this wretched place. Our gazes collided for a brief second, and I watched the sneer drip off Merrick's face.

I thrust an arm forward. A pillar of fire exploded and caught him in the chest. Merrick slammed into the ground with a cry of pain and began to beat at the flames with his hands. By the time the last lick of fire disappeared to reveal the charred shirt and skin beneath, I had crossed the room and pointed my sword at his throat.

Merrick gasped for breath. His eyes watered with pain and widened with fear. Slowly, he raised his blistered hands in surrender.

I smiled without a hint of humor. "You're a coward," I spat. "You've been hiding behind Brone's power your whole life, and now that you're without it, you're weak."

"You're weak, too," Merrick growled, a hint of desperation in his voice. "Don't talk to me about hiding when you've been—"

He stopped abruptly as a distant, rumbling bang echoed through the room. For a moment, we both paused, but I quickly recovered and pressed my sword into his skin again.

But before I could speak, another louder boom reverberated through the building. The tables and benches rattled. Merrick and I locked eyes in confusion.

Another boom echoed through the room, followed by three more, each one louder than the last. I craned my neck, scanning the ceiling and the walls, but there were no clues as to where the sounds were coming from. Something was happening, and I didn't have time to stand here and deal with Merrick. I flipped my blade around and whipped him across the face with the pommel of my sword. His unconscious form went limp.

I grabbed the rope Merrick had used on Jon and bound his hands together behind his back. Hopefully, he'd appreciate the irony after he regained consciousness. Then I unbuckled his sword belt and wrapped it around my own waist. This time, I made sure his sword was far out of reach by tossing it across the room, so it was out of sight behind one of the benches. Then, I turned and ran.

I burst into the hall, screaming Jon's name. The only response that met my words was an echo. My chest heaved. I spun in a frantic circle, trying to decide which direction to go, trying to guess where Brone could've taken Jon. Sudden commotion sounded from the far end of the hall, and I whipped around in that direction. It was the sound of people shouting. I sprinted toward the noise without hesitation.

This building must've been playing tricks on my mind. I thought I was running in the opposite direction from where I'd come, away from the fire, but for some reason the air was thickening with smoke. I rounded the next corner and sucked in a breath as I realized the air was not filled with smoke.

It was filled with *dust*.

One wall of the corridor was completely demolished, a huge, crumbling hole gaping in its center. Rubble covered the floor, chunks of stone strewn in every direction. A thick, choking cloud of dust hung in the air. Slowly, understanding dawned on me. Someone had just blasted into the Olum.

And I thought I knew who.

My pulse began to flutter. The dense cloud shifted, and I saw a familiar figure step through the haze and freeze. I squinted, then my jaw dropped.

"*Aris?*"

30

AILA

The entire wall erupted, knocking me across the corridor. The air filled with shouts and flying rock. I threw myself to the ground and curled into a ball, flinging my arms over my head, shielding my body against the far wall. Debris rained down, and I hissed in pain as a sharp stone sliced into my arm.

What is happening? Screams rose from every direction. It seemed neither my friends nor the Expos had any idea what was going on.

Then, just as quickly as it started, it was over. I slowly pushed myself to my feet, my mind spinning as I tried to squint through the dust. Then I spotted Ross, curled up on the ground, and my heart skipped a beat. He had been sitting against the very wall that exploded.

"Ross are you okay?" The words tumbled from my lips in a panicked jumble as I fell to my knees next to him, shoving rubble out of the way. To my relief, he sat up slowly. His hand immediately lifted to his cheek, and when he pulled it away, his fingers were red with blood. My eyes widened with horror.

"I'm okay," he said, dazed. "It's just a cut."

I let out a shaky breath and helped him to his feet. My nerves felt frayed; I'd had too many near-death experiences in the past thirty minutes alone.

"Aila." Ross's grip tightened around my forearm. "The Expos are still—"

He stopped short as the world exploded into chaos once more.

People began pouring through the gap created by the explosion. They were Exceptionals, I realized with a start, but none I had ever seen

279

before. Men and women, teens and adults, charged through the smoke, fearlessly wielding swords and maces and axes. They attacked the Expos before they even had the chance to stand. Ross and I stood there, stunned, as a battle unfolded right before our eyes. I had no idea who these people were, but as long as they were against the Expos, they were on our side.

Or so I thought, until one of the boys ran up to me and pointed his sword directly at my throat.

"Hands up, backs against the wall, now," he barked, wagging the sword under my nose.

I froze, out of confusion rather than fear. He couldn't have been older than thirteen. I found it hard to be intimidated.

"Now!" the boy snapped, waving his sword again. This time, I flinched.

"Arden!"

Chase appeared out of the dust, June at his side, his face lit up with a brilliant grin.

The boy spun around and pointed the sword at Chase's chest, but just as quickly dropped it. His eyes widened. "Chase, you're alive!"

"I can't believe this!" Chase's eyes glowed. "The Insurgence came to help? I can't believe it!"

"It was because of Aris and Storm," Arden said. Chase's eyebrows flicked up, and Arden nodded emphatically. "I know. Who would've thought that the kid who hates everyone and the kid who everyone hates would be able to change the hearts of the entire Insurgence? But here we are."

The Insurgence. I glanced at the surrounding chaos in wonder, but immediately noticed something was wrong. "Chase, where—"

I shut my mouth and quickly retreated back a step as Arden whipped his sword point back toward me.

Chase threw out an arm. "No, Arden, they're friends!"

The tip of Arden's sword dipped a bit. "Really?"

"Really." Chase pointed to Ross. "He could use some help. A wooden beam fell on his leg."

Arden's brow scrunched as he studied the wound on Ross's face. "Did it bounce off his head first?"

Ross shot me a questioning glance, but I just shrugged as Arden instructed him to sit down. Ross hesitated, clearly not quite over the fact that this boy had just held him at swordpoint, but Chase gestured for him to comply. I helped situate Ross so he was leaning against the wall. Arden knelt down and rested his hands on either side of Ross's wound. He closed his eyes, and what followed was a long, awkward moment in which Ross, June, and I exchanged baffled glances.

Then, Ross gasped, and I dropped my gaze to see his skin knit itself together before my very eyes. Arden lifted his hand to Ross's cheek and repeated the process. Soon, the streaks of blood were the only sign that a wound had ever been there.

Ross stood and tested his leg on the ground, then looked up at Arden. "Well done."

He just shrugged. "Now you owe me a favor."

"What—"

"I can heal you guys, too," Arden said, turning to the rest of us.

The cut on my arm was stinging sharply, but I shook my head and looked at Chase. "Brone's missing." Chase's eyes widened, and I added, "I'm going after him."

Chase waved away Arden, who was reaching for the gash on his head. "I'm coming with you."

I didn't object. I had been expecting this reaction, and besides, I had no desire to face Brone alone.

"Is Nylah here?" Chase asked Arden, who nodded. "Could you find her? Tell her we need her help right away."

Arden wrapped his fingers tight around his sword and darted off into the dust.

"Careful, now you'll owe him," Ross grumbled.

June stepped over to where a sword was wedged between two rocks and yanked it from the rubble. "We should arm ourselves." I blinked in surprise, and she rolled her eyes. "Yes, we're coming with you. Quit acting surprised."

The rest of us split and began to scour the surrounding debris. I kicked a rock aside and bent to retrieve the sword that had been trapped beneath.

"Where do you think Brone went?" Chase muttered, stepping up next to me with a sword already in his hand. "Does he have an office or something? Or do you think he left the building?"

"Close, but not quite."

I spun around, my blood running cold. Brone stood on the other side of the exploded wall, a few of his most trusted Expos filling the corridor behind him. Kala was among them. They stood tall, and grim expressions settled on their faces. Each of them held a sword ready in their hands.

But we were ready, too. Ross, freshly healed, lifted his sword and set his jaw. June stepped up next to me, her eyes trained resolutely on Brone. And Chase, bruised and bloodied, had never looked more fierce in his life. We had heard Brone's terms. We knew the risks. But we had made our decision and would defend it to the death.

So before Brone could say another word, before he could attack, I raised my sword. Judging by the approving sound Ross made, I finally got it right. Then, staring Brone dead in the eyes, I slashed my blade through the air.

We surged across the hall and met the Expos with blades drawn. I locked swords with Kala, and I immediately knew I was outmatched. I only got in two useless swipes before she put me on the defensive. Her sword cut through the air, and it was by pure chance that mine was in the right place to block it. She recoiled, then jabbed at my midsection, but not so quickly that I couldn't dart out of the way. The rest of the duel continued in similar fashion. Kala would attack, but just slowly enough that I had time to frantically block or dodge.

I was so busy trying to keep the point of her blade out of my way that I couldn't focus enough to go invisible. With my sword as my only weapon, I knew I was bound to lose, and I cast a desperate glance around to see if anyone was free to help.

It was a mistake, one that Kala had been waiting for. She stepped forward, twisted her sword, and drove it toward my leg.

This time, I didn't jump out of the way fast enough. The sharp edge of the sword sliced into my thigh, and I stumbled as pain shot through me like fire. I grabbed the wall for support and braced myself, eyes watering, for Kala's inevitable attack. But she just took a step back and watched me gasp for breath.

She was holding back. I knew full well she had the power to cut me into pieces, yet something made her hesitate. But we couldn't continue on like this, in a shaky stalemate. I needed to get back on the offensive, but I couldn't when I kept hesitating, as unsure of my next moves as I'd been in Ross's training lessons.

Ross's training lessons. If they had ever been for a greater purpose, this was it. June's words from a few weeks earlier echoed in my head. *Give yourself over to instinct*, she'd said. *Commit to your actions*. I was surprised how clearly the advice had stuck in my head, as if I'd tucked it away for this exact moment. *Instinct*, I told myself again, and suddenly I knew what I had to do.

I sucked in a breath and straightened up, clenching my jaw against the paralyzing pain that shot through my leg. I tried to channel the same reckless energy that had coursed through me when I first attacked Kala.

She had recoiled slightly, as if letting me catch my breath, and as I did, I gathered my wits about me.

And then I let them go.

I leapt forward and attacked.

The tables of the duel flipped immediately as I drove my sword forward. When Kala stumbled back out of reach, I didn't use the opening to consider my next move. Instead, I surged ahead, slicing my sword through the air, my blade whirling in every direction so that she was forced to back toward the half-destroyed wall.

All it took was a few more forceful attacks before I landed a blow. My blade sliced across her stomach, and Kala tripped on a piece of rubble, falling to the ground. Her sword flew out of her grasp, skittering across the floor.

I lifted my blade, but Kala croaked, "Wait."

If it had been anyone else, I wouldn't have hesitated. But Kala had been waiting for me the entire duel, and I owed her the same. "What?"

"Brone." Some dust must've gotten into Kala's lungs, because a bout of coughs hit her, cutting her off. Or maybe it was the ugly gash in her midsection that made it so difficult for her to breathe.

"The rebels are here. It's over," I told her, "and I'm going to find him next and let him know."

Kala shook her head and pressed a hand to the wound at her stomach, still struggling for air. "Spare him."

"He's a murderer!" I stared at her in disbelief. "I'm not going to give him the chance to keep killing Exceptionals."

Another head shake. Another cough. "He wasn't...always this way."

I seriously doubted that. I couldn't envision Brone as anything other than evil. "How would you know?"

"Because I'm...his cousin." Kala ground out the words before descending into another fit of coughs. The tip of my sword dipped slightly in surprise. I thought back to the time in Brone's office when she'd laid a hand on his arm. At the time, I'd been shocked that he'd let her do so. Now, I realized their relationship went beyond the Olum. "He was a little brother to me. I practically raised him. I just...I just want what is best for him."

I almost laughed. "Killing Exceptionals and trying to overthrow the government is not what's best."

"You know about that?" Kala's pained face flickered with surprise. She shook her head. "Of course you know about that. I always told him you were too smart to trust"

"Once the Earl knows what he's trying to do, it'll all be over."

"He's not trying to overthrow the government," Kala said faintly. "He just needs the Earl's power."

"Sounds like the same thing to me," I scoffed.

This conversation was pointless. No matter what Kala said, Brone's actions would never be justified.

But I couldn't help but feel a flicker of curiosity. What could've possibly turned Brone into the monster he was today? Against my better judgment, I hesitated, my blade quivering inches from Kala's neck.

"He's spent his whole life searching for his family," Kala rasped. Her gaze slid out of focus, probably from the pain. Or maybe she was becoming lost in a memory. "He wanted to find and end every last one of them."

My blood ran cold. I wondered with a start if the maps scattered around every inch of Brone's office hadn't been for finding Exceptionals after all. Maybe the maps marked where he had searched for his family. The maps weren't at all the calculated plans of a leader. Instead, they were a crazed search for vengeance.

Kala's next words sounded strained, whether from emotion or pain, I couldn't tell. "His parents treated him like dirt because he wasn't an Exceptional, and the one person who cared for him ended up dead because of it."

So, Mila's death was connected to Brone and his family. Things were beginning to come together, but not enough for me to see the whole picture. I was wasting time. Brone had let his anger control him, and nothing would justify all the horrors he'd done. I didn't need to hear the motives for his villainy; I needed to find him, or at least find Chase. Then we could end this once and for all.

I raised the hilt of my sword to knock her unconscious, but I had one last question. "Why should any of this matter to us?"

Kala gave me one final pleading look, not for herself, but for Brone. Her cousin. Her brother. The person she'd been trying all this time to protect. "There is one left," she whispered. "One last family member to destroy."

31

AILA

I found Chase and Brone at the same time, locked in a duel so vicious it had already driven them far down the hall to my left.

Of course Chase had taken on Brone. He was the most experienced swordsman, having started formal training before he even became an Exceptional, and Brone had no idea what he was up against. All these things should have worked in Chase's favor, but one look told me he was not winning the fight. Their blades were locked as Brone tried to force his down toward Chase's chest. Chase's forehead was beaded with sweat, and he grunted with the effort of keeping Brone's sword away.

I was invisible, so neither of them noticed my approach. I wasted no time in lifting my arm and aiming the dagger Storm had given me directly at Brone. But before I could throw, Chase spun around to Brone's opposite side, putting him directly in the dagger's path.

Brone lashed out, hitting Chase in the jaw with the pommel of his sword and sending him to the floor. I screamed in horror and flung the dagger at Brone. He had heard my shout and twisted to see the now visible dagger in the air. Brone jerked out of the way, and the dagger hit the wall, clattering to the ground.

But my unsuccessful attack had been a sufficient distraction. Chase lashed out with his sword from the ground, and the blade sliced deep into Brone's calf.

Brone's leg buckled under him, and he spilled to the floor with a pained shout. Now visible, I crossed the distance between us and leveled my sword triumphantly at Brone's throat. However, when I looked down the length of the weapon and straight into his dark gray eyes, I saw nothing but the usual collected calmness in his gaze. My face flushed with anger. He was the one being held at swordpoint, but for some reason, I was the one who felt thrown off-balance.

"We should knock him out," Chase gasped, picking himself up off the ground and sweeping his sweat-slicked hair out of his eyes. He had gained several more cuts in the duel, most noticeably a slice along his forearm. He rubbed at the ugly bruise forming on his jaw. "We'll tie him up so he can't get away."

I wanted to do more than just knock Brone out and bind him. He deserved more after what he had done to me, to Chase, and to every Exceptional who had lived. Chase must've seen something flicker in my face, because he laid a hand on my shoulder.

"Remember, we're better than him," he said, his hazel eyes boring into mine. "We don't want to do anything that would turn us into the same monster that he is."

I thought of how far Brone had let his thirst for revenge take him and looked away. "Yeah," I muttered, then turned my gaze to Brone. "We won't kill you, but we won't let you free. You'll get what you deserve when we turn you over to the Earl."

Brone finally dropped his gaze to his gloved hands. He fiddled with the leather, and although any other person might have mistaken it for nerves, he still seemed eerily impassive. *Too* impassive.

"I hate to disappoint you," Brone said at last, "but I'm afraid I'm not going to let that happen."

With a rush of horror, I realized just how wrong it was that Brone had shown no glimpse of fear since the Insurgence's arrival. I realized there was something else going on, another secret in the Olum that I had yet to uncover. But the revelation came far too late, and everything happened far too fast.

Brone ripped off his gloves and raised his hands. Chase screamed my name and slammed into me, sending me tumbling to the ground. A deadly sharp icicle shot from Brone's hands, cutting through the empty space where my head had been just moments before. It slammed into the wall, shattering into thousands of tiny shards. Chase was off-balance, and Brone was on his feet, his palm aimed at Chase's face.

Then, out of nowhere, a piece of rock flew off the ground and hit Brone square in the chest, knocking him back a step. I jerked my head around as a girl stepped forward. She lifted her hand, and another piece of rubble rose in sync, hovering in the air before her. She thrust her arm forward, and the rock flew at Brone, followed by another, and another, each forcing Brone back another step.

"Chase!" I shouted, and he dropped to his stomach just as another icicle zipped over his head.

The girl continued to whip rocks at Brone until, eventually, it became too much for him to continue attacking with his power. He flung up his arms. A wall of ice formed, frost crawling up from the floor until it reached the ceiling and solidified into an impenetrable blockade. It stretched from floor to ceiling and wall to wall, sealing Brone on the opposite side. The next few pieces of rock hit the ice wall and fell harmlessly to the floor, leaving little more than a dent.

My gaze locked with Brone's, and his face twisted into a brief, callous smile before he disappeared down the hall. I stared after him, trying to understand what had just happened.

When it came down to it, there was really only one explanation.

"Brone is an Exceptional." Chase said it first, his voice hollow with disbelief as he pushed himself to his feet, eyes glued to the ice wall. "*Brone* is an *Exceptional*," he said again, turning to face me. "*What?*"

I could only shake my head in astonishment. My mind was spinning too fast. It didn't feel real.

"That doesn't make sense, he hates Exceptionals," Chase said as he stood and started toward the ice wall. "Why is he...?" He trailed off and laid his palm against the thick wall of ice, as if to test if it was real. He turned around to look at me. "None of this makes sense."

I opened my mouth to agree that it didn't make sense; then all of a sudden, it did. "Oh, no," I whispered, horrified. All the pieces had finally come together, but the image that they revealed was not the one I'd expected to see. I stumbled back, leaning heavily on the wall.

"Aila?" Chase was by my side immediately. "Are you okay?"

"Brone killed Mila." The words didn't sound true as they fell from my lips. "Brone was the Exceptional who killed Mila."

Chase's eyebrows drew together. "I think I'm missing something."

The words couldn't leave my mouth fast enough. I told him about Mila, the girl Brone had loved, the girl who had been killed by an Exceptional. Now, after the fact, I realized his voice had been filled with guilt, because the Exceptional who killed Mila was him. Brone had said his family had been neglectful, and that's how Mila died.

I didn't want to think of how much Brone must've been ignored for his power to grow so out of control. I didn't want to think of how horrible the accident must've been to make Brone hate his family. I didn't want to think about it because I wanted to hate Brone, but for a moment, I couldn't help but feel pity for the horrible circumstances Brone had found himself in.

I felt pity because I knew exactly what it was like to know that someone I cared about the most was dead, and it was all my fault.

"Brone's going to come back," I said, turning away from Chase, my voice hollow. "We should be ready."

"Come back? After we defeated him?" Chase shook his head. "No, that doesn't sound right. He wouldn't risk it."

"Then where else would he go?" I said. "The only other person to go after is—" I stopped short, and Chase's eyes widened.

"No." At first, he said it quietly, but his voice quickly rose to a shout. "No, no, no!" He ran to the wall of ice and pounded on it with his fist, but it didn't so much as quiver. Chase whirled around, and the panic in his eyes was like none I'd ever seen. "I need to go rescue him."

Chase spun around and started down the hall, away from the ice wall, toward where the girl who had rescued us was standing silently.

My heart leapt into my throat. "No, it's too dangerous." I hurried to follow after, pain tearing through my leg from where Kala had cut me. I didn't want to lose Chase again, not so soon after we had reunited. "Storm will be fine. He has his power."

"And so does Brone." Chase didn't even turn around. "But Storm doesn't know that."

A beat passed in which I desperately searched for another excuse, but there was none. I was selfish; that's all there was. I knew Chase would do everything in his power to save Storm, and I was scared of what would happen when he did. But Chase's gaze had hardened, and I knew there was no talking him out of it.

"I'm coming with you." The words were out of my mouth before I could stop them. My heart raced at the thought of facing Brone again, but I lifted my chin as Chase turned to face me, his shoulders tight with tension.

"No, you're not."

"What, you don't think I can help?" I snapped.

"No offense, but you look like you're about to fall over."

"That didn't stop me from saving your *life*, though, did it?"

For a moment, the two of us stood there glaring at each other, tense and stubborn.

Then Chase's posture relaxed, and he took a step toward me. "I wish you could come. I hate being separated as much as you do. But you have to rescue your friends, and then you have something else important to do."

"What?" I said, folding my arms across my chest. I wasn't ready to match his calm tone quite yet.

"Not everyone in the Olum is on Brone's side. The captured Exceptionals, the other Expos you trained with—they all deserve a second chance. Even if things end badly for us, we win if we get them out of the Olum. The Insurgence owes it to them."

"Anyone else can do that," I insisted.

"But they'll only truly trust one of their own."

My confidence broke a bit. "Chase—"

He stepped forward wrapped and his arms around me. I immediately softened, hugging him the way I had every time one of our families left for a long trip when we were children. For a moment, I could pretend we were just kids, and this goodbye would only last until the other person got back from their great adventure.

But we were in the Olum, and this was no family trip. Chase drew back, and a sudden cold wrapped around me. He turned toward the girl who had saved us, who was waiting patiently.

"Nylah, this is Aila. Aila, this is Nylah. Her power will help you get everyone out of here safely. Okay?"

"Okay."

My voice shook, and Chase must've heard it, because his hazel eyes locked with mine. "You're stronger than people think, Aila, stronger than *you* think," he said, his voice full of certainty. "Yes, you've made mistakes, but you've learned, grown, and matured from them. And *that's* what matters."

We stood there for a moment longer, but I could tell with each second that passed, it was growing more and more agonizing for Chase to be here instead of helping Storm.

So, with difficulty, I forced a smile and said, "See you soon."

Chase grinned. "Definitely."

Our words sounded like nothing more than hollow lies.

Ross and June found us before we could find them.

Nylah and I had hurried off down the hall and away from the ice wall in silence, my thoughts clamoring too loudly for me to focus on any introductions beyond what Chase had given. But the second I saw Ross and June round a corner and rush toward me, all my worries flew out of my head to make way for relief.

"Aila!" June shouted, sprinting ahead of Ross to throw her arms around me. She had an ugly bruise on her jaw and a small cut on her shoulder, but other than that, she looked fine. I embraced her, feeling some of the tension drain out of me. But then she bumped into my leg, and I recoiled with a hiss of pain.

June's gaze dropped to the ugly gash on my leg, and she sucked in a breath. "What happened?"

"I fought Kala."

Ross drew to a stop next to June and gave me a skeptical look. "And you're still alive to tell the tale?"

I couldn't help but crack a smile. "I get it now, Ross."

"Get what?"

"Sword fighting. I understood what June meant about giving myself over to instinct. I just had to...let go."

A grin split Ross's face, brighter than the sun. "I told you I was a good teacher."

I rolled my eyes and noticed the cut running along the length of his left forearm.

Ross tracked my gaze and stuck out his arm proudly. "I know, I just keep surviving life-or-death situations."

"Seems to me like you just really want to have a scar to show off."

Ross gave me a sour look, then finally seemed to notice Nylah, lingering a few feet behind me. "You're not Chase."

"Obviously," June snapped, rolling her eyes at him. She stepped forward and extended a hand. "I'm June, and this is Ross."

"Nylah," she responded, and they shook hands.

"So where's Chase?" Ross said, his eyes darting around the hall. I could hear the sound of swords ringing against swords and shouts coming from nearby corridors, but for the moment, the hall we were in was deserted.

The reminder of the trouble Chase was heading toward cut through my relief. A shadow must've passed over my face, because June's eyes shot wide. "Is he—"

"He's alive," Nylah said quickly when I failed to respond. "We were fighting Brone, but he got away. Chase went after him."

"Brone got away in a three-to-one fight?" Ross shook his head in my direction. "Aila, I think your sword problems are contagious."

I didn't match Ross's smirk, and June noticed. She studied my face, and I saw her eyes widen in shock. "He got away because..."

"He's an Exceptional," I confirmed in a hollow voice.

Ross's eyes widened. "What?"

"He can shoot ice from his hands."

"*What?*" Ross's voice mirrored the shock that was still tearing through me. But June frowned, her eyebrows drawing together with concern.

"So Chase just went after Brone alone?""

"Yes." I gritted my teeth, my worry spiking again.

Ross gave an approving nod. "Of course he did. This guy sounds like a legend. Just wait until I introduce myself to him."

I hardly heard Ross's words. "He told me to find you guys. We need to release the other Exceptionals. They deserve a chance at freedom."

June's frown deepened. "Why would Brone leave?"

"We almost defeated him, so he's going to find Storm," I said. I felt a surge of frustration. "Look, we don't have time. Let's just do this so I can get back to Chase—"

"But Brone doesn't even *know* Storm," June objected.

I didn't understand why June was still stuck on the fact that Brone went looking for Storm, especially when we were once more racing against the clock. "Of course he doesn't, but he knows that they're on opposite sides. That's enough."

"Aila, this doesn't make sense." June shook her head and took a step away from me, and I could see the wheels in her head spinning. "This seems too personal. Why didn't he come back to fight the leader of the Insurgence, or someone who's actually *important?* He wouldn't go after a random kid without a motive."

I opened my mouth, about to snap that I didn't care about Brone's motives, just about getting back to Chase as soon as possible, when Kala's last words sprung unbidden into my mind. *There is one left. One last family member to destroy.*

Blood drained from my face. My stomach dropped like the floor had disappeared from beneath me, and I felt as though I was about to fall to my knees.

June was immediately at my side. "Aila, are you okay? I'm sorry—"

"It's Storm," I whispered with dread. June frowned, exchanging glances with Nylah and Ross. "Storm," I said again. "He's the last one. The last member of Brone's family to destroy."

It suddenly all made sense. Brone had taken an unusual interest in Storm when we first broke into the Olum, especially once I mentioned that Storm was adopted. But the reality of what this meant hit me harder than the revelation itself. If Storm was Brone's last living relative, Brone would stop at nothing to destroy him. He would kill anyone who got in his way.

And Chase was heading their way to do exactly that.

I nearly choked on my next words. "Chase—he's..." My voice broke off, and a horrified sob rose in my throat. "Brone's going to..."

June didn't need to hear anything else. She laid a hand on my shoulder. "We understand. Go after him."

I shook my head. "But I have to—"

"We'll get the Exceptionals out," June said, and Nylah and Ross nodded. "Just go."

"I—"

"Don't worry about it," Ross stepped up next to June, his blue eyes locking with mine. "June and Nylah will be fine. They have me." He flashed a grin, then added with a wink, "When you defeat Brone, tell him he's no match for Ross Erland's teaching skills."

I knew the right thing to do was argue, to say it was my duty to help rescue Exceptionals, and I was going to stick with it.

But in the end, I nodded and raced off in the direction Chase had gone. Chase and Storm would need all the help they could get, because they were about to come face-to-face with a man who would let nothing stop him from getting revenge.

32

STORM

Aris had been surprisingly happy to see me.

Even now, as I continued down the hall, away from him, I couldn't wrap my head around the fact that he had convinced the Insurgence to come. When I initially asked him, I had expected to be disappointed. But they were here, and according to Aris, they were winning. It was almost over.

Apparently, Aris had given a speech about how it was our duty to do all we could to stop the unjust killing of Exceptionals. He hadn't convinced Commander White, but he'd convinced nearly everyone else. In the end, she could hardly say no.

But my relief only stretched so far. Jon was still missing, and even though Aris had promised to keep an eye out for him, I became more hopeless the deeper I traveled into the Olum. Merrick had wanted me to find Jon, but maybe Brone didn't. Maybe it was all over.

I felt as though I'd been searching for hours when I rounded a corner and spotted double doors at the end of the hall. I shouted in frustration. I had backtracked. *This was all hopeless.* I aimed a furious kick at the closest door.

That's when I realized the doorway ahead of me was rectangular, unlike the arched opening to the refectory. And the door was shut tight, when I'd left the doors to the refectory open. My heart began to pound. I sprinted up to one of the wooden doors and shoved.

It swung open to reveal a room even larger than the refectory. The ceiling arched high above, but instead of being filled with tables and chairs, the room was completely bare. In fact, with the stone walls and floor and conspicuous lack of furniture, I could've mistaken it for the training room back at the Insurgence Base.

This was where Exceptionals were taught to become murderers.

I craned my neck, and my eyes wandered up toward the ceiling. I paused when I spotted gaps in the wall. The openings were positioned in strategic intervals about where the second floor of the building would be, providing balconies where people could watch the activity happening on the floor below.

Watch, or perhaps guard and make sure all the Exceptionals did what they were supposed to.

They were prisoners, not murderers, I realized with a start. In my mind, I had painted the Expos to be a bunch of traitors, killers, people who were cold-blooded and vicious. I couldn't have been more wrong. These Exceptionals were a bunch of kids trying to stay alive, just like me. They had probably spent their entire time here living with the knowledge that they were being watched, every day of the week, every hour of the day.

The door behind me crashed open with a *thud*. I spun around.

My breath caught in my throat.

A tall figure stood calmly in the doorway, backlit by the flickering torchlight from the hall beyond. His gloved fingers dangled lazily above the hilt of his sheathed sword, as if he thought he had won this battle already. I felt a spike of anger. *Brone*.

His voice was infuriatingly composed. "I wasn't expecting to find you here."

"Where is he?" I snarled. When Brone didn't respond right away, I ripped my sword from my scabbard and lunged.

But I had barely crossed half the distance when Brone tore off a glove and whipped up his hand. A jet of frost burst from his palm and slammed into my wrist.

I stumbled back. The frost crept around my wrist like a thousand tiny spiders until it formed an icy shackle. Numbness crawled up my arm. My fingers grew so cold that I could no longer keep hold of my sword, and it crashed to the ground. The stinging coldness took my breath away.

I wouldn't have believed what I was seeing if it weren't for the pain that roared through my arm.

Slowly, I lifted my head and looked at Brone with wide eyes. The very man who had made it his life mission to capture all Exceptionals was an Exceptional himself.

The cold grew so intense that it burned. I came to my senses and activated my power. The heat in my palms , and I placed my left hand over my right wrist, chasing away the coldness. The shackle of frost melted away until it was nothing more than a few droplets of water.

My attention shifted back to Brone, who had strangely not moved from his position in the doorway. Instead, he watched me carefully, his cold gaze pinning me to the spot.

I stooped and picked up my sword, this time keeping Brone at a distance. My voice shook. "Tell me where he is."

"I don't know who you're talking about," Brone said coolly, "but I'm sure whoever he is, he'll be dead by the end of the day, just like you."

I gave him a startled look. Merrick had lied. Of *course* he had lied. If Brone truly had Jon, he'd be using him as a piece of leverage. Just as quickly, my anger dissolved into relief. Jon was safe, at least for now.

But Brone was still blocking the only exit out of this place, and for the first time, I began to worry about myself. I was no match for Brone with his Exceptional powers. Slowly, I took a step back.

Brone countered it with a step forward. "I must say, I'm impressed by your resilience," he said. His dark gray eyes were glowing. He looked like a kid who was one step away from winning a prize, and I had the unnerving feeling that his prize was my life. "Not only did you break into my Olum—twice—but you're standing right in front of me, alive after all these years."

There it was again. A phrase spoken so offhandedly that I could almost ignore it, as if he had just delivered a joke I didn't get. But I was missing something, something important, and it unsettled me.

He took another step forward, and I warily raised my sword. "It's understandable, really. You're quite like myself. Do you know why I capture Exceptionals, even though I am one? It's to make up for a mistake others made when I was younger, when I couldn't protect

297

someone I loved. Now I have to make sure that no one misunderstands Exceptionals again. I'm really just trying to make sure history doesn't repeat itself." Brone's voice was smooth, too smooth, as if he was discussing plans for a holiday. "It's all about protecting the person you love."

Chase's words cut through my mind. *Sometimes, we're more like our enemies than we think.* I banished the thought with disgust, but the most disquieting part was that it rang true. I would do anything to protect Jon, and if someone killed him…I didn't want to think of what I would become.

This time, when Brone stepped forward, I took another step back, as if I could distance myself from the part of me that I shared with him. As if I could escape the fact that, if things had gone differently, I would be the same villain as Brone.

"You were a fool to come here," Brone said with a shake of his head. At his next step, I automatically curled my free hand into a fist. "And now, you're going to face the consequences."

Brone flung out his right hand. I dropped my sword and threw myself to the ground, but not fast enough. The deadly point of an icicle sliced open my cheek as it zipped by, inches shy from impaling me entirely. I hit the ground with a thud.

Blood began to drip down the side of my face.

So. He could bind me in shackles of frost and throw dagger-sharp icicles from his hands. How encouraging.

Brone whipped another icicle in my direction with a slash of his arm. I rolled out of the way and sprang up the second the ice cleared my head. Before he could attack again, I threw out both my hands.

Fire flooded from my palms and arced upward, creating a roaring wall of flame between us. I had to squint to make out Brone's next attacks through the smoke and shifting flame. Every icicle he tried to throw melted before it even reached the wall of fire I had created. He gritted his teeth in obvious frustration, and I couldn't help but smirk.

"Not as easy of a fight as you thought, huh?" I shouted.

The moment the words left my mouth, I wished I could take them back. My attention divided, and for a brief moment, the wall of fire flickered. I clenched my jaw and poured my focus back into upholding the flame, but Brone noticed the falter.

"See how long you can keep that up before you collapse," he called.

I wanted to snap back, but I didn't dare take my attention off the flames. Already, I could feel my energy draining. I couldn't keep this up much longer, and I needed to be ready when the wall dropped. My gaze landed on my sword, which I had stupidly discarded out of reach. The blade was red-hot from the heat of the roaring flame. Maybe if I lunged for it...

Just when I felt my power was on the verge of being exhausted entirely, I curled my hands back into fists and dove for the sword. As I stretched for the blade, I felt a cool wind brush past me as an icicle skimmed past my face. Too late, I realized I hadn't been its target. The ice slammed into the hilt of my sword and shattered, the force of the impact sending the weapon skidding away from me.

I landed on the floor with a grunt. Then Brone was there, emerging through the curtain of smoke to stand over me. His lips twisted in a smirk as he leveled a palm at my chest. "Still feeling confident?"

I threw my arm out, but to my horror a feeble flame flickered to life in my hand and then died. I tried again, but this time only a few weak sparks leapt from my palm. My energy had been drained, and now my power was useless. Slowly, I lifted my gaze to meet Brone's.

He must've exhausted his power, too, because he yanked his sword from its scabbard. I felt my resolve crumble.

"Wait!" I threw up my arms, this time to shield my face instead of use my power. "Wait, please! Don't hurt me."

Brone gave me a mocking look. "I thought it would be below you to beg."

So had I, but that was before I had a sword pointed at my face. I wasn't ready to die. I wasn't ready to leave Jon. I'd promised him I would come back.

"I'm sorry I broke into the Olum. It was a mistake, okay? I see that now, and I promise if you let me go, I won't bother you ever again."

My voice broke in desperation as I begged. "I won't even talk about this place. You can just forget about me. *Please.*"

"Your silence isn't enough to satisfy me." Brone's voice was suddenly sharp with anger.

"Please," I whispered. "Please, I've done nothing wrong."

Brone let out a bark of cruel laughter, but when I just stared at him in despair, his brows drew together. "You really don't know who you are?"

My heart stuttered. It was the same question Merrick had asked me earlier. "I-I'm Storm Dawson." Brone's gaze darkened, and my voice rose to a frenzied pitch. "I'm no one! I'm just a boy from a little farming town, and if you let me go, I can disappear."

"No." Brone shook his head. "No, you're not. You were adopted."

I hesitated. How did he know that? I fumbled for words. "I was so young, I hardly remember." Mostly because I had spent my whole life trying to forget.

"But you weren't adopted from another family in the town," Brone said. How did he know all this? "Where are you from?"

I felt rage mix with my fear. Brone was trying to squeeze every last ounce of dignity from me. "I...I don't know."

"Yes, you do," Brone growled. He dropped the tip of his sword until it hovered just inches above me. "Most people don't get a second chance, and I certainly won't give you a third."

"Fine!" I spat. "My mom lived in a Stone City! Satisfied? I'm from the Stone Cities."

To my surprise, Brone did look satisfied. His eyes slid out of focus for the briefest moment, then fixed on me with a penetrating stare. "I'm going to tell you a story."

I didn't want to hear a story, but I was the one with a sword at my throat, so I just pressed my lips into a thin line.

"My parents cared more about Exceptionals than they did me, and though their mistake cost them nothing, it cost me the life of one of the people I loved most."

"Mila." The name slipped out of my mouth before I could stop it. It was Brone's turn to look surprised. "Aila told me. That's why you created the Olum."

"But it wasn't enough," Brone spat. "Creating the Olum was the right thing to do, but it wasn't enough when my family was still alive and well, free to continue causing pain. The only way I could avenge Mila was by ridding the world of my parents and their descendants."

Horror hit me like a punch to the gut. Brone hadn't only killed Exceptionals; he'd killed his family. My stomach rolled with dread. For the first time, I knew exactly what this man was capable of.

"I had a younger sister, many years younger than me, and she realized what I was doing. When I sent people to find her, she was prepared," Brone growled. "She had a child, but before my men got to her, she hid the child away. This child has been the one thing keeping me from accomplishing my goal, because she hid him in a place she knew I would never find him."

My mouth went dry. Suddenly, I wanted nothing more than for Brone to stop talking. I didn't want to hear what he had to say. I didn't want to know.

My ears were ringing so loudly I nearly missed Brone's next words. "She hid him among the poorest of the poor, in a small farming town called Ferrol."

"No." I wasn't sure if I said the word out loud or just screamed it in my mind. The world started to spin. Everything felt wrong. This conversation, this man, this entire building. It was all happening too quickly for me to process. It couldn't possibly be real. But everything Brone and Merrick had been telling me proved otherwise.

We're more like our enemies than we think.

I tried to wrench myself away from him, but the point of Brone's sword dropped until it rested on my chest. My entire body locked, and I stared up the blade in terror. My vision blurred. My mother was Brone's sister. Brone was my uncle.

My life was the last thing standing between him and complete revenge.

Brone's face had hardened in resolve, and my eyes fluttered closed. *I'm not ready.*

"Leave Storm alone!" A fearless voice cut through the air. *Chase,* I realized in alarm. He shouldn't be here. And yet, my eyes flew open, and I saw him step into the room, his chin lifted, his sword raised, as confident and selfless as ever. "If you want him, you'll have to get through me first."

Brone twisted in surprise, just for a moment, but it was enough. I knocked his blade out of the way and kicked him in the shin. Brone fell, and I wrestled the sword from his grip as he hit the ground. He tried to shove himself to his feet, but I thrusted the blade forward, and it sliced into his side. Brone cried out, clutching his wound and falling back to the floor.

Then Chase was there, materializing seemingly out of nowhere and leveling his sword at Brone.

"Here!" he shouted, tossing me a rope. "Tie him up!"

I dropped Brone's sword and scrambled to bind his hands behind his back as Chase kept his own sword pointed at Brone's face.

Only after I triple checked the knot did Chase lower his weapon and retreat several paces across the room.

"Thanks," I gasped, adrenaline still coursing through me, my heart thundering against my rib cage. With my sleeve, I wiped at the blood still running down my cheek, but I could hardly feel the pain through the adrenaline coursing through me. "I'm so glad you're okay. After I set the hall on fire—"

"We all got out," Chase interrupted.

"I'm sorry—"

He smirked. "You've made worse mistakes." I hung my head, but Chase nudged me with his shoulder and laughed. "Storm. I'm kidding. You saved us all back there." He waited until I met his gaze, then smiled. "I'm proud of you."

My eyes widened, and I was at a loss for words as my chest filled with gratitude. I couldn't wait until this was all over, when I could finally introduce him to Jon. I opened my mouth to tell him so when his gaze cut over my shoulder to where we had left Brone. "We have to get out of here, Brone is—"

"—an Exceptional. I know," I said breathlessly. "But he's exhausted his power."

"Exhausted his power? What are you talking about?"

"We both used ours to the point where we lost all of our energy. But you're right, we should probably—"

"How long ago was this?" Chase interrupted.

"I don't know, five minutes, maybe. Ten." I let out a relieved chuckle. "It's all a blur, really." *But it was all over.* I felt like I had just crawled my way out of a living nightmare.

But one look into Chase's panicked gaze told me he still thought we were in it. "And you still don't have yours? Are you sure?"

I frowned. "Yes, I'm..." I trailed off, slowly curling my hands into a fist. When I unfurled my fingers, a ball of flame flickered to life in my palm.

There were no words to describe the horror that washed through me. "Chase—"

A shout echoed through the room, but I wasn't sure whose it was. Maybe it came from Brone, who, without warning, ripped his frozen bonds from his wrists and whipped both hands up, frost exploding from them in full force. Or maybe the shout came from Chase, who took the full brunt of the attack straight into his chest, the force hitting him so hard it flung him to the floor.

Or maybe the shout came from me as I realized my mistake. Chase crumbled, seeming to fold in on himself in agony. I twisted and sent a jet of flame at Brone. I heard him grunt as it hit him in the chest, but I was already scrambling across the floor to where Chase was curled and trembling. I shook, too, as I lifted Chase up and supported him against my knee.

"Chase, I'm sorry—"

"Not your fault," Chase ground out. He was pale, paler than I'd ever seen him, even paler than when I'd found him in the dungeons. His eyes slid in and out of focus.

My heart began to pound with dread.

Chase shut his eyes tightly, forcing out his next words between ragged breaths. "Have Aila…tell you about my power."

"What?" I asked, startled. Those sounded like parting words, like a dying request. My stomach dropped. "No, you're getting out of here. We're going to get you out of here, Chase. And then…and then we can start that school."

"We." Chase smiled weakly. "So that means you're not laughing at me anymore?"

"Stay with me," I begged. My eyes began to fill with tears, and I blinked rapidly. This wasn't happening. *Nothing was happening.* "You can't—"

"Fire," Chase interrupted, his faint voice still full of command.

I needed no further prompting. Two flames appeared in my palms, and I held them close to Chase's chest, hoping with all my might that they would create enough heat to ward off whatever Brone had done to him. To my relief, pain began to drip off Chase's face like water droplets on a melting icicle. Soon, his eyes fluttered closed, and he slumped to the ground, unconscious.

I shot to my feet and turned toward Brone just in time to see him beat out the last lick of flame with ice-encrusted fingers. His eyes flicked from me to Chase, and his lips curled in a cruel smile.

Fury tore through me like a raging bull, but this time, I wasn't going to let it control me. Instead, I replaced my anger with determination, and I lifted my arms. Two jets of fire exploded from my palms the same time a pillar of frost exploded from Brone's. The two elements collided in the middle, and the force of our raw power slammed into each other.

Then everything exploded.

The room erupted in light and sparks and jets of frost. A wave of force rippled outward, slamming into me and throwing me across the room into a wall. The breath flew out of my lungs as sharp pain shot up and down my back. I slumped to the ground with an agonized shout. Black crept in from the corners of my vision, and I could feel my body beginning to shut down.

Then, through the haze of mist and smoke that had filled the room, I saw a figure pick himself up off the ground.

For a moment, I thought it was Chase, but my stomach sank as the figure turned. I caught a glimpse of Brone's heartless expression as he limped across the room in my direction. I shot a desperate glance toward the doorway. For a moment, I considered escaping. I'd be gone before he reached me.

Then, somewhere in the dark recesses of my brain, I heard Chase's clear, confident voice. "*Whatever it takes.*"

Suddenly, I wasn't in the Olum, but in a narrow alleyway, Chase's grip on my shoulders the only thing keeping me from collapsing.

"*We'll find a way.*" It was like Chase wasn't unconscious across the room, but instead right in front of me, speaking in a voice as clear as day. "*We'll sneak out of the Insurgence Base, find the Expos, something. Anything. Whatever it takes.*"

And we had. Against all odds, we'd pushed through and broken into the Olum, just like Chase had said. I couldn't let it end here. Chase *had* done whatever it took, helping me even when he faced life in a jail cell, even when he faced death. The least I could do was put up a fight.

All these thoughts flashed through my mind in the time it took for Brone to take three long strides toward me. On his fourth step, I made a decision. I would fight, even though Brone would inevitably win. And when the time came, I would let Brone get his revenge, if that's what it took for my friends to make it out of here alive.

On Brone's fifth step, I felt all the tension drain out of me. I blinked away the darkness that clouded the edges of my vision and clenched my jaw. I could do this.

"Whatever it takes," I muttered, then shoved myself to my feet.

Pain tore through every part of me, and I braced an arm against the wall to keep from collapsing. I clenched my jaw and forced myself to straighten just in time to see Brone send a jet of frost at me.

I countered Brone's attack with a wave of blistering heat that caused the frost to melt away. I extinguished each icicle with a ball of fire, melted each icy blast with flame, but I didn't attack. I wasn't giving up; I was giving myself over.

I was giving my friends a chance.

I slowly retreated up until I reached the corner, my back colliding with the wall opposite of where Chase still lay. My vision swam, and it took all my strength to stay standing. Brone swept his arm through the air and sent hundreds of tiny little ice darts toward me. I was so distracted trying to avoid getting pegged in the face that when he flung out another jet of frost, I was unable to dodge. It hit me in the stomach, knocking the air from my lungs. I gasped as a searing cold filled me, followed by a burning numbness. The frost crawled across my abdomen and up toward my chest, the cold so painful that I couldn't do anything but stand there, my eyes watering with agony.

And then the spreading stopped. The frost had formed a case across my stomach and spread onto the stone behind me, pinning me against the wall. I clenched my fist instinctively, but the cold was so deep that I couldn't even tell if my power was working.

Brone stopped in front of me, his expression devoid of triumph, devoid of anything but decades worth of burning hate. He lifted his hand, and, to my astonishment, a weapon began to form in his palm. Layers upon layers of frost built on each other until he was holding a sharp ice dagger.

I sucked in a breath, but not at the dagger. I felt a small yet promising flicker of warmth in my palm. It wasn't enough for me to melt my bonds entirely. I knew it was too late for that. But maybe, I could take Brone down with me.

"Look at me," Brone snarled. "I want to see your eyes when I finally finish what my parents started."

I looked up, and when I did, I felt peace wash over me. I finally understood. I had been trying all these months, and in fact, my entire life, to get what I wanted. But now all I cared about was saving as many people as I could, and I didn't feel angry anymore.

My only regret was that I wouldn't be able to tell Jon goodbye.

Brone lifted his arm and pulled back, the ice dagger aimed at my heart. I felt energy drain into my palm. In the end, I wouldn't need the energy anyway.

What happened next seemed to occur in slow motion.

Brone brought the ice dagger down the same time I whipped up my palm and released a burst of fire. All the energy drained out of me at once, and I hardly had enough in me to feel a final stab of fear as the dagger descended.

A flash of movement. A grunt. Blood.

But no pain.

I barely had time to register what had happened, barely had time to understand that the blood was not my own, barely had time to recognize the wide, hazel eyes filled with pain and the same reassurance as when I had first seen them, before I was swallowed by a cold, endless darkness.

33

AILA

As soon as I heard the explosion, I knew with certainty that it was coming from Chase's direction. I tried to move as fast as I could, but my leg screamed with pain, and my vision grew blurrier with every step. Adrenaline was the only thing that kept me going as I wove my way back into the chaos of the battle.

The fighting had spread out across several halls. Most of the people I passed were locked in vicious weapon duels, but others were fighting with powers. I nearly got hit by an Insurgent when she lurched through a portal that materialized in front of me, but I twisted out of the way just in time. A few steps later, I spotted an Expo whose skin turned into stone each time the Insurgent swung their weapon.

I also passed people whose fights had ended badly. Both Expos and Insurgents alike were on the ground, clutching at wounds and groaning in pain. I passed a few Insurgents who lay unmoving, and I hoped they were only unconscious.

I was picking my way through the rubble near the explosion when a rock beneath me shifted suddenly. I tried to catch myself on the wall, but it was no use. I hit the ground, and pain tore through my leg. No matter how hard I tried to stand, my leg refused to support me. I let loose a scream of frustration.

"Aila!"

Arden broke through a crowd of Insurgents, and I almost melted in relief. His gaze zeroed in on my leg. "I'll help you!"

308

I wanted to object, wanted to keep pressing forward and find Chase, but given that I couldn't even stand, I wasn't in the position to argue. Arden dropped to his knees beside me and laid a hand gently on my wound.

The skin slowly stitched itself together, and I was grateful for the relief from the pain.

"Where's Chase?" I asked the second he finished, shooting to my feet.

"I don't know," Arden said. His voice quivered, and I was reminded just how young he was. "I've been keeping an eye out for him, but—" He stopped short as his eyes dropped to my hand. I'd discarded my sword long ago, needing a free hand to prop myself up against the wall, but I still clutched the dagger Storm had given me. Arden's eyes widened. "That's Chase's dagger. Is he—"

"I don't know," I interrupted. "Did you hear that explosion just a bit ago? Where did it come from?"

"Down there." Arden pointed toward the training rooms and Common Areas.

"Thanks." I almost ran off, but I couldn't just leave Arden standing there, looking suddenly lost in the midst of a battle that was too big for him. "You're doing great, Arden. Out of everyone here today, you're saving the most lives."

Arden nodded, looking a bit more confident, and I took off down the hall with newfound strength. I skidded to a halt in front of the trainees' Common Area. The door was ajar, and I slipped inside.

A boy looked up as I entered, and I was about to leave because he obviously wasn't Chase, but I hesitated when I realized he was guarding someone. Merrick was propped up against one of the wooden tables, his hands and ankles bound tightly. The boy noticed me pausing in the doorway, and Merrick tracked his gaze, his eyes darkening in anger.

"She's an Expo! Get her!"

I didn't stick around to see if the boy would listen to Merrick, instead continuing toward the first training room. When I turned the corner to find the hall was hazy with smoke, and the door was propped open, I broke into a flat-out sprint. I stopped short in the doorway, my heart dropping when I saw the scene that was unfolding.

Storm was pinned against the wall, but my view of him was half-blocked by Brone. Before I could even step into the room, Brone jerked his arm down at the same time Storm whipped up a hand. Without thinking, I lifted Chase's dagger and chucked it at Brone.

The world seemed to slow. I stood, frozen, as the ball of fire and the dagger hit Brone simultaneously, the fire in his chest, the dagger between his shoulder blades. At the same time, Storm's eyes dropped closed as he braced himself for the deathly blow of the ice dagger.

And then, out of nowhere, Chase...

Chase...

Jumped in front of Storm and took the dagger for himself.

"*Chase!*" My guttural cry echoed off the walls, raw with terror. I stumbled into the room as Chase, Brone, and Storm all collapsed to the ground.

Blood was everywhere: On Storm, on Chase, on Brone, rushing through my ears and making it impossible to hear even as I screamed Chase's name.

I fell to my knees at his side, tears streaming down my face. I knew before I even reached for him what had happened. The dagger was embedded in his chest, his hand splayed around it as if he had fallen clutching at the wound.

I sobbed in panic. I didn't know what to do. Should I pull the dagger out? Should I wipe up the blood? Should I bandage his wound? I didn't have a bandage. I reached for Chase's wrist, seeking out a pulse.

When I touched his skin, it was ice cold.

"Medic!" I screamed, although I knew there was no one near enough to hear. "Arden! Someone help! I can't—I can't—" I broke off, gasping for breath through my choking sobs. I grabbed his wrist again. There had to be a pulse. There *had* to be. "Help!" I cried again. "Help! Please, anyone!"

I was trembling all over, my eyes so filled with tears that I nearly missed the tiny flutter in his wrist. But I did notice when Chase's eyelids flickered. For the briefest of moments, his lids cracked open, and I caught a glimpse of his hazel eyes. The edge of his mouth quirked up in the tiniest smile, then his eyelids dropped closed.

His breaths were so shallow that his chest hardly moved, and when his eyes flitted open again, there was no mistaking the goodbye in his gaze.

"No," I choked out. "Chase, hang on, please. Help is coming."

Chase's eyes shut again. I could barely feel his pulse anymore.

"Just hang on, Chase," I begged. My voice broke. "Don't go. Please, don't go."

Suddenly, I didn't care about the blood. I just wrapped my arms around my best friend for the last time. "Please, don't go. I don't want you to go, Chase. I don't want you to go. I don't want you to go."

I didn't know how long I stayed there with my arms wrapped around him, begging for him to stay with me. I didn't know how long it was until my desperate cries turned into silent sobs.

But I was entirely aware of the moment that Chase Kader's chest rose and fell with his final breath.

34

STORM

The day I became an Exceptional, I was certain it would forever be the worst day of my life.

I thought it was all over after that day. Even when I woke up, alive in the Insurgence Base, I knew there was no erasing the Exceptional mark. There was no escaping the life that awaited me. From that point on, I would be tied to the X on my left hand, tied to that horrible day when the Securities dragged me home for the last time.

But I was proven wrong when I saw the real Expos drag Jon away. The pain I'd experienced that day was worse than any pain I'd ever felt, because I was helpless to do anything as my little brother was pulled into a far worse life than the one I'd been living.

And again, when our first attempt at rescuing Jon failed miserably and landed me in a cell in the Insurgence Base, I had felt a crushing defeat and the sense that my life would never be the same. The sense that things had changed drastically for the worse.

But at least all those times, I had hope. Sometimes I didn't realize it, but there was always a flicker of something deep inside, the possibility that things could change, the hope of a second chance.

But now, there was nothing. Not even the faintest tremor, the barest flutter, because there was no bringing back the dead.

When I awoke from my unconscious stupor to see Aila bent over Chase's unmoving body, the pain that tore me open was like nothing I had felt before. Suddenly, it didn't matter that I could hardly walk, or that my face and arms were covered in thousands of tiny cuts and bruises. I couldn't feel anything past the agony that ripped my heart into pieces. I didn't even have the strength to scream, didn't even have the strength to cry. I just collapsed on the ground next to Chase and stared at his lifeless body, knowing that this time, there was no second chance. My best friend, Chase Kader, was dead.

"This isn't fair," I whispered when I finally found the strength to speak.

Aila, who had moved off to my right to give me some space, jerked her head up to look at me.

"He doesn't deserve this." I turned to look at her. "It shouldn't have been him. He—" A sob escaped, and suddenly, I was crying, gasping for breath. "It's not fair that I get to live and Chase doesn't. It...it was supposed to be me."

My entire body shook. I felt empty, cold, scared. I was more scared than when I became an Exceptional, than when Jon was taken away, than when Aila betrayed us, because this time, I was alone. I was going to have to take every next step in life without Chase by my side, and I didn't know how I would do it. I didn't know what to do.

Then, I felt Aila's arm around me, and with it came a sudden, startling rush of clarity. I *wasn't* alone. Today, we had both lost a friend. We were both feeling grief. I had been pushing her away, insistent on hating her, when really she was the only one this entire time that I could truly relate to.

We're more like our enemies than we think. I didn't know whether to cry or laugh. Even with Chase gone, he was still helping me change.

"It wasn't supposed to be you, Storm," Aila murmured. "Chase took that dagger for you for a reason, and now you need to find that reason and live your life so his last decision is worth it."

I shook my head, choking on another sob. "It's my fault. He wouldn't have been here if it weren't for me—"

"We both made mistakes, but Chase's death was not one of them. It was his choice to give you a second chance."

A second chance. "He doesn't even know half of the mistakes I made. He wouldn't have given me a second chance if he did."

Aila was silent for a long time. When she finally spoke, her voice trembled. "Did Chase ever tell you about his power?"

I remembered one of the final things he said to me: *Have Aila tell you about my power.* It had been one of his best kept secrets. I sucked in a trembling breath and shook my head.

"He could sense things. He had a sort of...intuition." Aila's eyes glistened as she gazed softly at Chase. "He could sense when something had gone wrong, or when someone was lying. He could...he could sense the good in people."

My chest shuddered, but my tears were momentarily gone.

"He's always known there was good in us, even when it seemed like we couldn't stop proving him wrong."

I opened my mouth to reply, but my throat was so thick with emotion that I had to shut it again. Of course Chase had always seen the good in us. He always saw the good in everyone, even Aris, even when we didn't see it ourselves.

Aila's voice was no more than a whisper. "He took that dagger for you because he sensed that it was the right thing to do. He *knew* it was the right thing to do. You have to trust that decision."

My gaze dropped back down to Chase. I had only known him for such a small part of my life, and yet he had changed everything for me. He had been kind and selfless, all the way to the end.

I lifted my head, my gaze locking with Aila's. "We're going to get through this," I murmured, my voice shaking. "We'll make him proud."

Aila smiled, and finally, I felt that little flicker of hope ignite inside of me again.

35

STORM

The door at the other end of the room burst open.

I heard footsteps, shouts, the shuffling of feet. Then, "Storm!"

My head jerked up, and I barely had time to react before Jon was there, throwing himself into my arms and clinging to me as if I was about to slip away. I immediately embraced him, holding him just as tightly as he sobbed into my shoulder. I would have been crying, too, if I had any tears left to cry.

"You're okay—I was so worried—it's over, the battle is over—they just need to find Brone, but when we couldn't find you—" Jon tightened his arms around me. "You're okay, you're *okay*—" His rushed words dissolved as he buried his face back into my shirt.

"Yeah, I'm okay," I whispered. "We're both okay."

Jon sniffed and drew back, his concerned gaze flying to my cheek.

I had almost forgotten about the wound, but now that I remembered, I felt it stinging sharply. In fact, my entire body ached, but at least none of my cuts were bleeding anymore. "I'm fine," I insisted, then slowly took in the rest of my surroundings.

The first thing I noticed was the cut above his eye, a small yet ugly scrape that made my gut clench. Then my attention shifted, and I realized the room was slowly filling with Insurgents and Expos alike, bustling with activity as the Insurgence began to line cuffed Expos against the wall. I spotted Aris just a few feet away. He had probably just arrived with Jon. I opened my mouth to thank him, then paused.

He was standing stock still, staring down at Chase's form. Jon spotted Chase, too, and inhaled sharply.

Aris's eyes were dry, but he was shaking his head slowly, as if unwilling to comprehend what was before him. I stood up and walked to stand next to him. "It was Brone." My voice was hushed. "He's an Exceptional with ice powers. He bound me to the wall and threw an ice dagger at me and Chase—" I immediately cut off; the memories were still too fresh.

"That's how he deserved to die," Aris said, his voice thick. "A hero."

I nodded, tearing my gaze away from Chase's body to stare at the floor. "He gave me a second chance."

"He gave everyone a second chance." Aris wasn't crying, but his voice shook with grief. "He came up to me, a week or so before you ran away. He...he was the first person to ever confront me and let me know how much of a jerk I was."

I raised my eyebrows. If I'd known that's all Aris needed to be humbled, I would've told it to him ages ago.

"I was angry at the time, but there was something about the way he said it. Like he wasn't going to let that stop him from caring about me."

Eventually, Aris, Jon, Aila, and I stepped back, letting other Insurgents move forward and have their moment of grief. I was only now realizing how much of an impact Chase made on all of us, and how much more of an impact he would've made if his time hadn't been cut short.

It took a while for someone to notice Brone. I had hardly even noticed him, lying just a few feet away from Chase. One of the Insurgent medics rushed over, then looked up in surprise.

"He has a pulse!"

Another time, I might've felt disappointment, but all I felt was empty. I had seen enough death today and didn't need to see more, even if it was the death of the enemy.

Medics swarmed Brone's body in a flurry of balms and bandages, and the first medic turned to a group of Insurgent members who were watching with worried expressions.

316

"Go get Commander White, and tell her we found Brone alive." As they hurried off, the medic shook his head and turned back to Brone. "He's going to have a lot of questions to answer when he wakes up."

We watched in silence for several seconds before I turned to Aris and Jon. "Did you guys find each other?"

Jon suddenly looked away as Aris said, "I bumped into him while he was looking for you."

I shot Jon a stern look, and he just shrugged.

"It's okay," Aris said. "I kept him away from the battle…as best I could." He cast a sidelong glance at Jon's wounds.

The conversation fell into an awkward silence, the ease of our earlier interaction having long since trickled away. All I could think about was how hard I had been on Aris. I'd been so focused on his flaws that I hadn't seen any other part of him.

I gave a little cough. "I, uh—thanks for watching out for him," I said uncomfortably. "That was…um." I cleared my throat.

"No problem," Aris said quickly, sparing me from further embarrassment. I caught a glimpse of Aila's amused expression over his shoulder and scowled. "He hardly needed me, anyway," Aris continued. "Even without his power, he's got guts."

"What?" I rounded on Jon, who offered me a tentative smile.

"Surprise?"

"You got your power? When were you planning on letting me know?"

"Later," Jon said, although I could tell by his glare in Aris's direction that he'd been hoping to keep it a surprise. Suddenly, he grabbed my hand. "It's really cool, though."

"What is—ow!" I yelped as a shock jolted through my arm, our skin zapping the moment it touched. I jerked my hand back and shook it out, glowering at Jon, who grinned.

"I just got it today," he said eagerly. "I still think yours is cooler, though."

I opened my mouth to agree when I was cut off by commotion across the room, followed by the unmistakable click of boots on stone. Commander White broke through the crowd of Insurgents who were still lining up the captured Expos. She strode toward us with the same air of confidence and authority she'd had on my first day at the Insurgence, despite the fact that she was clearly limping.

She stopped short next to the medics and started barking commands. Brone was still unconscious, but someone locked him in special cuffs that covered his hands, and he was rolled onto a stretcher and carried out of the room. I let out a breath. He wouldn't be able to hurt anyone anymore.

Commander White's eyes landed on Chase's body, and I saw her breath catch. She stood there, staring for several moments, then turned away abruptly, but not before I spotted the tears glinting in her eyes. Eventually, she commanded nearby Insurgents to remove him from the room. It was hard to breathe as I watched them lift him onto a stretcher, lay a white sheet over his body, and carefully carry him out. Even the commander stopped to watch him go, her gaze softer than I'd ever seen it.

When his body disappeared through the doors, I dropped my head. Jon's hand slipped into mine, and my throat tightened.

Commander White approached to give us a brief update. Apparently, Nylah had partnered with June and Aila's other Olum friend, Ross, to release the imprisoned Exceptionals. Those who they had rescued, and all who said they were no longer loyal to Brone, were being held in the refectory, where I had dueled Merrick.

Suddenly, the commander grew quiet, her gaze darting between me and Aila. At last, she said, "I believe I have the two of you to thank for this, and I do not mean that in a bad way."

I shook my head and began to speak, but Commander White gestured for silence. "I know you both made mistakes, but you dared to act when no one else would." There was another pause, then Commander White made eye contact with Aila and said, "I apologize for not doing anything more forward about the Exceptionals until now. I have let you down."

"What matters is that you came," Aila said.

The sound of raised voices suddenly spilled into the room from the hall, and I turned just in time to see a man burst through the doors,

318

followed by a contingent of soldiers. Their uniforms were adorned with the Earl's insignia.

"What's going on here?" the man at the front bellowed. "We got a report about a disturbance at the Olum. What—" He stopped abruptly, his eyes darting around the room, widening when he spotted Merrick bound and surrounded by armed Insurgents.

"That's Dion, one of Earl Nicolin's officials," Aila told Commander White with wide eyes. "He comes here for updates. Brone's been lying to him, but I think Dion was starting to catch on. This is our chance. We can fix this."

For the first time, I realized just how much we still had to do before Exceptionals were truly free. The pain didn't just stop at the Olum; it spread throughout the entire country of Rosan.

Next to me, Commander White nodded resolutely. "I must speak to him. Would you accompany me?"

As the two started off in Dion's direction, I turned to Jon and cracked a grin. The grief was still there, threatening to break me down again, and I wasn't sure if it would ever fully go away. But there were things to celebrate, too, like the fact that I was standing face-to-face with my little brother again.

Aris, who had still been lingering nearby, must've noticed something in my expression because he excused himself to go talk to a medic, leaving Jon and me alone for the first time in what felt like years.

"So," he said, grinning. "I'm an Exceptional."

An unexpected laugh bubbled in my throat. "Yeah. You sure are." So much had happened since Jon and I had last been together in Ferrol. Neither of us knew where to start. I didn't know how to put into words the joy that was filling my heart, so full it felt like it was going to burst.

An uncontrollable grin was on Jon's face as he asked, "What happens next?"

What happens next? It was a good question, and I was beginning to feel less afraid about not knowing the answer.

"Honestly? I don't know. I truly don't know." Jon nodded, as if he had been expecting this answer. "But it doesn't matter," I added, "because whatever we do, we'll be safe, and we'll be together."

"Good," Jon said, twisting his face into a mock scowl, "because if you try *one more time* to send me to a utility closet while you risk your life, I'm zapping you."

I rolled my eyes and threw an arm around Jon's shoulder, pulling him into a headlock. "Don't forget the fire, Jon, don't forget the fire."

And suddenly, even after all that had happened, even after becoming an Exceptional, fighting the Expos, and losing my best friend...I realized my plan had worked. The journey to get here had been hard, but now I saw it was as valuable as the prize of Jon and I standing here together, facing a future of possibilities.

Aila found me sometime later, perched on top of the climbing wall in the corner of the second training room. My left leg was pulled up to my chest with my injured arm slung over it, and my right leg dangled fearlessly over the edge. I had used to perch this same way atop the buildings of Carsley and relax after a long and successful day.

Except today, I wasn't in Carsley. I was in a makeshift hospital, watching Jon with eagle eyes as Arden treated his head wound. It looked like the two of them were getting along nicely. I was guessing how long it would take them to become friends when Aila scrambled over the lip of the climbing wall.

She dropped down next to me with a huff, and without even looking in her direction I said, "I got up here in half the time."

Aila shot me a glare and bumped into me with her shoulder, frowning when I yanked my injured arm out of reach. Her eyes then landed on the jagged cut that was still on my cheek. I had wiped off the dried blood, but it was still a bright, angry red.

"You should have Arden take a look at that."

"Yeah," I said. To be honest, I kind of wanted to let it heal on its own. Then I would have a scar, something that would remind me of everything that had happened and everything I needed to continue to fight for.

But of course, I didn't tell Aila that. She'd probably make fun of me for it.

The two of us lapsed into silence as my gaze returned to Jon. Arden had just finished healing his wound, and as I watched, my brother touched his forehead, his eyes widening with wonder. Jon glanced around, searching the corners of the room until he spotted me up above. His eyes lit up, and he pointed to his head, as if to say, *Can you believe it?* I grinned and flashed him a thumbs up.

"You really love him, don't you?" Aila said, watching our exchange with a soft gaze.

"Well, I don't know," I said, leaning back and propping myself up with my elbows. "I just decided to risk my life and everyone else's for the fun of it, you know?"

Aila laughed, but the sound quickly filtered away. "No, I mean…I understand now."

I looked at her.

"I understand why you risked everything for him. Seeing the way you look at him, how much you care about him…" Aila let out a breath. "Well, I would've done the same."

I wasn't sure how to respond to that, so instead, I kicked the back of my heels against the training wall and let my gaze travel across the rows of the healed, wounded, and dead. There were some people I didn't even know down there, stretched out on cots while white-clad Insurgence medics raced between them. I spotted Ross telling a story so animatedly that the medic couldn't keep him still long enough to bandage his arm.

I pushed myself up straight and took a deep breath. "Aila, I need to tell you something." She glanced over and nodded for me to continue. "I…Brone is…" The words caught in my throat, and it took effort to finally force out, "Brone is my uncle."

Aila was silent for such a long time that I didn't think she was going to respond. When she did, her words were not at all what I expected. "I figured."

I blinked. "What?"

"Kala said something, and it made me realize there was a bigger reason behind what Brone was doing. I can't forgive him, and I don't pity him, but…I suppose I understand him."

I nodded. I felt the same way. "I don't want to tell Jon yet," I said haltingly. "Is that…wrong?"

Aila fixed me with a firm stare. "You and Brone share nothing but blood. He is not your family, and he never will be. That word will always be reserved for Jon. But…you don't have to be ashamed of your past. Don't let it trap you."

I dropped my eyes and pretended to study the cut on my arm. The past *had* been trapping me, and her, too.

"Aila?" I said again, more hesitantly this time.

"Yeah?"

"I'm sorry."

She blinked in surprise, and let out a quick, startled laugh. "For what?"

"We've just been…butting heads ever since we met, and Chase had definitely noticed, and…" I trailed off, and Aila turned to face me. For once, she didn't look judgemental or condescending. She just waited for me to continue.

I cleared my throat again, then my words tumbled out in a rush. "I've probably been coming across as a huge jerk, and if you walk away from here only remembering me as that annoying kid who tried to light you on fire, then I did something very wrong."

Aila stared at me, and I knew right then that I was doing a terrible job at apologizing. "I never thought of you like that."

"I just don't want to be remembered as another enemy."

"No," Aila said, before I could get another word out. "I'll only walk away thinking of you as the person who helped me do the most impossible, rewarding thing ever. It wasn't just your fault that we didn't get along, and we're on the same side now." She hesitated, a flicker of uncertainty crossing her gaze. "Right?"

"Right," I agreed hastily.

We fell silent once more and turned back to watching the bustling activity below. With a start, I realized that a huge weight had been lifted

322

off my shoulders. The chains of guilt had been broken, and for the first time in a long while, I didn't feel like all my mistakes were haunting me.

One glance at Aila told me she felt the same.

"You know, it's almost like he's not really gone," she said after a moment.

I dropped my gaze. I knew exactly what she meant.

"I mean, I know he's dead, but it's like he's still here. You can see him in every act of kindness the people are doing down there, you can hear it in the way everyone talks about him." Aila took a deep breath and looked at me. "It's like he's in our hearts."

I couldn't think of another word to add. Even though he was gone, the impact he made on our lives wasn't going away anytime soon. It was as if he was with us now, reminding us to make good decisions and to see the best in others, even though he wasn't around to actually tell us.

Brone might've thought he defeated us by killing Chase, but he was wrong. Chase Kader would always be kept alive in the hearts of everyone who had ever known him.

Epilogue

AILA

It was an unusually warm day for mid-October, and the sun beat down on my shoulders as I strode across the cobblestone street, heading in the opposite direction of where I wanted to be. I was sweating, but not because of the heat.

I was sweating because of nerves.

It had been five months, and part of me was ashamed it had taken me that long to work up the courage to be here today.

"Do you want me to go with you?" Storm had asked earlier that morning. He'd been sitting on a crate, his back against the wall, snacking on an apple and watching Jon and Arden unpack more crates. They were filled with items from the Olum and had been sitting unopened in a storage room in the Insurgence Base since the battle. Finally, a group of us had decided to do something about them.

Standing next to Storm, I'd marveled at how much he had changed since we first met. Sure, he was still stubborn, impulsive, and at times, disrespectful. But behind the curtain of grief that never quite left his eyes, a certain brightness glowed. Gone was the guilt and fear that used to haunt him. Gone was the anger that he'd nearly let control him. He'd walked through fire and come out on the other side more mature than ever.

We both had.

"No, I need to do this on my own," I responded, turning away from him to open the long, thin crate next to me. I pulled out some old

324

brooms and tossed them in a pile before shooting him a look over my shoulder. "Aren't you going to help?"

Storm had, in fact, not helped unpack the crates, but his offer of support meant so much that I wasn't too annoyed. Although I had lost one friend, over the past several months I had found another in Storm. He by no means could replace Chase and would never quite be the same to me as Ross and June, but we could relate to each other in a way I couldn't relate to anyone else. We had both experienced the loss of someone very close to us—experienced it, but also grown from it.

We had decided to break for lunch at noon, and I set out shortly after. It was my first time walking in public alone since the battle, and I fought the urge to keep my hand concealed behind my back. It was hard not to notice the stares cast in my direction and the way people avoided me as I wound through the stone streets of Bedrock.

Despite this, our country had come a long way regarding Exceptionals since the Battle of the Olum. That's what people were calling the Insurgence's stand against the Expos. I don't know which Insurgent started it, but it had spread beyond the walls of the Insurgence Base to towns all over Rosan. Ross had made a valiant effort to change the name to Ross Erland's Victory Over the Expos, but as June immediately pointed out, it didn't quite have the same ring to it. So the Battle of the Olum stuck.

There were other bigger victories to celebrate. It had taken many hours of explanation and conversation, but we had finally managed to convince Dion—and through him, Earl Nicolin—that Exceptionals were not corrupt and dangerous, just different. It had taken even more time and conversation, but finally the earl had made an official announcement: Exceptionals, when found, would no longer be reported and taken away.

The farming and trading towns had been the first to accept this new protocol, then the business towns, with the Stone Cities following with more reluctance and time. Storm had been unsurprised.

"The Stone Cities are used to having the earl do the thinking for them, but the towns have always been more free," he had told me after a discussion with Commander White about the most recent developments. "It'll always take the Stone Cities more time to react, more time to change."

I watched as a mother pulled her daughter to the other side of the street when I passed. Storm's words were true.

A cloud passed briefly over the sun, casting me in a cool shadow for one glorious moment as I turned the next corner. On the far end of the street was the Security Station. Normally, on a day like today—right in the middle of Mission Week—a squad of Expos would be waiting inside for a report of an Exceptional. But now, the building just sat there, quiet and empty, another symbol of how far Rosan had come.

People were slowly beginning to realize that Brone was truly just a power-hungry murderer, but still, not all Exceptionals were still wanted. At first, the Insurgence had welcomed every unwanted Exceptional into the Base, but we all knew there would soon be too many.

That's when they started constructing schools, all over Rosan, where Exceptionals would be taught to responsibly control their powers. At first, many families balked at the idea of taking their child out of their regular school or job to send them to these institutions, especially if the distance of travel meant they would be gone all day. Commander White had quickly found a solution by requiring Exceptionals go to classes only three days of the week until Exceptionals were deemed responsible enough to stop attending. Until then, there was a strict prohibition on the use of Exceptional powers without supervision of an instructor.

There were many loopholes, of course. Some of the Exceptionals who were trained today could use their power for harm in the future, and the blame would always fall back on the Insurgence. There would always be some element of fear, some element of resentment between the normal public and these strange Exceptionals with special powers. But for now, we were doing the best we could. I was proud to be a part of the group working to change the country for the better.

The closer I drew to the heart of the city, the more familiar the streets became. I passed Bedrock's school just as the last of the students jogged down the steps. Two small boys and a girl, probably around ten years old, caught my attention. Their eyes were bright with laughter as they exchanged glances, then took off down the street in a race.

A sad smile came to my face. It felt like a different lifetime, but that had once been Warren, Chase, and me racing each other home from school.

Home. The word shot a pang through my heart, and I forced myself to continue on my way. The longer I hesitated, the more I risked talking myself out of what I needed to do.

But I had to do something else first, something even harder than delivering the news of a death to a person's loved ones.

I turned onto the streets I knew better than my own name. I passed the alley where I had played street games with Chase and Warren for hours until we were exhausted and muddy. I passed the practice hall where Chase had learned to use a sword, a skill that had saved my life.

I passed the bakery that I had run inside, crying for help when I realized that Chase was an Exceptional.

And then, suddenly, I had arrived. The house was built of stone with chiseled steps leading to the doorway, the dead lillies in the flower box the only difference between this house and all the others. It used to be my job to water those lilies. I stared at them for a second longer, then took a deep breath. I climbed the stairs and rapped my knuckles twice against the heavy wooden door I had pushed open so many times before.

I stood there for so long that I began to wonder if anyone was even home. Then, suddenly, I heard footsteps come from inside. My heart seemed to slow as the handle turned, and the large door swung open to reveal a boy I knew so well.

We both sucked in a breath, staring at each other, momentarily frozen in time.

Then, I said, "Hi, Warren. Can I come in?"

My brother's gaze widened with shock, but not fear. There was not a single trace of fear in his eyes as he pulled the door open wider, stepping aside so I could enter.

We had always been taught to fear the Exceptionals.

But now, finally, it seemed like that was starting to change.

ACKNOWLEDGEMENTS

When I first had the idea for this book 5 years ago, publishing it seemed like an impossible, far-off dream. I am so excited to finally share my novel, but I would not have reached this point without the help of so many important people.

First, a huge thank you to Scott Hertzog, who was an integral part of the revising and self-publishing process. Without you, this book would still be a half-formed plan. Also, a big thanks to Kaitlyn Roth for reading and giving feedback on one of my final drafts. The time and perspective you put into this novel played a large role in the final product. Mrs. Mayo, I also want to thank you for the excitement and belief you had in my writing. It was so encouraging to have someone take the time to read my work, and if it wasn't for you, I would have never known about the independent study. Thank you all.

I would like to thank all of my friends, both at church and school. I was going to list names, but there are genuinely too many of you. Just know that if I ever talked to you about my book, you are included in this thanks. Even if the conversation was short, and even if you were just asking if there would be an audiobook, it meant so much that you were willing to listen to me talk about my novel. To my church friends, it means a lot that you all asked for signed copies. I apologize in advance, I don't have the prettiest signature. To my school friends, after so many years, I am happy to finally share with you the novel I was working on in Spanish class.

A huge thanks also goes out to my teachers, specifically Mrs. Swope, Mrs. Becker, Mrs. Kinderwater, and Mr. Telesco. Not only did I learn so much in your classes, but you all played a huge role in encouraging my creativity and author dreams early on. You were some of the first people to motivate me to keep writing creatively, and each one of you gave me invaluable words of encouragement that I remember to this day. You have inspired me more than I can say. Thank you.

Last but not least, I want to thank my family. It took hours of work to get my book to this point, and without them, this would not have been possible.

Thanks to my extended family, including grandparents, aunts, uncles, and cousins, especially those of you who were my first audience when I wrote stories for your birthday gift.

Dad, thank you for always being an example of how to work hard and honor God. Your influence has impacted more than just this book. Mom, thank you for making me take typing lessons when I was seven. You were the first person to encourage me in my writing. Liam, thanks for writing and reading with me when we were young. I am blessed to have you as an older brother. Lydia, thank you for staying up late and letting me tell you and Zoe stories instead of going to sleep at our sleepovers. Also, thanks for being the second shortest Howell so I don't have to worry. Caleb, thank you for being the first one to listen to a *very* rough plot explanation of *The Exceptionals*. I'll be here if you ever want help rewriting *Blood Moon*… And Asa, thank you for sharing my love of telling stories and making videos. I love you really bad.

I am so grateful for all of you who encouraged me through this process. Thank you.

ABOUT THE AUTHOR

CLARA HOWELL is seventeen-year-old with a love of storytelling. She learned to read at age four and started writing short stories when she was seven, and has been an avid reader and writer ever since. She lives with her parents and four siblings in Eastern Pennsylvania, where she fills her time with school, theater, writing, creating videos, and going on one too many trips across the country in a travel trailer. *The Exceptionals* is her first published work.